Ascension

Ascension

GREGORY DOWLING

Thomas Dunne Books
St. Martin's Press
New York

THOMAS DUNNE BOOKS.
An imprint of St. Martin's Press.

www.thomasdunnebooks.com
www.stmartins.com

Library of Congress Cataloging-in-Publication Data

Names: Dowling, Gregory, author.
Title: Ascension / Gregory Dowling.
Description: First U.S. Edition. | New York : St. Martin's Press, 2016. | "A Thomas Dunne book." | "First published in Great Britain by Polygon, an imprint of Birlinn Ltd in 2015"—Title page verso.
Identifiers: LCCN 2016027612| ISBN 9781250108524 (hardcover) | ISBN 9781250108531 (e-book)
Subjects: LCSH: Murder—Investigation—Fiction. | GSAFD: Suspense fiction. | Mystery fiction.
Classification: LCC PR6054.O862 A94 2016 | DDC 823/.914—dc23
LC record available at https://lccn.loc.gov/2016027612

Our books may be purchased in bulk for promotional, educational, or business use. Please contact your local bookseller or the Macmillan Corporate and Premium Sales Department at 1-800-221-7945, extension 5442, or by e-mail at MacmillanSpecialMarkets@macmillan.com.

First published in Great Britain by Polygon, an imprint of Birlinn Ltd

First U.S. Edition: September 2016

10   9   8   7   6   5   4   3   2   1

Venice, under the Dogeship of
Pietro Grimani (1741–52)

I

I should not have interfered. I would have avoided a good deal of trouble if I had listened to that faint inner voice of prudence – or if I had listened to Bepi, a not so faint outer voice.

"Leave them alone," he said in his terse Venetian.

"Why should we?" I said.

"They'll have their reasons."

"Yes, but what sort of reasons?"

"That's their business."

All good sense. Bepi is a practical man, as gondoliers have to be. And why should he quarrel with a scudo for doing nothing, when the whole afternoon's work would have earned him at best half as much? That was what this *ganzer*, whom he had never seen before, had given him, as a reward for *not* offering his services to the new English arrivals here on the edge of the lagoon. I had not been given anything myself, so self-interest might have played a part in my urge to interfere.

There is always a good deal of bustle around the landing stage at Fusina around mid-afternoon, which is when most of the carriages arrive bringing the foreign visitors from Padua. Many of them take the slow barge down the Brenta Canal, which takes them all the way into Venice, but some want to put off to the very last the moment when they commit themselves to water. And for these passengers that moment occurs here, at the landing stage of Fusina.

So in the hours before sunset the gondoliers, *ganzeri* – literally, the "hookmen" who pull the gondolas ashore – and guides cluster around, offering their services, mostly in a few practised phrases of Venetian-accented French. My fluent English is naturally a great asset when the milords arrive, and by now the gondoliers accept my right of precedence with these passengers. And they all know that Bepi and I are a team, so they let him move forward as well, together with Bepi's brother, Tonin, who takes care of the baggage.

But this time we had been pre-empted by a *ganzer* new to us: a wiry-looking man, with grey hair pulled back into a pigtail, who had leapt off a gondola rowed by two men dressed in black. Bepi did not know them, which is fairly unusual, especially since they were both wearing the red caps of Castello, just like Bepi himself.

As soon as the hired carriage bringing two English gentlemen and a servant arrived, this *ganzer* had darted forward, cutting in front of Bepi. "These are for us," he had said.

Of course, it often happens that private gondoliers are sent to Fusina to pick up specific passengers, but the two gentlemen had given no signs of expecting a pre-arranged escort – and then the *ganzer* had made it perfectly clear that this was not the case by pressing a coin into Bepi's hand and saying, "Leave them to us."

Bepi, after a glance at the coin, had shrugged and strolled back towards me. At which point I had expressed my perplexities.

"Yes, but what sort of business can it be?" I said, to myself as much as to Bepi. I looked at the two Englishmen. The types were clear enough: a young English nobleman on his Grand Tour and his "bear-leader" or tutor. The young man looked amiable enough: he was gazing around at the scene with frank interest. Presumably all very different from the decorous orderliness of his home, where his mother would have bidden him farewell with a stately bow of the head and his father with a manly handshake. Here at Fusina a family of Venetians were exchanging raucous shouts, hand-slaps, kisses and lively embraces with relatives who had crossed the lagoon to meet them. Gondoliers and servants in bright liveries were transferring parcels and trunks to waiting boats and yelling at one another for no apparent reason, and across the lagoon the towers and domes of Venice shimmered in the golden haze of early spring sunlight. The scene appeared to fluster the tutor; he was in his late thirties, with a slightly lopsided wig, and an expression of anxiety on his round face that might have been habitual but now looked especially acute. Their servant hung back, a squat young man with an expression of frank suspicion on his face, as the *ganzer* took charge of their luggage. Only the young aristocrat appeared to have noticed the view across the lagoon, and was clearly appreciating it.

I made up my mind and moved forward. "Excuse me, sir," I said in English, doffing my tricorn hat. I heard Bepi give a resigned groan behind me.

The young man swung round towards me. "Oh, hello," he said. His voice was as amiable as his expression.

"I hope you won't mind my addressing you like this. I thought I had best tell you about the man who's transferring your baggage to his boat."

The *ganzer* had stopped to listen. He did not understand a word but his expression was suddenly suspicious.

"Oh yes? What about him?" asked the young man.

"It is just that he seemed exceptionally keen to take charge of you and your belongings. He actually paid my gondolier to hold back from offering his own services."

"Really? Is that usual?"

"Not at all, sir."

The *ganzer* came forward and addressed me aggressively in Venetian. "What are you pushing in here for? What are you saying to him?"

"I'm just letting him know about your odd transaction with Bepi here. I thought he ought to be warned."

"Your Bepi seemed happy enough to take the money. Now get out of it." And he gave a nod to one of the gondoliers, who came towards me. He was a hefty man, with a pockmarked face like the kernel of a walnut, and I began to think Bepi probably had a point. Still, it would look feeble to back down right away.

"I just thought the gentleman ought to know so that he can make an informed choice." I hoped my voice sounded more confident than I felt.

The *ganzer* gave another nod to his gondolier and suddenly my shoulder was gripped by something that felt like a vice.

"Tell your man to get his hands off me," I said.

"I say," said the Englishman, "what's going on?"

The tutor put in a word: "Oh dear, this all seems rather uncalled for. Had we better, em . . ." But he clearly had no idea what to propose; this was a contingency for which his travel guides had not prepared him.

Suddenly my shoulder was released. I swivelled and saw that the walnut-faced man had been jerked away from me by Bepi. They stood facing each other; Bepi was quite a bit shorter than the other man but that did not seem to bother him. He darted a quick smile at me but then his eyes went straight back to his opponent.

"Thanks, Bepi," I said, and rubbed my shoulder. I put my hat back on.

Without taking his eyes off the other gondolier, Bepi pulled out the coin he had been given and tossed it to the *ganzer*. "Here, I've changed my mind."

There was another flash of metal and this time it marked the sudden appearance of a knife in the walnut-faced man's hand. The babble of voices all around us seemed to stop for a moment, and then it was resumed with an added note of shrillness. Bepi tensed.

The *ganzer* spoke. "Leave it," he said to the gondolier. For a moment or two the walnut face seemed on the point of cracking, and then the man thrust the knife away inside his jacket. He gave us a vicious scowl and turned away. The *ganzer* stood still for a second or two, his dark eyes fixed on us. Then, with one lithe snake-like movement, he stooped, picked up the scudo from the grass and pocketed it. "I'll remember you," he said to me, and followed the gondolier towards their boat.

"Thanks," I said to Bepi again.

He shrugged. "Couldn't just leave you, I guess."

"I'll make up that scudo," I said, then added, "as soon as I can."

He flashed another smile, laconic this time. He knew my financial situation better than I did.

"What's going on?" said the Englishman.

"They've changed their minds," I said. "We can take you to the city."

"Then we must get our baggage back," he said.

I looked towards the landing stage. The black-clad gondoliers had put the last trunk down and were looking towards the *ganzer* for further instructions. There was a moment when it seemed the *ganzer* was toying with the idea of loading the luggage on to their boat anyway, but then he evidently thought better of it; he gave a quick flicking gesture of summons, stepped nimbly into the gondola and they pushed off.

"That seems to have been settled," I said to the Englishman. "Maybe we should have thanked them for taking it at least to the water's edge."

"Who are they?"

"I don't know," I said, "but they seemed very keen to have the honour of taking you into Venice. Are you expected?"

He gave a quick glance at his tutor, who still appeared flustered. "Not as far as I know," he said.

"No, no, certainly not," said the tutor, in quick nervous fashion. "How could we be? We have sent word to the English Resident, but we didn't specify a date."

There seemed little point in pursuing this issue. "Well, gentlemen, if you wish, our gondola and sandolo are at your disposal. Have you already decided on a inn?"

"We were told the Queen of Hungary is reliable," said the young man. "But would you mind telling me who you are? You're English, aren't you?"

"English-Venetian," I said. "My mother was Venetian but I grew up in England. So I speak both languages and if you wish I can offer my services as *cicerone* during your stay here. Bepi will be happy to provide transportation."

The young man glanced at the tutor. I had come to realise that the rules varied regarding control of the purse strings for these tours. It really depended on the instructions that had been given to both tutor and pupil by the family; and that depended, I suppose, on the amount of trust the fond parents felt they could repose in their offspring's behaviour during his first excursion beyond the confines of Albion.

I used a formula I had developed for these occasions. "If you wish to consider the matter I will attend to your baggage." This allowed the young man to conceal the possibly embarrassing fact of his limited financial responsibility. He nodded with a touch of relief and I turned to Bepi.

"Let's get the luggage on to the barge. Regina d'Ungheria."

He nodded. He had recognised the inn's name; he had picked up a few English words over the last few months working with me. Inn names, the principal sights of Venice, numbers – these last with reference to zecchini, and so never beyond single figures.

"Let's hope there's no more trouble," he said, gesturing out to the lagoon. Our recent rivals had set off towards Venice, but at present they seemed to be lingering some twenty yards off.

"You've really never seen them before?" I said.

"Not the gondoliers. But the *ganzer*, I've a feeling I've seen him somewhere. Not on the water. There's something about the way he moves . . ."

I remembered the lithe, serpentine body. "Distinctive, definitely," I said.

"They're leaving," Bepi said with a note of relief. They had been joined by another gondola, which had set off from the shore a few moments earlier, and now both boats began to row towards Venice.

"Who was in that second gondola?" I asked.

"Not sure; a gondolier from San Marcuola, I think."

"Yes," I said thoughtfully. I turned to our customers. "Sir," I said, "do you have any special reason to go the Queen of Hungary?"

"Only that I heard it was good. Why?"

I gestured to the lagoon. "Our friends from earlier . . . you saw they were waiting out in the lagoon?"

"Well?"

"They were waiting for someone to tell them which inn you will be staying at."

"Oh really," he said with a touch of disbelief.

His tutor spoke up; there was a quiver in his voice but he was clearly decided. "Sir, we cannot afford to take any risks. Let us take these people's advice."

"In that case, can you recommend a inn?" said the young man, turning to me.

"The White Lion is equally good," I said. "Close to the Rialto."

"And don't tell me, it's run by your brother," he said, and gave a sudden barking laugh, which made several people around us jump.

"You can believe that if you wish," I said levelly. "And you can decide to hold to the Queen of Hungary. It makes no difference to me. The prices of the two inns are more or less the same."

"All right, let's get devoured by your Lion." Out came that bark of a laugh again. "As for your services beyond today, let's see how things go, shall we?"

"As you wish," I said, with a polite bow, trying not to let my frustration show. It would not help my chances for him to see just how much I needed the job.

2

We were soon on the water, inside the *felze* of Bepi's gondola. The servant was travelling with the luggage in Tonin's sandolo. Introductions had been made. I had presented myself as Alvise Marangon, professional *cicerone*; I had omitted the further qualification of out-of-work artist. The young man was Mr Boscombe and his tutor was Mr Shackleford. They had been travelling through France, and then Milan, Verona and Padua: the usual Grand Tour. It was to conclude in Florence, where his uncle lived. He had introduced himself as Mr Boscombe, so it seemed that he was not actually a nobleman; none the less, everything about him – his clothes, accent, and demeanour – indicated that he came from a wealthy and privileged background.

He was, in fact, quite clearly the usual young English traveller, with an amiable enjoyment of the scenery, a mild interest in the antiquities, and, I suspected, a more lively appreciation of the possibilities of amorous dalliance and bacchanalian revelry. Shackleford clearly took his tutorial duties with some seriousness, as he began to read aloud from a travelogue by some earlier visitor: "The approach to Venice across the lagoon offers charming prospects of the city's numerous bell towers and domes –"

"Oh, do leave off, Shackleford. We can see the damned prospects for ourselves."

"It never hurts to benefit from others' experience," he said rather huffily, putting the book down. I had the feeling that this was a conversation they had had many times over.

I suppose I could have taken this as a cue to inform them myself of the height, date and architectural style of each bell tower, but I sensed that this might not be the likeliest way to win Boscombe's favour. Probably not Shackleford's either, since I could be seen to be challenging him in his own role. It was a game that had to be played with great tact.

"So how did you end up here, Mr Marangon?" asked Boscombe.

"Well, you could say that I started out here," I said. "I was born in Venice, but my mother moved to England when I was still a child."

"Oh, really? Why was that?"

I had learned by now how much of my past it was prudent to reveal. For some reason it seemed more acceptable to most Englishmen to learn that after my father's death my mother had won the favours of an English nobleman than that she had been an actress and singer in a travelling theatre company. But even her profession became more acceptable (or less unacceptable) if I emphasised the fact that she was, after all, Venetian. What would have been scandalous in an English-woman could be seen as charming exoticism in a foreigner.

"My mother was widowed when I was a child. She moved to England when she was offered financial support by an English nobleman."

"Dashed decent of him," said Boscombe, with little attempt to conceal his amusement.

"So she thought," I said, my voice as neutral as possible. There was little need to go into her years of precarious hand-to-mouth existence in progressively less respectable quarters of London, her intermittent frequentation of the theatrical world, and her single-minded if unconventional devotion to my upbringing.

"So you went to school in England?" said Shackleford. He was clearly still puzzled by me, and perhaps a little wary.

"I had an English education, yes," I said, simplifying things a little.

"And when did you come back to Venice?"

"Two years ago, with an English nobleman on his Grand Tour."

"Really?" said Boscombe. "What was your position?"

"I wasn't his tutor," I said, rather unnecessarily. They were hardly likely to have conceived such a possibility, since I was only a year or two older than Boscombe. "He wished to have an artist who could record some of the scenes for him."

"So you're an artist," said Boscombe. His tone suggested that he had suspected as much; I was a foreigner, after all.

"I have endeavoured to be," I said. "But I think the fact that I speak Italian played a greater part in Lord Somerset's decision to engage me."

"And then you ditched him."

"We parted by mutual accord," I said. We had achieved a state of mutual detestation by the time we reached Venice, and his decision to show his opinion of my sketch of the Rialto Bridge by throwing a glass of wine at it had been the deciding factor. It had not been one of my best efforts but I still resented the waste of good wine.

"And you stayed on?" said Shackleford. "Wasn't that a little imprudent?"

"You must remember that I was born in Venice. And there were relatives I could call on." They had not proved particularly welcoming, but there was no need to go into that. After all, why should they welcome a poor relation, the foreign son of a cousin who had disgraced herself by joining a theatrical troupe? The gondolier Lord Somerset had used had proved more helpful in setting me on my feet. Which was why we were now travelling in his gondola.

Boscombe had had enough of my reminiscences. "Tell me, do you know the nobleman Piero Garzoni?"

"Sir . . ." Shackleford broke in, as if dismayed by the question.

"I have heard of him," I said, after a curious glance at Shackleford. "I can hardly claim his acquaintance."

"Well, no, I didn't expect you to be the fellow's friend," said Boscombe, with his sudden laugh.

"I believe he has very few friends," I said. "He lives a rather retired life, by all accounts. He only attends the Great Council when absolutely obliged to do so." He was actually a notorious recluse, and all sorts of rumours abounded about what he got up to in his ancient Gothic palace on the Grand Canal.

Boscombe lowered his voice: "Is it true that he engages in the Rosicrucian mysteries?"

"Sir," said Shackleford in a pained voice.

"I cannot say," I declared with complete truth. I had only vaguely heard of these mysteries, mainly from a distant acquaintance of mine, the ex-abate Giacomo Casanova, who claimed some familiarity with them, though I could not say with what degree of seriousness.

"I think we would do better to refresh our mind on the history of the republic," Shackleford said earnestly, referring again to his book. "We are told here that it was founded by refugees from the city of Aquileia, fleeing from the brutal incursions of Attila the Hun . . ."

His voice droned on. Boscombe gazed vacantly and amiably out of the window, while the names of doges and saints flitted past him, together with dates of treaties, naval battles and sackings of cities, all testifying to the steadily growing power and splendour of the Most Serene Republic of Venice. As we entered the Grand Canal (and the Fourth Crusade) I murmured an apology and stepped out of the felze to confer with Bepi.

"No sign of trouble?" I said.

Bepi gave a shrug. "Nothing I can see."

I gazed at the busy scene around us. I always took pleasure in sharing the first view of Venice with our clients; it allowed me to see the city with fresh wonder. If there was one advantage I had over Bepi (and, of course, over all Venetians), it was that I could remember my first view – at least my first adult view – of the city. And at the same time I could share in his own personal pride in the city: after all, had I not spoken the dialect since infancy? I could thus indulge in both pleasures: that of the wide-eyed visitor and that of the all-knowing native.

At this early evening hour, with the setting sun behind us casting a reddish-golden glow on the upper storeys of the palaces, the city was at its most splendid. Gondolas and barges, sandolos and ferries thronged the water. There was the usual hubbub of warning cries, salutations, quips, insults and challenges, together with a few songs, romantic or bawdy, and lamps were already lit in the prows of the more prudent crafts, adding flickering dots of brilliance to the scene. Shackleford's voice had faded out behind me. I hoped they were both enjoying the spectacle. If they were not, they did not deserve to be here.

By the time we approached the Rialto it was definitely dusk. The inn had lamps blazing beside the great Byzantine arch of its entrance, but the adjacent palace was unlit, being currently under restoration, and dark shadows were cast on the right-hand side of the inn by the scaffolding that covered its façade.

"Is this it?" said Boscombe, peering out of the *felze*. "It looks rather old."

That was an understatement. The Leon Bianco is situated in a palace that dates from the thirteenth century. "I can assure you that the rooms are very comfortable," I said.

"Your brother can be trusted, eh?" he said, and gave that bark of a laugh again.

I smiled dutifully, and then called out to the porter, who was peering out from the entrance. "An English milord and his tutor! Do you have rooms, Andrea?" Even if Boscombe had mentioned no title, all wealthy English visitors were milords.

"Ciao, Alvise," said Andrea, in his cracked Venetian. He gives the impression of being only a little younger than the palace itself. "Yes, we can accommodate them. Second floor, with a view on to the canal. How many servants?"

"Just one valet," I said. "He's coming with the baggage in Tonin's sandolo."

We were soon standing in the inn's large entranceway. The landlord, Sior Scarpa, had come down himself to greet the new arrivals, and was bobbing and smiling and saying "Plee-eesa", his one English word. Bepi's brother had arrived in the meantime, and the servants were busily unloading the trunks and cases. Boscombe and Shackleford looked a little uncertainly at the draughty entranceway, with its cracked marble walls and shadowy statues.

"You must think of this as the stables," I said. "The real hallway is on the first floor, as in all Venetian palaces."

Bepi sidled up to me. "Well?" he said.

"I think so," I said. "At least they haven't said no. I think it'll depend whether they like my brother's rooms."

"Your what?"

"Just a running joke with milord," I said. "I'd better help settle them in, then I'll let you know."

But I had no real doubts by this point. Sior Scarpa knows how to treat his English clients, and the first floor, with its polished mirrors, blazing chandeliers and stuccoed walls, always makes a fine first impression. By all accounts the bedrooms are warm and the bedding clean, so Boscombe would have to be exceptionally fastidious to object.

"Any sign of our friends?" I asked Bepi before I followed Boscombe up the stairs.

"Just one watcher in the entrance. But I think he's an Inquisitors' man."

I nodded. New foreign arrivals at all large inns were quickly reported to the Inquisitors; by tomorrow Boscombe and Shackleford would already figure in a register somewhere in the hidden chambers of the Doge's palace, no doubt with full details on their financial status, sexual preferences and shoe sizes. Or so most Venetians liked to believe.

Minutes later I rejoined Bepi and told him that we were hired for that evening and the next day at least. "They want a trip to the Piazza and I think Mr Boscombe would like to find a gaming room. But first he wants me to take the tutor to the Regina d'Ungheria to see if there is any post awaiting them there."

"Do you want help?"

"I know the way," I said. "And it's quicker on foot."

"That's not what I meant."

"I know. But let's not get things out of proportion. I'll be careful."

Bepi looked doubtful but nodded. It was strange that I should be giving lessons in calm realism. Bepi, after all, is the man for whom the adjective "laconic" was invented.

The tutor now came down the stairs. He had changed out of his travelling garments and presumably put on his best city clothes. He still somehow contrived to look dusty, as if he had been scrambling in the cobwebby corners of some uncatalogued library. His wig seemed designed to look lopsided; it matched the peevish curve of his mouth, and I got the impression that this immediate trip to the other inn had not been his idea.

"Well, shall we go?"

"Yes, certainly," I said. "It will be quickest to walk."

"Will we need a link-boy?"

"A *codega*? I don't think so. The main roads towards Saint Mark's Square are well lit."

We left the inn by the land entrance and immediately found ourselves in the crowds thronging towards the Rialto. Shackleford looked around. "I thought people would be wearing masks," he said.

"Carnival is over," I said. I had come across this before with foreign visitors, who presumed Venetians wore masks all year round.

"Ah, so you only wear them for Carnival," he said.

"Well, no, there are other times of year as well. Feast days, like

Ascension, and the period immediately afterwards; the theatre season, from October till Christmas . . . and then for various high days and holidays. And you'll need them if you go to gaming houses, as I believe Mr Boscombe wishes to do."

"Well, my feeling is that an early night would do us both good," he said.

"No doubt," I said, "but I think you can understand that a young man, in Venice for the first time . . ."

"I suppose so," he said with a sigh. "But I would appreciate it if you did not encourage him."

"I merely obey instructions."

"You also make suggestions. This inn was your idea, after all."

"That was in response to what appeared to be a definite danger."

"Are you sure you didn't exaggerate?" Could they not have been just eager *ciceroni* – like yourself?"

"Mr Shackleford," I said, "I have been doing this job for over a year now and I have never before seen a rival offer money in order to secure a client."

He made no answer. I had the feeling that he had put forward this notion more from a desperate wish to believe that it was so than out of any genuine conviction.

I decided to ask the obvious question. "Do you have any idea why these people should be interested in you?"

"No, no, absolutely not," he said at once. "I don't understand it at all."

The answer was too quick. He had already decided to deny all knowledge. There would be no point in persisting.

"Well, even so you might like to consider buying a tricorn hat," I said. "You can pull it down over your forehead and it works almost as well as a mask."

The purchase made, we passed through Campo San Bartolomeo, always the busiest small square in the city, with crowds criss-crossing from Cannaregio, San Marco and the Rialto. As we approached the small side street where the land entrance to the Regina d'Ungheria inn is situated I could sense that he was growing more and more nervous; when I told him to pull down his hat he seemed to have an urge to tug it almost as far as his mouth.

Instead of turning into the side street, I indicated that we should proceed towards the bridge from which there was a view of the water entrance to the inn. A man in a *tabarro* and *bauta* was standing idly on the bridge; he did not look at us. He was tossing a coin in his hand. It was as if he were posing as the spirit of Carnival just for Shackleford.

We walked on down the other side of the bridge. Shackleford made a half-turn, as if about to walk back to the inn, and I hissed: "Keep walking."

We reached the large basin, busy with gondolas, just before the entrance to Saint Mark's Square and at last I spoke. "Did you recognise that man on the bridge?"

"On the bridge? He was wearing a mask. How could –"

"It was the man from Fusina. The one who wanted to take you to your inn."

"How could you tell?"

"I couldn't swear to it in court, but you may remember the way he moved. Supple and snake-like. It was him."

"Oh, dear. What –"

"There's another way to approach the land entrance." I indicated a *calle* to our left. It led towards the Frezzeria, the narrow but busy shopping street that runs parallel to the western end of Saint Mark's Square. We made our way along it, turned left at the end and then immediately right into a narrow alley that led to a little bridge. "Don't turn round as you cross," I said. This was the only weak point in our alternative route; the bridge was just yards away from the other where the watcher stood. We must do nothing to attract his attention.

I hoped the night would work in our favour. We would be just two dark figures against a dark background. With luck his attention would be on the water, where he was expecting to see a gondola arrive. I forced myself to gaze rigidly ahead.

The land entrance to the inn was quiet. We climbed the staircase to the hallway of the inn. A large woman with an apron came forward and looked at us enquiringly.

I took off my hat and bowed. "Madam, I have brought this English gentleman. He wishes to know whether any mail has arrived here for him or for his young companion, Mr Boscombe. They had meant to stay here, but have had to change their plans."

"Ah, the English milord," she said, nodding. "Yes, there have been enquiries."

"Really? Could you tell me who?"

She looked at me a little suspiciously. "And who are you?"

"Alvise Marangon, at your service. Professional *cicerone*. I have brought clients here in the past," I said, with my most winning smile. Well, I had once dropped a drunken German at the entrance, after he had vomited over Bepi's gondola.

She sniffed and said, "I don't know who. He was masked. Just wanted to know if the milord had arrived. Then he went away. There are a couple of letters."

She reached into a drawer and pulled out two letters, both with unbroken seals. "So the gentleman is not staying?"

"Unfortunately not," I said.

"Can he prove who he is?"

I translated this for Shackleford. As usual he looked both flustered and automatically suspicious at the request for information, but then he said, "I have Mr Boscombe's signet ring." He pulled it from his coat pocket, and she handed over the letters.

"Who left those?" I asked her. This was, perhaps, none of my business, but since I had been pulled into their secret game of hide-and-seek I felt I had a right to find out about the rival team. In any case, Shackleford could not understand.

"It was a boy," she said, "an impudent brat." Then she added, "But he won't try that sort of nonsense again." She looked at her hand with some satisfaction, as if she could still see the imprint of a freshly smacked cheek.

Shackleford had broken the seal on one of the letters and was reading it eagerly.

"Good news?" I asked conversationally.

He glanced up. "Everything is as it should be," he said. He concluded his reading and put the missive carefully into his coat pocket, along with the other one, its seal still unbroken. "Shall we go?"

I looked at him. There was a fresh pink glow to his cheeks, and his eyes looked brighter. One might even have described his wig as being at a rakish angle, rather than just lopsided.

"Yes, certainly," I said. I thanked the woman and we set off, replacing our hats.

When we got outside I glanced around. There was no sign of any watcher and we set off towards Campo San Luca, where I glanced back.

"Ah," I said.

"What's the matter?"

"I think, though I can't swear to it, that we have company."

3

"Oh dear, oh dear." He had instantly returned to his state of flustered nervousness.

"We can try an experiment," I said, and indicated the narrow alleyway opposite us, which led to Calle dei Fabbri. Taking it would thin out the crowds around us and make any follower easier to distinguish.

When we reached the end of the alleyway I looked round again and saw a dark-cloaked figure entering it in our wake. I thought I recognised the lithe, supple gait, and turned immediately right into Calle dei Fabbri. "Quickly," I said. "Into the first shop."

Seconds later we stepped into the welcome gloom of a bookshop.

"How can I –" began the small figure behind the desk.

"Sior Fabrizio," I said, doffing my hat, "please let us into the back room. I'll explain later."

Fabrizio wasted no time on questions but opened the door behind his desk and waved us through. Seconds later Shackleford and I stood in a dark, cramped space surrounded by stacks of leather-bound volumes, loose papers and a general smell of mustiness.

"We'll just wait until we can be sure he's gone past the shop," I whispered.

The tutor said nothing. He was breathing heavily and irregularly, as if we had run a race. I imagined he was not used to this sort of agitation.

A minute or so later Fabrizio opened the door, so that the lamplight fell in upon us.

"Do you wish to stay here indefinitely?" he said. He is a small man, in his early fifties, whose air of scholarly mildness is deceptive; cross him on a point of Latin grammar and you unleash a tiger.

"Did anyone come in – or look in?" I said.

"You know what a thriving business I run," he said drily. "I think I had a client last February ..."

"I wasn't asking about your sales figures," I said. "Just whether anyone looked in through the window or the door."

"There was one man, in a mask and a cloak. He looked in very briefly. Somehow I don't think he was a booklover, but in that he is little different from most of the inhabitants of this city. Are you going to introduce me to your friend?"

"Of course. Mr Shackleford, this is Signor Fabrizio Busetto," I said, switching back to English, "owner of the best bookshop in Venice."

We stepped out of the dark back room into the slightly less gloomy precincts of the shop itself. Bookcases in polished wood with curious curlicued carvings stood all round, even creating a series of small narrow corridors on one side of the shop. Their shelves were filled with volumes bound in darkly gleaming leather. I could see Shackleford's own eyes gleaming in response, as he took in his surroundings. I guessed this was his kind of setting.

"An English gentleman," said Fabrizio, switching to French, a language he presumed Shackleford would speak. The tutor mumbled a few words of courteous, heavily accented French and the two men shook hands.

"We'll stand over here for the moment," I said, retreating into one of the dark book-lined corridors, and beckoning my companion to follow me. "Just in case our friend comes back up the street."

"Is this trouble with your landlord again?" asked Fabrizio, switching back to Venetian. "Or another sacristan you forgot to tip after enjoying a private view of the Tintorettos?"

"I don't know who it is," I said. "But they seem very interested in my client."

"They? Not just our friend in the cloak and mask?"

"Well, he had gondoliers. They've been after us since we left Fusina. And the client refuses to say who they are."

"Father," came a new and far more attractive voice. "What's happening?"

Fabrizio's daughter came down the stairs in the corner of the shop that lead to the apartment above. Three voices in the shop were presumably enough of a novelty to arouse her curiosity.

"Ah, Lucia," he said. "Alvise has joined us, with an English friend, and they are apparently on the run from the forces of evil."

Lucia came towards us and as usual I began to wonder if my wig was straight and my shirt clean. I knew my tongue was going to prove twice as large as usual in my mouth, so that I would stammer and perhaps even slobber. It is not just that she is extremely attractive; it is that unlike most girls of her age (nineteen) she will stare you straight in the face and laugh if there is anything to laugh at. And in my case there usually seems to be. Her supreme confidence can perhaps be attributed to the fact that she grew up without a mother to tell her that young ladies are supposed to lower their eyes bashfully in the presence of men (Fabrizio's wife died in childbirth and no other female relative was willing to take on the task of her upbringing). Certainly it never crosses her father's mind to give her any instructions. I imagine he once told her to put away her toys when she was about three and is still reeling from the experience.

"Knowing Sior Alvise I expect it's his landlord," she said, fixing me with her dark eyes.

"I suggested that and he fiercely denies the allegation," said Fabrizio.

"Not fiercely," I said, making my usual awkward bow in her direction. "Just truthfully for once. I paid my rent last Saturday."

"I thought the bells of Saint Mark's rang with unexpected fervour that day," she said. She gazed at Shackleford. "Who is this gentleman?"

I performed the introduction, and Shackleford made an even more awkward bow than I had done, which was a minor comfort. I imagine he had never met quite such a self-assured young woman before.

"Ah, just a moment," said Fabrizio, who was gazing towards the window. "I think your friend is back again." He spoke without turning to us. "Stay where you are."

Lucia looked towards the window as well. "Do you want me to go and ask what he wants?" she said.

"No," I whispered. "Pay no attention to him."

"He's going," said Fabrizio, with a sigh of relief.

"Let me ask a great favour," I said. "Would you mind taking Mr Shackleford back to the Leon Bianco? I just want to find out a little about this man. Then I'll go straight to the inn."

"You're going to follow your follower?" said Lucia. The idea seemed to amuse her. "Yes, I'll take your friend back."

"No, Siora Lucia, I meant your father . . ."

"I know you did. But he has a shop to run."

"Lucia," said her father, "I think the shop could manage –"

"Hush, Father. I know what I'm doing."

And of course he said not another word of protest. Neither did I. "Thank you, Siora Lucia," I said. "Please be careful."

"And you too," she said.

I wondered briefly whether she was truly concerned for my safety but guessed she just had little confidence in my powers as a pursuer. Well, she was probably right. But there was only one way to find out.

"Which way did he go?" I asked Fabrizio.

"To the right, towards the Piazza," he said. "Be careful." He did sound concerned.

"I will," I said. "And Siora Lucia, please do not take a direct route to the inn." I turned to Shackleford. "This lady will take you back to the White Lion. I'm going to follow our friend."

"What? Who –" Now he was seriously flustered but I had no time to make reassuring noises.

"I'll see you back at the inn very soon," I said, and made towards the door. "Thank you so much, siora – and thank you, Sior Fabrizio, for the refuge."

"Don't worry, Alvise." Then, as if the idea had just struck him, he added: "Next time you could come and look at the books. You might even like them." But I was already out in the street and staring down the Calle dei Fabbri in the direction of Saint Mark's Square. I pulled my tricorn well down over my forehead and set off, trying to vary my gait by hunching my shoulders up and swinging my arms. I could see the cloaked figure ahead of me; he had clearly given up all idea of following anyone, and was walking briskly and purposefully, without any sideward or (fortunately) backward glances. There was no mistaking that wiry nimbleness of movement. He weaved around the other pedestrians in the narrow street with a panther-like grace.

He passed under the Sottoportego dei Dai and about fifteen seconds later I did the same, emerging into the sudden breadth and beauty of Saint Mark's Square. The hectic days of Carnival were gone; there were no raucous crowds in elaborate costumes and masks, no troupes of dancers or trapezists spinning through the air, although anyone unfamiliar with the place might have assumed from the number of people in exotic dress that Carnival was not quite over, until closer study revealed that those in Turkish costumes were indeed Turks, and in Armenian dress Armenians . . . and above the throng the great red pennants with the golden lion of Saint Mark flapped proudly from the flagpoles.

My man headed diagonally across the square towards the booths selling wine and cakes at the foot of the great bell tower, making for the coffee shop closest to the water. Now he began to look around and I joined a group of Croatian tourists. But then I realised he was looking for someone among the people sitting outside the coffee shop and so with a smile and a nod I detached myself from my politely puzzled Croatian companions and sidled towards the coffee shop myself.

The *ganzer* had approached someone at one of the tables. I could not see his features – the only lanterns were behind him – but I thought I could make out that he was wearing a nobleman's cloak. The *ganzer* hovered a few feet away until the man at the table acknowledged his presence with a raised hand and a few words of vague greeting. He did not invite the other man to sit down, which was not surprising, if he really was a nobleman. However, from the posture he adopted, with his head raised towards the *ganzer*, he was clearly interested in what the other man had to say.

I realised there was no way I was going to be able to overhear their conversation. And unless I got a little closer I was not going to be able to identify the seated man. Could I do so, without letting myself be seen? It was worth the risk, I thought. I walked forward as casually as possible, at the same time drawing my little sketchbook and a black crayon from my inner pocket. If the man would turn his head towards the light I might be able to get a likeness of him.

As the *ganzer* talked on, however, the man's position remained unaltered. There seemed only to be a stiffening of his shoulders, as if he were irritated by what he was hearing. Then he spoke a few short sentences, and the *ganzer's* pose became apologetic; with rather flamboyant gestures he threw out both arms, as if to say, "What would you have me do?" I guessed that the story of the failed interception of

Boscombe and his bear-leader had come to its climax – or rather anticlimax. And he could not even tell him which inn the men were staying at.

Just at that moment my crayon-holding arm was gripped and I jerked my head to the right and saw my old acquaintance, Walnut Face. I could only presume that he had been keeping an eye on things from beneath the portico.

"What are you doing?" he said in a quiet but threatening voice.

I almost answered in the same low pitch but fortunately realised in time that this would be a mistake. I said loudly: "Do you want your portrait too, sir? Just eight lire. It'll only take ten minutes."

As he attempted to grab the sketchbook, I twisted away, holding the book at arm's length. "Ten lire, if you want it full face . . ." People were turning to stare at us. "Please, sir," I called out, as he made another attempt to grab the sketchbook, "don't be impatient. You're not the only one wanting a portrait."

His grip on my arm loosened as he became aware of the growing public interest in our little private dance. "Give me that drawing . . ."

"No, sir, I can't do that. It's not of you."

I darted a glance towards the coffee shop and saw that the seated man and the *ganzer* were also looking our way. Walnut Face, I could tell, was itching to reach for his knife again. That would not go down well with the officials responsible for public decorum in the square but their disapproval would be of little comfort to me as I lay in a pool of blood. I squirmed free from his grasp and turned and ran across the square, swerving past the cluster of conveniently companionable Croatians, weaving around other groups of visitors and revellers, and heading towards the arch of the clock tower. I heard no footsteps behind me and by the time I reached the comforting gloom of the archway I felt able to slow down. The Mercerie, the main shopping street between San Marco and the Rialto area, was crowded as usual, and it was impossible to move fast without attracting attention. I forced myself to a semblance of calm, put my sketchbook inside my coat, adjusted my coat and tricorn, and walked on with as casual an air as possible.

4

I took a roundabout route back to the bookshop, deciding it was worth calling there before going to the inn. When I arrived Lucia was just divesting herself of her cloak. Her father looked a little concerned.

"All well?" I asked.

She turned to me. "I didn't get lost, if that's what you mean. And no one seemed to be interested in us."

"I meant – people not being interested in you. I'm glad no one was."

"Not your prettiest compliment," she said, "but I suspect you mean well."

I did not try to answer that. "Thank you, both of you. You've been extremely helpful."

"My dear Alvise," said Fabrizio, "are you going to honour us with an explanation?"

"There isn't very much I can tell you," I said, "but I'll do my best." I told them what had happened at Fusina and then the business with the change of inn.

"*Cospetto*," said Fabrizio; it is his strongest imprecation and is roughly equivalent to "Dear me". "Should you not inform the authorities?"

"Mr Boscombe seems against it," I said. "They both say they have no idea why anyone should be concerned with them." I turned to Lucia. "Siora, did Mr Shackleford say anything to you?"

"You think he might have felt more inclined to reveal all to a helpless maiden?" she said.

"Well, yes. I think you might be better at persuading a middle-aged man to confide his troubles than I am."

"You are full of compliments today, Sior Alvise," she said. "Sadly, I learned nothing of any consequence. He likes our bookshop and hopes to pay it another visit. He wished to know if we have any of the English authors but I said only in translation, and he asked which authors, and I said, we have William Shakespeare, we have Thomas

Hobbes and John Locke, and of course Mr Samuel Richardson, and he wished to know if I had wept over the vicissitudes of poor Pamela, and naturally I replied that I have . . ."

"And all this was in which language?"

"French, and a smattering of the English I have acquired from you."

"I didn't know I had imparted any English."

"Dear Sior Alvise, don't I regularly hear you talking to the clients you bring here? Do you think it is beyond my wits to acquire a word a two of your barbarous tongue?"

"I realise I'll have to be careful in future what I say."

"I have also been reading *Pamela* in English. Slowly but steadily."

That was how I remembered the plot of the novel developing so it seemed a suitable method. "Did you meet Mr Boscombe at the inn?"

"No. When we arrived the landlord informed us that the milord had decided to take a little trip along the Grand Canal with your gondolier friend."

"Ah. Well, I'm glad Bepi is being kept busy."

"I think," she said speculatively, "that Mr Boscombe might have decided to take the opportunity to enjoy the spectacle of the Grand Canal without the added benefit of architectural and historical information."

"You're probably right," I said. "I suppose I can be a little tedious."

She laughed. "My barb wasn't directed at you." And then she added, "This time."

"Ah, yes, I have heard Mr Shackleford in full flow," I said, "and I can understand the desire to escape from it."

"But what about you? What were your adventures after you dashed away so precipitately?"

"Yes," said Fabrizio. "What happened? Did you find out anything about the man?"

"I followed him as far as the Piazzetta in front of the Doge's palace. There he met with a nobleman."

"Indeed? Did you know him?"

"I couldn't see his face, but from the cloak he looked rather like a barnabotto," I said. Barnabotti are the impoverished noblemen who, being obliged by law to keep up the appearances of their rank, are provided with cheap state-owned accommodation in the neighbourhood of the church of San Barnaba. "I wanted to make a sketch of him but couldn't see his face properly. But I did do the man who was following us."

I pulled out my sketchbook and showed it to them. Like other accomplishments that my erratic education has equipped me with, my talent for portraiture is not sufficient to guarantee me a living but is occasionally valid enough to solicit a nod of approval from friends and acquaintances. Lucia went so far as to say "Bravo", and for once there seemed to be no irony in her voice. The compliment was not unearned, I think; I had done full justice to the man's sharp, cragged features.

Fabrizio pondered. "It is a good portrait and I'm sure I will recognise the man if I see him again, but I can't say I know him."

"I'll know him too," said Lucia. "He looks like a tough character. And you say he was talking to a nobleman."

"I think so. He certainly seemed deferential enough."

She kept her eyes on the picture and eventually said: "Sior Alvise, you have a skill with the crayon. Why do you not try to develop that?"

"I have tried," I said. "I think I told you that I first came to Venice as a travelling artist. But I could not make a living."

"You did not persist, I think."

I could have made an ironic quip about bowing to the superior knowledge of the world she had accumulated over her many years but did not, mainly because I suspected she had a point. So instead I shrugged and said, "Siora Lucia, you may be right. But at the moment I have another job."

"Showing bored English boys works of art they are not interested in and the way to the gambling houses and stews."

"Lucia!" This time her father was angry.

She gave a half-shrug herself. "My language may be unrefined but I think Sior Alvise will find it hard to contest the accuracy of my remark."

"I try to overcome their boredom," I said. "And I'll admit that I suggest the safest gambling houses. As for the other thing, they don't seem to need much guidance in finding their way there."

"Lucia," said Fabrizio, "there is no reason why Sior Alvise should have to defend the perfectly honourable way he has chosen to make a living. It is good to know that there are young people interested in this city's heritage and eager to pass on their knowledge. And for someone who did not grow up here, Sior Alvise is remarkably well informed about our city."

"With many thanks to you," I said, "who have been so generous in lending me books." His books had helped to fill the many gaps in my education. I had grown up amid actors and actresses, singers and performers, with occasional lessons from private tutors when my mother could afford it, and two much-resented terms at two different boarding schools, both of which I had run away from. Even though I had somehow managed to acquire a steady reading habit, not wholly confined to theatrical scripts, and a love of art, partly inspired by the Italian scene-painter my mother had taken up with for a few years after her noble patron had finally tired of her, there were many areas of learning where I was painfully aware of my deficiencies.

He smiled. "Well, keep bringing your charges' tutors to me. Every so often I even manage to sell them one or two."

5

The moment I reached the land entrance to the Leon Bianco I was greeted by Bepi. "Something's up," he said. Brief and to the point as ever.

"What?"

"They're saying they've been robbed."

"Ah," I said. "And you don't mean they're contesting the bill."

"No. Robbed in their room."

"How –"

"You'd better ask them. I took Milord for a short row down the Canalazzo and when I got back there was the tutor wailing and moaning about thieves and bandits and God knows what."

I climbed the stairs to the piano nobile. In the grand reception hall, Sior Scarpa was distraught; he seemed to have taken over the task of wailing and moaning. Shackleford and Boscombe were a good deal calmer. Indeed, Boscombe looked completely unruffled. Shackleford just seemed a shade more flustered than usual. Some of the serving staff were standing around, looking anxious but clearly not knowing what to do or say until orders should be issued.

"What happened?" I asked, addressing Sior Scarpa in Venetian.

"Sior Alvise, please tell them, nothing like this has ever happened before. This is a respectable inn."

I translated, hoping that someone would soon tell me what the unprecedented happening was. Boscombe nodded and said, "Tell him we're not blaming him."

I did so, and before Sior Scarpa could burst into a flurry of grateful exclamations asked quickly: "Can you tell me exactly what happened, sir?"

"Well, after you'd gone, I decided it would be rather pleasant to go for another ride with your gondolier friend, just up and down the river, you know . . ."

"It's the Grand Canal," I corrected him automatically.

"Whatever you say. And when I got back there was Shackleford leaping around and tearing his hair out."

I glanced at Shackleford. It was difficult to picture this.

"I was certainly perturbed," he said, with a touch of reproach in his voice. I could also hear a note of definite nervousness. "When I returned from our expedition with the good lady, who was most helpful, by the way . . ."

"I think Shackleford is quite smitten," said Boscombe, and he gave his sudden noisy laugh.

Shackleford continued, determinedly ignoring this sally. "When I returned I went straight to our room. The moment I opened the door I could see something had happened."

"What?" I said.

"My trunk had been opened and tampered with. Clothes and other items were strewn over the floor."

"Was much taken?"

The two men looked at each other. I got the impression that they both wished they had agreed on an answer to this question.

Then they spoke together. I think Shackleford said "Nothing significant" and Boscombe "Just a few trinkets", and then they looked at each other again and opened their mouths, as if about to qualify their statements, but no words emerged.

"Well, shall we go and check?" I said.

We set off towards the staircase to the upper floor, with Sior Scarpa behind us continuing to reassure us about the respectability of the establishment.

It was the first time I had seen the guests' rooms and I could see that the praise for the establishment was merited. It struck me that my whole apartment could fit into the room where Boscombe and Shackleford were accommodated, and there would still be space left over – perhaps inside the wardrobe with its decorated doors – for my local tavern; some of the clients might even find it airier, if the doors were left ajar.

The size and splendour of the room, with its blazing chandelier and the large windows giving on to the Grand Canal, meant that the disorder mentioned by Shackleford made little immediate impact on the eyes. The travelling trunk lay open on the floor before the bed, and one might at first have mistaken the scattered sprawl of garments all around it for a careless attempt at Carnival decoration. But another glance made it clear that these things had been pulled out and cast around in great haste. There had been both urgency and speed in the search. And from Boscombe's and Shackleford's earlier reactions it sounded as if whatever it was that had been sought had been found, but they were unwilling to reveal what it was.

Sior Scarpa repeated: "This has never happened before. Never before. A respectable establishment."

I went over to the window. I was remembering the view of the palace as we had approached it by gondola. I leaned out of the left-hand window, peering out on to the canal. The view was attractive enough: gondolas with flickering lanterns bobbed below me, and on the other side of the canal lamps flared above the doorways of the taverns around the Rialto market area. However, this was not what I was interested in. I gazed to the left and could made out the dark fretwork of the wooden scaffolding on the adjacent palace. There was about a four-foot gap between my windowsill and the nearest wooden planks.

"You left this window open?" I asked Boscombe.

"Yes, certainly," he said. "It was damned stuffy. You think the villain got in through there?" He joined me at the window. "He'd have to be pretty damn nimble."

"Yes," I said.

"And of course anyone could see him from the canal," he added.

"I suspect no one would pay too much attention," I said. "It's dark up here, after all."

"Some sneak thief," he said. "Does this happen a lot?"

"Not according to our host," I said, gesturing to Sior Scarpa, who was once again urging upon us the unprecedented nature of this event. "The scaffolding might have made it a special temptation. And if you were known to have something especially valuable …" I left the sentence dangling.

He clearly felt no need to retrieve this conversational loose end. "Just the usual stuff for travellers," he said. "Anyway, there's no need to make a fuss over it."

"You don't want to report your loss?"

"No. Least said and all that."

"Sior Scarpa will be very relieved," I said. I turned back to face the room and translated Boscombe's decision for the benefit of the host, who immediately switched from profuse declarations of sorrow to ones of gratitude. I glanced at Shackleford, who also seemed relieved. It was clear that they had no wish for any assistance from the authorities in recovering their lost property, whatever it was.

"All right then, Benson," said Boscombe to the valet, who had been hovering in the doorway. "You might as well tidy up this mess now."

Sior Scarpa had already barked orders to two of his servants, who had started picking up some of the garments. Benson snatched them from their hands, an expression of outrage on his face. Seeing the risk of an international incident I addressed the two local helpers in Venetian: "Better leave it to Milord's man." They shrugged and made for the door.

"Milord," said Sior Scarpa, "I would like to offer you dinner this evening. Please, you will be my guest."

When I had translated this Boscombe said, "Oh, very generous. Thank you." Then he turned to me. "Afterwards how about a trip to the Piazza? And perhaps a little gaming, if you know of anywhere?"

"Oh, sir," protested Shackleford, but this was clearly part of a well-rehearsed routine. He must raise his token objections but Boscombe would go ahead and do just as he pleased.

"Certainly," I said. "I could return in a couple of hours or so, when you have had time to rest and dine."

And so it was agreed. I went downstairs and informed Bepi of the plan. He was sitting in the draughty entranceway, playing dice with another gondolier and Andrea. Bepi nodded. "So we're hired," he said.

"Yes. By the way, just how upset were they when they discovered the theft?"

"Well, I came back with Milord and the tutor was standing here waiting for us, and he started gabbling away. He seemed in a fair state."

"Yelling? Screaming? Crying?"

Bepi shrugged. "Gabbling."

As that was Bepi's word for all foreigners' conversation this was not much help. But then he added: "He kept pointing upstairs and saying something like *takeeneet*, over and over."

"Ah," I said. "I don't suppose you saw anyone on the scaffolding next door?"

Another shrug. "I wasn't looking. At that time of day you have to keep your eye on the other boats. Some of these young gondoliers . . ."

I said, "I know, I know." The deplorable lack of skill of the new generation of gondoliers is one of the few topics Bepi is loquacious about. He is, of course, referring to rowers about ten years younger than he is, at most.

"And you didn't get the idea that any of our friends from Fusina had turned up again?"

That caught his attention. He looked up from the dice. "You think it was one of them?"

"I don't know," I said. "But I can't help wondering."

"Well, maybe they've got what they want now and they'll leave us alone," he said. His eyes went back to the dice.

"Let's hope so," I said. "But I still wonder."

"Well, keep wondering," he said, making it clear he had no intention of wasting his time in such a fashion. Speculation for speculation's sake is never going to be one of his weaknesses. He had now turned all his attention to the demanding activity of shaking the dice.

"All right. I'll see you later," I said. Probably our good working relationship depends on the fact that we know better than to share our leisure hours.

I set out towards the Rialto again. With so much time in hand I could actually have gone home; my small apartment is in the parish of San Giovanni in Bragora, about twenty minutes' walk away, but there was nothing to eat there and I was hungry. One of the things that had taken me longest to learn in my adult Venetian life were the complicated rules that regulated the various kinds of eating and drinking establishments in the city. A *furatola* could not serve any food reserved to the *luganegheri* (sausage-makers), nor could they add cheese, oil or any kind of fat to their foods. If they were caught selling wine, they would be fined heavily and banished from the city for a year. The *magazeni* could serve wine, but no food – or at least no cooked food. The *malvasie*, the most refined of these establishments, sometimes frequented even by noblemen, served fine wines (including the wine that gave them their name, malvasia or malmsey) and biscuits. In the end, of course, it was my pocket that dictated which I could go to; I usually took whatever basic dish was on offer at the nearest *furatola* and then endeavoured to get rid of the taste with a glass of Cyprus wine from a malvasia. There was always local gossip to make up for any culinary deficiencies.

The topic that accompanied my bowl of *sguazzetto* – boiled pig trotters and veal – in Corte dell'Orso that evening was the rather unusual one of a local murder. A *gnaga* had been found stuffed down a well.

I was mildly relieved to find I was not the only one who had no idea what a *gnaga* was. The host expressed puzzlement and the group of gondoliers who had brought the subject up roared with laughter at his ignorance.

"*Gnagaaaaa*," said one of them, imitating the sound of a cat on heat.

"They killed a cat?" said the host. This did not seem to warrant the excited tones with which they had been discussing the event.

"Come on now, Martin," said the loudest gondolier. "Don't play the innocent. You must have seen these types at Carnival." The whole group now joined in the caterwauling, one of them adding to the performance by strolling around the courtyard in an exaggeratedly feminine fashion, one hand on his hip and the other wafting kisses to the upper windows. I remembered having seen a group of men in women's clothes and cat masks miaowing coquettishly at the crowds during Carnival. I had thought it was just one of those one-day jests, but apparently it had lasted long enough to earn the performers a new name. And a watery death for one of them.

"Where was it?" said the host.

"Over at Santa Maria Mater Domini," said the performer.

"Well, I won't drink any water there for a while," said the host.

6

As we waited for Boscombe and his tutor to descend from their meal I asked Bepi if he knew anything about the murder. He gave a grimace and said, "Nasty business."

"Who was he?" I said.

"Young man from the Friuli. He was selling himself."

"And they've no idea who did it?"

He gave his all-purpose shrug. "I don't think they're looking very hard."

"I expect his family would like to know," I said.

"His mother came here from the country," was all he said. Bepi comes from a large family and his tightened mouth and eyes told me he was making the painful comparisons.

There was the sound of footsteps on the grand staircase and Boscombe and Shackleford appeared. The young man had put on a splendid light-blue jacket and cream-coloured shirt with frothy frills at the neck and cuffs. His wig was freshly powdered and he was carrying a stick with a gold handle. Shackleford was his usual shabby self, with a dark cloak over one arm. Their shining cheeks and benevolent expressions suggested they had dined well. As I gazed at them I felt my *sguazzetto* rising to my throat; I obviously had not drowned it in sufficient wine.

"Tomorrow we have to call on the Resident," said Boscombe. "You know who that is?"

"Of course, sir. Mr Murray is very well known. He always receives in the morning, but not too early."

"I imagine not. Shouldn't imagine most visitors here are dawn-lovers, hey?" He gave his barking laugh. "Unless they haven't been to bed yet. So let's go and see this Piazza I've heard so much about. And then a little gaming . . ."

Shackleford was too mellowed by wine even to make his token protest.

We boarded the gondola and made our way down the Grand Canal. It would, of course, have been far quicker to walk, the curve in the canal adding an extra twenty minutes to our journey, but speed was hardly the point, and no gentleman of any standing was going to make his entrance into the Piazza by jostling through the crowds down the Merceria.

I confined myself to pointing out one or two of the more notable palaces – Palazzo Grimani, Palazzo Pisani Moretta, Ca' Foscari, the magnificent Ca' Rezzonico, which was finally being completed, the beautiful Ca' Dario and, of course, the great church of Santa Maria della Salute – and Boscombe smiled at them, while Shackleford did his best to remain awake. We emerged into the great open stretch before the Piazzetta, amid a host of other gondolas, bobbing towards the landing stage. There was a good moon shining down on us, and the classical façade of San Giorgio Maggiore shimmered across the water.

Bepi steered us in gently to the landing stage, where a busy *ganzer* stood ready to offer his hand to those passengers whose clothes warranted his attention. That category did not include me, so I leapt ashore unaided, while the *ganzer* fawned over Boscombe. A coin or two exchanged hands.

"Why couldn't we stop there?" asked Boscombe, pointing towards the pillars of San Marco and San Todaro. "That would seem the obvious place."

"Venetians never walk between the pillars, Sir," I said. I knew this was one of the anecdotes visitors enjoyed – far more than the date of the Palazzo Ducale or the architect of the Marciana library – so I immediately transformed myself into the professional *cicerone*. "It's supposed to bring bad luck. The pillars were brought to Venice from Acre in the twelfth century, and a reward was offered to anyone who could work out a way to raise them. The man who succeeded asked for the right to set up gaming tables between them and the state agreed, but then also made it the place for public executions."

"Wouldn't have thought that would put people off," said Boscombe, "knowing what gamblers are like, eh?"

"You're right," I said, "as you can see." I gestured towards the tables where a cluster of cloaked figures was hovering around a small table on which dice were being rattled. "Mind you, they usually stop while an execution is carried out. But even so, Venetians still prefer not to pass between them."

"Ah," said Shackleford, "wasn't there a doge who walked through them?"

"Yes," I said, a little surprised. The tutor had clearly done his preparatory studies. "Doge Marin Falier. He landed in Venice on a foggy evening and couldn't see where he was going and passed through them unawares. And it proved a bad augury as he ended up being executed himself. Beheaded."

"Oh, really? Between the pillars?" asked Boscombe.

"No, that was not thought suitable. In the courtyard of the Doge's palace." And I gestured towards the great Gothic building facing the waterfront.

"He's still remembered, is he?" asked Shackleford. The story of the treacherous doge seemed to have woken him up.

"Well, among those interested in history," I said. "And you could say they ensured he would be remembered by doing their best to stamp out his memory. They covered up his portrait in the room of the Great Council in the palace with a painted black drape, and so of course it's the only one everyone notices."

"Wasn't he an alchemist?" Boscombe asked.

"I've never heard that."

"Isn't he the one in –" he said, turning to Shackleford.

"Yes," Shackleford cut in quickly, "that's the one. But it's not important."

"So he walked between these pillars," said Boscombe. "Well, well."

I was surprised by this sudden manifestation of interest in medieval history. For some reason Shackleford, with equal suddenness, now seemed desirous of changing the subject. "Well, shall we see the square?" he said abruptly.

Boscombe accepted the diversion equably enough. He gazed at the crowds of people, all heading towards the Liston. "So that's the Piazza, is it?"

"That is the Piazzetta," I said. "We are looking on to the side of the church of Saint Mark. The Piazza lies in front of the church, a much larger open space, as you'll see."

"Well, let's go and join the merry throng, eh? And if there's anyone of note you can present us to, all the better. Especially if they're female, eh? Ha?"

"Certainly, sir. Shall we ask our gondolier to wait for us?"

Boscombe waved a hand rather vaguely; clearly the journey home was the last thing on his mind.

I turned to Bepi and said we would follow the usual rules; if we were not back by two he could consider himself free to go home. He nodded; he had already pulled his dice from his pocket. A gondolier needs inner resources for the slack moments.

We strolled towards the Piazza. Both Boscombe and Shackleford were looking with interest at the crowds. At this time in the evening all sorts of people can be found parading between the waterfront and the clock tower: finely dressed noblemen and their retinues, *cittadini* with stiff clothes and stiff wives, working men and women come to stretch their tired limbs and enjoy the spectacle of splendour laid on freely by the city, prostitutes, artists, performers, gamesters and torch-bearing children offering their various services. Near the great bell tower lounged a group of burly arsenalotti; they have the specific job of keeping order when the Great Council is in session, but even when there is no session a group of them can often be found there, just reminding the city that they exist. There is little enough for them to do at the Arsenale itself nowadays.

I glanced towards the coffee shop where I had earlier seen the nobleman and the wiry *ganzer*, and then looked around to see if there was any sign of Walnut Face. I caught no glimpse of any of them; several hours had passed, after all.

"This is the Liston, is it?" asked Shackleford.

"That's right," I said. His guidebook was clearly well informed. "To our right is the Doge's palace, which was built –"

"No dates, please," said Boscombe. "It was built. That's enough for me. Damned fine building, no doubt. So he lives there, does he?"

"The Doge? Yes, certainly. It is also the seat of government. And to our left is the Marciana library."

"Books, eh? Your sort of place, then, Shackleford."

"Undoubtedly, sir," said Shackleford. "I believe it has a priceless collection of Greek manuscripts."

"Well, don't let me hold you back. Go in and wallow."

"I have no doubt it will be closed at this hour, sir," said Shackleford, with a strained smile. "But I will certainly pay it a visit during the day." However, he seemed far more interested in the strolling people than in the building; his eyes were continually flitting over the crowds. Well, even tutors are human, I thought, and probably the village square back home offered a rather more restricted array of human types.

One particularly flamboyant specimen of humanity was strutting towards us: a young man who gave an immediate impression of being made of silver. Closer observation revealed that it was mainly his coat and wig that exuded an argentine shimmer; his complexion tended more to a powdery paleness, with just one beauty spot delicately placed high on his right cheek. He held what seemed to be an ivory cane, although it might just have been of a polished light-coloured wood; he was apparently being led by a poodle, whose white fur was as elaborately curled and powdered as his wig. He dispensed indulgent smiles to left and right, which were returned with equal benevolence for the most part. Venetian crowds are a tolerant lot on the whole.

I glanced at Shackleford to see how this spectacle would strike him and saw that he too was smiling. I was reminded of the look of eagerness I had seen when he opened his letter at the inn.

"My goodness," said Boscombe. "Don't see many like that at home."

The young man heard the English words and turned towards us. "I have no doubt you do not, sir." He spoke in English himself. The voice did not ring with the silvery fluting tones one might have expected, but was rather breathy and hoarse. It had just the slightest hint of a foreign accent, one that I could not identify.

"Ah, you speak English."

"I have been granted that privilege," he said, with a slight bow. Now that we were up close, I could see that he was not as young as he had first appeared; beneath the pale powder were delicate lines that suggested he was in his late thirties at least. "You are just arrived in this city?"

"First time," said Boscombe. "Being shown the sights. History and all that." He waved vaguely to the architectural vestiges of 'history' that surrounded us.

"History is an illusion. The real truths of this cosmos are perpetual

37

and unchanging. But let me present myself. I am Count Gelashvili, of Mtskheta." (I use the spelling I learned from later research; at the time all I caught was a sudden spluttering of frothy consonants.)

"Of where?"

"The ancient capital city of the kingdom of Georgia," said the count.

"Ah, yes," said Boscombe, with his usual vague amiability.

"Georgia, sir," said Shackleford. "On the eastern shores of the Black Sea." From his eager tone one might have got the impression that he had been yearning for the day when he might meet a true Georgian.

"That is correct," said the count. "But geography . . ." He waved a fluttering hand dismissively.

"Is an illusion?" I suggested.

The count's eyes turned towards me, but only for one flickering moment. Then they dropped towards his poodle, as if the creature were far worthier of his attention. "Sit, Zosimos. We must learn the virtue of patience." The dog obediently lowered its haunches, and cocked its head, gazing earnestly up at its master. Probably we were expected to take this as a model for our own behaviour.

Boscombe presented himself, and then Shackleford. The count lowered his head in two formal bows. Then Boscombe gestured towards me and said, "And this gentleman is our *cicerone*."

This time the count's eyes remained perfectly still, with not the slightest flicker in my direction. "All too often the mercenary guides in this city miss the essence of things, with their insistence on tedious dates and names."

"I suppose it's our fault for living in a world of illusion," I said, straining to keep my tone light.

"I suspect an intention of mockery," he said, still without glancing at me, "but words that come from the darkness of spiritual ignorance cannot touch one armoured in illumination. They pass by me as the idle wind which I regard not." He studied Boscombe's face, which looked a little blank at these words. "You, milord," he said, "are at an early stage on the path towards full illumination."

"Oh, ah, yes," said Boscombe. "I suppose I am."

"You have some acquaintance with the Egyptian rites?"

"Oh, I see. Well, yes, actually. I knew a chap in England –"

"Sir," said Shackleford, with an apologetic cough. "Is this the place?" And his eyes gave a quick dart towards me. Well, it was good to know that I had not actually become invisible.

"Come now, Shackleford," said Boscombe. "This gentleman here is clearly one of the Enlightened. You said that we might meet someone here."

"Yes, but let us not forget all discretion," he said. I do not know whether it was embarrassment at being shown up as a believer in this farrago, but he was almost squirming.

"Ah, I see," said Boscombe. He turned back to the count. "Perhaps we could exchange cards? You are staying in Venice?"

"Nothing is certain on this lower plane of life," he said. "Venice holds my physical body for the moment. But for how long . . ." He allowed his voice to tail off into silence, suggesting that at any moment he, like his words, might fade into oblivion.

"Ah, well, here's my card," said Boscombe, bringing out a mono-grammed slip from his waistcoat pocket. "We're staying at the White Lion."

The count took the card and slipped it into a pocket. "But I believe in taking immediate advantage of circumstances, for no encounters are truly fortuitous; all can be traced to a superior design, had we but the power to see it. Take the tide at the flood."

"I suppose so."

"So perhaps you will join me," the count said, "in my stroll."

"That is very amiable of you," said Boscombe. "We'd be delighted. We were thinking of visiting some place of, em, entertainment," he added in a slightly apologetic tone. Perhaps he feared that such an intention indicated too great an attachment to the lower plane of life.

"I applaud you," said the count. "Games of chance have their instructive side, especially for those who know that chance is always an illusion. I can certainly introduce you to an establishment where a gentleman of your standing will be made most welcome."

"Sir," I put in, "it may not be my place but I think I should offer a warning –"

The count became instantly aware of my existence. "I think there is no doubt that it is *not* your place."

I ignored him and went on doggedly. "Saint Mark's Square is well known as a venue where new visitors are sometimes taken advantage of." I glanced towards Shackleford; this was surely where he should come in with one of his little moralising platitudes in support of my warning. But apparently he was as beguiled by the count's performance as his pupil and was gazing at him with an expression not unlike the poodle's.

"I think I can judge for myself," said Boscombe, a touch of irritation in his voice.

I realised I was going to lose this battle. Well, I would at least make sure that I got paid as promised. "Do I understand you wish to dispense with my services?" I said, in as level a voice as possible.

"Yes, thank you. You've been very helpful but now I think we can cope for ourselves."

"Very good, sir. I'll just remind you that you engaged me for the whole evening."

The count now gave a little laugh, probably intended to be as silvery as his shimmering coat; actually it sounded cracked. "I think we now know where the interests of our *cicerone* lie."

"I have a living to make, like most people," I said. I added, "And an honest one . . ." I allowed the sentence to trail off pointedly.

The count gave another of his fluttering gestures, waving the remark off like the idle wind. "Give the man his 'h-onest' wage," he said. He gave breathy and ironic voice to the aspirate.

"Yes, of course," said Boscombe. There was just the faintest hint of embarrassment in his voice.

"There is also the gondolier," I reminded him.

"And what could be more h-onest than a gondolier?" said the count, stooping to pat his poodle.

I made no answer to that. I reminded Boscombe of the price that had been stipulated and he pulled the sum from a purse. Shackleford turned and examined the façade of the Marciana library, as if these sordid commercial transactions had nothing to do with him.

"And what time would you like me to meet you tomorrow?" I said, as a purely token gesture, knowing what the answer would be.

"How the h-onest man insists!" said the count. He had found a line of banter and clearly intended to stick with it.

"Well, perhaps we can leave things as they are," said Boscombe. "Many thanks for all your help. Hope you find some other client."

"I have no doubt I will," I said, lying through my teeth. "In the meantime, let me offer you a card, should you decide to avail yourself again of my services."

I gave him the small printed card I had had prepared on a rather extravagant whim a few weeks earlier. It gave my name, listed my services ("Professional *Cicerone* and Adviser to Travellers of all Nationalities; fluent Italian and English") and my address ("Salizada del Pignater, San Giovanni in Bragora"). "Should you need me, I live above the *magazen* in the salizada." I realised how unlikely it was that a wealthy English gentleman would come seeking my services in the back streets of Castello but I told myself, a touch dishonestly, that I owed it to Bepi to make this gesture, desperate though it might seem.

"Yes, of course," said Mr Boscombe. He put the card away with his purse without looking at it.

I gave a stiff bow to him and then to Shackleford, who made a fumbling show of being surprised at my departure.

"I trust your new acquaintance will live up to the glittering promise of his outward appearance," I said. As a parting shot, it was not quite as arrow-sharp as I would have liked; I would probably wake up around three o'clock knowing exactly what I should have said. I turned and walked back towards the waterfront, just catching behind me a final cracked laugh from the count and the words "So h-onest!" Well, his was not exactly a lethal shaft either.

Bepi looked up from the game of dice he was playing with two other gondoliers. "Ah," he said.

He did not have to make it sound quite so inevitable, I thought with a touch of irritation. "Yes," I said, "we've been dumped."

"So what did you say this time? Argue with them over the height of the campanile?"

"You know I always defer to the client," I said. "There was just that one time with that arrogant Scot who thought he could correct my Italian. And my knowledge of Venetian history. And art history . . ."

"Yes, I remember. Anyway, what got you riled this time?"

"Nothing. They just decided they preferred a Georgian count with a poodle."

"A what?"

"A count from Georgia. Who is apparently armoured in illumination, which must make a difference."

Bepi gave a puzzled flick of an eyebrow and I added, by way of explanation, "He talked nonsense about Egyptian rituals and spiritual planes which seemed to go down well with Mr Boscombe. And with the tutor, to tell the truth."

One of the other gondoliers looked up. "Ah, that fellow. He's out on the Liston most evenings."

"Who is he?"

"Nobody knows. Some foreigner. But he lives in Palazzo Garzoni. With the nobleman Piero Garzoni."

"Ah," I said. That was a curious coincidence.

"Oh, him," said Bepi. "Walks around with two arsenalotti, as if he expects to be assassinated."

"That might not be the only reason he likes to have them around," said the other gondolier, with a snigger. That, of course, was one of the rumours that circulated about the nobleman.

"Well, anyway, we've lost the clients," said Bepi, returning to practical matters.

"Yes. But they paid us for today. Not quite as much as you'd have got if I hadn't interfered this afternoon, but I'll make up the difference."

Bepi gave a generous wave. "Those people needed taking down a peg or two. Don't want that sort around Fusina. So I suppose it's back there tomorrow."

"I suppose so," I said. "Meet you at the usual place tomorrow afternoon. Thanks, Bepi."

And so ended our brief association with Mr Boscombe and his tutor.

Or so I thought . . .

7

Over the next week Bepi and I found an English family by the name of Higgins who wanted an occasional short gondola ride and an occasional short introduction to the splendours of Venetian civilisation, for which they were prepared to pay an occasional and much-reduced fee (usually after much *sotto voce* wrangling between husband and wife, while their two sons, aged twelve and ten, took advantage of the situation to start a fight).

I did not see Boscombe or his tutor during that week, although Fabrizio told me the latter had called again at his shop and passed an hour or two browsing and eventually buying a second-hand copy of Francesco Sansovino's *Venetia, città nobilissima et singolare*. As far as he and Lucia could tell, Boscombe and Shackleford were happily settled in the city and there appeared to have been no further episodes involving snake-like pursuers or infiltrating burglars. Lucia gathered that Boscombe was much taken with his new acquaintance, the Georgian count, who had introduced him to an exclusive casino, where he had even won some money. It sounded a fairly typical story; it would be interesting, and probably a little depressing, to hear what happened on subsequent visits to the same casino. As for the more esoteric interests of the count, the subject had not arisen in their conversation. Discretion remained Shackleford's rule in this area, it seemed.

The English family had no interest in strolling the Liston in the evening – the boys tended to become fractious, or at least more fractious, around seven o'clock – and so I had no chance to renew my acquaintance with Gelashvili. I heard that Boscombe had been seen on the evening parade together with the count.

On 16 April, as Bepi rowed us back from a visit to San Giorgio Maggiore, I mentioned to Mr and Mrs Higgins that for the Feast of Saint Isidore there was always a grand procession in Saint Mark's Square, with the Doge and all the authorities, followed by a Mass in the basilica. As good Protestants they wanted nothing to do with any Papish nonsense in the church, but they thought the boys might enjoy watching the procession; they had been rather disappointed to find that not everyone in Venice wore masks all the time, as they had been led to believe, and maybe a little pomp and ceremony would be some kind of compensation.

"Who was this Saint Isidore?" said Mrs Higgins, "and why should they celebrate him?" It was always she who asked the questions, usually in a suspicious tone; the premise for all her actions was the notion that anything done in this city – and probably everywhere outside England – had as its primary aim the extortion of money from guileless visitors, and she was not going to fall for it.

Knowing the likelihood of this question, I had prepared myself. "He was martyred under the Emperor Decius on the island of Chios and his remains were brought to Venice in the early twelfth century."

"Why?"

"Well, the veneration of saints' relics is common in the Roman Catholic world," I said, trying not to sound too apologetic. As this remark only provoked a snort from Mrs Higgins, I went on: "But there's a historical reason for the procession as well. The day of the Translation of his body was April the sixteenth and that happens to be the day that Doge Marin Falier was condemned to death."

This was met with blank silence; they clearly had not done the same preparatory reading as Shackleford and Boscombe. I went on: "In 1355 Marin Falier attempted to overthrow the Venetian state."

"I thought you said he was doge," she said.

"Yes, you did, you know," said her husband, eagerly nodding. He would put in the occasional comment to show that he had not fallen asleep.

"Yes, but being doge doesn't mean you have absolute power," I said. "Quite the contrary. Almost everything the doge does has to be approved by the Senate or the Great Council. And he wanted absolute power, like the other rulers in Italy at the time, and so he conceived a plan, along with a number of malcontents, to slaughter all the members of the Great Council. Unfortunately for him one of the conspirators warned someone in the Council and so word got out; all the conspirators, including the doge, were caught and executed. Ever since then the Venetian state has commemorated his execution, as a warning to the ruling doge of the limits of his power."

The boys wanted to know the details of the execution and were disappointed to hear that the procession did not involve a re-enactment of the beheading.

"And you say we'll see the doge and everyone," said Mrs Higgins.

"All the authorities that count in the city."

"And they'll all be dressed up in their finery."

"All in their ceremonial robes of office," I assured her, knowing that if she suspected that just one minor senator was missing a button or a frill there would be arguments over my fee ("such a disappointment for the boys after all they'd been promised"), but also knowing that if there was one thing the Venetians could be relied upon to do, it was to put on a good show.

And so it proved. We arrived in the square in time to see the grand procession setting out from the Doge's palace: first came eight officials bearing silk standards (two white, two red, two sky-blue and two green), followed by six officials blowing silver trumpets; then the *comandadori*, pipers, shield-bearers and the Doge's cavalier with the Missier Grande (head of the *sbirri*) on his right and the *scalco* on his left. Six canons in scarlet copes came next followed by two ducal *gastaldi*, four secretaries of the Council, the Doge's chaplain, two lower chancellors, and the Great Chancellor between two equerries, one bearing a gilded chair and the other a cushion of gold cloth. Next came the Doge himself, in a gold cope with a white stole around his neck and the ducal cap perched awkwardly on his wig; he peered out vaguely at the crowd, attempting a benevolent smile, and there were a few half-hearted cheers from some onlookers, but it was mostly appreciation of the spectacle rather than any warmth towards the man himself. Pietro Grimani had not endeared himself to the Venetian populace, who remembered how frugal had been the largesse he had scattered on his election day; still, he was their doge and nobody was actually going to denigrate him – not on a popular feast day, with foreigners around. His golden train was borne by four officials in scarlet liveries; to his right walked the papal nuncio, and to his left the imperial ambassador. A great golden cope was held over the Doge's head, protecting him from the weather – in this case, the sunshine – by an official in scarlet robes; behind him came a lengthy train of other ambassadors, legates and office-holders including the Heads of the Forty, the Leaders of the Council of Ten, the Cavaliers of the Golden Stole, and representatives of various institutional bodies.

Through sheer English determination and skilful use of elbows and a walking stick the Higgins family had managed to push their way to the front of the crowd – not exactly oceanic, since this was actually a fairly minor festival by Venetian standards – near the Caffe Florian; I had followed, a trifle apologetically, in the wedge-shaped gap created immediately in their wake, so that I, too, found myself in the front line.

"So that's the Doge," said Mrs Higgins, with a sniff. Clearly she had expected something grander.

"Is he going to get his head cut off?" asked Frederick, the younger Higgins child, who had not fully understood the intricacies of my earlier explanation.

"No one's going to be beheaded," I said, and realised that once again, quite contrary to my intentions, I was sounding apologetic.

"And who's that man on the roof?" asked Peter, the other boy.

"On the roof?" I swivelled to look in the direction he was pointing. At the far end of the square, on the roof of the building flanking the church of San Geminiano, which stands directly opposite the basilica of Saint Mark, was a figure dressed in black. He was holding something round in his hands, like a large cannonball. The procession was heading in his direction; once it reached the far end of the square it would make a broad U-shaped turn in order to move back towards the basilica.

"I expect he's just gone up there to get a better view," I said.

"He's going to throw it," said Peter.

He had indeed raised his arms above his head, and he stayed poised in this position for a few seconds. As far as one could tell from below, he was not especially tall but he was certainly broad. Suspended in that menacing position he was almost like an allegorical figure of brute force.

Other people in the crowd and in the procession had now caught sight of him and an excited buzz was arising, even above the sound of the pipes and trumpets. The procession had begun to lose some of its stately dignity; it was no longer moving forwards at a slow but steady pace. Some of its components had halted, others were hesitating and one or two were frankly moving backwards; there was a certain amount of stumbling and bumping, with all the consequent treading on heels and trains. The music itself had fallen for the most part into inharmonious squeaks, with just one steadfast trumpeter determinedly playing on; maybe he simply had not noticed what was happening.

Venetian crowds are generally well disciplined and there has never been any need to marshal them with armed guards, so the only people with any weapons were the ornamental halberdiers. And unless the man on the roof jumped down and tried to strangle the Doge with his bare hands, it was unlikely their halberds were going to be much immediate use.

The squat dark figure threw his missile and there was a general scattering in the area immediately beneath his vantage point. From our position we could only see the round object plummet into the crowd, not the actual target – whatever the target was. The next instant the figure on the roof had disappeared: it happened so fast it was hard to say whether he had just vanished into thin air or had dropped into a waiting skylight. There was a sudden scream from the area where the object had been hurled: it was not a cry of pain but a female yell of pure horror. It was taken up by other voices, until there was just a general high-pitched babble. The crowd around us was getting agitated; the procession was breaking up, so that it was now difficult to distinguish between onlookers and participants. I said to the Higgins family, trying to sound firmly in control of things: "I think we had best withdraw."

"Nonsense," said Mrs Higgins. It was as if I were yet again trying to swindle her.

"My dear," said her husband nervously, "I think it might be prudent . . . the boys, you know."

"We don't want to go now!" said Peter.

"You're not going to see anything in this confusion," I said grimly.

"You think so?" Peter said, with a defiant glance at me. And suddenly he wormed his way through the apparently impenetrable barrier of people ahead of us and disappeared, heading in the direction of the point of greatest turmoil.

"Oh, dear," said Mr Higgins. "You shouldn't have challenged him."

"Get after him!" snapped Mrs Higgins. "No, not you," she added, seizing her husband, who had made a half-hearted gesture of pursuit. She made a firm snatch at the younger boy with her other hand and then stood rigidly firm, like the bell tower.

I set off after Peter, pushing and elbowing and squeezing until I somehow managed to get within sight of the determined little figure, still pressing onwards. Fortunately he was wearing a bright blue coat, which was easy to see in the crowd.

A few seconds later I caught up with him and grabbed his arm. He resisted my backward tug, yelling, "I want to see!"

Since we were now so close to the heart of the hubbub it seemed a little ridiculous not to make the final penetrative thrust; I, too, had some natural curiosity. So, still holding tightly on to his arm, I pushed between two priests and found myself on the edge of a jostling circle of people, most of whom were looking horror-struck. The perimeter was being kept steady by a number of burly arsenalotti, who had clearly been deputed to this task by some quick-thinking officials in the procession, and at the very centre of the circle was the object that had been hurled.

It was a human head.

The position in which it had come, so to speak, to rest was, unfortunately, with the severed neck towards us, so that we had a grim view of dark, matted arteries and skin; beyond that we could see a white staring face with an open-mouthed, open-eyed expression which in other circumstances would have been comic. The headgear, too, might have been amusing in another context: I could just make out the curious details of a cat's ear protruding from the top of the head.

And now amid the confused babble of voices I heard the word "Gnaga" being repeated all around us, adding an odd feline intonation to the tumult.

I looked down at the boy beside me. His face had taken on the same round-eyed, round-mouthed expression as the severed head. It was clear that the comic elements of the spectacle were lost on him too. That was a relief.

"Come on, let's get back to your mother," I said.

He allowed himself to be led away. We found the rest of the family still standing where we had left them, while the crowd seethed and surged around them. I had not really expected his mother to swoop on him with a tearful rib-crushing embrace so I was not over-surprised when she greeted him with a severe "What have you to say for yourself?" without even bending towards him.

He muttered sulkily, "I wanted to see." And then, having plucked up some courage in the last thirty seconds, he added, with a note of justificatory pride: "They chopped someone's head off. I saw it!"

"Nonsense," said his mother automatically.

"I'm afraid it's true," I said. "I really think you had better take him away. I think it's been a bit of a shock."

"Someone's head?" said Mr Higgins.

"That was what was thrown down," I said.

"It was all bloody and messy!" said Peter, with an evident desire to taunt his younger brother, who had not had the privilege of beholding this spectacle.

And inevitably Frederick started to wail. "I want to see."

"Madam," I said firmly, "this is no place for children."

She accepted this and announced: "We will return to our inn."

We made our way back to the gondola. I realised there was no need to tell Bepi what had happened. Gondoliers pick up news long before anybody else in the city; they seem to have an instant network of contacts, each one equipped with that spider touch, so memorably described by Alexander Pope, which, "exquisitely fine / Feels at each thread, and lives along the line".

As Bepi manoeuvred us out into the lagoon, he just said to me: "Another *gnaga*."

"So it seems," I said. "I only caught a glimpse. It was not pleasant."

"Someone's got it in for them," said Bepi.

"And for the Doge," I said.

"Yes," said Bepi. "That is strange."

I do not think he said it out of any special love for the present doge. Like all Venetians he simply had an unquestioning respect for the order of things as they are in the city. Venetians will grumble about almost everything but they would never dream of trying to change anything.

8

The shocking event had the immediate effect of putting an end to the Higgins family's sojourn in the city. The decapitation of a male prostitute was not exactly the kind of edifying and instructional experience that the parents had hoped for. The next day they left for Padua, Frederick still bewailing the fact that he had not seen the gory head and Peter taking every opportunity to remind his brother that he had done so by making unconvincing imitations of the expression on the face. Even his father was driven to tell him to stop it.

With my wages in pocket and no new client I took the opportunity to call on Fabrizio. It was always good to get a sane perspective on things.

When I raised the subject that was on everyone's lips he shook his head, slowly and sadly. "There's something sinister behind this."

"Well, yes," I said, a little disappointed by the obviousness of the statement. "Murder, sedition . . ."

He shook his head more briskly this time. "No, that's not what I meant. There's more to it. I'm talking about the deliberate symbolism."

"Symbols of what?"

"Well, that's what I would like to understand. The procession of Saint Isidore commemorating the beheading of Marin Falier, and a beheaded prostitute. The previous one . . ."

"Was stuffed down a well," I said.

"Exactly. And this one, the rest of the body . . ."

"Burned." They had found the decapitated corpse in a baker's oven, charred and unrecognisable.

"Exactly. The legend of Saint Isidore tells us that, among his various sufferings, he was thrown into a well and thrust into a furnace."

"Ah," I said. "So these aren't just random acts of violence."

"No. But the pattern is not clear. In fact, you have to be a bookseller with time on your hands even to know the legends that surround the life of Saint Isidore. It's almost as if there is a private message."

"Addressed to whom?"

"Well, I doubt they had me in mind. The Inquisitors may well have done the same reading as me, but I don't think they will communicate their suspicions to the public at large. So for the moment, despite the glaring publicity of the actual crimes, the message remains private and cryptic."

"You think it might be a religious fanatic?"

"It's possible. A devotee of Saint Isidore. He is a protector of sailors – just as Saint Mark is. In fact, you could consider him a kind of poor man's substitute for Saint Mark. But why St Isidore should have a particular objection to *gnaghe* . . ."

"Well, I imagine any especially religious person might consider them offensive." I only needed to think of the lady in the apartment above mine, who, between one church visit and another, had told me that the two victims had practically asked to be killed.

"Yes, but there is a great difference between being offended and being ready to commit murder. And very spectacular and risky murder."

"Yes," I said. "And a very well-planned one." The figure that had appeared on the roof and hurled the bloody trophy had climbed there from an empty apartment; after his gesture he had dropped back into the apartment, stripped off his black disguise, which was later found on the floor, and managed somehow to slip into the crowd unobserved, helped by the fact that no one was watching the back of the building at that moment.

"I wonder whether it can have been done by one person," Fabrizio said. "Think of the whole business of dragging a corpse to a disused baker's shop, lighting the fire . . ."

Lucia entered the shop at this moment. She had a laden shopping basket; the smell of fresh bread filled the room. It was a comfort to know some bakeries were used for kinder purposes.

"Sior Alvise," she said, with a smile.

"Siora Lucia," I said with a bow.

"You have left your English family?"

"They have left me," I said. "Or rather they've left Venice. The episode with the head was too much."

She grew serious at once. "Ah, I can imagine. You weren't there in the Piazza, were you?"

"I'm afraid I was. And one of the boys had the misfortune to see it."

"Ah." She winced. Then she added, with a touch of rueful realism: "But knowing boys I'm sure he'll have got over it."

"All too quickly," I said. "But it was undoubtedly a shock at first."

"And think what it must be like for the poor family," she said.

"Well, as I said, they've left now."

"I meant the family of the murdered man."

"Ah yes, right. Have they found out who he was?"

"Another young man from the Friuli, come here to try to make a living. I'm sure it wasn't his first choice of career."

I could tell that her father was embarrassed again. This was not the kind of topic he would have chosen for conversation with his daughter. "My dear, perhaps you should put the shopping away."

She smiled. "Don't worry, Father. I don't intend to engage in a discussion with Sior Alvise on the ethics of prostitution, whether female or male."

"My dear . . ."

"But a word of common pity seems the least we can offer this wretched victim," she went on undeterred. Then, presumably out of common pity for her father, she changed the subject. "Have you heard any more of your young English gentleman?"

"No," I said. "I don't really expect to. Has his tutor looked in again?"

"No," said Fabrizio. "But I have heard that his pupil was not so fortunate on subsequent visits to the gaming tables."

"Well, what a surprise," I said. "And I suppose our Georgian count is encouraging him to try again."

"So it seems. They attended the private *casino* of his Excellency Loredan, I believe."

"Well, perhaps the count will teach him how to turn base metal into gold and so all his problems will be solved," I said. "Anyway, it's not my problem. I'm just surprised that his tutor didn't make the slightest objection when the count turned up. He is such an obvious *frappatore*." I used the Tuscan word for swindler that Goldoni had made popular.

"There's something strange about Mr Shackleford," Lucia put in.

"Strange?" I said.

"Yes. I suspect his scholarship is not so profound as he claims."

"What makes you say that?" her father asked.

"I don't know. It was an impression I got when we talked here in the shop the other day. When I started talking about Virgil he steered the conversation away. In fact, at a certain point I realised he just wanted to be left alone with the books."

"That is hardly unusual in a bookshop," observed her father mildly.

"Yes, but it wasn't just a desire to browse in peace, I think."

"I think I'd steer the conversation away if we got on to Virgil," I said.

"Yes, but you don't claim to be a tutor and a classical scholar."

"No, just a humble *cicerone*. Oh, and the name comes from Marcus Tullius Cicero, Roman consul and orator and –"

"Bravo, Sior Alvise. But you do see there's a difference between your job and that of a private instructor for a scion of the English ruling classes?"

"Yes, I know. I just show them the way to the gambling houses and the –" I pulled myself up short, with a glance at Fabrizio, who was frowning.

"I spoke out of turn the other day," Lucia said, with a slightly embarrassed smile. "I apologise."

"I'm glad to hear you say so," said her father.

"Have you forgiven me?" she said, turning her dark eyes full on me.

When she looked at me like that I would forgive her anything. "There was nothing to forgive, signorina. You gave me food for reflection."

"You are generous to say so," she said, and her smile became broad and dazzling.

Realising that I would melt unless I turned away I spoke to Fabrizio, choosing a different topic of speculation. "I wonder if I'll ever find out what those people who were following Boscombe wanted. And whether they're connected with the Georgian count."

"In this city everything is connected with everything else," said Fabrizio. "But the knots that tie them are usually so intricate that you can rarely follow the threads from one end to the other."

"I wouldn't bother trying in this case," said Lucia. "I'm sure you can find better things to fill your time with."

She might have been right. But as it turned out I was not to have much choice in the matter.

9

I was pulled into the intricate web the very next night. The first intimation of my newly entangled state came in the form of hard, insistent pummelling sounds. I passed from a confused dream in which the two bronze Moors on the clock tower were pounding me with their long hammers to an only slightly less confused realisation that the urgent knocks were being administered to my bedroom door (which is also my front door, my apartment consisting of just the one room).

I sat up. The gaps above the window shutters told me that it was still dark. I guessed that I had been asleep only a couple of hours.

"Who is it?" I called out.

The knocking ceased. "It's me, Boscombe," came a muffled voice.

This made little more sense than my previous notion that the Moors had come to life. "What –"

"Just open the door, please!"

I pushed the bedclothes from me, stumbled across the room and turned the key.

A little light from the tavern on the floor below seeped up the stairs and I could just make out his face, white and anxious, above a dark cloak. I thought he was even shaking.

"Please let me in," he said. "I need to sit down."

I stood aside and he stumbled in. I wondered if he was drunk. Then I told myself the man was no longer employing me and so I said out loud: "Excuse me, sir, but have you been drinking?"

"No, really. Not a drop. Where can I sit? I can't see anything."

I groped for my tinderbox and a tallow candle. A few moments later the young man's tense figure was visible by its flickering light. He was definitely pale; he looked out of breath and his eyes darted nervously around the room.

"I'm sorry," I said. "If I had known you were coming I would have tidied up." I pointed to the little table by the window and my one stiff chair. "You can sit down there, sir."

He crossed the room, picking his way through the scattered clothes and piles of books, and sat down with a grateful sigh.

"To what do I owe –" I began.

"He's dead," he said abruptly.

"Who?"

"Shackleford." He said it almost impatiently, as if it were obvious.

"I'm sorry," I said clumsily. "My condolences –"

"He was killed."

"Killed?"

"Yes, killed!" His voice had risen several notches so that it was almost a scream. "Murdered!"

"But who – how –"

Suddenly he bent over the desk with his face resting on his left arm and started sobbing.

Like all men faced by another man in tears I felt at a loss. Fortunately he got a grip on himself and sat up.

"Sorry," he said with some difficulty. "Shouldn't have done that."

"Don't worry," I said. "Just tell me what happened." I forgot the difference in rank as I spoke.

He was too upset himself to notice the lack of deference. "I didn't know where else to turn," he said. "Then I remembered your card and found I still had it. The people downstairs told me where you lived."

"Very kind of them," I said drily. Carlo and Giovanna who ran the tavern would presumably see nothing odd in someone calling on me at two in the morning. The tavern usually closed around one thirty; it had taken me a few months to habituate myself to sleeping through the buzz of voices and even the occasional rowdy choruses from the regular clients, and then through the clatter of pots and pans that would accompany my dreams for half an hour or so after closing time. My first night in the apartment had made it clear to me why the rent was so affordable. The tavern was officially just a *magazen*, which was only supposed to serve cheap wines, but the *luganegher* next door, run by Carlo's cousin, provided sausages and other forms of meat, and there was a constant to and fro between the two establishments; it was clear to me that all the washing up was done in the kitchens of Carlo's *magazen*.

"You see, there's no one else. I don't think I can trust anyone. Not the count. Nor his Excellency Loredan . . . I don't know whether I can go to the Resident, not after this."

"After what?"

"I'm going to tell you. Wait. Wait." He sat there breathing hard for a few moments.

I waited. To try to relieve the tension I picked up a few stray garments and discreetly pushed my chamber pot under the bed, out of sight.

"You see, I followed him," he said.

"Your tutor?"

"Yes. I felt sure he was up to something. I never believed that theft, you know."

"Theft?"

"Yes, you remember. The night we arrived at the White Lion."

"Ah yes. You didn't believe it? You mean you didn't believe there had been a burglary?"

"Well, I did at first. But later . . ." He looked sharply at me: "Did you believe it?"

I shook my head. "I had my doubts," I said. "But as I didn't know what was supposed to have been taken, I kept my suspicions to myself."

"It was the book," he said.

"What book?"

"About Marino Faliero." He used the Italian, rather than the Venetian, form of the name.

"Ah," I said. There had to be a reason why things kept coming back to a fourteenth-century doge. "So why would anyone steal a book on Marin Falier? What sort of book was it? A history book?"

"Well, I didn't know exactly, because it was in Italian. But Shackleford told me it explained the Rosicrucian mysteries. Because Marino Faliero was one of the first initiates."

"I've never heard that," I said. "But if you say so. Or rather if Mr Shackleford said so."

"I had better start at the beginning," he said.

"That would help."

"The book was in my father's library. I was no bookworm, no point pretending that, but my father used to like this book and take it out so I recognised it when I saw it in Shackleford's luggage."

"In his luggage?"

"Yes. I had the impression there was something he was hiding. He would close his trunk whenever I came near; rearrange his clothes to cover something. So one day in Milan, when he wasn't around, I had a look. Thought he might have some erotic pictures or something. And I found my father's book. So naturally I asked him about it." He was breathing more normally now and his voice had lost its agitated tone.

"And he had an explanation?"

"He was very embarrassed. He apologised over and over again. He said he intended to return it when we got back to England but this journey was too good an opportunity to miss. He wasn't likely ever to be able to come to Italy again. He had thought of asking permission but then decided he couldn't bear the idea of being refused. I mean, my father is dead but my mother probably would have said no, out of respect for his memory."

"Too good an opportunity for what?"

"That's the point. He told me the book dealt with Marino Faliero's explorations of the Rosicrucian mysteries and that in Venice there was a man who could probably make use of the knowledge. The nobleman Piero Garzoni."

"And you believed him."

Boscombe seemed a little startled by this question. "Well, why shouldn't I?"

"Tell me," I said, "did Mr Shackleford know that you were interested in these things? Rosicrucian mysteries?" I resisted the temptation to add "and that sort of nonsense".

"Well, yes, of course. He shared my interest. Although he had to keep quiet about it in front of my mother, who doesn't understand these things. And he said we shouldn't mention it over here, either, since the authorities don't approve of such things. That's why we didn't tell anyone when the book was stolen."

"But he could have just decided to tell you that story about Marin

Falier as a way to win you over, after you had caught him out with the book. And you admit you haven't read it."

This was clearly a new idea for him. "But surely —"

"It's just that I have never heard anyone claim that Marin Falier had anything to do with the Rosicrucian mysteries."

"The count said it too!" he said, with an air of slightly desperate triumph.

"Ah, the count," I said.

"He is a true initiate," he said. "Even if . . ."

"Even if what?"

"Well, I realise now he took me to some rather shady gambling places. But I suppose a man like that has to make a living like everyone else. And he certainly knew the rituals."

I decided this was not worth pursuing right now. We needed to get to the murder. "So you followed Mr Shackleford."

"Yes," he said. "Over the last few days I began to think he was hiding something from me again. He was definitely acting suspiciously."

"You think he still had the book?"

"Well, I began to wonder. The story of the burglary had come from him. You'll remember that I came back from my ride in the gondola to find him very upset, complaining that we had been robbed. But no one else saw anything. Nothing else had been taken."

So it was possible for Boscombe to have his suspicions aroused, I thought. It probably took him a little longer than most people — and possibly a series of relentless losses at the gambling table helped.

"But," I said, "there were people after that book."

"Yes, that's true."

"Who were they?"

"I don't know. I'm not sure whether Shackleford knew. But it made me realise the book must contain some very important secrets. So naturally I was sorry it had been stolen. However, it wasn't the end of the world. I thought we could still try to meet this nobleman Garzoni and that would be interesting. And then we bumped into the count and that was a real stroke of luck, since he was actually living with Garzoni."

"Very lucky," I said.

"So for the next week or so the count kept meeting us, taking us to gambling houses, showing us some of the sights of the city. And he said he would introduce us to his Excellency Piero Garzoni but it wasn't easy, the nobleman was a very retiring man, he would have to choose the right moment . . ."

"Right. And when did you start wondering about Mr Shackleford and the book?"

"Well, he would go off on his own. Nothing wrong with that, of course. I mean, goodness knows I didn't want him with me all the time. Especially in the evenings . . . But if I asked him what he had been doing he always sounded a little shifty. I did have another look through his luggage, actually; I mean, the fellow is in my service, after all. Didn't find anything. But I began to wonder. And then one evening I heard the count and Shackleford talking together and I heard the count say, 'You've got it, haven't you?' and Shackleford said, 'No, no, I swear it's been stolen.' And then they must have realised I could hear them and they changed the subject."

"So the count knew about it."

"Well, it seemed so."

"So maybe that encounter with the count in the square wasn't quite so unplanned." I was remembering the letter that Shackleford had found for himself at the Queen of Hungary, which had seemed to cheer him.

"Oh, you think so?" Boscombe was struck by this. After a few seconds, during which I could almost hear the cogs of his brain whirring as he adjusted his mind to this new notion, he said: "Well, this afternoon he received a note at the inn. He kept it to himself but I could see it made him thoughtful. In the evening he asked if I was going out with the count, as usual, and as it happened I wasn't. I had decided to have a quiet evening for once; I mean, you can't drink and play every night, you know."

"No, I imagine not," I said.

"I could see this rather put him out. Anyway, I retired to bed early. And later I heard him creeping out. So I thought, well, now let's see what you're up to. And so I followed him." The tremor returned to his voice. "Why didn't I just challenge him? It would have been so much – so much better."

I didn't say anything. I didn't want to affect his flow of thoughts at this point.

He went on. "Well, he obviously knew where he was going. Much better than I did. After all, I've always got around the city by gondola. This was the first long walk I'd been on. We crossed that square with the man on the horse at one point."

"The statue of Colleoni. Campo Santi Giovanni e Paolo."

"Yes, a big church. And a big building with a white façade next to it. Lions on the façade. That was where I had to be careful to stay some way back. Then he turned right, crossed a bridge, maybe two bridges, and entered a house. I waited for a while, maybe as long as ten minutes, just keeping my eye on the door. Nobody else went in or out."

"Could you hear any voices?"

"There was a tavern nearby which made a fair bit of noise so I couldn't hear anything from the house. At one point I thought I heard some kind of cry and a thumping noise . . ." He fell silent as his mind clearly relived these moments. "So then I thought, well, I've come this far. I might as well see what's going on up there. The door opened with just a push and there was a staircase. I went up. Of course it was all completely dark and I didn't have a lantern. At the top of the stairs there was just a little light coming from under a door so I presumed that was where Shackleford was. So I stood outside the door for a while, just listening. Couldn't hear anything. I pushed the door."

Another pause. His eyes turned to the candle, as if seeking comfort in its flickering light.

"And there he was. Blood everywhere. I must have let out some kind of cry. That was presumably what roused the people in the other apartment."

"So you were seen?"

"Yes. Not at once. Wait . . ."

He swallowed and started again. "He was sitting propped up against the wall, and he was staring straight at me. I mean, his eyes were open. And there was a big gash across his throat. Blood all down him. And on the floor. I slipped in it." He looked down at his foot, as if to see if there were still stains. "Nothing I could do for him. I mean, he was clearly dead."

"So what did –"

"Wait. That's not all."

I waited.

"He was dressed in women's clothes. And he had these cat's ears on his head." He paused. "It wasn't funny."

"I imagine not."

"And there was no one else there. No one. Just me and him."

"Did you search the place?"

"There were two rooms. All very luxurious. You know, lots of little carvings. Painted ceiling. A small chandelier – with candles still lighted. A table – for gambling, I presume. And a bed in the second room."

"A *casino*," I said. That was the name for these discreet sets of rooms, which usually belonged to noblemen: places where they could indulge in private gambling and other intimate activities. Boscombe must have been familiar with the word, since he had been regularly visiting the *casino* of the Loredan family.

"Yes. And he just lay there." He paused, and then said very simply: "Poor Shackleford."

"So then?"

"I panicked. I just wanted to get away. I opened the door. And at that moment the door on the other side of the landing opened and a woman looked out. She stared straight at me – and then she must have seen Shackleford behind me, because I hadn't closed the door yet. And she screamed."

"And you ran for it?"

"I tried to say something like calm down, signora . . ."

I winced. "So she must have heard you weren't Venetian."

"I suppose so. I wasn't thinking. Then I ran. And she just kept screaming. By the time I got to the bottom of the stairs I could hear other doors opening. And people looked out of the tavern as well."

"And you came straight here."

"Yes. Well, not straight. I had to ask the way. You were the only person I could think of who might be able to help. All I had was your card, so I had to ask people for directions."

"Right." So fairly soon word was going to get round that a man with a foreign accent had been seen fleeing the scene of the murder and then asking for directions to my house. He might as well have left a trail of bloody footprints. Perhaps he had done that too.

I said slowly: "You realise that you will probably be traced to this house."

His eyes widened. "You won't give me away."

"Sir, I'm not sure what you think I can do for you."

"Hide me! I didn't do anything ... I can't ..."

I waved my hands around the apartment. "Hide you where?"

"Help me escape then. Your gondolier friend. He can take me to the mainland."

"Sir, Bepi has a living to make in this city. He can't take such a risk."

He had got to his feet and put his hands to his face. I realised he was quite likely to break down in tears again.

I spoke as calmingly as possible. "Sir, what you must do now is collect your thoughts and decide what you are going to tell the authorities. You cannot run away from this. Remember you are a man of good birth, from a nation that is respected. You will be treated with deference. There is an English Resident in the city who will do what he can for you. Running away would be the worst solution."

"What will my mother say? My family?"

"Didn't you say you have family in Italy? In Florence? You must write to them."

He grabbed at this. "Yes, my uncle. And his daughter, my cousin. "

"Tell me their names."

"Mr Hugh Boscombe. His daughter is Clare. She's intelligent. She'll know what to do. We grew up together. She'll vouch for me."

"What do they do there?"

"My uncle is a clergyman. And an antiquarian. He studies – you know, antiquities and that."

Not as useful as a diplomat or a lawyer, and the clerical qualification would not count greatly in Roman Catholic Venice; still, a respectable enough activity. It might help.

"Tell me again about the *casino*: you're sure there was no one else there?"

"No one."

"And no one came out while you were waiting outside?"

"No. But they must have – I mean, there must be another way out. The window. Something."

"Did you have time to look properly at Mr Shackleford?"

"What do you mean?"

"Did he look as if had put on those clothes by himself?"

"I don't know. He was covered in blood. I didn't stop to look at his – the way he was dressed."

"Even though he was wearing women's clothes?"

"Well, I could hardly help noticing that. But I didn't look to see if he'd done the stays up properly . . ." He gave a grimace as he realised how incongruously comic this sounded. "He'd had his throat cut!" he said in a sudden high-pitched cry.

"And was there a weapon?"

He stopped to think. "Yes. A big knife. Covered in blood. I didn't touch it."

It struck me that I had better get dressed. If I was going to receive the *sbirri* I would prefer to do it in more dignified apparel. I muttered an apology and started gathering my clothes.

"Are we going to go back there?" he said, with clear dismay.

"No," I said, taking off my nightshirt. "Not unless they take us there." I could hear new voices in the tavern below. I found yesterday's clothes; they would have to do for another day. I imagined that the next few hours might bring about a certain amount of sweating, so I saw no point in putting on a clean shirt.

"They?"

"The people who have arrived at the tavern downstairs and are now asking about the arrival of a foreign gentleman."

"Oh, my God."

There were footsteps on the stairs. Boscombe gave a desperate look at the window but I shook my head. "Stay calm," I said. "React with dignity."

There was a knock at the door. I opened up. Two figures stood there, one of them holding a lantern. They were clearly *sbirri*: nobody else has that same look of menacing surliness, usually combined with a certain lack of sartorial flair.

"How can we help you?" I said, making myself sound as Venetian as possible.

"Looking for the *foresto* who just got here," said the larger *sbirro*, the one holding the lantern. His accent had the rising intonation of western Dorsoduro, the area around San Nicolò, where nearly all the *sbirri* came from. His expression of surliness was exacerbated by a jagged scar that seemed designed to emphasise the downward tendency of his mouth.

"He is ready to answer your questions," I said, "but you will probably need me as an interpreter."

"That's no problem," he said. "We've got irons for both of you." And his colleague held up two sets of fetters. I think he gave a surly grin as he did so, but it was difficult to tell as most of his face was hidden behind a matted forest of black hairs.

"That won't be necessary," I said. "We're not going to try to escape."

"Rules are rules," said the man with the jagged scar. "Hands behind your backs."

I translated for Boscombe. He gave just a faint whimper of protest but then obeyed. A few seconds later we both had our arms shackled behind us and were being pushed towards the doorway.

"Are you going to let me lock the door behind us?" I said.

"Don't worry. We'll look after your little house," said the scarred man. "We'll keep it real nice for you."

When we got out into the street I realised there were other *sbirri* waiting there. Carlo and Giovanna had come out of the tavern and were talking to them. Many of the windows around us were open, and curious faces were staring out.

"Don't worry about this," I said to Carlo and Giovanna. "It's all a mistake. I'll be back later."

Carlo looked sceptical but Giovanna gave me an encouraging smile. "I'm sure it'll all be sorted out," she said. "We'll keep everything nice for you." The fact that she used the same expression as the *sbirri* was not encouraging, however motherly her tone. I could see three *sbirri* making their way upstairs as we talked. Well, there was nothing more incriminating for them to discover than my chamber pot, I thought. They were welcome to it.

The man with the scarred face prodded us forward and off we went, to our first night in custody.

10

Half an hour later I was standing in a small room somewhere in the Doge's palace, with my arms still tied behind my back and just one *sbirro* – the hairy one – by my side. Boscombe and I had been separated some minutes earlier, although I had not realised it at the time. I had no idea where in the palace I was, having lost all sense of direction since being pushed out of the gondola into the prison courtyard. It was only because I had realised, at a certain point during our scrambling up dark stone staircases and along cold stone corridors, that we were crossing the Bridge of Sighs that I knew I was now in the Doge's palace itself: the heart of Venetian government – and of Venetian justice. But after that moment of recognition another series of torchlit staircases, twisting corridors and secret doorways had me newly bewildered. I suspected that this was not unintentional on the part of my captors.

Venetian justice. For me, as for most citizens of the Most Serene Republic of Venice, these words were not entirely reassuring. I knew that many of the stories of what went on in the back rooms of the palace were exaggerated; I knew that executions were comparatively rare today and that it was not true that secret denunciations dropped by malevolent spirits into stone lions' mouths resulted automatically in the arrest and secret dispatch of innocent victims. I knew these things – or, at least, I had known them up until a few hours ago. I felt a little less sure of them now.

The room was narrow and lit by just one small chandelier with a few flickering candles. There were no windows. The walls on two sides were lined with tall cupboards; the door of one was slightly ajar, allowing me to see that it was crammed with sheaves of paper and books with dark leather covers. The furniture consisted of one desk against the far, narrow end of the room, with two chairs behind it. I guessed it would not be a good idea to ask if I could go and sit on one of them, though I was now aching with tiredness and tension.

A figure in a dark cloak scuttled into the room, sat down at the desk and pulled a large book and a quill towards himself. He was not quite as daunting a figure as I had been expecting: round cheeks, a pair of glasses that glinted in the candlelight and a slightly lopsided wig. I should have felt relieved, perhaps, but the very softness of his features was in fact rather disturbing in its incongruity.

Then came the *colpo di grazia*. In walked the Missier Grande.

Every Venetian knows this figure. Leader of the *sbirri*, in direct contact with the Council of Ten, responsible for law and order throughout the city. His jet-black robe with its huge sleeves and white fur trimmings marks him out, and usually he only has to appear in the midst of a crowd for everyone to fall silent. He never carries a weapon and even when not flanked by cudgel-bearing *sbirri* can impose order by his presence alone.

I had only ever seen him from a distance before that night, but was familiar with his lean, hard features. He stared straight at me and I saw that his eyes were of an icy blue. He sat down without glancing at the other man, who had scrambled to his feet at the moment he entered. Still without turning his head he put up his left hand; the man in glasses placed a sheet of paper in it. The Missier Grande glanced down at the paper for a second and then straight back at me.

"Alvise Marangon," he said. His voice was quiet and level, the voice of a man who knew he never had to shout.

"That's my name, Illustrissimo," I said, trying to reproduce his own quiet confidence and failing.

"Son of Alvise Marangon, clerk at the Arsenale. And Fiammetta Visentin, actress."

"Yes, Illustrissimo."

"You have lived in Venice for nearly two years, having grown up in England."

"Yes," I said again. There was really no need for me to say anything. There was not the slightest interrogative tone to any of his sentences.

"And you have worked as a *cicerone* mainly for English visitors, with a regular licence, usually with the help of Bepi Zennaro, gondolier."

He gave the merest glance at the sheet of paper in his hands as he spoke; either he was a very fast reader or he already knew all these details about my life. I preferred to think he was a fast reader.

"You ceased to be a *cicerone* for Signor Boscombe" – he pronounced it *Boscombay* – "a week ago."

"Yes, Illustrissimo," I said again.

"And yet tonight Signor Boscombay came running to your house after murdering his tutor."

"He says he did not do it," I said.

He ignored the remark. "He came running to you. Why is that?"

Now that a question came at last, I found myself unprepared for it. I floundered for a few seconds and then said: "He knows no one else. No one who speaks English, that is."

The man in glasses started writing; his quill squeaked as it darted over the paper in front of him.

"Were you going to help him escape?"

"No," I said. "I told him it would be useless to try. And as he is innocent he must trust in the Venetian system of justice."

"He was seen following his tutor. His tutor entered a *casino* alone. A few minutes later Signor Boscombay entered the same house. He emerged a few minutes later in an agitated state. The woman who lives in the house opposite saw the dead body of Signor Boscombay's tutor in the room behind him and raised the alarm. No one else was found in the apartment. No one else could have fled the apartment."

"It sounds bad for Signor Boscombe," I said, "but I am convinced he did not do it. He liked his tutor."

"Did the two men engage in sodomitic practices?"

The scratching of the quill pen halted for a few seconds in momentary consternation.

"I am sure they did not," I said. Well, certainly not with each other. I saw no point in voicing this qualifying remark.

The quill scribbled away.

"Do you know if Signor Shackleford was in the habit of wearing women's apparel?"

"I am sure he was not," I said.

The Missier Grande just stared at me, his eyes boring into me like honed blue icicles. Then he spoke again: "Why was he following his tutor?"

"He told me he wanted to know where he was going. He suspected Signor Shackleford of having stolen something from him."

"What?"

"A book about Doge Marin Falier."

There was a momentary flicker in the blue eyes; I could not tell whether it was of surprise, disbelief or puzzlement.

"And why did he think his tutor had stolen it?"

"He didn't know. It was a book that had belonged to his father, which his tutor had removed from the family library."

"And why?"

"Well, according to Signor Boscombe, the tutor told him that the book contained cabalistic secrets and he thought someone in Venice would be able to interpret it."

"Someone?"

Was I justified in bringing in another name? That of someone about whom I knew nothing? But this was a murder investigation. "The nobleman Piero Garzoni."

The blue eyes did not flicker now. "Did Signor Boscombay have any dealings with nobleman Piero Garzoni?"

"It seems he never met him," I said. "He met a certain Count Gelashvili, who claimed to know the nobleman, but the count did not effect an introduction."

The quill did not even hesitate as it came to the foreign name.

"We know all about Count Gelashvili."

Well, of course you do. Perhaps you can even pronounce the name of his home town.

"Illustrissimo," I said, after a brief pause, "please allow me to repeat: I am fully convinced that Signor Boscombe did not murder Signor Shackleford. Signor Boscombe is a rather ingenuous young man, given to gambling and certain esoteric interests, but he is not a murderer." Then, trying to think of an argument that would bear more weight, I added: "And he comes from a respectable English family."

"He is not a nobleman," said the Missier Grande.

"No," I said, "he has no title, but he is an English gentleman. I am certain that his family is a distinguished one."

The blue eyes were not impressed. In Venice you are either of noble

68

birth or you are not. The Missier Grande himself, of course, is not a nobleman, and no doubt for that reason appreciates all the more acutely just how important it is to be one.

"He tells me his uncle lives in Florence and should be contacted. He is a distinguished antiquarian . . ."

But not a noble one. The blue eyes continued to remain icily imperturbable. After a pause he said: "Naturally the English Resident here in Venice will be informed of what has happened. He will take whatever steps he considers appropriate."

"Perhaps I could help," I said.

"No." The word came out with sudden force. "This must be the end of your dealings with Signor Boscombay."

"But I could help interpret . . . He speaks no Italian."

"The English Resident will provide whatever assistance is needed. Signor Marangon, your involvement with this man is now over."

"But he —"

"He does not need the assistance of a hired guide, the son of an absconding actress and a treacherous clerk at the Arsenale."

As if in reaction to the iciness of his tone, I felt my blood suddenly surge to boiling pitch. I took an involuntary step forward and immediately a hairy hand gripped my shoulder.

I forced myself to speak calmly. "My mother did not abscond. She left Venice to seek work with a travelling theatre company. And she never ceased to instil in me a love for her native city."

"Most laudable in her, I'm sure. I see you do not defend the reputation of your father."

"I know nothing about my father," I said.

"I imagine not. Your mother is not likely to have boasted of his accomplishments. In any case, the fact remains that you can be of no assistance to this English gentleman. And if you wish to keep your licence as a *cicerone* —"

His voice did not trail away in a series of menacing dots. He simply allowed his sentence to conclude with this significant conditional.

I swallowed. "I understand."

He nodded to the *sbirro*, who had not let go of my shoulder. "Take him to a cell."

"I'm not being released?" I said in dismay.

He merely stared at me. I realised that a direct question was always going to be a mistake. As was a plea. I shut up.

I was made to turn and marched towards the door at the rear of the room. More bewildering corridors, staircases, flickering torches, courtyards, creaking doors . . . and then suddenly I was in a cell with a chamber pot, a bench and a bed containing a sleeping figure. The *sbirro* locked the door and moved away; the last vestiges of light left me groping for the free bench.

There is no point in recounting the next twenty or so hours in any detail. I got some sleep. I had limited conversation with my Croatian cellmate, who eventually woke up still drunk and convinced that I was the devil. I did little to disillusion him since I certainly felt quite hellish. We ate some greyish sludge and drank some filthy water and listened to the bells outside to get some kind of idea of how much time was passing. I wondered how Boscombe was faring.

Eventually, with no explanation whatsoever, the cell door was opened and I was accompanied along the various corridors and staircases until I found myself outside on the Riva degli Schiavoni. Alone. It was night-time again. I imagined the day's custody was simply intended to show me that they could do it. They certainly had not needed all that time to go through my belongings.

II

My apartment was not the disaster area I had been gloomily envisaging. There was no missing the fact that it had had visitors, and it would be hard to claim that they (or my landlady) had "kept it nice" for me: clothes had been tossed around, books pulled from the shelf and my bed stripped. However, they had not actually torn the books apart or the clothes to shreds, nor had they caused any purely wilful damage. The impression I got was that they had carried out a routine search, and not an exceptionally diligent one. Perhaps they felt they already had all the evidence they needed. After all, the murder weapon had been left at the scene of the crime.

The only fortunate thing in this whole mess was that it had not interfered with any pressing engagements. Bepi and I had no clients at the moment and we had agreed to take a couple of days off. One just for a rest (which I had taken on the bench of the prison) and the other so that Bepi could attend to certain domestic matters. His mother, a powerful figure by all accounts, had a new bed that needed installing, if I had understood correctly.

I made no attempt to tidy things up. I just took off my shoes and lay down on the bed, wondering idly whether Siora Zennaro's new mattress would contain as many inexplicable rocky protuberances. I drifted into a troubled sleep, grateful that the ambient noise was now limited to the distant rumbling of Carlo's snores.

This time it was a much less invasive noise that woke me. It did not need to be so loud, since I was only skimming the surface of sleep. It was a scraping noise at the shutters on the window. My first thought was of pigeons, which sometimes squabbled on the windowsill, ever since I had made the mistake of scattering crumbs there.

But pigeons do not actually pull the shutters open. I turned over and gazed towards the square opening, which was gradually filling with grey half-light, as the shutters were prised apart.

I lay completely still. My first thought was that the *sbirri* were back again. But then, even amidst the mental fog of semi-dormancy, I asked myself why they would choose this means of ingress, when it was so easy to batter the front door down.

Before I could form an answer to this question a dark shape filled the grey square, pushed the hinged window panes apart, hoisted itself on to the sill and leaped into the room. It was all done with supple speed and ease of movement; this was someone used to this mode of entering buildings.

Even as it happened – even before the intruder landed on the floor – I let out a startled gasp. It was not a scream, I swear, just a gasp, but it was enough to give my visitor a start. Clearly he had not expected to find anyone in the room.

I could have had the advantage at this point, but wakeful urgency clearly won out over sleep-befuddled confusion. The next instant the figure had hurled itself on to me and pinioned me to the bed, gripping both my arms. I lay there, frozen with terror, gazing up at a featureless black head, in which I could only make out the whites of the eyes. "Quickly," it hissed. There was no corresponding movement of a mouth and the word sounded muffled, so presumably there was a full facial mask. In any case, I realised that the word was not directed at me. Confirmation came from further sounds of scrambling at the window.

I twisted my head in that direction and saw another dark figure appearing there – larger and less supple than the one now holding me tight. Again it was impossible to distinguish any features.

"What do you want?" I managed to say, but the next instant a hand was clamped over my mouth. The figure looming over me had released my right arm to do this, but the instant I raised that arm in a gesture of resistance, the other figure, now inside the room, had gripped it, and this grip was even tighter and harder than the previous one. A memory stirred somewhere inside me but there was no way I could wrestle it to the forefront of my mind; terror and confusion had full rein over my faculties for the moment.

The two men exchanged a few grunting words, which I didn't catch, and then I was hoisted to a sitting position and my arms were forced behind my back. The pricking sensation at my throat, I realised was caused by the point of a knife that was being held there by the larger man.

I forced myself to concentrate on one thing at a time. These two men were clearly too strong for any effective physical resistance on my part. I was going to have to rely on my mental powers, and something told me that I might have the advantage there. Perhaps it was just the fact that they had not expected to find me at home; this suggested, at the very least, a failure in planning.

"Where is it?" said the smaller man, in an urgent whisper.

"Where is what?" I said, concentrating hard. That flickering memory of an instant ago must have meant something, I thought. I needed to track it down in the tortuous tunnels of my mind.

"You know," the sibilant voice said. "What the Englishman brought you."

Trouble, I thought; nothing else. Out loud I said, "He didn't bring anything. He came here out of terror."

The knife-point pushed in a little way. Even as I gasped, I managed to grab hold of the coat-tails of that memory. The vice-like grip on my arm was extremely similar to the vice-like grip I had felt on my shoulder some weeks earlier at Fusina. And in my mind there loomed the figure of the walnut-faced man—who had pulled out a knife on that occasion, until told to put it away by the *ganzer*.

And I made a further connection, linking the lithe movements of the *ganzer*, as I had seen him at Fusina and then in the streets of Venice, with the supple leap and spring of the first man, as he had scrambled into the room a minute earlier.

I had no doubts. These were the same men. The *ganzer* was speaking in a deliberate breathy whisper, presumably to disguise his voice, but I thought I could identify it.

Did this help me at all? If I were to say "I know who you are", would they fall back, confounded, and then scramble over each other in a desperate attempt at flight? It seemed unlikely. Indeed, the fact that they were doing their best not to be recognised was an indication that they did not intend any fatal harm to me. It would be foolish to jeopardise that position.

"Where is it?" the *ganzer* repeated.

"Look, I swear I don't know what you mean," I said, with almost perfect honesty. I had an inkling what they were after, but certainly no idea where it was. I was sure Boscombe had not brought it with him.

The *ganzer* was now kneeling on the bed behind me and he was busy tying my wrists with something. Presumably he was the kind of man who always travelled with a spare bit of rope in case he needed to manacle anyone. His voice came from right behind my left ear. "We can make you talk."

"Look, if I knew anything I would tell you," I said, this time with absolute honesty.

"Have a look around," said the *ganzer* to the other man, shoving a piece of cloth in my mouth.

The large man had found my candle and tinderbox, and flickering light was cast over the room. The two men were dressed in dark, tight-fitting clothes and both wore full facial masks – black ones, with no openings for the mouth. They had no cloaks and I imagined that this probably had something to do with the fact that they had planned to climb up to my window. I was only now getting to grips with the fact that they had somehow got up there. Had they used a ladder? It seemed unlikely, but so did any other solution.

The big man began throwing things around in a totally unsystematic attempt at a search. I made pointless mmffing sounds of protest, which were naturally ignored. After a minute or so the *ganzer* said: "This is a waste of time. Let's take him where we can question him properly."

They blindfolded me with some greasy piece of cloth and then prodded me towards the door. My immediate fear now was of falling down the stairs without being able to put my hands out protectively, and as I reached the landing I began to shuffle cautiously until another shove from behind pushed me forward. I realised that one of them was now walking in front of me, which was a slight relief; my fall would not be unbroken.

Somehow I got to the bottom of the stairs without injury and I felt the breeze as the leading man opened the front door.

There was no sound outside. The two men hastened me along the *salizada*; then suddenly prodded me to the right. Unless I missed my guess we were now heading towards Calle del Pestrin; we reached it and turned left along it, which would bring us to the Rio di San Martin. There was no bridge here. Were they just going to shove me into the canal?

But as we got to the water's edge the big man jerked me to a halt with a hand on my shoulder. From the sounds that followed I gathered that the *ganzer* had lowered himself into a waiting boat; a few seconds later the big man, to my consternation, lifted me bodily and more or less dropped me after the *ganzer*. I found myself staggering on the swaying boards until steadied by the *ganzer*'s hands, and then I was rudely thrust into what I guessed, from the increased darkness and stuffy smell, to be a cabin. I found a seat and perched on it. A moment later the boat was moving.

And now I lost all sense of orientation. Partly it was due to panic, partly to my attempt to concentrate my mind entirely on the question of what to do next; the two impulses were, of course, in conflict. I gradually forced the latter to quell the former, with the aid of slow, measured breathing and sheer force of will.

I took stock of every part of my body, particularly my wrists, in an attempt to see what my chances of escape were. Wriggling and twisting and chafing my hands did not offer any real grounds for optimism. I turned my attention to the gag, and twisted my head so that it rested against the rough wood of the cabin wall; perhaps if I rubbed it hard I could work the cloth down . . .

"Stop that!" came the *ganzer*'s voice. So I had not been left alone.

I sat still. For want of anything better to do I listened hard to the outside noises to try to work out where we were. There was just the noise of the oar, the steady swishing of the water and an occasional human voice from a nearby house or street, but nobody saying anything useful like "What a lovely night, here in Campo Santa Maria Formosa."

I do not know how long we travelled; sheer terror can rob one of all sense of time and place. Eventually, though, the boat came to a halt; I could hear it scrape alongside the stones of the canal bank before rustling noises told me that the big man was mooring it.

The *ganzer* prodded me and I moved in the only direction I could – out of the cabin. One possibility was flickering in my mind: I could throw myself overboard. The splash would be some kind of signal, if anyone were around, and once in the water I should be able to work the gag out of my mouth. Would the water slacken or tighten the rope binding my wrists? I did not know, and the moment of hesitation as I pondered this point lost me the opportunity to find out, if that was what it had been. "No tricks," muttered the *ganzer*, pushing me towards the side of the boat.

There were some scrambling noises and the boat rocked wildly for a moment or two. It is only with hands tied behind the back and a blindfold over the eyes that one realises how much one relies on arms and sight for balance, reassurance and (obviously) contact with the world.

Then I felt the big man's hands grip me round the waist and I was heaved bodily, as helpless as a baby in swaddling clothes, on to firm ground.

It was clearly the water gate of a building. There were slimy steps beneath my feet and the general atmosphere of enclosure and damp that comes from such spaces. Things seemed darker through the blindfold. I was prodded forward. A few more steps upward, then a corridor, and then another even more grimly enclosed space, where I was guided to a bench and made to sit.

The two men conferred at a short distance, speaking in low and indistinguishable voices. Then the *ganzer* spoke to me. "Stay sitting there. Any move and you get it. Clear?" Then there was silence. After a minute or so it struck me that they might both have left and so I made a move to stand up.

"Sit down." It was the big man's voice, a few yards away.

I sat down. So the *ganzer* had gone. Why? To obtain more effective tools of coercion? I decided to concentrate all my mental efforts towards an assessment of my current situation. It was either that or go mad.

Where was I? Once again I had that strange sensation of unexplained familiarity. There was something here that reminded me of places that I knew well. What was it? Well, given the circumstances it must have to do with either sounds or smells. Or possibly both.

Sounds. At the moment there were very few. From outside there was just the faintest sloshing of canal water and the occasional cry of a seagull: we were still in Venice. Inside there was just the breathing of the big man and nothing else. I shifted on the bench and it creaked slightly. Nothing to get hold of there.

Smells. Venice always offers an abundance of these, ranging from the delightful to the disgusting. Here I could smell nothing from the canal, neither the seaweedy tang of summer days at sunset nor the shitty stink of certain backwaters at low tide. And we were clearly a long way from any fish market or coffee shop or spice counter or fresh bakery; there was no hint of food or drink, just a musty but not unpleasant tickle in my nostrils that came from . . .

Wood.

That was it. A lot of wood.

Not a sawmill or a carpentry shop: it was not the sweet pungency of sawdust-filled air, of freshly carved planks or poles, but the scent of a place where such planks or poles were used abundantly, where the floor and ceiling were of wood, which creaked when they were trodden on . . . a place where wooden objects were shifted around . . . a furniture shop? No, that would not explain the sense of familiarity.

And suddenly I knew where we were. Or, at least, in what sort of place we were. It was one I knew well, one I had practically grown up in. We were in a theatre. And we were not sitting among the benches and stools of the spectator area; we were backstage.

Even as I realised this my brain grasped another of the delicate sensations perceived by my nostrils: I could just sense the faint traces of paint that always hang around the storage places in theatres.

And now I knew why the *ganzer* had always struck me as familiar: he was a zany. I had probably seen him on stage, in one of those frantic unscripted comedies in which he, as masked Harlequin, threw himself around the stage in a series of acrobatic comedy routines. The kind of routines that Goldoni, with his character-based plays and insistence on fidelity to the written script, was gradually making unfashionable. It was no surprise that no one had recognised my portrait of him; zanies always performed in masks. But his moving body had struck both me and Bepi as familiar.

In strictly practical terms none of this made my situation any less problematic. It was not as if I could use my recognition of the location to effect an escape. But it did slightly – just slightly – take the edge off my fear. Somehow it was difficult to imagine a zany doing anything really terrible to me.

I sat there mulling over this new knowledge. I even found myself dwelling on childhood memories: running around the dressing rooms of theatres all over England, wherever my mother was performing; being petted and spoiled by motherly actresses and singers, yelled at by directors and stage-hands; listening to good and bad music, to good and bad performances of Shakespeare and Dryden and new comedies from Italy . . . and then helping with the painting of scenery: daubing green woods for *As You Like It* and Scottish mountains for *Macbeth* and turbulent waves for *The Tempest*, and always getting in the way. I must have been insufferable at times.

There were new noises from outside. A distant door being opened and closed; not the water gate this time. There were footsteps and quiet voices. I recognised the *ganzer's* quick muttering. And a new voice, elderly and urgent; at least, that was my first impression. But I could not make out any words.

The footsteps did not come into the space where we were. Instead, I heard the big man move towards the door – and then, I was almost sure, leave the room.

I shifted on my bench. Nothing happened. I started to stand up. Still no reaction. So he had left me.

Now I could hear the voices above me and the ceiling creaking, and my sense of location became even more precise. I was underneath the stage, and they had chosen to confer on the boards themselves. Perhaps that was the first place a zany would think of going – even for a secret talk.

If there was one thing that was true of all stages in all theatres, it was that there was always the space for that most essential of links between front- and backstage: the prompter's box. Probably they had not reckoned on my recognising where we were. I sat down again and slid along the bench in order to create the least possible noise. The muttering continued above me, and occasional shifting footsteps. At the far end of the bench I became aware that the sounds of the conversation were becoming definitely sharper. I stood up, keeping the wall to my left, and moved towards the voices. At a certain point I bumped against a wooden obstruction, which I worked out was a ladder. And now the words were distinctly audible. I had reached the point of access to the prompter's box.

"But why here?" This was the elderly man.

"We need somewhere to question him, Excellency. Without anyone seeing or hearing." This was the *ganzer* – the zany. He addressed the other man as 'Excellency'; either he was a nobleman or the zany was one of those who scattered titles with sycophantic haphazardness. I guessed the former, and made the further guess that this was the man I had seen him talking to in the Piazzetta.

"Do you think he knows anything?"

"I don't know. He doesn't seem very intelligent." I decided to take that as a compliment to my acting skills.

"What have you asked him?"

"Just if he knows where it is."

"And you didn't say what it is?"

"No. But I'm sure he knows, Excellency." So maybe my acting skills were not quite so well honed as I thought.

"And how did you question him?"

"Well, I just asked him. Nothing more." There was a pause, and then the zany added, "Not yet."

Another pause. "Well," said the nobleman, "are you going to question him . . ." another pause, "further? With other methods?"

"That was why I wanted you to come. I thought you might know what to do."

"Me?" This was a high-pitched Venetian "*Mi?*" I could not tell whether the tone were surprise, outrage or just panic. Then, as the nobleman continued, I guessed – to my surprise – that it was probably the last of these. Or at the very least it was nervousness. "Why should I know what to do?"

"You've worked with the magistrates, Excellency," said the zany. "You must have interrogated people. Used the rope." I knew the rope: not for whipping, but for suspending a prisoner from a beam, sometimes for hours.

"No, no . . . it's hardly ever used now. It's sometimes threatened, but that's all." Well, that was one state secret the old man's colleagues would not be pleased to know he had revealed.

"Well, let's threaten him," said the zany. "But you should do it. It will sound better coming from a new voice."

"All right. But if he doesn't know anything, just get rid of him."

"You mean . . . ?" The zany was clearly disconcerted.

"Get rid of him. Take him away from here. Free him somewhere out in the lagoon or something."

"Ah."

I could sense relief on the zany's part. I was getting the impression that these men were far from being the ruthless bloody bandits they wanted me to take them for. This did not make me any fonder of them, but for the first time I found the knot at the pit of my stomach slackening somewhat.

"Hey," said the zany suddenly. "What are you doing here?" For one panicky moment I thought I was visible to them; then I realised he must be addressing the big man.

"I just wanted to know what you –" said the big man slowly.

"Get back down there! He might have got free by now!"

There was a sudden clatter of footsteps and I hastily shuffled back to the bench, trying to resume the same posture and position as before. I was just in time.

They entered the room, and there was a moment's silence as they gathered in front of me. I did my best to assume a look of stupid helplessness. It was not very difficult.

One of them pulled the gag from my mouth. I resisted an urge to spit and contented myself with slow and heavy breathing.

"My friend tells me you have not been helpful," said the old man. He had adopted a harsh whispering tone, presumably with the double purpose of disguising his voice and frightening me. It was surprisingly effective. I was very glad I had overheard the foregoing conversation.

"I don't know what he wants," I said.

"I think you do."

"If it's this book . . ."

"So you do know," came the hoarse whisper.

"The Englishman told me about it, but that's all. He didn't give it to me."

"So why did he come to you?"

"He doesn't know anyone else here – anyone else who speaks English.

He thought I might be able to help him to escape. Which I couldn't, of course."

"We have ways of making you remember," said the old man.

"Not if there's nothing to remember," I said. "I swear to you. Why should I lie? Do you think I care about his wretched book?"

There was a long pause.

"I think you may be telling the truth. But I warn you, if it turns out you do know more than you say, we will punish you in ways you can only dream about."

I had the sensation he was now enjoying himself, and I began to suspect something about this man. He was a lover of the dramatic. There must be a reason why his two henchmen had brought me to a theatre. Most theatres in Venice were financed by the nobility; I guessed that this particular nobleman had a stake in the one we were in. Sometimes it was a purely commercial venture, but in many cases it indicated an attraction towards the world of fictitious thrills, laughter and tears. I suspected that he would have loved to be an actor himself; precluded from such an activity by his rank, he had taken up the next best thing: sponsorship and possibly directorship of a theatre.

And now he was taking the opportunity to play the lead role in a stirring drama, complete with diabolical villains and cruel torments.

Well, I could not applaud but I could gratify him by letting out a whimper. The sooner this whole farce was over, the better.

Some minutes later I was back in the boat, as helplessly gagged and trussed as ever. The nobleman had come to the water gate to hiss a last melodramatic "Remember what I said . . . ".

More twisting and turning through the quieter canals of Castello and then I could tell from the breeze on my face and the cries of seagulls that we were out in the open lagoon, where I was unceremoniously dumped on the muddy shore of a remote island. Their last gesture was to slacken the knot on the rope binding my wrists.

A few minutes later I had struggled free of rope, gag and blindfold. I was on a tiny island somewhere between Murano and Burano and I could see the boat that had brought me there: a tiny dark shape making its way back across the lagoon towards the sun-gilded towers of Venice.

12

A couple of Buranello fishermen took me back to the Fondamenta Nuove. I fortunately had a couple of coins in my pocket and once I had let them know that my being stranded on the island was the result of an unlucky bet they lost all curiosity about my predicament. I was just another mad Venetian.

When I arrived home, before entering the front door, I looked carefully at the building. I saw that by skilful use of the protruding stone frame of the ground-floor window, a gap in the brickwork above that, and a combination of athletic dexterity and foolhardiness, it would indeed be possible to climb up to my own window. I was not intending to try. There was just some slight comfort in the knowledge that my assailants did not actually possess the power of flight. This comfort, of course, was counterbalanced by the thought that it could be done again.

That afternoon, having caught a few hours' sleep, I made my way to Fabrizio's bookshop.

"Ah," he said, as soon as I entered. "You've been released."

"So you know."

"Only what all Venice knows. And I've managed to strip away some of the more lurid accretions to the story. For example, I find it hard to believe that you and Mr Boscombe had spent the evening together at the Ridotto, losing thousands of zecchini each."

"Why else would I be wearing these old clothes?" I said with a rueful smile. "But go on. Tell me what you've heard. And then I'll tell you what happened, as far as I know."

He gave me a summary of the stories that were going the rounds. At the core of them was the news that an English gentleman (some said a lord, some a scholar, some a priest) had been murdered by his friend (some said a lord, etc.) while they were playing some perverted game. His account became a little stilted and nervous at this point because Lucia joined us in the shop while he was giving the details. He passed on to all they had heard about my involvement; it was simply reported that the murderer had taken refuge with me.

"Tell us what happened," she said, gazing at me with troubled dark eyes.

I gave them a rough account of the story up to the same point. When I told them about Boscombe's description of the dead body, Lucia drew in her breath and said: "That poor man."

I remembered that she had spent some time with Shackleford and made a sympathetic murmur. When I reached the moment of my brief encounter with the Missier Grande Lucia gave another sharp intake of breath and Fabrizio said, "*Cospetto*."

"It was a frightening moment," I acknowledged. I told them how I had been warned to stay away from the whole business.

"Good advice," said Fabrizio.

"Yes," I said. "Nothing I would like better."

"Why do you say that?" said Lucia, looking sharply at me.

"It seems I'm not going to be allowed to." And I went on to recount my subsequent nocturnal adventure. For some reason I left the details of where I thought I had been taken vague.

"You've had a busy couple of days," Fabrizio said. "Tell me again: what was this book?"

"A book about Marin Falier."

"I wonder . . ." he said pensively.

"What?"

"Well, this reminds me . . . It's a curious story." He turned to a bookcase behind him and ran his fingers along the volumes, humming the while; he nearly always did that when browsing. "Ah, here we are. A curiosity – and one which will mean more to you than it does to me. Literally so."

He passed me the volume: a small leather-bound book, clearly very little read. I opened it at the title page:

AN ACCOUNT OF THE LIFE OF
DOGE MARINO FALIERO
DEFENDER OF THE MOST SERENE REPUBLIC OF VENICE
MARTYR FOR THE CAUSE OF REPUBLICAN FREEDOM

"It's in English," I said, with puzzlement.

"Your scholarly perspicacity never fails to astonish," said Lucia.

"This can't be the book," I said. "Boscombe specifically said he couldn't read it because it was in Italian."

"Let's see," said Lucia thoughtfully. "Is it possible for a book written in one language . . ."

"But why would the Boscombe family have the Italian version?"

"Well, that I don't know," said Fabrizio. "The curious thing is that I only know of the English version. It caused a little stir when it first appeared in London."

"A stir?" I said. It seemed unlikely.

"Oh, not among the English."

"And why a stir?"

"You know the story of this doge?"

"Yes, of course."

"So you will understand that describing him as a defender of the republic is provocative, to say the least."

"Yes, but why should Venetians worry about what some English historian says?"

"Turn the page," he said.

I did so. The same title was repeated but this time it was followed by the words BY A VENETIAN NOBLEMAN. Then, in smaller script, and below a sharp dividing line, came WITH AN AFTERWORD BY A SECOND VENETIAN NOBLEMAN AND A PREFATORY POEM BY A THIRD VENETIAN NOBLEMAN. Finally came the details of the publisher: Printed for J. Knapton at the Crown in St. Paul's Church-Yard, 1721.

"You can imagine," Fabrizio said, "that the idea that three Venetian noblemen were prepared to write a defence of one of the most notorious villains in Venetian history was considered a little troubling. But as nobody was ever able to discover any further details of these noblemen, in the end the book was dismissed as being a hoax by an unscrupulous English publisher."

"I see," I said.

"But now you tell me that an Italian version of the book does exist."

"And as far as we know no one ever translated it into Italian?" said Lucia.

"No, my dear. It was considered best simply to ignore it."

"So the Italian version . . ."

" . . . must be the original," I concluded.

"It would seem so," said Fabrizio.

"May I borrow this?"

"I can't think of anyone better suited to do so."

Lucia was frowning. "Sior Alvise," she said, and then paused.

"Siora Lucia?"

"You haven't forgotten the warning of the Missier Grande?"

"No," I said. "But I don't think it extends to taking an interest in medieval history."

"Perhaps not," she said, "but please be careful. In any case, there are two questions I'd like to ask you. First, is there nothing we can do for Mr Boscombe?"

I smiled gratefully at her. "Well, if you could take it on yourself to contact his relatives in Florence, it would be good."

"Of course. Why didn't you say so sooner?"

"It seemed an imposition . . ." She gave an impatient click of her tongue so I changed the subject. "And your other question?"

"Are you going to report what happened to you last night?"

"Well . . ."

"It is possible that your information could help Mr Boscombe."

"Possible," I said, "but not certain. And my impression is that coming out with an accusation against an unidentified nobleman will not help my own position."

She frowned. "You may be right. The problem is that word 'unidentified.'"

"Exactly," I said. "If only I had been able to get a proper view of him the other evening in the Piazzetta."

"You thought he was a barnabotto," said Fabrizio.

"It was just a vague impression, I couldn't see him clearly but from where I was standing his cloak looked, well, shabby."

"That is hardly definite evidence."

"No," I said. "But I'll recognise his voice if I hear it again."

"No," said Lucia.

I looked at her in surprise. "You don't think so?"

"I mean that you will not spend your time hanging around the taverns of San Barnaba trying to identify this man."

Fabrizio nodded. "Lucia is right. You had better stay out of things. The Missier Grande's spies are everywhere. We'll contact the relatives of Mr Boscombe and leave things in their hands."

"Very well," I said meekly.

Lucia looked hard at me. "You mean that?"

"I promise not to lurk in the neighbourhood of San Barnaba," I said.

She still seemed a little suspicious but I changed the subject by giving them what little information I had on Boscombe's relatives in Florence. Fabrizio told me that he had heard that the English Resident had arranged for Boscombe's servant, Benson, to be sent home, so that was one problem the fewer. Having sorted out these practical matters I left the shop and made my way to Bepi's house. I did not often call on him at home, our relationship being a strictly professional one, and I was not too sure that his mother approved of our partnership; she probably felt that Bepi could have done better by finding fixed work with some noble family. She was a large lady, with a voice to match, and it was clear that her sons (I was never sure just how many there were) went in awe of her.

The family lived in the warren of back streets in the parish of San Giuseppe (or Sant'Isepo, as the locals called it), beyond the Arsenale. It wasn't an area I knew well but I knew better than to ask for the Zennaro family; probably a fifth of the inhabitants of eastern Castello shared the surname. I made my way down the fondamenta alongside the canal that flanked the church. The alleys to my left were all festooned with washing; the housewives of Castello were taking advantage of the spring sunshine.

In the street where the family lived a group of small children was playing some elaborate skipping game under the benign gaze of three old women dressed in black, who were sitting in a row in the sunshine outside the first house.

One of the old women caught sight of me and immediately called out, "Bepi, it's your foreign friend."

The last time I had been here, as far as I could remember, was about ten months earlier. This woman should be working for the Missier Grande. Perhaps she was. The children stopped their game and looked at me with open-mouthed interest.

There was a buzz of voices from within the house and a few seconds later Bepi appeared at the front door, looking dusty and sweaty. "Alvise," he said. "What's up?"

"Nothing special. Have you time to talk a moment?"

He looked nervously over his shoulder and said, "Well, if you're quick."

"Are you really a foreigner?" asked the smallest child, a boy aged about six, with huge awestruck eyes; he might have confused foreigner with demon from the underworld.

"I'm as Venetian as you," I said, with technical correctness but knowing it was a lie.

"Bepi!" came a thunderous female voice from inside the house; I *swear* the walls shook.

"Coming, Mamma!" He gave me an apologetic shrug and smile. "Five minutes . . ." he said and disappeared inside. He was never as biddable as this with our clients.

"New bed," said the old woman nearest to me by way of explanation.

The children resumed their elaborate game, with occasional glances at the foreign intruder, and I waited, listening to the voices inside the house and trying to count how many people were engaged in the drama of the installation. I thought I could distinguish at least twelve voices, ranging from ancient to very young, and the discussion seemed to be about the position and orientation of the bed, taking into account the direction of the prevailing winds, the effect of early morning light and the desirability or otherwise of hearing the local church bells. Every so often the dominant female voice would roar something along the lines of "Of course, I'd ask Bepi for his opinion but I know he can't concentrate on anything while his foreign friend is waiting for him."

Bepi would mutter some inaudible response and I would try to look as if I had not heard anything, while the three old women all stared at me, shaking their heads in sorrow.

Eventually, just when I was on the point of leaving, Bepi appeared at the door again, this time wearing his red cap, and said, "All right, let's go for a walk."

I gave a vague nod of farewell to the children, who went on with their game, and to the old women, who shook their heads again as if our departure confirmed all their darkest suspicions, and Bepi and I strolled down the fondamenta. I mumbled some apologetic remarks about disturbing him, and he shrugged and said, "Not a problem." Obviously he was going to pretend that I had not heard a word of the conversation inside the house and I was expected to play along.

"I wouldn't have come if it wasn't important," I said.

"All right."

"Have you heard about our previous clients?"

"The murder? Yes, of course."

"You know I was taken to the Doge's palace?"

"And you were released this morning. Yes."

All this was obviously well established. I said, just a little nervously, "Does your mother know . . ."

"Yes. But it doesn't matter."

I guessed that it made little difference to her whether I was a possible throat-cutting maniac or not; the salient fact was my failure to be a wealthy nobleman.

"And then I got kidnapped," I said. And I told him the rest of the night's events, including my conviction that I had been taken to a theatre.

I had undeniably caught his attention this time. After all, he had had dealings with the two men himself, and I suspect that despite his wish to stay out of things some resentment lingered.

"I knew I'd seen him before," he said. "That smooth way he had of moving. Of course."

"So do you know the theatre?"

"Teatro Santa Giustina," he said without a moment's hesitation. "I must have seen him in dozens of shows. And his gondolier was probably one of the company too."

"That makes sense," I said. I had lost my bearings in the boat, but I knew the theatre had to be somewhere in eastern Venice.

"It closed down about six months ago," he said.

"And that makes sense too. Why else would the zany have become a hired tough?"

"It couldn't take the competition. You know: all these wars."

He was referring to the bitter battles among the various theatres in the city; it was all too likely that the old-fashioned knockabout comedy of a theatre like the Santa Giustina had not been able to stand up to the rivalry of such innovators as Carlo Goldoni and the *capocomico* Girolamo Medebach.

"So who was managing the theatre?"

He pondered. "I heard of a few names. But the only one that fits your description is nobleman Zanotto."

"Zanotto. Is he a barnabotto?"

"Well, if he isn't already he's likely to become one. He had a lot of money tied up in the theatre, but he doesn't own it; the Tron family does. His interest is in the company."

That was unusual; the involvement of noble families in theatres was usually confined to the dignified (and remunerative) business of ownership of the building and its effects. Zanotto's theatrical yearnings must be very powerful.

"An old man?"

"Must be in his seventies."

"Thank you, Bepi. That's very helpful."

"Why? What are you going to do?" He stopped and turned to stare at me as he spoke. It wasn't often that Bepi was so direct.

"Good question," I said slowly. He didn't say anything, he just kept his gaze fixed on me. "I just need to know if it was him. Then I can think of something. But I'm not going to take that kind of treatment without hitting back." I paused. "Missier Grande or not."

He made a curious whistling sound which I was unable to interpret.

I said, "But this is entirely up to me. I'm not going to involve you."

He was staring across the canal at the façade of the church. It is not one of Venice's most famous buildings but it has a charming bas-relief of the Adoration of the Magi over the doorway. "Let me show you something," he said after a moment.

"Yes, of course," I said, a little surprised.

"Of course, I don't know about all the art in the city, like you," he said. "But I do know this church."

"I'm sure you do," I said. Well, it was his parish church.

He led me across the bridge and we entered the church. I had been there before and remembered vaguely a fine Veronese of the Adoration of the Shepherds behind the high altar and a monumental tomb to a doge on the left-hand wall. Bepi crossed himself, nodded to the sacristan and led me to the last altar on the left-hand side. The altarpiece consisted of another bas-relief, almost life-size, of the Nativity but he directed my attention to the altar front beneath this. Again in bas-relief was a curious stylised representation of a sea battle, with golden war-galleys arrayed in curved lines on a background of green waves.

"Lepanto," said Bepi.

Venice's greatest ever naval victory, and a turning point in the struggle against the Ottoman Empire. It is celebrated in huge pompous canvases in the Doge's palace, but the graceful economy of this tribute was far more moving.

"And look above." Bepi pointed to the predella beneath the altarpiece, which bore three delightful carvings of Venetian galleons, complete with sails, rigging and fluttering pennants.

"They made me want to become a sailor when I was a boy," he said.

"I can imagine," I said. I was still uncertain what point he was making.

"You see," he said, "there are times when I wonder what we're doing. You know."

"Um," I said uncertainly.

"Not you and me. Or not just you and me. This whole city. Is it all just about Carnival?"

"And gambling," I said, remembering his ever-ready dice.

"And then I think of Lepanto and remember that we did count for something."

"And so?"

"So yes. We can't just let them walk all over us."

"Nobleman Zanotto isn't the Ottoman emperor," I said.

He gave an impatient snort. "That's not it."

I realised my answer had been inappropriate, and tried to salvage things. "I think I know what you mean. But there's still no reason why you should get involved."

He was clearly already embarrassed at having revealed so much of himself. "Let's go."

"Where?"

"To the theatre. Check it out."

"And your mother's bed? Is that all done?"

He eyed me suspiciously. "Don't worry about that."

"All right. I'll try not to." I realised it was a dangerous subject for jokes. "Let's go then." I changed the subject as we walked out of the church. "How many of you are there in the family?"

"Four brothers, two sisters. We're all gondoliers except for my youngest brother Giacomo. And my sisters, of course."

"What does Giacomo do?"

"He works in the Arsenale." He said this with a sad shake of the head, as if it were a shameful family secret. "He's a caulker."

We went to Bepi's gondola, which he kept moored on the canal close to his house. I suspected that when things got a little too difficult in the house he would invent maintenance jobs here, and spend happy hours polishing his brasses.

As ever he refused my offer to help with the rowing and we headed out to the lagoon. As we emerged into the great open space, with the city's towers and domes glittering ahead of us and the dazzling water dotted with a host of coloured sails and gondolas and barges, my spirits lifted as always. "Not a bad way to go to work every day."

I half expected him to make some laconic comment along the lines of "Try it on a foggy winter morning", but instead he grunted: "It's not bad."

We made our way past the broad canal leading towards the Arsenale, past the Ca' di Dio and past the church of the Pietà, where the orphan girls still performed the music written by the red-headed priest who had died some ten years earlier. Bepi swung the gondola into the next canal and we made our way northwards, passing the church of Sant'Antonin, the little School of St George of the Slavs and the adjoining hospital of the Knights of Malta. Just beyond this, on the opposite side of the canal from the baroque church of Santa Giustina, and at a corner formed by two canals, stood a tall, almost windowless building: the Teatro Santa Giustina.

Bepi brought the gondola to a halt beside the large water gate, whose heavy wooden door was closed.

"This must be where we entered," I said. I looked around. There were a few people crossing the little square in front of the church, none of whom paid any attention to us, and three small boys playing with a dog. An old man paused on the bridge that led down to the theatre front and spat meditatively into the canal just ahead of us, but there was nothing personal in it.

"Let's try the front entrance," I said. Bepi swung the gondola around and we moored alongside the square. The three boys eagerly offered to help with the rope and Bepi allowed them the illusion of indispensability. I fished in my pockets and found a coin, which seemed to satisfy them. "We'll keep an eye on it," said the smallest boy, who had a surprisingly deep voice that clearly conferred authority.

"Keep an eye out for Turks or Nicolotti," said Bepi indulgently.

We crossed the bridge and looked at the front of the theatre. It had a rather forlorn-looking marble façade, with classical pillars. A short flight of stairs led up to the large double doors, which were also closed. There was a peeling poster to one side of the door, advertising a "Commedia Nuovissima" by Abate Chiari; the emphatic adjective itself already hinted at the decrepitude of the product.

"I've had some good times here," Bepi said, with a touch of nostalgia.

I pushed at the door without much conviction. "It's locked," I said.

"Well, only one thing to do." He called across the canal to the boys. "Come over here!"

They came running over the bridge, without a backward glance at the gondola.

"How can we get in there?" said Bepi, jerking his thumb at the theatre.

"Round the side," said the small boy without a moment's hesitation. "It'll be a squeeze for you, though."

"Fat Piero managed it," said one of the other boys.

The memory of Piero's exploit convulsed them all in laughter.

"Did he get out again?" asked Bepi with a half-smile.

"Don't know," said the small boy. "Maybe you'll find his body."

And they all dissolved into giggles again.

"But there's nothing left worth stealing," said the small boy, clearly wishing to be helpful.

"We're just checking it out," Bepi said, with an air of vague authority.

They led us into an alley alongside the theatre and pointed at a window about five feet above the ground with a loose shutter. It turned out to be a scramble as well as a squeeze but we managed it, finding ourselves two minutes later inside a dusty store room.

"Always ask the local children," said Bepi. "Especially with a big abandoned building."

"I just hope we don't find Fat Piero," I said.

"Recognise this place?" he asked.

"Not exactly," I said. "But let's find the stage."

The storeroom gave on to a corridor which led us out into the foyer.

The atmosphere of abandonment was pronounced here. Where the chandeliers should have hung glittering from the ceiling there dangled two despondent chains. Marks were visible on the walls where items of furniture had been removed. Only the stucco decorations remained on the walls and ceiling, together with a dimly visible fresco of gods and goddesses romping on robust clouds.

We walked through a colonnaded doorway to the vast gloom of the auditorium, our voices automatically descending to whispers.

"Is this it?" Bepi said.

"It has to be." My senses had already picked up the familiar atmosphere of tangy mustiness. "I was under the stage."

We picked our way carefully forward. The rows of chairs had gaps, but most of the furnishings were still present, too cumbersome to move. We climbed the short flight of wooden stairs leading up to the stage.

"I've never been up here before," said Bepi in an awestruck voice. The lure of the stage seems to affect everyone, one way or another.

"I grew up in places like this," I said.

"Really?" Bepi was clearly surprised. He had never asked me about my background. I always had the impression that he had decided early in life that most people were unfathomable and just had to be taken as they were. Maybe for the first time ever I had told him something about myself that impressed him.

There was a noise from the foyer. Someone was turning a key in the main entrance door.

Bepi and I immediately darted to the side of the stage. We held our breath and listened hard. There were two voices, talking animatedly.

"It's them," I whispered to Bepi. I recognised the elderly complaining tone of Zanotto and the sharper voice of the zany. They seemed to be arguing as they entered the auditorium.

"There's no need to repeat yourself," Zanotto said. "I understand your position. And that of your friend. And as soon as I manage to sell my share . . ."

"You know as well as I do, Excellency, that there's no certainty of any sale."

"Don't be so pessimistic."

"Excellency, your financial troubles are *your* troubles. You hired me and the others for a special job. We did what you asked."

"Well, not entirely."

"Only because the book wasn't there. We can't be blamed for that."

"But I pay for results."

"You pay for our time and our work. While we were actors you paid for our performances on the stage; now you pay for our performances off it. We've done the show we were hired for. And we're not going to repeat it."

"I'm not going to ask you to do anything again. I just need you to be a little patient." Zanotto's voice was growing agitated.

"Especially now there's this murdered foreigner as well. We want nothing to do with that."

"Well, of course not. My only concern was to get hold of the book so that nobody would make any connection . . . But let's leave that. All I ask is a few days' patience."

"We've been very patient, Excellency. But patience has a limit."

"Just a few days. And, of course, if you can help in clearing this place up, things will happen that much faster. We must make a good impression if the sale is going to go through."

"You know that the problem isn't what the theatre looks like, Excellency. There are just too many theatres."

"Yes, but this is the only one in eastern Venice. There's a whole area of the city that loves a good show . . ."

" . . . and doesn't have any money."

"Always so pessimistic."

"Always so realistic, Excellency. Why else did the theatre close?"

"Temporary problems. It just needs fresh writers, perhaps better musicians . . ."

"And you think your impresario will really buy your share in a company with no writers, bad musicians and a potential audience of cheap gondoliers and arsenalotti?"

I could sense Bepi bridling at my side. I put a restraining hand on his arm.

"He expressed an interest," said Zanotto, in a plaintive tone.

The zany gave an expressive snort. Then he said: "So what do you want me to do? We can't polish the chandeliers if there aren't any."

"No, but you can bring some of the better-looking props on to the stage. Some classical pillars, a painting or two . . . there must be some such things left backstage. Appearances do count."

"Good cue," I whispered to Bepi, and strode out on to the stage. I heard Bepi heave a sigh behind me; Zanotto and the zany both gave a gratifying gasp. I could see their upturned faces just beneath the stage, mouths and eyes wide open.

Now I had to follow up with something equally dramatic. "Greetings again." Hm.

"What . . . How . . ." stammered Zanotto. He was a small man, whose elaborately curled wig was in absurd contrast to his shabby nobleman's cloak.

"Good to see your faces this time," I said.

The zany suddenly leaped on to the stage and lunged towards me. I had forgotten his amazing agility and reared back in alarm. Not quite the effect I had intended.

The next instant Bepi was by my side. "Back off."

The zany backed off. He stood a few feet away, glaring at us both.

"I can't jump around like you," said Bepi pleasantly, "but I can break your arm like a twig." A pause. "Even if I am just a cheap gondolier."

"And I would applaud," I said. "I'm pretty angry, you know."

"You have every right to be so," said Zanotto, in a fawningly conciliatory tone.

"Excellency," muttered the zany, "better not say anything."

"I don't care what you say," I said. "I've already heard enough from both of you."

"But you haven't heard what was behind all this," said Zanotto.

"Excellency," muttered the zany again.

But there was no stopping Zanotto. "I assure you I would never have taken such drastic steps had it not been necessary."

"Necessary for you," I said. "To protect your reputation. But why should I care?"

"Why indeed?" he said. "I fully understand. It was unforgivable."

"And rest assured I won't forgive," I said.

"Of course not. But you do see that my men went beyond their instructions . . ."

"Excellency," said the zany. And this time his voice had a tone of menace.

"You told your *bravi* to break into my house in the middle of the night," I said. "That's already unforgivable."

"We are not *bravi*," muttered the zany.

"What could I do?" Zanotto said. "I heard of this terrible murder, that the murderer had made his way to your house. And that you were in custody. I felt it was important for me to be sure . . ." He paused. He was clearly wondering how much I knew.

"To be sure that I wasn't hiding the seditious book you wrote on Marin Falier."

He winced. That had gone home. "Hardly seditious. Injudicious. And of course I didn't write it."

"So you wrote the afterword. Or the poem."

"Not that either. I see you don't know the full story." He shook his head. "My full shame."

"Excellency . . ." said the zany for the fourth time.

"It all comes down to sordid financial gain," he said. "But I was hard pressed – I still am – and I yielded to temptation."

"What are you talking about?" I said.

"It seems you know about the absurd book that was written by three Venetian noblemen. One of them was my brother."

"Your brother?"

"Now deceased. He lived in England twenty or thirty years ago. Recently I heard with some alarm from an acquaintance that a young Englishman was bringing out a copy of the Italian original, which would make it perfectly clear who the three Venetian noblemen were."

"And you wanted to spare your brother's reputation."

"Ah," he said. "Yes, that too. But I confess that was not my first thought." In a kind of nervous twitch, he adjusted his wig. "I am not a rich man."

"So I gathered from your earlier comments."

"My family has lost much of its wealth. We had property in Greece, which was lost to the Turks. Then there were unfortunate speculations. Some, I will confess, I lost at the gambling tables . . ."

"Do we need to know all this?" I said impatiently.

"I am just explaining the temptation to which I was put. The last straw was the closure of this theatre, in which I had unwisely invested what little fortune I had left. So when I heard of this book it struck me that the possession of it could be a potential means . . ." He coughed.

"Of blackmail," I concluded.

"That is an unfortunate word," he said.

"And who were you going to blackmail?"

"There is no need to call it that. I thought of the book as a possible instrument to help to persuade two old acquaintances to . . . to . . ."

"To pay you hush-money."

"To make me a loan that they might otherwise have been reluctant to offer."

"And who were these old friends?"

"I see no reason why I should tell you. I have made my confession; there is no need for me also to play the . . . the informer." He even managed to draw himself up with an air of rediscovered dignity as he spoke.

"Piero Garzoni," I said.

He assumed a look of stony-faced stolidity. But I could tell I had hit home.

"Bepi?" I said.

"Yes?"

"What shall we do?"

"Leave the scum," he said briefly.

Zanotto bristled. "Whatever my faults I would remind you that I am still a member of the Venetian nobility."

"Noble by the cloak," said Bepi ironically.

"I will not be insulted by a . . . by a . . ."

"Gondolier," said Bepi. "The backbone of this city." Then he added, with heavy irony: "Excellency."

Zanotto decided to accept this last word as a sop to his ruffled dignity. "I think it best if we take leave of one another at this point."

I gave him a quick nod, which he could choose to interpret as a bow if he were that desperate, and to the zany I said: "Don't ever come near me again. Nor your big friend."

Zanotto asked one last question. "So you do have the book?"

"I've only seen a copy of the English version," I said. "I know nothing of the Italian original."

I did not look to see if this answer satisfied him. Bepi and I descended from the stage and walked out of the auditorium.

As soon as we were in the foyer I said, "How did that go?" Even as I said it I realised how preening it sounded. But it seemed that Bepi too was pleased with himself.

"We did all right, didn't we?" he said.

I gave him a smile. "It was pretty good, for a first time."

He shook his head. "There's no denying it does something to you."

"What?"

"Being up on that stage. Never thought I'd have that experience."

We walked out through the main door, to the consternation of the three boys, who were staring towards the side alley by which we had entered.

"Did they catch you?"

We smiled indulgently. "We sorted them out," I said.

"But that was the zany!" said the smallest boy. "He's really something."

"So are we," said Bepi.

He flipped another coin at them and we made our way to our gondola. There was definitely an extra spring in Bepi's step.

I hoped he would get over this soon.

13

That evening I read the *Account of the Life of Doge Marino Faliero*. Or, at least, as much as I could bear. The writer had clearly read his Machiavelli and seemed to have taken the pages on Cesare Borgia as his main model. But there was none of Machiavelli's cool detachment and cynical realism. This was simple power-worship. Or rather worship of what should have been power – real power – if only the Venetian system of government had not been so absurdly short-sighted as to cut down the only forceful ruler the city had ever had. Marin Falier, according to the book, had seen the dangers of weak government and had naturally desired the same kind of power that various despots were assuming for themselves in the numerous *signorie* arising in Italy in his time; the writer made comparisons with the Visconti, the D'Este, the Medici, all to the detriment of the outmoded Venetian system.

The fact that the city for many centuries both before and after Marin Falier had not done too badly, in terms of commerce, influence, culture and general prosperity, under this feeble system of government did not seem to cross the writer's mind. Maybe it would have done even better under a real ruler. Or maybe all that counted was that the right sort of people would have respected such a ruler.

One thing was perfectly clear from the text: it had to be a translation. I wondered that anyone could ever have doubted that. Almost every sentence suggested an Italian original: "It was the year 1349 and so tragic in its effects was the pestilence that struck the entire peninsula that there seemed to be scarce possibilities of a future resurrection from this fatal condition of misery and despair . . ." Would any English writer, unless under the influence of drink, pen such a combination of words as "scarce possibilities"? But then I guessed that the book had actually found very few English readers. Why on earth would anyone willingly subject themselves to such excruciating prose?

The 'prefatory poem' was an embarrassing paean to Falier in limping heroic couplets. I guessed that the artificiality of nearly all the rhymes could be ascribed to the fact that it too was a translation, but decided that even that consideration failed to justify so dire a couplet as:

> And tragic was the loss that fatal day
> On which so great a man they chose to slay.

The afterword praised the courage of the author without entering into the merit of his argument. It read like a piece of dutiful hackwork, and it was difficult to imagine that the writer of the book could have been greatly thrilled by such desultory praise.

For relief from this torture I read a canto of Pope's *Rape of the Lock* and felt much better for it.

At Fusina the next day Bepi and I found an English clergyman travelling with his elderly mother and were promised a week of gainful employment. There were, I was relieved to see, no lasting signs of histrionic compulsions in Bepi. Possibly the highly respectable nature of the only audience we had (whose greatest pronouncements of approval or enthusiasm as we swung into the Grand Canal were "How very charming" and "Goodness me") served to repress any temptations towards the flamboyant in my partner, who limited himself to an emphatic "Ecco" when we approached the Rialto Bridge.

After we had delivered them to their inn with a promise to collect them at nine o'clock the next morning I made my way to Fabrizio's shop to return the book on Marin Falier. He and Lucia were interested to hear my reaction.

"If you're thinking of ordering bulk copies of the Italian version, should it turn up," I said, "I would advise caution."

"Not compulsive reading?" said Fabrizio.

"Tedious in the extreme," I said. "I think nobody need worry about its possibly subversive effects on the populace."

"I don't think anyone ever was worried about that," said Fabrizio. "But they did want to know who had written it."

"Well, I've identified one name," I said. "Nobleman Zanotto:

deceased brother of the man who owns a share in the Santa Giustina theatre company."

"How did you find that out?" said Lucia, looking sharply at me.

"I asked the brother. Or rather, he told me."

"You *have* been investigating, then," she said.

"I had to find out who kidnapped me," I said. "Nobody else was going to do it."

"And how did you do it?"

"Well, I didn't hang around San Barnaba," I said. "I promised not to, remember?"

"That wasn't the point –"

"I first identified the place I had been taken to, with the help of Bepi."

"Your gondolier? Did you warn him . . . ?"

"Of course. He was even more eager than I was." And I went on to give a full account of the previous day's events.

"So Zanotto is a blackmailer," said Fabrizio. "Well, it's no great surprise to anyone who has observed the family's fortunes."

"What happened exactly?"

"The usual story: he dissipated the family's remaining fortune for the most part at the gaming tables. He hangs around the Broglio hoping for – well, let's put it charitably and say hoping that his vote can be of service to those who need it."

"Hoping for bribes, you mean."

Fabrizio lifted his hands defensively. "I did not say that."

It would perhaps be unfair to say that Lucia snorted; however, the derisive intention was clear enough. Her father winced: "My dear, I know you have had no female examples to learn from . . ."

She put her arm around him. "Yes, Father, I know. Decorum and duty. I will retire to a dark corner of the room and resume my needlework and you will not hear another peep from me."

I managed to resist snorting myself. Her father merely gave a wry smile and went on: "For the last year or so he has had some kind of official post in the customs office, which probably helps him pay some of his bills. It's apparently a renewable position."

"And his brother?" I asked.

"I seem to remember that he was in England for a while, in some ambassadorial capacity. I had no idea he was a writer or interested in history. But then perhaps he only wrote the poem. Or the afterword."

"So now you can identify your kidnapper," said Lucia. "Will you go to the Missier Grande with the information?"

"What do you advise?" I said, meaning it. I really had not taken a decision.

She frowned. "It seems Zanotto had nothing to do with the murder. If his interest was just to get hold of the book for blackmailing purposes, why would he kill the man who had it? Especially since it sounds as though he still hasn't managed to get his hands on it."

"Exactly," I said. "I have no interest in protecting Zanotto, but . . ."

"No point in creating unnecessary trouble," she said. Her voice was neutral; as usual I could not tell whether she approved or disapproved.

"And the other name," I said, addressing Fabrizio. "Piero Garzoni. Can you tell me anything about him? All I know is that he's something of a recluse."

"Well, yes, I can. He's a client."

"Oh yes? What sort of books is he interested in?"

"Well, Venetian history for a start."

"Aha," I said.

"Obviously guilty," said Lucia. "What more evidence do we need?"

"And books on occult matters. The Rosicrucian mysteries. The Knights Templar. The Cabal. All that sort of stuff." He sounded weary.

"I see," I said. "And did he have, does he have, any English connection?"

"I'm scarcely an expert on his family history but it's possible he travelled there. Perhaps he visited Zanotto. I don't recall ever hearing of his having any diplomatic or ambassadorial function. He was mainly connected with the Arsenale."

"Really?"

"Yes. He held various roles there: member of the Collegio alla Milizia, provveditore, sopraprovveditore . . ."

"Sopra-sopraprovveditore," I suggested.

"There probably is such a role," said Fabrizio, "only they don't give it an official name. His first title, I believe, was Provveditore alli Biscotti."

"Supervisor of the biscuits?" Was Fabrizio gulling me?

"Very important role. Essential to have someone reliable guaranteeing the supply and the quality of the basic diet of our sailors. Remember, we invented the biscuit."

One of many Venetian claims to creative priority. I did not attempt to question it.

Fabrizio went on: "But he was dismissed from his last post at the Arsenale a few years ago. There was some scandal connected with the treatment of workers there. I think it was under his aegis that it was decided to extend certain punishments accepted on our ships to the workers who make those ships – flogging, for example – and a worker died after being beaten."

Lucia winced. "Such things are barbarous wherever they are done," she said.

"They say he still has arsenalotti servants," I said. "Faithful ones."

"Oh, there were some there who loved him," said Fabrizio.

"Probably those who administered the floggings rather than those who received them," said Lucia.

"Probably so, my dear. In any case, they seem to be the only people with whom he has any dealings. He lives alone in his palace on the Grand Canal; other family members have either died or abandoned him."

"He sounds exactly the kind of person who could have written that dire book," I said.

"Yes," agreed Fabrizio.

"Except . . ." began Lucia, and then paused.

"Except?"

"Except that he doesn't sound the sort of person who would be ashamed to have written it."

"Good point," I said.

"But Sior Alvise . . ."

"Yes?" I always knew that she was going to say something serious when she addressed me in this formal fashion.

"Please don't persist in these inquiries. It would not be safe for you."

"Don't worry," I said. "I've found out what I needed to know. I'll stay clear from now on."

And I thought I was telling the truth.

The first indications to the contrary came a week later when Bepi and I were at Fusina again waiting for new arrivals from Padua.

Our clergyman and his mother had paid us well and thanked us copiously. They had not asked me any questions I could not answer, or for which I could not invent plausible answers ("How deep is the Grand Canal?"), and they had professed themselves satisfied with the sights they had seen and the acquaintances they had made; both of them had nodded with a kind of strange personal satisfaction as they said this and I wondered whether each had had some clandestine encounter of a kind that would for ever remain a secret from the other. Well, I would never know. I waved them off with a certain affection as I jingled the unfamiliar plurality of coins in my pocket.

And now Bepi and I watched a new carriage draw up and disgorge another oddly assorted pair of English travellers: a middle-aged gentleman in dark breeches and jacket and a young fair-haired lady in a frothy confection of pink and yellow silk. It was a warm evening and both were clearly relieved to be stepping out of the carriage. The man was bare-headed and was mopping his brow, while the young lady was waving an elegant silk fan. Their servants, a short stocky man with a shaven head and a pink-cheeked girl, stood nearby gazing around with the usual air of Anglo-Saxon wariness.

I approached, doffing my hat. "Good evening, sir; good evening, madam. May I offer my assistance? I have a gondola . . ."

"Non preoccupatevi, signore," said the man, in atrociously accented Italian. "Possiamo fare da soli."

I bowed and said, "As you wish, sir."

"Oh, Father," said the girl. "There's no need to make things difficult for ourselves. If the young man has a gondola let's use it, for goodness' sake."

She was busily smoothing out the creases and kinks in her dress, and at this point she was adjusting the lacy frills around her décolletage, apparently unaware of the fact that this delicate operation had captured the eyes of every gondolier, porter and errand boy within a hundred yards. Even the customs officer's dog seemed transfixed.

She turned to me and I guiltily jerked my eyes up to meet hers, which were large and blue. She was decidedly pretty, with delicately rouged cheeks and her hair in a pile of carefully cultivated curls.

"Per favore," she said, "vogliamo andare all'albergo del Leon Bianco." Her accent was no less atrocious than her father's but was somehow infinitely more charming. Maybe it was due to the fact that she made her request sound like a heroic enterprise that only I could carry out for her.

"Sì, signorina," I said, wondering how much longer we would keep up the pointless exercise of speaking in Italian, but judging that it was not up to me to stop.

"Lo sapete?" she said.

I guessed that she meant lo conoscete? and replied that I did know it.

"Mio cugino," she began.

And I broke in: "You're Mr Boscombe's cousin."

She was startled but recovered her equipoise a second later. "That is correct. And you . . . ?"

I introduced myself, and Bepi as well, who seemed even more transfixed than the dog by her adjustments to her décolletage but managed to pull himself together sufficiently to effect a stiff bow, and then gestured towards his gondola.

"We accompanied your cousin to the Leon Bianco, just as we are doing with you now," I said.

"And do you know what happened to him?"

"I do, signorina," I said gravely. "Probably better than most."

"Father, you hear this? This gentleman knows all about poor Freddy."

"Does he indeed?" He seemed unimpressed. I guessed that he had doubts about the appropriateness of describing me as a gentleman. He reached inside the carriage and pulled out a wig, which he thrust on his head with little regard for symmetry. His daughter immediately reached up and carefully adjusted it, an action he scarcely seemed to notice, presumably because it was so routine.

I made the necessary transport arrangements, directing their servants, along with the baggage, towards Tonin's gondola. A few minutes were occupied with the delicate operation of introducing Miss Boscombe's hooped skirts into the cabin of Bepi's gondola; once this operation had been successfully concluded they re-expanded miraculously and further rearrangement of her décolletage was required. I realised that the only way to impose discipline on my wandering eyes was to engage in conversation with Bepi outside the cabin until these final amendments had been effected. It gave me the chance to fill Bepi in on the identity of our new clients. He nodded thoughtfully but made no comment.

When a reasonable amount of time had passed I re-entered the cabin and gave a brief account of the time I had spent with their relative, up to the last fateful encounter. For the moment I omitted the book about Marin Falier from the story, just telling them that Boscombe had decided to follow Shackleford, because he suspected him of being engaged in some shady dealings with someone he had met in the city.

"And so the letter we received came from your friend the bookseller?" Miss Boscombe asked. She had a way of looking at you directly with her large blue eyes which seemed to suggest that you were her only means of salvation.

"That's right," I said.

"And he is now languishing in prison."

"Well, yes," I said, "although I'm sure that as an Englishman of gentle birth he is being treated with all due –"

"Have you been to see him?" Mr Boscombe interrupted bluntly.

"I am not allowed to."

He snorted, as if that was just the sort of excuse he had expected.

"The Missier Grande – that is, the . . . er, the chief magistrate – specifically told me –"

"But Mr Marangon," said Miss Boscombe, her blue eyes brimming with reproachful moisture, "how can you say that he is being well treated if you haven't seen him?"

"The Venetian state has no desire to provoke the hostility of his majesty's government," I said. "And I am sure that the English Resident in Venice –"

"We were told in Florence that Mr Murray is a well-known drunkard," said Miss Boscombe.

I found it difficult to deny this with convincing force. "Mr Murray takes his duties very seriously, even if –"

"It's because my nephew ain't a lord," stated Mr Boscombe. "That's all they understand here. If you haven't got a title, as far as they're concerned you're no better than dirt. Even if you belong to one of the oldest families in the land."

"Mr Boscombe, I am sure that if you speak to the authorities here and make it clear that your family –"

"As good a family as any in England," he said. "Even if my brother did marry a –"

"Father," said Miss Boscombe sharply.

"Well, you know what I think," he said, and settled into a sulky silence, gazing out over the lagoon.

"Yes, Father. But that is hardly the point. Not when poor Freddy –"

Another snort and a few muttered words, which might have been an unclergymanlike "damned fool", which she resolutely talked over: "When poor Freddy is accused of an absurd crime with no evidence against him."

"Well," I said, "that is the problem. Your cousin put himself in a very invidious situation."

"Mr Marangon, do you really think my cousin would kill his own tutor?"

"Of course I don't, Miss Boscombe, not for a moment. But he managed to make it look very much as if he had done so."

"It's not as if it was any great loss," muttered Mr Boscombe.

"I'm sorry?"

"Father," said Miss Boscombe, in automatic reproach.

"Well, by all accounts this Shackleford fellow was a pretty shady character."

"He seemed perfectly respectable to me," I said, a little surprised.

"Typical of my sister-in-law."

"What?"

"Hired the fellow without getting any proper references, just because he talked so fine. And because she was desperate to get the boy out of the country."

"Father," said Miss Boscombe, now squirming with embarrassment.

"Well, you know it's true," he said.

"Yes, but it's not the point."

"So Mr Shackleford wasn't Mr Boscombe's regular tutor?" I asked.

"No. He just wormed his way into the family, after the story about the village girls got out –"

"Father!"

I realised that a direct question about the village girls did not really befit my role so I attempted a circuitous route. "Are you suggesting that Mr Shackleford was not really qualified for the role?"

"Oh, I expect he has a smattering of Latin and Greek. She met him in Bath, while she was taking the waters. Trying to get over the shock of that business –"

"Father!"

Maybe the direct route was better after all. "Miss Boscombe," I said. "I have no interest in the private affairs of your family but I think it would be helpful if I had a fuller picture of Mr Shackleford and his relations with the family. It would make it easier for me to give you relevant information that might help you to establish the truth of this affair."

She turned those brimming blue eyes on me. "You think you can help?"

"I can certainly provide you with information about Mr Shackleford. But it would be useful to know a little more how he came to be tutoring your cousin."

"Well, we only know what my aunt wrote to us. We have been living in Florence for over a year now. My father, as you may have heard, is a leader of the Anglican community in the city –"

"He doesn't need to know about me," her father cut in. "The story is quite simple. Frederick was sent down from Oxford for gambling and general unruly behaviour. His mother decided to keep him at home and he got involved with a set of rogues in the neighbourhood who filled his vacant head with blasphemous nonsense about cabals and the Rosy Cross and God knows what . . ."

"He's not a bad boy," said Miss Boscombe. "He just gets easily led astray. And I think that in his own way he's looking for spiritual comfort."

Mr Boscombe snorted. "I suppose he never thought of going to his parish church – or even talking to me."

"Father, how could he do that?"

"The boy can write, can't he? Anyway, to cut a long story short there was a scandalous incident in the village involving the rogues he'd fallen in with and some local wenches. They were carrying out some sacred Egyptian rites, if you can believe it, and the wenches started screaming, the neighbours intervened, and there they all were, as naked as newborn babies but a lot less innocent. My sister-in-law had to pay a good deal of money to hush everything up. After that she decided Frederick must go abroad with a tutor, and since she never takes the trouble to think things over carefully she hired the first plausible-sounding scoundrel she met in Bath."

"Father, we don't know he was a scoundrel."

"We don't know anything about him at all. That's the problem. Apparently she just liked the way he talked about Virgil. As if she knew the first thing about Virgil."

"That does fit in with something my friend at the bookshop hinted at," I said, remembering Lucia's doubts about Mr Shackleford's classical scholarship.

"There you go," said Mr Boscombe. "Smooth-talking charlatan. Who knows what he was intending to do with the lad." After a pause, he added darkly: "What he might have done already."

"Do you know anything about a book your brother owned?" I asked. "A book in Italian about the fourteenth-century doge Marin Falier?"

"My brother owned a lot of books. Hardly ever read them." There was a touch of bitterness in his voice. I guessed there was a touch of the younger brother's resentment here.

"This was a book your brother was apparently quite fond of, according to your nephew."

"Weren't many of those –"

He was interrupted by his daughter. "Father, try to be more helpful. You know there was more to Uncle James than you're making out."

He gave a sort of snorting noise, which could have been anything from contempt to contrition, then started again. "Well, yes, when he was younger James fancied himself as a thinker. Even got mixed up with some so-called philosophical scholars in town. You know the sort: people interested in Locke and Newton, that sort of stuff."

"I see," I said. I guessed it would be difficult to get him to be more precise.

"And then there's the family history. We were for Parliament, you know. And we paid for it when the Stuarts came back. Well, we're loyal enough now to king and country but my brother went through a patch when he got interested in the old family traditions and started reading up on the civil war and republicanism. Didn't last, of course, like all his enthusiasms."

"Did he have any Italian acquaintances? Specifically, Venetian?"

"Well, yes, I believe there were one or two he met in town. And he had them down to the family seat on at least one occasion. Couldn't tell you who they were. I do remember him getting interested in Venice as an example of a successful republic. But he was always taking up notions and then dropping them."

"Does the name Zanotto mean anything? Or Garzoni?"

He frowned. "Garzoni. Yes, that name is familiar. Little fellow? Talks in a low voice?"

"I don't know. I have never met him myself."

"Well, if it's the man I'm thinking of, there was something odd about him. He'd come to England to study ship-building techniques . . ."

"Ah, that sounds likely," I said.

" . . . but apparently he'd already decided he knew all he needed. He seemed to think there was nothing an Englishman could teach a Venetian about ships."

"That too sounds quite likely," I said. It was probably the attitude of most of the Venetian population, although they would not necessarily say so to your face. Diplomacy is another art in which Venetians are well schooled.

"Arrogant fool," said Mr Boscombe, who had clearly attended a different school. "Just the kind my brother would be influenced by. Always looking for someone to follow. Like his son."

"So he was a forceful person, this Garzoni?"

"Well, he was if you were malleable enough. Like my brother. Though they did have some falling-out, as I remember. Never got the full details. But I had my own concerns, studying for the Church."

"Yes, of course," I said. "When you say a falling-out, do you mean they argued over something?"

"James never argued. Didn't know how to. He blustered. Anyway shortly afterwards our father died and all of a sudden James became the traditional country squire, all hunting and fishing and never picking up a book to save his life. And no foreigners around the house any more."

"Father, you're exaggerating. But it's true that Uncle James was a very changeable sort of person. I think Freddy takes after him in that." She turned to me. "What is this book you mentioned?"

I gave them a fuller account of my last encounter with Frederick Boscombe, telling them about his discovery of the book in Shackleford's baggage and its consequences. I did not go into my own subsequent adventures with nobleman Zanotto and his henchmen. One thing at a time. I attempted to lighten things towards the end of the journey by bidding them enjoy our entrance into the Grand Canal. But although they gazed at the spectacle it was clear that appreciating the sights was not the first thing on their minds.

When we reached the Leon Bianco, Sior Scarpa offered them the same rooms that their relative and his retinue had occupied, declaring how sorry he was about what had happened and assuring them of his firm belief that all would be resolved soon. I wondered whether there was still a matter of an unpaid bill, which, for him, would be one of the questions most urgently in need of resolution. Miss Boscombe had her usual dazzling effect on the staff of the inn, of which she seemed radiantly unconscious.

"When can we see poor Freddy?" she asked me, as I prepared to leave them for the evening.

"I think the easiest thing will be to arrange matters through the English Resident," I said.

"Can't we just go to the prison and demand to see him?"

"That would not be wise," I said, trying not to wince at the notion.

Mr Boscombe, slightly to my surprise, agreed with me. I was half expecting him to propose relying on sturdy national persistence but it seemed he was more realistic than that. "From what I've seen of the Venetians," he said, "you won't get anywhere by claiming to know better than they do." And so we arranged that Bepi and I would take them there the next morning. I wondered whether I should suggest that Miss Boscombe dress a little more soberly for the encounter if she wanted to draw Mr Murray's attention to the facts of the matter, but decided it was not worth it. She would at least be sure of getting his attention.

14

And so it proved. John Murray was his usual bleary self in the early morning (around eleven o'clock) but not so bleary that he could not focus on Miss Boscombe's cleavage (nestled within the gorgeous slopes of a sky-blue dress this morning). He received us in the splendid reception hall of his palace on the Grand Canal, frescoed figures of the family of the former owners cavorting with indulgent deities on the ceiling.

Mr and Miss Boscombe presented themselves while I hovered in the background, feeling distinctly supernumerary, until summoned forward. On hearing my name the Resident frowned: "Aren't you the fellow young Boscombe went running to? I thought the authorities told you to stay out of things – until they call upon you to give evidence."

"I'm here solely in the capacity of *cicerone* to Mr and Miss Boscombe, whom I met quite by chance at Fusina yesterday."

"In that case," he said, "I'll kindly ask you to wait outside. And perhaps Mr and Miss Boscombe will think of hiring another *cicerone*." He turned to them. "There is nothing to be gained by antagonising the authorities here."

I bowed and took my leave, faintly cheered by a dismayed "Oh" from Miss Boscombe. I was escorted down the grand marble staircase by a black servant in yellow livery. Bepi, sprawling in the stern of the gondola enjoying the spring sunshine, looked up as I made my way towards him.

"Sacked again?" he said.

"Not quite. Or at least not yet. We'll see when they come down."

I explained what had happened and Bepi nodded philosophically. His only remark was: "Pity. Wouldn't have minded another week with her in the boat."

"A little out of reach for the likes of us," I said.

"We can always look," he said. After a pause he added: "And she doesn't seem to mind being looked at."

About fifteen minutes later the Boscombes appeared in the entrance hall. He wore his customary expression of surly truculence while she appeared flushed and angry. "Honestly," she said, "the absurdity of this."

"No more than I expected," he said.

"Is something the matter?" I asked.

"They will let us know when we can visit Freddy," she said with haughty indignation. "Let us know!"

"But I'm sure it'll be soon," I said. "They have no reason to make things difficult for you."

"And we are advised to sack you," she said.

"Ah," I said.

"But I can assure you that is the last thing I will do."

"Ah," I said again. After a pause, I went on: "Thank you. But I don't want to make things any more difficult for you than they already are."

"Nonsense," she said. And that was clearly settled. Certainly her father made no protest other than a throaty muttering that could have meant anything. "Now you can take us to see your bookseller friend," she added imperiously.

"Certainly," I said.

I doubted Fabrizio was going to make any sales.

Half an hour later I was making the introductions in the bookshop. We switched to Italian, and Fabrizio and Lucia uttered polite and mendacious compliments on the Boscombes' mastery of the language of Dante. Lucia went on to express her entirely sincere sorrow at the situation of their relative, her glistening dark eyes testifying to the veracity of her words.

Miss Boscombe asked what she knew of Shackleford and Lucia explained her doubts about him, at the same time assuring them that he had seemed perfectly respectable and that what had happened to him was appalling. Fabrizio added that Mr Shackleford clearly had been interested in books, as he had spent many happy moments browsing among his volumes.

Lucia was shocked to hear that they could not immediately go and visit their relative, but she hoped they would not have to wait long. She was sure that the truth would emerge soon.

"Perhaps," said Miss Boscombe. "But I think we might have to help it along a little."

"Yes, of course," said Lucia. "And if I can do anything . . ."

Her father made a clucking noise which was quite as enigmatic as Mr Boscombe's mutters had been, but could have been expressing some reservations.

"Well," said Miss Boscombe, "I think the first thing will be to visit the place where this dreadful murder happened. And I think our *cicerone* can help us there."

"But signorina," said Lucia, with a touch of agitation, "the authorities have forbidden Signor Alvise to have anything more to do with this case."

"I'm sure Signor Alvise will not be so weak as to allow that to prevent him from doing his duty," she said. (Her Italian was not quite as grammatically accurate as this rendering might suggest but this was the essential message.)

"It is not a question of weakness," said Lucia with some asperity. "Signor Alvise is a resident in this city and has to abide by its laws."

"I cannot believe there is any law that forbids a gentleman from assisting a lady in distress. Goodness me, I'm not asking him to lead a rebellion, just to show me the way to a house."

"Signorina," said Lucia, "I can do that just as well as Signor Alvise."

"Perhaps," she said, "but I would feel safer in the presence of a man." After a quick glance at her audience she added quickly, "A young man, who knows the city." She turned to me, her delphinium-blue eyes brimming with supplicant tears. "You will not abandon me?"

What could I say?

Even without looking at Lucia I could sense her steadily rising indignation. She said quietly but firmly, "Signorina, this is not fair." She turned to Mr Boscombe. "Signore, you must realise that this is not necessary."

He made a throat-clearing noise and said: "I leave these things to my daughter."

I half expected Mr Boscombe and Fabrizio to shake hands on the sentiment but of course they did not. Fabrizio mumbled a few words to the effect that perhaps Signorina Boscombe should listen to what Lucia was saying, but Signorina Boscombe simply touched my elbow and said, "*Andiamo.* Thank you for your time, signorina, signore." She gave the slightest hint of a curtsey and turned towards the door. Mr Boscombe muttered a few formal words and headed out of the shop as well.

I gave Lucia an apologetic half-smile. "I'll be careful."

She did not smile back. She just said: "You are being foolish, sior, but I suppose it is not entirely your fault."

And on this cold note we parted.

Bepi rowed us to Campo Santi Giovanni e Paolo. I had told him briefly why we were heading there and he had shrugged and said, "Well, I hope you know what you're doing."

"So do I," I said.

We drew up alongside the square and I helped them step out of the gondola. Miss Boscombe was becoming quite practised at this and it took her no more than thirty seconds to readjust her clothing once on dry land. Quite enough to gather the attention of the entire neighbourhood.

Father and daughter ignored the occupants of the square and gazed instead at the splendid architecture: the marble façade of the Scuola di San Marco with its fine late fifteenth-century sculptures, the great gothic mass of the Dominican church towering into the blue sky, and the bronze statue of Colleoni sneering down at us from his equally supercilious steed.

A few words in my role as *cicerone* seemed appropriate.

"Statue by Verrocchio," I said. "The condottiere Colleoni."

"I beg your pardon," said Miss Boscombe, startled by the name.

I had momentarily forgotten that she spoke Italian. I wondered whether I should point out the condottiere's coat-of-arms, with its three testicles, and decided not to.

I was about to lead the way across the square when Mr Boscombe said: "I'll stay and look at the church."

"Oh, Father," she said, but with no special emphasis.

"You know you don't need me. And I've got no questions to ask."

"Very well then," she said, and I had the distinct impression that she was far from minding his decision. "But don't wander off and get lost."

"Don't be silly, dear." He stumped off towards the church, his wig and hat askew as usual. This was decidedly unusual; there were certainly few Venetian fathers who would so casually leave their unmarried daughters alone with a *cicerone*. However, I was not going to complain.

"Mr Marangon," she said, "please lead the way."

"Certainly, signorina," I said, and did so. I thought I heard a faint sigh of envy from Bepi behind me as we set off across the square.

As we walked past the statue she gazed up at it. "Colleoni," she said, but pronouncing it quite distinctly as "coglioni." And then she said, "Oh goodness me," and emitted an embarrassed little laugh.

"Signorina?" I said.

"Nothing," she said. And she gave me a sidelong smile. "Quite a man, this condottiere of yours." She had clearly seen the coat-of-arms.

It was my turn to be startled and she obviously enjoyed my confusion. "Pray do tell me more about him," she said with breathy eagerness.

"I really can't tell you that much," I said. "As so often in these cases the statue is now far better known than the man. Indeed, the man is really only known, other than to historians, because of the statue."

"And yet he looks so proud and sure of himself," she said. "What a lesson for us all. All forgotten – even his manly attributes." And she said this last phrase with such an air of innocence that I wondered whether I had misread her earlier remarks.

We walked towards the eastern end of the square and the narrow lane that led towards the canal. I was remembering Frederick Boscombe's description of his night-time walk, and accounts I had heard later from others; I was fairly sure I knew where the house was.

"Oh, goodness me," she said. "Some of these narrow streets. Hardly wide enough for one's skirts."

"There are many much narrower streets," I said.

"Well, maybe we'll have a chance to explore them later," she said. "That could be most intriguing, Mr Marangon. But now we must concentrate on our reason for being here."

"Well, of course. It should be over the next bridge. This, on our right, is the tavern your cousin mentioned."

We mounted a bridge, on which stood an idle figure in drab clothes gazing at the view. It was worth gazing at. Looking to our left from the top of the bridge, we could see the canal divide into two prongs alongside the flanks of a wedge-shaped palace, which rose from the water like a sturdy vessel. In the other direction the canal broadened and was flanked by a number of fine palaces with marble frontages.

On the other side of the bridge I began to look at the front doors to the houses, although I was well aware that it would be absurd to expect any visible sign of the momentous event after all this time.

"Why don't we ask the man on the bridge?" she said.

I don't know whether it was just typical male reluctance to ask for help but my instinct was to resist this suggestion. However, before I could say anything she called out to him, in her comic Italian: "*Dov'è la casa del delitto?*" Where is the scene of the crime?

He grunted that it was the second house on the left and we thanked him and pulled the bell rope. There was just the one.

Seconds later a window opened above us. No face appeared but a creaky female voice asked who we were. Miss Boscombe answered that she was a relative of the poor Englishman. Not an exhaustive answer, but after another few seconds the door was opened, clearly pulled by a string from above.

I led the way up the narrow staircase. There were two doorways off the first landing, but only the one to the right was open. In the doorway stood a small lady with a head that seemed to be at least twice as large as it should be. In better lighting, as she stood aside to let us pass into the hallway, it proved to be composed mainly of an elaborate wig of stiff yellow curls. I found it less disturbing to focus my attention on these curls than on the face beneath, which was coated in a thick patina of paint and powder in a vain attempt to conceal its web of cavernous corrugations. She wore a dress with as profound a décolletée as Miss Boscombe's, but it merely provided another reason to keep my eyes fixed on the stiff curls.

"Can I help you?" she said, in a throaty whisper that was clearly intended to be seductive but was as cracked as the face. I do not think she had any particular designs on us; this was just her habitual mode of address.

"Signora," Miss Boscombe began.

"Signorina," the lady corrected her at once.

"I beg your pardon, signorina. I am a relative of the Englishman who was arrested following the murder in this apartment last week."

"Ah, the murderer."

"No, I assure you. My cousin is entirely innocent. We've come to try to find out what happened."

"I've told everything to the *sbirri*. And to the magistrate. And to the Missier Grande. That should be enough."

She spoke in thick Venetian and I could see that Miss Boscombe was having problems. I translated into English for her.

"But signora – signorina," Miss Boscombe protested, "try to understand. They aren't interested in finding the truth. They just want to arrest someone. And even better if he's a foreigner."

The door on the opposite side of the landing opened and another small lady appeared there. Her plain grey dress and hair were in total and welcome contrast to those of her neighbour. "Haven't you created enough scandal?" she said indignantly, addressing all of us indiscriminately. "Can't we be left in peace?"

"Signora," said Miss Boscombe, "please excuse us. I've only come for –"

I cut in, guessing that a few words in Venetian would work better than this heartfelt but laboured explanation in bad Tuscan. "Siora, this young lady is the cousin of the Englishman who was arrested. She just wishes to establish the truth of the events of that night."

"I saw him there. Brandishing a knife. A monster. Covered in blood. And that other man. Lying there. All in a pool of blood."

This came out in a series of clipped Venetian phrases, each one a miniature picture of horror, like a sketch by Piranesi. She had clearly told her story many times over and had perhaps even come to relish her part in it. I guessed that it would be difficult to get her to go back to her original impressions – for example, to remove the brandished knife from Mr Boscombe's bloodstained hands.

The lady in the opposite doorway drew herself up to her full height, which even with the wig was far from towering, and said: "I cannot be blamed for what my clients choose to do when they rent my rooms."

"Everyone knows what people rent your rooms for," said the lady in grey. "And we've had enough of it."

"My rooms are rented by some of the best names in the city," said the lady with the wig. "There has never been any scandal until this unfortunate affair. And no one is more harmed by it than me."

Miss Boscombe was looking from one to the other, trying to catch the odd recognisable word in the torrents of vehement Venetian.

"Up and down. All night long," said the lady in grey. "And the noises that come from in there . . ."

"I'm sure you sit with your ear to the door," said the lady with the wig. "Just jealous of anyone still able to enjoy life. Snooper."

The lady in grey looked as if she were about to explode. Then she said, "You've got a nerve: that to me! You know perfectly well –"

The lady with the wig was suddenly eager to close the argument. "That's enough," she said loudly, drowning out her neighbour. She turned to us: "Come in."

We were hustled into the apartment and the door was closed behind us, while the other lady continued to protest as vehemently as ever, if more indistinctly.

"I am so sorry," said the lady in the wig. "Some people do not understand true refinement. I am sure that two young people like yourselves have more appreciation of the finer things in life." And she gave us what was presumably intended as a winning smile, but unfortunately revealed a chequered wreck of a mouth. "This is my little *casino*, which can of course be rented by the day, the week or the month." She had switched automatically to her sales pitch, regardless of the reason we had given for our visit.

Miss Boscombe and I looked around. We were standing in a small hallway with ornately decorated mirrors on three sides. On the ceiling were frescoes of damsels in clearly vain flight from leering gods; ornamental stucco frisked and frolicked in lascivious coils and curves at the tops of the walls.

"You can see how elegant everything is," our hostess went on. "Only the best artists and decorators –"

"Signorina," I said, "we're not here to rent the rooms. You will remember –"

"Of course," she said. "How foolish of me." She let out a girlish giggle that sent a shudder up my spine.

"What a place," said Miss Boscombe in English. "Is this where she lives?"

"No, I don't think so," I said. "At present she's trying to rent it to us."

"Well, you can put a stop to that."

"I have done so."

"Not my style of place," Miss Boscombe added.

I was a little disconcerted by this but returned to the lady, who was looking at us warily. "Signorina, we wish to find out what happened that night."

"Well, of course I wasn't here. I was in my apartment upstairs. The first thing I knew was when that woman there started screaming . . . dreadful noise."

"Well, it must have been a horrific sight."

"Yes," she said, realising that it hardly suited her role to remain unaffected by such an event. "Dreadful. The poor man."

"Did you know him?"

"The poor victim? No, no. Never seen him before."

"So who had rented the room?"

"I've been through all this with the magistrates. I've told them that I don't know."

"But you must have spoken to someone. They must have paid you."

"Sior, the very nature of the service I offer means that I guarantee discretion. I never ask for names."

"Yes, but –"

She went straight on. I imagined that she had been repeating this defensive line unremittingly for the last week. "You know as well as I do that our hardworking senators and lawmakers and merchants need somewhere to relax occasionally; they must be allowed to shake off the heavy responsibilities of their office with some moments in the company of friends. A little card-playing. Some gentle music. Sympathetic female companions . . ."

I saw Miss Boscombe give a little smile. The lady was enunciating her words very carefully for our benefit and I supposed that Miss Boscombe's ear was becoming attuned to the dialect.

"Yes, but you must have spoken to one of these hard-pressed servants of the republic, even if he didn't give a name," I said. "There is the matter of payment, after all."

"Well, yes," she said. "But as I said to the magistrate, it was someone I had never seen before and he was wearing a mask."

"A mask?" I said. "At this season?"

"I was a little surprised, but I imagined he wanted particular discretion. He called on me the night before it happened and asked to book the rooms for one night. He paid in advance and I gave him the key and promised to leave everything ready. As of course I did. The card table was prepared . . ." She gestured towards the room beyond and we walked into it.

It was occupied mainly by a round table with a gleaming dark surface; four elegant curved chairs were placed around it. Above us was another fresco with gods lying listlessly on comfortable cushions of cloud. Another door to the right gave on to a room containing a large canopied bed. From where we stood I could see that the frescoes here had lost all pretence of coyness: the fleeing damsels had all been outrun and everywhere one looked plump buttocks and breasts were being palpated by the triumphant pursuers, while the doomed maidens raised resigned faces to the heavens.

"Goodness me," said Miss Boscombe, in English.

"A very fine artist," said the lady. "Appreciated by those who understand true refinement."

I returned to the question of the masked man. "Did you recognise his voice?"

"No, no. Except that he was a foreigner."

"Ah," I said.

"As I said to the magistrate, he pronounced his words strangely, and he didn't speak Venetian."

"A foreigner from where?"

"Well, I didn't ask that, of course."

"No, but could you tell from the accent? For example, did he sound like this young lady?" I gestured to Miss Boscombe.

"Oh, nothing like that," she said. "The lady has a charming voice."

"I'm referring only to the accent," I said. "Did your customer not have a charming voice, then?"

"No, it was hoarse. And as I said, his accent was funny. German perhaps. Or French."

Or Chinese or Russian or Arabic, I added to myself. The lady clearly was no linguist.

I turned to Miss Boscombe. "Have you been following?"

"Something about a man in a mask?" she said, in a questioning tone.

I nodded and explained the details of the booking of the apartment. She asked: "Are there many places like this in Venice?"

"Well, it's not uncommon. Many of the noblemen keep them. And then there are some who just rent them when they need them, like this one. I don't know that they are all decorated like this."

"No, it's quite remarkable." She gazed at the frescoes with frank curiosity. "Some of the postures seem a little improbable."

"Yes," I said, a trifle awkwardly.

"I'm sorry," she said, with a smile. "I don't want to embarrass you."

"The lady likes the pictures?" asked our hostess, with a gap-toothed leer.

"She's fond of art," I said stiffly. I tried to move the conversation on. "Tell me, signorina, is there another entrance to the apartment?"

"No. Why should there be?" she said; her response was suspiciously swift.

"Well, my friend's cousin said that when he entered the apartment and found the murdered man there was nobody else here. So the question is how did the killer escape?"

"I don't know anything about that," she said. "I wasn't here, as I've already said."

"May I inspect the windows?"

"They were all shuttered from within," she said. "My clients like privacy."

It did not take long to inspect the entire apartment. There was just the little entrance hall, the room with the gaming table, the bedroom, and a little dressing room just off the last. The hallway had no windows but took light from the other two rooms if the doors were left open. The gaming room had one window looking on to the calle from which we had entered; the bedroom window looked on to a little courtyard. The lady showed us how the shutters closed, with a heavy bar that precluded any possibility of anyone leaving through the window and closing it behind them.

"Are we sure the shutters were closed?" said Miss Boscombe.

"Well, she says so," I said. "There is just one thing . . ."

"What's that?"

"Something her neighbour said. Let's have another look at the bedroom."

"I certainly have no objection," she said.

But as I turned back in that direction our hostess stood in the doorway blocking the access. "I've answered all your questions. Now I really have to return to my apartment."

"We really do need another look at that room," I said in English to Miss Boscombe. "Have you got any money?"

"How much will be required?"

"I'll ask." I said, and turned to the lady. "My friend and I would love to spend some time enjoying the artistic treasures of the bedroom. Can you tell us how much it will cost us? For half an hour?"

I could see suspicion battling with avarice in her eyes. Eventually the latter won out. "Well, how delightful. I could see the young lady was curious. Three zecchini."

"Tell her one," said Miss Boscombe, who had understood the price.

We did not take long to come to terms and, with another leering smile, she moved towards the front door. There she turned and gave us a last indulgent farewell: "Ah, young people . . ." Then we were alone.

"And now what, Mr Marangon?" said Miss Boscombe, turning to me with those big blue innocent eyes.

"I want to study those frescoes," I said.

"Really? Do you need to?"

"Well, I've a feeling we'll discover they conceal something," I said, when I had regained control over my voice.

"They seem to conceal remarkably little," she said.

I could tell that she found my awkwardness a source of amusement, which helped me to resist her very obvious charms. God knows I was tempted, but I suspected that any amorous dalliance would lead to far more trouble than it was worth. It was also likely that the dalliance would in any case be very limited; I did not think that she would really let a mere *cicerone* get much further than an awkward kiss and a squeeze.

But I did heave an inward sigh as I tried not to think of what there was to squeeze.

I walked into the bedroom and gazed at the wall opposite the bed. "You remember the neighbour? Her last words?"

"I understood very little," she said.

"She took umbrage at being accused of snooping. And she said something along the lines of 'You dare to call *me* a snooper' . . . *ficcanaso* was the word she used."

"Implying . . ."

"Well, let's see," I said, studying the decorations on the wall. A few moments later I pointed to the stucco work above a particularly salacious scene of a faun and a nymph. "There."

"Oh goodness me," she said. "Colleoni himself would be envious . . ."

"Above that," I said. "Look between those two coil-shaped pieces of stucco."

"Ah, yes," she said. "A hole."

"A spy hole," I said. "From the house next door. Which undoubtedly also belongs to our hostess. And no doubt she gets one rent from those enjoying the bed in here and another, a little reduced, from those enjoying the spectacle in there."

"How very sordid," she said. "But does this help us?"

"Well," I said, "I suspect there is also a means of communication." I looked at the mirror on the same wall, a large rectangular sheet of glass in an elaborate frame of carved and gilded wood. It appeared to be solidly fixed to the wall.

"Aha," I said, after a few moments. "Look."

I pointed to the left-hand side of the frame. Concealed behind carvings of Mars and Venus were two metal hinges. "It's a door," I said. "We just need to find the opening mechanism on the other side."

She ran her fingers down the various carved figures on the right-hand side. "If I can judge from the lady's taste I would suspect . . . ah, yes." She gently caressed a virile figure with a swelling loin cloth. "Yes, here we go." There was a click as she pressed the wooden bulge and the mirror swung forward from the wall. "Well, there will be a certain appropriateness if a phallus proves the means of salvation for my cousin," she said with a smile.

"No doubt," I said.

We gazed through the doorway, which led into a plainly furnished room; it was fairly gloomy, presumably because the windows were shuttered.

"Shall we explore?" she said, preparing to step through.

"Well, why not?" I said.

There was a sudden loud hammering at the front door of the apartment.

I felt a sudden jolt of apprehension, like a fist to my stomach.

"Who will that be?" she said, clearly quite untroubled.

"I don't like to think," I said, half tempted to dive through the doorway, as if a land of salvation must lie beyond the mirror.

"Open up! In the name of the republic!"

"How very grandiose," she said. "What can they want?"

I closed the mirror-door, turned round and walked towards the front door. There was little point in putting off the inevitable.

As I suspected, the man we had seen on the bridge stood there on the landing, flanked by two old friends, the *sbirro* with the scarred face and the hairy one.

Scarface's mouth grinned, although the jagged downward scar did its trick of maintaining an overall appearance of surliness. "Well, who would have thought it."

At that moment Miss Boscombe emerged from the bedroom. The two *sbirri* gave her a clearly appreciative look and Scarface said: "Congratulations, son."

"I'm here as *cicerone* to this lady, who is the cousin . . ."

"*Cicerone*, eh?" said Scarface. "Anyway, don't bother explaining it to us, son. Keep it for the folk at the ducal palace."

"Who are these people?" Miss Boscombe asked me in English.

"*Sbirri*," I said. "I think we're under arrest."

"For what?"

"Well, I'm certainly under arrest," I said. "For disobeying the authorities."

"Nonsense," she said.

"Come on then," said Scarface. "We've got irons for you again, and even for the lady if she wants to make trouble."

"It won't be necessary," I said. "I'll persuade her."

She understood this. "Persuade me to do what?" she said in Italian. "To come to the ducal palace," I said.

"Well, what an excellent idea," she said. "Isn't that just what I wanted to do?"

It was that easy. I managed to persuade the *sbirri* to let us pass by Campo Santi Giovanni e Paolo, so that we could collect her father. "The more the merrier," said Scarface, with a grim smile. He agreed not to use the irons, since we were being so very accommodating.

Her father was emerging from the church as we entered the square and he muttered a few inarticulate syllables as I explained the situation. His daughter told him that it was all for the best because now we were going to the ducal palace and we would be able to explain everything. He looked sceptical but accepted the inevitable.

Bepi had found some colleagues to play dice with in the square and took the news that we would not be requiring his services immediately with his usual laconic resignation.

"I'll send word," I said, and then added, "As soon as I can."

15

Half an hour later I was back in the narrow room with the single chandelier where I had been questioned by the Missier Grande a week earlier. Once again I had been separated from my companions at a certain point in our wanderings through the twisting corridors and staircases of the palace, and found myself with just the hairy *sbirro* for company.

I stood in front of the long desk, as I had done before, and waited. It was midday this time, rather than the middle of the night, but it made very little difference in this windowless room. Probably forty minutes passed and I found myself wiping sweat from the back of my neck. I could not tell whether it was the heat or my nerves.

The same little bespectacled man came bustling in as before, and sat down, and started scribbling in a large book.

I continued to wait. The Missier Grande chose to break the pattern by abruptly appearing from behind me. My start no doubt afforded him satisfaction. He took his place at the table alongside the little man.

"So, Alvise Marangon," he said, quietly and levelly as ever. "You chose to disobey my orders."

"Illustrissimo," I began.

He raised a hand. "You will be able to offer your excuses to the jailer later. I'm certainly not going to listen to them."

"But Illustrissimo..."

My shirt collar was suddenly gripped from behind and I felt the hot stinking breath of the hairy man close by my ear. "Shut up."

I shut up. My collar was released.

"You will, however, answer my questions."

"Yes."

"Who suggested the visit to the *casino* of Signora Padoan?"

"The young lady," I said. "She's the cousin —"

"I know who she is."

Well, of course he did. "Has she told you what we found?"

The Missier Grande made no acknowledgement of my aborted question. "And you raised no objection?" he asked.

"I told her I had been ordered to stay clear of the affair, but I thought that she might need . . ." I faltered to a stop, realising how lame it sounded.

"She is an attractive young lady," he said, and it sounded like definitive proof of her iniquity.

I said: "She's very worried about her cousin."

"Which is none of your business."

"Well, no, but she's a foreigner, and –"

"There is an English Resident in this city. And I believe he was very clear on this subject to you."

"With all respect to Mr Murray," I said, "I did not feel that he intended to exert himself very greatly in this matter."

To my surprise he did not try to cut me off. I realised he was gazing at me in a strangely speculative fashion. He remained silent for a few seconds, and then he addressed the *sbirro* behind me. "Please leave us."

Without a word the *sbirro* turned and walked out. When the door had closed behind him the Missier Grande spoke again. "Signor Marangon, are you a courageous man?"

Was this the way he introduced the threat of the rope?

"It is hardly for me to say," I said, and hoped the quiver in my throat was not audible.

"It would seem that you are endowed either with stubborn courage or with inordinate stupidity."

"Maybe something of both," I said, trying to sound jauntily off-hand.

"It may be so," he said. "And it may be that the state will need both qualities."

"The state?"

"The Most Serene Republic of Venice. You could perhaps be of service."

"Well, I'd be happy to help."

"Be quiet." He paused for a moment. "You will have to learn the gift of silence. It doesn't seem to come easily to you."

It was clearly better not to answer this, so I nodded.

"You presumably know that the republic employs a number of

confidenti. I myself am responsible for some of them; the Inquisitors for many more. Most of these *confidenti* are little more than private snoopers."

"A Venetian pastime," I said.

He shot one icy blue glance at me and went on: "Idle people, reporting on noblemen who go out without a cloak. On noblemen's wives who spend too much on their Sunday lunch or use too many coloured ribbons in their hats."

The sumptuary laws of the republic lay down very strict guidelines for all such matters, guidelines that are forever being pushed against until the Senate is forced to revise them. Which does not mean people cannot be fined for breaking them; it usually depends on who the Inquisitors are at any given moment.

"This is not to say that such *confidenti* are useless. All such information has its value," he said. His eyes ran round the cupboards and bookshelves in the room, presumably crammed with such serviceable jottings. "However, I am also responsible for a number of *confidenti* who provide information of a more vital nature. *Confidenti* who must never allow themselves to be suspected of playing such a role, and therefore do not give the impression of being watchful or, indeed, especially intelligent. It seems to me that you have the requisite qualities."

I didn't think he was being complimentary.

"At the same time I suspect you are not without resources. You are clearly linguistically gifted, since your Venetian seems flawless to me, despite the fact that you were raised in England. And your theatrical background might also prove useful."

He paused. I waited, definitely intrigued.

"Now, you presumably know that my area of competence extends no further than common criminality in the city. Anything connected with crimes against the state, with treason, with political chicanery, with foreign intrusion into Venetian affairs, is in the exclusive jurisdiction of the three Inquisitors. However, the dividing lines are not always clear, and before I refer matters to them I need to know precisely which category of crime we are dealing with. Once a matter has been referred to them it is out of my hands."

I nodded. He had not said so, but I gathered that he did not feel the hands of the Inquisitors were necessarily the most efficient. For most

Venetians such a sentiment would have been close to blasphemy; the three Inquisitors were held in even greater awe than the Missier Grande himself – a fact that I suspected irritated the Missier Grande.

"So let us come to the point. Nobleman Piero Garzoni." He paused again and I wondered whether the time had come for me to make another remark.

"Yes?" I said.

"You mentioned the nobleman in connection with Mr Boscombay, referring to the fact that Mr Boscombay was hoping to meet him. And you referred to the Georgian count who appears to have been taken into nobleman Piero Garzoni's confidence."

"Count Gelashvili," I said.

"I suspect that the count is merely a common fraudster whose aims are purely mercenary, so no international complications need worry us here. Exactly the same considerations apply in the case of Mr Boscombay and the murder of his tutor. However, the case of nobleman Piero Garzoni is more complex."

"The case?" I said.

"To put it very simply, we need to know what nobleman Garzoni is up to."

"Ah," I said. Probably I looked and sounded very stupid as I did so. And presumably that was all to the good.

"I suspect you have already heard something of this man: his former connections with the Arsenale; the fact that he lives a somewhat isolated life. And, as you yourself mentioned, his cult of Doge Marin Falier."

"Well, I only thought that perhaps –"

"He makes little secret of his feelings on this subject. But we need to know whether those feelings have led him into any possibly criminal activity. However, investigating a member of the nobility is always a delicate matter. We must avoid unnecessary scandal and possible resentment. For this reason I need someone who can investigate intelligently and discreetly – but also someone I can deny all knowledge of should the investigation come to light before any useful results have been achieved."

"I see," I said. "And that would be me."

"That would be you. I am making you an offer, Signor Marangon.

I will lay aside all charges against you for having flouted our explicit orders in exchange for your co-operation in investigating the activities of nobleman Piero Garzoni. But as I have indicated, should anyone question what you are doing I will deny all knowledge of your activities and will see to it that you receive the prison sentence you clearly deserve."

"Thank you," I said, keeping my tone as neutral as possible.

He nodded. "I see that we understand each other. Your knowledge of English may be of assistance to you in this matter. We can lend you a copy of the book you have already mentioned in this regard, of which we only possess an English version. It may provide a useful starting point."

I was about to say that I had already seen the book but fortunately stopped in time. Fabrizio would not thank me for drawing attention to his ownership of the item. Instead I said: "So where do you suggest I go from there?"

"Signor Marangon, the offer I have made is based on my intuition that you possess a certain resourcefulness. If I am mistaken I might as well just have you sent straight to prison."

"With all respect, Excellency, this is the first time I have been hired as a *confidente*. I thought there might be certain standard procedures."

"The essence of this activity is that nothing is standard. But you can talk to my assistant here, Signor Massaro, who will give you whatever practical instructions are necessary." He waved to the little bespectacled man, who did not cease his steady scribbling. "He will also decide on a suitable emolument."

Things were already looking up, I thought.

"Just one instruction I can give you," he went on. "You are a *confidente*. That means you tell *no one* of what you are doing, not even your closest friend. Because remember this: if it turns out that we have to send you to prison after all, any person you have informed of your activities will accompany you there. Good day."

"Illustrissimo, just one last thing," I said urgently, as he turned towards the door.

"Be brief."

"In that *casino* we found that there was another way out."

"Ah yes, the door behind the mirror."

"So you know."

"Did you really think my men would have failed to search the place thoroughly?"

"So the evidence against Mr Boscombay . . ."

"I am not here to discuss that case, Signor Marangon."

"But you will be talking to his cousin –"

"Good day. You can discuss all other practical matters with Signor Massaro." With a final nod, he left the room.

And so I became a confidential agent of the Most Serene Republic of Venice.

16

The little man introduced himself as Sior Marco Massaro, *cittadino* from the parish of San Polo. In time I came to know Sior Massaro well and to appreciate his knowledge of the intricate workings of governmental machinery. He spent his life scurrying around the more secluded corners and corridors of the Doge's palace, like a busy ant in a formicary. His devotion to the Missier Grande was total and he would never presume to question or contest any of his decisions. I was to discover that he had an almost instinctive contempt for nearly every other branch of the administration, even though it was always expressed in the guarded language of officialdom.

"The Missier Grande is the key to the whole administration," he said as he took me into another tiny office, lined on all sides by dark cupboards. This, it seemed, was his own small kingdom.

"And the three Inquisitors, the Council of Ten?" I said, naming the most revered institutions in the city.

"They play their part, of course," he said, as if referring indulgently to keen little children. "But in the very nature of things, they cannot get as firm a grip on matters as does the Missier Grande."

I realised he was referring to the temporary nature of these appointments. It was an essential feature of the Venetian system of government that the more power a position conferred, the shorter was the term of office. Inquisitors held the post for a year; they could be re-elected but usually were not. Their powers were in theory vast: they could, for example, order secret executions, which helps to explain why they were held in such awe by the Venetian populace. But in Massaro's view of things, I gathered, they were little more than a series of bumbling functionaries, who barely had time to learn how the system worked before they were substituted by the next set of appointees.

Of course, he would never express himself in such openly disrespectful terms. What he did say was: "You see, it is thanks to people like me, who keep all the papers in order and understand the regulations, that things get done properly." He waved a hand at the document-crammed cupboards all around us. "And the Missier Grande realises this and appreciates just how important we are."

"So he treats you well?"

"He appreciates us," he repeated, with a note of dignified pride. "It makes a great deal of difference, you know."

"I'm sure it does," I said. The Missier Grande clearly knew how to inculcate loyalty.

"I wish it were true of all our government officials," he said. He was about to add something but suddenly shook his head, as if to expel any possibly seditious thoughts that had taken lodging there. "But, dear me, we need to concentrate on the matter at hand. First of all, let me file the record of our recent meeting." He pulled open a cupboard, drew out a large ledger with a series of apparently random letters and numbers on its spine and placed the closely written pages inside it. The ledger was returned to the cupboard.

"You know where everything is?" I asked.

"That is my job," he said. "And if I don't know where something is, I know whom I must ask."

"And does everything also have to go the Inquisitors?"

He seemed shocked at the suggestion. "Goodness, no. They wouldn't be able to cope. Indeed . . ." He was suddenly seized with quiet laughter as he remembered something.

"What's the joke?" I asked.

"There was one occasion when the Inquisitors did insist on receiving copies of our more important documents. Dear me." The memory was clearly a hilarious one; his little shoulders quivered convulsively. "The Missier Grande knew just how to deal with that. He had copies of absolutely everything sent to them as it arose, hour after hour. After a few days it was they who begged him to stop." Probably nothing so amusing had happened in the Doge's palace since the banquet laid on for Henry III of France.

"Is this rivalry a good thing?" I asked.

"It's not a question of rivalry," he said stiffly. "The issue is a clear demarcation of areas of competence." He really spoke like that. I was to get used to it – even to grow strangely fond of it. "There is also the fact that the role of the Missier Grande has been unfairly denigrated. It is undeniable that certain holders of the office in the past have proved unworthy of it. But the present Missier Grande has fully restored its honour and prestige. And anyone who attempts to deny this clearly does so with malicious intent."

"Well," I said, "there is the fact that by nature of the job he has to consort with *sbirri* and *zaffi*."

"And no one has done more to improve the quality and reliability of those men," he said.

I remembered Scarface and the hairy man who had arrested me and felt a little doubtful. But it probably was not worth arguing the point.

"What do you think the Missier Grande expects me to do?" I said.

"To investigate nobleman Piero Garzoni," he said, as if puzzled by my question.

"Well, what does that mean? Am I supposed to follow him around in disguise? Or just to study the files you've already compiled?"

"Well, of course you can consult our files," he said.

"There's no 'of course' about it. Remember I'm entirely new to this world. Do you have extensive files on him?"

"Well, naturally we have reports. And the Inquisitors will have their own files as well."

"And do you have access to their files?"

"I can gain access," he said, with the quiet complacency of a skilled workman. "If you come back tomorrow I can promise to have everything ready for you."

"I can't just go and potter around in the archives myself?"

He managed to check his horror at this notion and said, after gulping a few times: "You would not know where to start looking. And access to files is of course restricted."

"Well, yes, I suppose so." I did not say that I had just wanted to see the expression on his face. "Tell me, why do you think he's keeping the Englishman in custody, given the evidence of the other way into the *casino*?"

"My job is to gather information and make sure that it is available to those who need it. It is not my place to speculate on that information or to attempt to make any deductions from it."

"I see," I said. "But you must have an opinion?"

He looked pained at my insistence. "I can only repeat –"

"Don't worry. I get the point," I said.

But then, after giving a glance around the room, as if to make sure there were no other gatherers of information lurking in the cupboards, he leaned towards me and said in a low voice: "I can tell you that the Missier Grande has been known to keep someone in prison in order to deflect attention from the real suspect while evidence is being gathered against him." Then, straightening up, he said: "That, by the way, is a purely unofficial remark."

"Don't worry," I said. "I'll omit it from the record of our meeting."

He looked momentarily puzzled, and then disapproving. Official procedures were not a matter for mockery.

I went on to another question, closer to my heart: "An emolument was mentioned . . ."

"Ah yes. Here we have to base our judgement on established criteria for such financial transactions. Which means we take into account the estimated time required, the level of complexity of the case, and the social standing, the level of education and the experience of the agent in question. And so, making an assessment in line with comparable precedents, I would place you in category 3A and assign you, for the moment at least, a monthly stipend of thirteen zecchini."

I did my best not to whistle. This more than doubled my average income. Maybe I could buy myself a new wig.

"We will lay down ten zecchini at once," he went on, "so that you can make any necessary purchases. Funding for extra expenses will possibly be available in future, but only with a detailed and written justification of each item."

"Coffee in the Piazza to keep me alert?"

The answer came immediately, without any hesitation, or any hint of a smile. "We would need documentation proving that you had selected your coffee house on sound criteria, whether financial or logistical or a combination of both."

"And you will file away this documentation?"

"Of course," he said. "Now I require you to sign certain documents and then you will be free to go. We will meet again tomorrow morning, when I shall have assembled all the relevant files on nobleman Piero Garzoni."

"Do I come back to the palace?"

"No. Henceforth we will meet at the Missier Grande's private offices, in the Piazza. Far more discreet. I'll give you all necessary directions and passwords required."

The next twenty minutes were spent signing and counter-signing lengthy documents, none of which I had a chance to read through properly. I might well have been signing my soul away, along with all my property (my books and two sets of clothes). I was then bustled down the familiar narrow corridors and staircases; it was difficult to believe that this was the same building that hosted the splendid chamber of the Great Council, with its massive celebratory canvases by Tintoretto and Veronese. Occasionally I caught a glimpse through half-open doors of people working at desks in rooms adorned with gleaming oil paintings and dark wooden panelling. We emerged into the sunlight of the great courtyard, where senators and noblemen stood conversing with eager petitioners and lawyers. Sior Massaro took his leave of me, with a brisk formal bow, and I headed out into the Piazzetta, wondering whether anyone was asking what I was doing there, at the heart of Venetian government, and deciding that if anyone had noticed me, they probably presumed I had been delivering cakes from one of the Piazza's coffee houses.

I went home, comforted by the feel of the shiny new ducats but otherwise more than a little perplexed, and wishing there was someone I could talk to about my new position.

The first thing I had to do was let Bepi know that for a while at least he would have to find alternative employment. Without offending him, and without telling him the truth. Perhaps an edited version might work.

I found him at the gondola station by the church of San Moisè, which is where he goes between regular jobs. He was playing dice with two other gondoliers and he looked up as I approached. "So?" he said.

I shook my head. "I've been warned to stay clear."

He shrugged. "Well, there'll be others. Fusina again this evening?"

I shook my head again. "No. I'm sorry, Bepi. It's not just the Boscombes; I've been told to stay clear of all travellers for the moment."

Just for a second I saw Bepi looking startled, a new phenomenon. His two mates looked almost equally surprised: presumably they too thought of him as wholly unrufflable.

Then he caught control of himself. "For how long?" he said, his voice flat.

"Until they tell me."

"Well, that's a nuisance," he said. *Una seccatura* was his expression; I'd heard him use it in the past to describe new mooring charges, freak storms and an over-long sermon by his parish priest. Now the loss of his livelihood.

"You're telling me," I said. "I'm sorry, Bepi. You can look around for other work, of course. It's me, not you."

"All right."

"It'll make your mother happy," I said, unable to resist.

He shrugged. "If I tell her."

"I hope it won't be for too long," I said.

"So do I."

"Thanks." I was oddly touched. "We make a good team."

"It works," he said. "Well, let me know when things change. You know how to find me."

"Of course," I said.

And that was done. Bepi returned to his dice and his fellow-gondoliers and I to my secret life.

The next people I had to lie to were Fabrizio and Lucia at the bookshop. This would be a little trickier, I guessed. And I was right.

As I entered the shop Lucia was dusting the books in the corner bookcase, while her father sat at the desk with a volume of Ariosto. Lucia gave me a brisk "Bondì, sior" with only a fraction of her usual smile, while her father was his usual amiable self.

"Good afternoon," I said. "I thought you might like to know what happened this morning."

"Ah yes," said Fabrizio.

"How kind of you," said Lucia, with chilling courtesy.

"We managed to establish that the *casino* where Shackleford was killed did have another way out," I said.

"Well, that's excellent news," said Fabrizio.

"I trust you have informed the authorities," said Lucia.

"Well, yes," I said, "of course."

"And I'm sure they were most grateful for the information," she went on. "Did they compliment you on your continuing interest in the case?"

I put on a look of apologetic regret. "Well, as you can imagine, they weren't too pleased that I had ignored their instructions."

"Really?"

"And they've told me I'm to stay away from foreigners for the moment."

She said, in the same tone of cold sarcasm: "Well, what a surprise." All of a sudden the pose collapsed and her next words were uttered in a tone of complete dismay. "Oh, Sior Alvise, how awful." She took a step towards me, her dark eyes full of solicitude.

I suppose I should have felt pleased at the success of my performance. "Don't worry," I said awkwardly. "It's just temporary."

"That stupid woman," she said.

"My dear," said Fabrizio, in mild reproof.

"Oh, I'm sure she meant well," she said, "but it was so unnecessary."

"Well, we did find out about the other exit from the *casino*," I said, "which will help her cousin." I thought there was little point in letting them know that the Missier Grande had already known all about it.

"Yes, of course," she said. "But I'm sure you needn't have been involved. Tell us, how did you find out about it?"

I gave them a brief account of our visit to the *casino*, remaining vague on the décor of the place and the activities that presumably went on there.

"How squalid," said Lucia. "So people would pay to spy on other people while they . . ." Her voice trailed off, presumably to the relief of her father.

"Yes," I said. "I expect some people don't mind being spied on."

"We are a city of performers," Lucia said.

"How very true," I said, wondering for a moment whether she had guessed something.

Her father, understandably enough, decided to change the subject. "And so, Alvise, what do you propose to do now?"

"Well," I said, "I've decided to treat this enforced rest period as an opportunity to further my studies."

"Bravo," he said. "That's what I like to hear."

"In particular, it strikes me that it could be helpful for me to find out a little more about the areas of occult and arcane mystery that seem to interest so many of our visitors."

"Ah," he said, the single syllable clearly indicating his disappointment.

"Sior Alvise," said Lucia, "you're not serious."

I persisted, addressing her father. "You were telling me about nobleman Piero Garzoni and his interests. You said he had bought some books from you on such matters."

"But why should you wish to follow his example?" said Fabrizio, clearly bewildered.

"Oh, it's not his example that interests me. It's just that my clients are often curious about such matters and it would clearly help me to be well informed, while remaining clear-headed and detached."

"Sior Alvise," said Lucia, "you're blathering and you know it."

"Lucia, my dear, there's no need –"

"No," I said, "it's good that she should speak her mind. I'm not offended." I turned to her. "Siora Lucia, it may not be to our taste but perhaps we should try to understand the fascination of these matters." I was suddenly struck by another possible line of approach. "For example, should I encounter another traveller like Mr Boscombe, so easily susceptible to any *frappatore* with a vague knowledge of such things, it will be easier for me to protect him if I'm able to counter his arguments."

"Perhaps," she said, but she did not sound convinced. "Are you sure that's the real reason?"

"I'm not going to become an occultist," I said.

"Siora Boscombe has nothing to do with this?" she said, looking straight at me.

It was good to have something I could honestly deny. "No," I said, looking straight back at her, "I swear it. And besides, I've been told I am not to see the lady again."

"No need to swear anything," she said.

I realised that my underlying sense of guilt had made me overplay my part. I still had a good deal to learn as a performer. I turned back to Fabrizio. "So, Sior Fabrizio, as a start, it might be a help to know what books Piero Garzoni was interested in."

"Why particularly him?" he said.

"Well, I have to start somewhere and it seems that Mr Boscombe was drawn towards him because of what he'd heard about him," I said, hoping it sounded convincing.

"Very well," he said, a note of resignation in his voice. "Let me see if I made a note of the titles." He turned to a ledger on his desk. "Of course, I'm not denying that many of these texts are of great interest; it is just that they are also liable to abuse by all sorts of charlatans and *frappatori*. I myself can see the fascination of the alchemical works and given time would certainly like to learn more about the Philosopher's Stone. Ah, here we are." He ran his finger over a page covered in his neat handwriting. "The *Corpus Hermeticum* of Hermes Trismegistus in Marsilio Ficino's Latin translation, *Alchymista Christianus* by Pierre-Jean Fabre, *Le sommaire philosophique* by Nicolas Flamel – and then a good counter to that, the *Archidoxa* by Paracelsus . . ." He turned the page and continued to read, but my head was spinning by this time and I only picked up the thread again when he mentioned the Rosy Cross: "*The Chymical Wedding of Christian Rosenkreuz* by Johann Andreae, the *Fama fraternitatis Roseae Crucis* . . . extraordinary title, begins in Latin and continues in German . . . *oder Die Bruderschaft des Ordens der Rosenkreuzer*. Do you read German?"

"No," I said.

"Ah, pity. That might be helpful. Still, so long as you can cope with the Latin . . ."

"Just about," I said, a little doubtfully. "Can I buy these books from you?"

"How will you afford them?" he said. "Especially if you have no work at the moment. One or two I can lend you, others you will undoubtedly find at the Marciana library."

I decided it was not politic to flaunt my newly acquired zucchini, since I could not think of any convincing explanation for them, and so expressed great gratitude for the loan. I left the shop laden with leather-covered Latinate learning; I had decided to start with the Rosy Cross.

Lucia accompanied me to the door, still clearly perplexed by my choice of reading matter. "Sior Alvise," she said, as I left, "do remember your promise to remain clear-headed and detached."

"I'll do my best," I said. "If you hear of an explosion in the parish of San Giovanni in Bragora you'll know my search for the Philosopher's Stone has gone wrong."

It was not much of a joke but she awarded it a courteous smile and I took my leave.

Giovanna was standing at the door of the tavern chatting to a customer as I arrived with my burden. "More books," she said, shaking her head sorrowfully. She clearly hated to see a young man go astray in this fashion.

"Siora Giovanna," I said, "I'll do my best to turn the pages quietly."

She looked puzzled for a moment and then gave a roar of laughter, causing the customer to jump and spill his wine. "Sior Alvise, you're so *spiritoso*."

"And you're my best audience," I said. Which was true. "Can I take up a jug of your best *malvasia?*" I knew I was going to need some form of sustenance. "Oh, and I can settle my account."

"It looks as though your meeting with the *sbirri* brought you luck," she said as she handed me the jug of wine.

"Just some clients who finally paid," I said. Giovanna's remark was probably quite innocent but I hoped she would not repeat it to anyone else. I was beginning to realise how full of pitfalls a double life could be.

17

I spent much of the night struggling with the Rosy Cross, in Latin and Italian. I had not realised until now that there was – or, at least, there was supposed to have been – a man of that name: Christian Rosenkreuz. After several hours poring over the various books until their different typefaces began to swim before my eyes in the flickering candlelight, I was not very much closer to understanding what the members of the Brotherhood of the Rosy Cross were in search of. I passed on to Hermes Trismegistus and found myself equally baffled, as I tried to understand whether he was a god or a philosopher, Greek or Egyptian, pagan or Christian.

As the buzz of voices below my apartment gave way to the familiar clattering of pots and pans, I decided that for my purposes it was probably better to take a definite position on certain questions and then force everything to accommodate itself to that position – probably a standard enough academic approach. Hermes Trismegistus was therefore Egyptian, I decided, to be identified with the god Thoth. The more exotic and distant, the better. Similarly, Brother Christian Rosenkreuz had travelled, in the fourteenth century, to Damascus and lived in Egypt, which was where he had discovered the foundations for his "order", possibly in the writings of Hermes himself. This way I only needed to concentrate on those texts that supported my interpretation, which simplified my task. Maybe I could even work out a connection with Marin Falier. It was the same century, after all.

Eventually I snuffed out the candle and got a few hours' sleep; crosses and circles and moons and suns and pyramids and all-seeing eyes floated through my dreams on a steadily sloshing sea of cheap *malvasia*. I was achieving *spagyria*, Paracelsus might have said . . .

The next morning I got up when the Marangona sounded, the bell with my name that announced dawn and told the *marangoni* of the

Arsenale that it was time to start work. It was a long time since I had turned up early at the well head in the nearby square and so I found a different set of women there to make more or less good-natured fun of me as I stood there with my single bucket. None of them asked me about the *sbirri*, but I could tell from one or two sidelong glances that I would provide a fruitful topic of conversation the moment I left them.

After I had washed and refreshed myself I set off towards Saint Mark's Square. Preparations there were already under way for the great feast of the Ascension in three days' time. Along the sides of the square great stacks of planks and piles of painted wooden columns were waiting to be assembled into the elaborate colonnade of booths that would take over the square for the duration of the holiday. For a couple of weeks the coffee shops would lose their view of the square, looking instead on to the backs of these booths; nevertheless they would probably not do too badly, given the numbers of visitors who would be flocking into the city, some of them from small towns that had no coffee shops at all.

At this hour in the morning the shops had that curious early morning mixture of raddled-looking clients who had not yet been to bed and grumpy-looking ones who had just got up. I probably looked somewhere in the middle. I treated myself to a cup of coffee at Florian's, sitting at one of the tables and watching the people on their way to their offices, workshops, schools . . .

It felt like my city. After all, I was being paid to protect it, wasn't I?

Although I did not as yet know what from.

After draining my coffee I set off towards the sunlit western end of the square. Close to the church of San Geminiano, in the north-western corner, was the Missier Grande's headquarters; I learned later that he had an apartment above the offices.

There was no name or number on the door, as Sior Massaro had warned me. One simply had to know where the offices were; if one did not, one was the wrong sort of person, who would have no business with the Missier Grande. Now I knew; now I was the right sort of person. As I climbed the dark stone staircase I had a momentary hankering for the days when I had not known – which is to say all the days in my life before today.

On the first-floor landing was a monumental arched doorway, with a door slightly ajar. I pushed it. A young man in dark clothes sat at a desk by the door and said: "Yes?"

"*Ruppemi l'alto sonno ne la testa / un greve truono,*" I said. This line from Canto IV of the *Inferno* was today's password, Sior Massaro had informed me.

He nodded and indicated I should go straight through the door behind him, which led into a large room with windows looking on to the square. Immediately facing me was a long desk; apart from the windows it was very much like the office in the Doge's palace. Once again the walls were lined with dark bookcases and cupboards.

Facing me sat Sior Massaro. Maybe this was where he spent the night.

"I'm not too early then," I said.

"Of course not," he said. What a suggestion. "Here are all the relevant files." He indicated a pile of ledgers and manuscripts on the desk.

It was almost as intimidating as the pile of books on Rosicrucianism.

"This is all on nobleman Garzoni?" I said.

"Well, it's not all we have, but it's all the relevant information," he said.

"Can I take them all down to the coffee shop and browse through them there?"

"I trust that is a joke," he said.

"Yes. I'm sorry."

"Very amusing." He picked up his quill and scribbled something on a sheet.

"Oh dear," I said. "Has my joke been filed for future reference?"

"You know it's my duty to keep records. Now, I need you to sign a few documents before you start consulting these."

"Of course you do," I said. "And I'll sign my joke as well, if you like."

"That won't be necessary." He pushed the documents towards me and I started signing, vowing to myself to reduce my joke-telling to the bare minimum.

"Can I take notes?" I asked.

"Yes. You'll see that the second document you just signed specifically confers that privilege."

A few minutes later I pulled the pile of manuscripts and ledgers towards me and started to leaf through it. "My God," I said after another few minutes, "there are records of every single thing this man has ever done."

"I like to think we've done a fairly thorough job in his case. We could have kept closer observation during his years abroad, perhaps."

"When he was in England."

"That's correct. I see you already know something of his life."

"That's about all I know," I said. "So I have a good deal to learn."

"You can take the documentation into that office where you won't be disturbed," he said, pointing to a door to his left. It was a small room with devotional paintings from the previous century on the walls, mostly of saints in dark craggy landscapes; nothing that was likely to distract me from my reading.

And for the rest of that morning I sat at the desk in this room and took notes. It was not just a series of official documents, like the registration of his baptism, his wedding, his appointments in the various posts he had held (and Fabrizio was right – he really had been Provveditore alli Biscotti at the Arsenale); there were pages and pages devoted to observations of his private life. For example, with regard to the wedding, in addition to a copy of the certificate, there were reports on the number of guests, the amount that had been spent on the feast, the clothes worn by both bride and groom, the speeches that had been made . . .

"Who provides all this information?" I said, almost appalled, when Sior Massaro looked in about half an hour later.

"Well, who do you think?" said Sior Massaro.

"An army of snoopers," I said.

"That's right," he said. "People like yourself. What would we do without you?"

I winced. Quite possibly he had not meant it maliciously.

I began to build up a picture of Garzoni's life. The family had always been important in the life of the republic, and in the previous century they had acquired considerable wealth through their holdings in the Levant. The Turkish advance had not been as damaging to them as it had been to other families, since they had always managed to find a channel for their trade, sometimes even in the midst of war between Venice and the Ottoman Empire, with the aid of useful connections in

Constantinople. Even now, despite the fact that Piero Garzoni had eschewed all direct intervention in commerce, he still held a considerable fortune, thanks to the possession of property in Venice, on the mainland and on Corfu. His long involvement in the Arsenale had been financially rewarding as well, since the family owned areas of forestry in the Friuli which supplied timber for the fleet; questions had been raised in the Senate about a possible conflict of interests but no individual act of malpractice had ever been proved against him.

He had spent some time in England early in the century, probably at the same time as Zanotto's brother, although detailed documentation was missing. As Boscombe's uncle had thought, he had gone there to observe new ship-building techniques, but there was no record of his having introduced any major innovations on his return to the Arsenale.

He had married into another wealthy family, his bride being Elena Foscari. However, she had died in childbirth a year after the marriage; the baby had not survived. Piero Garzoni had shown no inclination to embark on a second marriage, despite the fact that the family now risked extinction. There was just one nephew, the son of his deceased sister, who had married beneath her years before and had been cut off from the family as a result. Garzoni had probably never spoken to his nephew, who owned – oh, the shame of it – a cheese shop in western Dorsoduro.

I found documentation on the scandal that had led to the nobleman's final resignation from his post as Sopraprovveditore; Fabrizio's account had been more or less accurate. After the regulation that permitted flogging for arsenalotti had been brought in at his personal insistence, a worker in the caulking section had been flogged for insubordination and had subsequently developed gangrene and died. Pressure from above eventually led to Garzoni's resignation, but it had clearly required a good deal of pressure, and that exerted from especially lofty locations.

Since then he had become something of a recluse, devoting himself to his historical and occult studies (the reports were rather vague on this, so I could only be grateful to Fabrizio), and rarely leaving his palace on the Grand Canal. After his wife's death he had reduced his household to a minimum, and now shared the palace with three ex-Arsenale workers and the mysterious Count Gelashvili.

All I had to do now was go there and find out what he was up to, then come back and let the Missier Grande know. After that it would be back to my guide work as usual, I presumed. Or rather, I hoped.

Around midday I pushed the documents away and stretched, noticing as I did so that I was imitating the pose of St Jerome on the wall opposite me, as he raised a large stone high in the air. Perhaps a little breast-beating on my part would not come amiss. I certainly did not feel proud of the way I had spent my morning.

I returned to the main office, where Sior Massaro was still at his desk, poring over new reports. I had heard several people call on him during the morning, presumably bringing the results of their observational activities. I had not seen anyone, nor had I heard the words of most of the conversations, but I had been able to get some impression of the tones and timbres of the callers. I had been struck by the variety of voices: all ages, both sexes, apparently most classes, usually but not always with a Venetian cadence. Many recognised the appropriateness of speaking in low, stealthy tones, but for one or two the conversation with Sior Massaro was clearly just part of their daily routine, and they chatted away in casual, breezy tones. I even caught enough of what they were saying to gather that they began by chatting about the weather or their health before passing on to delivering their confidential reports.

All colleagues of mine.

"Have you read enough?" he said.

"For my purposes," I said.

"Good. Have you decided how you are going to approach this case?"

"Yes."

"Good. You needn't tell me. In fact it might be better if you didn't, because as the Missier Grande indicated we do not officially know anything about this operation."

However, despite this disavowal, I was pleased to see that he was human enough to be curious. I said, "I'm going to use what I'm good at."

"Very sound idea." He waited.

And I realised that I wanted to tell him. After all, there was no one else I could talk to about it.

"I'm just following the suggestions of the Missier Grande himself. He mentioned my theatrical background. So I'm going to put on a show."

"A show," he said, sounding a little doubtful.

"I get the impression that nobleman Garzoni likes spectacle. That's the best explanation for his having taken in Count Gelashvili."

"I see."

"I simply have to put on a better show than the count. And that's where my main skill might be useful."

"And what's that?"

"I'm a good improviser." My highly varied upbringing had forced this skill upon me. I was expert in nothing, almost certainly because I lacked the gift of persistence (this was clearly Lucia's opinion), but there were a number of things I was quite good at, and, perhaps more important, I was good at assessing when and how to put these things to use.

In fact, I had everything one needed to become a first-rate *frappatore*. Just like Count Gelashvili.

18

I made my way to western Dorsoduro. Perhaps the nephew could throw some light on his uncle's personality, even if only through family hearsay. For my purposes any extra titbits of information might be useful.

I found the cheese shop near the church of San Nicolò dei Mendicoli; this area of the city has its own definite character, which can be summed up in one word: fishiness. Everything in the area is permeated with the tang of fresh and not-so-fresh fish. The alleys that slope down to the lagoon are lined with glistening tangles of fish-nets; everywhere you look are barrels and chests either crammed with squirming heaps or coated with the silverily gleaming evidence of their passing. The streets themselves are slippery with sloughed scales and oily innards.

The inhabitants, whether bearded fishermen, busy traders or sharp-tongued fishwives, mostly appear to wear clothes of a squamous consistency, and the children, who weave in and out of the crowds like darting minnows, all seem to be playing elaborate games with oyster shells and crab claws. The accent is different, with a rising intonation and truncated syllables, almost as if one were hearing the voices through water. The separate nature of this area of the city even has official recognition, with the local population being allowed to elect their own "doge", usually a leading fisherman, who is received by the Doge himself in the ducal palace after his election. I imagine that fastidious Doge Pietro Grimani washes his hands thoroughly after greeting his piscatorial counterpart.

The cheese shop was in a quiet street close to the church, and the owner had decided to do his best to combat the overwhelmingly marine atmosphere by hanging a number of pungent goat-cheeses around the doorway. It almost worked. I entered the shop and breathed in the rich crumbly odours with pleasure.

"Sior, can I help you?" came a voice from behind the counter. Leonardo Mantovan, as I knew him to be called, was a small man in his mid-thirties; he wore no wig but pulled his thinning hair back in a neat pigtail. He had a vaguely harassed look; maybe that came from trying to sell cheese to fishermen. In any case, there was nothing to indicate that he was the nephew of a nobleman who lived in a palace on the Grand Canal.

"Sior Mantovan?" I said.

"That's my name," he said. "And whom do I have the pleasure . . ." He did not finish the question; he allowed it to fade away into inaudibility, like a crumbly ricotta in your fingers. I noticed that he did not have a Nicolotto accent. But then I remembered that he had grown up in Cannaregio, after his mother had left the family home.

"My name's Alvise Marangon," I said. "I hope you won't mind my troubling you with some questions about your uncle."

"Which uncle?" he said, giving me a sharp look.

"Your maternal uncle," I said.

"Ah. Well, I've never spoken a word to him in my life. And why are you interested?"

"I'll be quite honest," I said, meaning it – more or less – but knowing the instant I'd said it that it was the surest way to be disbelieved. "I'm enquiring on behalf of the Missier Grande."

'You're a *sbirro*?" he said, looking at me with narrowed eyes. As he lived and worked in this area, a certain wariness was understandable. Most of the city's *sbirri* are from this parish – it's probably the only career open to anyone not fond of fish.

"Not exactly," I said, "just someone appointed to make discreet enquiries."

"And so you come and talk to a shopkeeper about him."

"Of course, I can't guarantee your discretion but I thought it worth trying. You might be able to tell me something that you heard from your mother."

"Well, I certainly never heard anything good about him from her."

"I imagine not."

"Enquiries about what, anyway?"

"Leo!" came a shrill voice from a room beyond the shop. "What's going on?"

"Just a customer asking some questions, my dear." His voice became as harassed as his face when a large woman appeared in the doorway, her hands holding a wet cloth, which she was clearly in the process of wringing. She fixed me with a glare that intimated that my neck was next in line.

"Are you here to buy cheese?" she said.

"Well, I'll take a little of that pecorino," I said, pointing at the counter, and her husband quickly picked it out and placed a knife over it in interrogative fashion, so that I should indicate the required amount.

"You weren't talking about cheese," she said accusingly. Her accent was definitely Nicolotto. I hoped that mine was not too obviously Castellano; I could imagine her in the front line during the regular fights between the two factions on the Bridge of Fists.

"No," I said. "I was asking your husband some questions about his uncle. On behalf of the Missier Grande."

I had not really hoped that the name would send her fleeing back in terror to the kitchen. "A *sbirro*," she said contemptuously, and gave a sudden savage twist to the cloth, which dribbled a few last drops.

"We're investigating a question of inheritance," I said. "It seems that on the island of Corfu some local families have contested the passing of some parcels of land to the Garzoni family, since certain local bye-laws were ignored; the contestation dates back to the early years of the century and we are hoping that family members who retain any records from those years might be able to throw some light on the matter."

"My mother didn't have any papers," said Mantovan. "She was cut off with nothing beyond the clothes she was wearing."

His wife snorted. "She didn't have to accept that treatment. But you know she liked to play the martyr."

"My dear, some respect, please. My dear mother –"

"Yes, yes, she's dead, God rest her soul, but you know what I think."

He clearly did and made only a token attempt to defend his parent. "She married for love, and she knew what to expect. It was a courageous decision –"

"Which she spent the rest of her life complaining about."

"She didn't complain, my dear."

"No, she just sat there and sighed. And we were all expected to commiserate."

I imagine that the older Siora Mantovan must have been disappointed in her expectations, at least with regard to her daughter-in-law.

"So there are no family papers," I said tentatively.

"Nothing," said Mantovan.

"I wonder if you can tell me anything about your uncle."

"What's this got to do with the inheritance?" said Siora Mantovan.

"Nothing directly," I said, "but it all helps us to build up a picture. We need to know about his involvement with his overseas estates. And perhaps your mother will have reminisced about her early days."

"Never stopped," said Siora Mantovan.

"Now that's not quite true, my dear."

"Never let an opportunity to let us know what a great sacrifice she had made go by. No wonder your father lost the will to live. 'Oh, in the palace we always used *silver* forks for fish . . .'" She said these last words in a crude caricature of an aristocratic accent, and fluttered the tortured cloth as if it were a brocaded fan.

"Did she talk about her brother?" I asked.

"All the time," said Siora Mantovan, just as her husband said, "Occasionally."

"And what did she say about him?"

"Well, she was understandably rather resentful," began Siora Mantovan.

His wife cut in: "Of course she complained about his cruelty but the fact was she obviously admired him."

"Admired him?" I said in surprise.

"My dear, you know that's not true."

She went on regardless: "She was always telling stories about how cruel and unpitying he was, how obsessed with the family honour. But so was she."

"My dear, that's an absurd thing to say. How can you imply she was cruel?"

"No, obsessed with the family honour. And you know that's true."

"Well, naturally she took some pride in —"

"She never stopped talking about the Garzonis, and what they'd done for Venice, and their role in the battle of Lepanto. She made one big mistake in her life and spent the rest of it looking back at what could have been and comparing her feeble husband with her strong brother –"

"My dear, you're talking about my father here."

"Oh, you know I never had anything against your father. Felt sorry for him. But it was clear your mother wished he had some of the Garzoni rigidity." She looked at her own husband, and the expression on her face clearly suggested that she understood the feeling. I would not have been too surprised at this point if she had made explicit an underlying sexual reference. I guessed that these arguments were nothing new between them; the wife probably welcomed any chance to return to the subject, even if offered by an inquisitive *sbirro* who was probably not going to buy more than a few grams of pecorino. I wondered whether she had married Mantovan thinking that the connection might provide her way out of this fishy quarter of the city; if so, she was making her disappointment plain.

"What sort of stories did she tell about her brother?" I said, trying to lead the conversation back to the territory of usefulness rather than mere gossip.

"Oh, there's one story she was always telling," said Siora Mantovan. "About when she was fifteen years old and wanted to go to church one Sunday wearing a new dress she had been given by a family friend. Her parents insisted that it was not suitable – too many frills, or something – and they had a great row. Her brother didn't say a word but he put an end to the row by simply tearing the dress off her and throwing it on to the fire."

"Ah," I said. It was a feeble reaction but I was trying to take in the picture this created. Tearing a dress from a girl's body suggested something far more disturbing than merely a wish to protect the family's honour.

Mantovan spoke up now, possibly eager to ingratiate himself with his wife by agreeing with her. "Yes, she often told that story. She said she could never forgive him for it. He did it in front of the servants, as well. And her parents didn't say a thing; they were probably shocked but they never said a word of reproach to her brother."

"But there was always something strange about the way she kept telling it," said his wife. "I had to ask her to stop doing it in front of the children." Then she looked sharply at me. "Does this help your investigations? Properties on Corfu, wasn't it?"

"Well, not directly, of course," I said, "but it helps us to understand nobleman Garzoni."

"And his sister," she said. "Well, are you going to buy that cheese?"

"Oh yes, of course," I said, and I turned to Sior Mantovan and indicated the portion required, making it larger than I really needed.

Another customer entered the shop at that point and I guessed there was little point in trying to obtain any further information. I paid for the cheese and thanked them. Siora Mantovan gave a final wrench to the cloth by way of farewell and disappeared into the inner room. Sior Mantovan offered me a weak smile and turned to the other customer. "The usual?" he said. I sensed relief in a return to routine.

19

In the early evening of the next day I approached Palazzo Garzoni.

Put like that it sounds simple; in fact it was quite otherwise. My approach to the palace had taken most of the day to prepare. I knew that gaining entrance was going to be difficult: not necessarily the most difficult thing I was to do over the next few days (this premonition proved most grimly true), but certainly something that would require forethought and planning.

And so I thought and planned thoroughly. From all I had heard, nobleman Garzoni did not throw open his doors to all and sundry. I would have to make it clear that I was definitely not sundry.

First, I decided there was little point in trying to outshine Count Gelashvili sartorially. In fact, I was going to do the exact opposite: I was going to out-dark him. I spent a significant portion of my earnings on a completely new set of clothes, in which everything, from shoe-buckles to tricorn hat, was black: as richly and deeply Plutonic a black as money could buy. I even managed, in an obscure shop in Cannaregio, to discover a wig of jet-black yak-hair curls; the shop-owner assured me (quite mendaciously and also unnecessarily) that they were going to be all the rage. I carried an ebony cane and over my shoulder I slung a dark leather satchel containing a couple of books, my sketching materials and a few other assorted items. I had even toyed with the idea of painting my teeth black but decided that might be overdoing things.

Then I needed something to set off this Stygian guise. What better than light? And so at the landing stage of San Tomà, immediately opposite Palazzo Garzoni, I hired a gondola with two gondoliers and four torch-men. The gondoliers were men I had never seen before, as far as I knew, and I hoped they did not know Bepi — and that Bepi would never get to hear of this exploit. (Well, this hope applied to all my acquaintances in the city — almost certainly a forlorn one, given the infinite reticulations of the city's network of gossip.) The torch-men were taken from a nearby tavern at the extortionate price of one scudo each for their services. All in all this was proving a highly expensive production. It had better work.

I asked for a gondola without a cabin; this was easily obtained, as the station at San Tomà also serves as a landing-stage for the cross-canal ferry; the gondolas used as ferries have no seats or trimmings and a wider girth.

I had been wondering whether I should try to invent a story that would convince these six sceptical Venetians of the innocence and rationality of my proceedings but decided that it was not worth the bother; I would never manage to come up with a fiction that would withstand serious scrutiny, or even hold out against a sardonic quip. So I just fell back on using a marked English accent so that they could attribute the whole performance to the eccentricity of foreigners.

As luck would have it our final departure from the landing stage took place in a gathering storm. Clouds almost as dark as my own clothes were massing over the grand Gothic façade of Ca' Foscari to our right; far off to the left the Rialto Bridge gleamed as if it had absorbed the last fitful rays of the setting sun before black clouds had swallowed it. The water had taken on an ominous dark sheen, setting off the numerous bobbing lanterns of the boats, which were all making hastily towards their mooring stations.

I looked across at Palazzo Garzoni. There were flickering lights in the windows of the piano nobile and I thought I could detect faces in the side rooms. This was a good moment to set off.

I stepped into the gondola and stood in the very centre of it. Two of the torch-men took up position in front of me, and two behind. I told them to move as close to the side of the boat as possible so that I would be plainly, if darkly, visible in the centre. And, as already agreed, they now kindled their torches till they were blazing furiously and then raised them high in the air. The gondoliers pushed off and swung the gondola round so that we were pointing straight at Palazzo Garzoni. We moved forward.

I do not think I have ever felt quite so conspicuous. This was, of course, the point of the whole exercise, but it did not make it any the less excruciating. Up until that moment I had been firmly pushing away all thoughts of public opinion; I realised that I had to take on the mentality and personality of a born showman – someone like Count Gelashvili, for instance. Otherwise I could not hope to succeed. This meant systematically crushing any inner doubts and endeavouring to achieve a state of pure external appreciation of my own performance; I had to reach the point where I was viewing the whole spectacle from some imaginary gallery in the clouds.

I almost succeeded. A distant roll of thunder I took to be divine applause and I even found myself thrilling to it. But then somewhere inside me a little voice said: "Please God don't let Lucia see this." Why Lucia should have come to mind at that precise moment I would have been hard put to it to explain.

The thunder continued to roll. Other gondolas were bobbing and swivelling around us and somewhere a gondolier raised an ironic cheer. The flames from the two torches in front of me flared back so that I felt their warmth against my cheeks. I stared up at the Gothic façade of Palazzo Garzoni and saw movement at the windows above. We came nudging against the poles beside the palace's water entrance and the gondola swung round and came to a halt by the seaweedy steps. The large wooden door remained closed and the windows on either side showed no sign of light or life.

Then a voice called from the balcony above. "What do you want?"

The accent was eastern Castello; I guessed this was not the nobleman himself.

I shouted back: "I have a document to deliver to nobleman Garzoni. He will be interested in it." And I lifted my satchel above my head invitingly.

There was silence. The torch-men lowered their torches and one of them spat into the canal, while the gondolier behind me muttered: "It's going to piss down." I told him peremptorily to keep quiet, thinking how glad I was that he was not Bepi.

Then there was a flicker of light in the windows beside the water entrance. I heard a scrabbling of chains and keys. The door was scraped open and we found ourselves staring at a man in dark clothes holding a small lantern. He had a round face that glistened in the lantern-light. The eyes, however, were small and sharp. They flickered quickly over the gondola to fix on me. "Give it to me," he said and stretched his hand out.

I reached into my satchel and pulled out a neatly rolled scroll tied with a black ribbon (the ribbon in itself had cost me another hour of searching, but I had decided consistency mattered).

He took it from me and without saying another word closed the door again. A few seconds later the ground floor was dark again.

"Now what, sior?" said the gondolier behind me.

"We wait," I said, trying to sound perfectly calm.

We stayed there another five minutes. Lightning flickered in the sky and the first raindrops began to fall. I could sense dissatisfaction growing all around me; I quelled the first muttered imprecation with another peremptory "Silence" but I knew that my hold over them was slackening. And if the rain got any heavier . . .

And it did. It was as if the gods suddenly overturned a celestial bathtub. The torches went out with hisses and our clothes were instantly pasted to our skins. Suddenly all six men were protesting.

"One minute," I said, trying to make it sound like an order rather than a plea – and at that moment the water-gate scraped open again.

"He says come in," said the same round-faced man.

"Thank you," I said. I distributed what remained of the men's pay and then stepped onto the slimy steps by the entrance. I had a sudden image of myself slipping and tumbling head first into the canal, which would have spoiled the effect somewhat. Fortunately this did not happen and I reached the top of the stairs, where I turned and said to the six men: "You need not wait."

They made no more than a concerted muttering, fortunately covered by another crash of thunder; I imagine each of them said something along the lines of "To tell the truth, esteemed sior, that had not been our intention." I gave them a last wave and strode through the doorway. I heard the gondola push out into the rain-churned canal, carrying six men I hoped never to meet again.

I turned to the man by my side. "And so please lead me," I said awkwardly keeping up my exaggerated English accent.

He placed his lantern in a bracket, closed the door, turned a large key and fastened a rusty chain. Each movement was careful and precise.

Then he took hold of the lantern again and walked ahead of me. He did not say a word and neither did I. His round face suggested plumpness but in fact his body was trim and sleek; he walked with a kind of fussy precision, as if counting and measuring each step.

The entrance hall was the usual large cold space with posturing statues. We made our way to the monumental staircase on the left-hand side. This led to the great *salone* on the piano nobile, which was only slightly less cold and bleak than the entrance hall below; large canvases on the side walls provided the only visual attraction, apart from the view on to the Grand Canal at the far end. There was no furniture, apart from a table by the window with two simple chairs drawn up to it. On the table stood a single candle; this, apart from the torch in my companion's hand, was the only lighting. I glanced up. There were two large multi-branch chandeliers but their dingy appearance suggested they had not been used in years.

At the table sat a man wrapped in a nobleman's cloak. With symbolic appropriateness lightning flickered outside as he raised his head to stare at me. His head was against the window and the candle was to one side so I had only a vague impression of a cadaverous shape, with shadowy pits where his features should have been; a few fluttering strands of white hair glistened in the candlelight. He wore no wig. I saw that the document I had delivered was laid out on the table in front of him.

There were two other people present; it was odd that I had not noticed them first because they were far larger – or at least broader – than anything else in the room. They were both sitting at the window staring out at the rain. One had a mane of red hair and the other greasy black locks that hung straight down either side of his face like a wet towel placed there by a barber. They wore dark clothes and, apart from the hair, shared certain bovine features and a fixed dullness of expression; I guessed them to be brothers. Neither of them had done more than glance at me before going back to the more interesting sight of the rain.

"Did you create this?" said the man in the nobleman's cloak. His voice was quiet and indistinct, as if it reached me from the other side of the Grand Canal.

"I did, Excellency."

The man with the lantern went to the other side of the table, so that he was standing beside Garzoni, as if protecting him. He glanced briefly down at the document and then went back to staring at me. He was a man in his early fifties, with an expression of what I guessed was permanent peevishness on his round, glistening face; the decision to invite me upstairs had certainly not been his. There was something clerical about him; I could imagine him working alongside Signor Massaro, in fact. But I would not attempt to crack a joke with him.

I looked back at Garzoni. Now that the lantern-light was closer to him I could see the features more clearly; however, although the shadows had lessened, the pits remained. His eyes were like pinheads at the bottom of twin mine shafts, and deep declivities ran down the sides of his face in jagged but parallel lines. His mouth was drawn inwards, suggesting a sparseness of teeth, an impression confirmed by the indistinctness of his pronunciation. He was looking down at the sketch on the document and the cryptic words written around it.

I had drawn the Great Pyramid and hovering over it Thoth, pictured with the body of a man and the head of an ibis; he held a writing tablet and a pair of compasses. Both the pyramid and Thoth were ingeniously (though I say it myself) incorporated into the upper branches of the conventional Cabalistic image of the tree of life, the three uppermost circles forming the angles of the pyramid, and the two sloping sides running parallel to the two arms of Thoth's compasses.

Within the lower circles I had placed cryptic images bearing some relationship to the elements associated with each circle, but also making connections with Garzoni's own life and ambitions, as I had read them. For the circle of power, for instance, I had placed a scourge, adding bloody tips to the knotted ends of the ropes. For kingship I had placed a crown, but one that incorporated the distinctive shape of the Venetian ducal cap. And for glory I had reproduced the image of the black drape that covered Marin Falier's portrait in the Doge's palace, but with a sceptre on one side and a sword on the other.

And beneath all this farrago of pictorial insinuations and hints I had written some cryptic words in English:

The crown that crowneth all
Ariseth from a fall
He who would hold power
Waits not upon the hour
Show mercy not to those
Who spurn the cross and rose

The doggerel rhymes had come almost randomly to me but I felt confident in my abilities to wrench a suitable meaning out of them if interrogated. And I had no doubt that I was going to be interrogated.

"Who are you?" said Garzoni eventually, still looking down at the document.

"A wandering seeker of illumination," I said, maintaining the English accent. "I was born in the Scottish highlands but have travelled both east and west in search of enlightenment. My name is Umbriel." I judged it unlikely that he would have read *The Rape of the Lock*.

"And what are you doing in Venice?"

"I came here in the footsteps of the artist Giorgione, having seen his painting of the Three Philosophers in Vienna. Giorgione was clearly one of the truly Enlightened." I had decided to stick as far as possible to areas where I might have an advantage over my interlocutor, and had guessed sixteenth-century art to be one of these. "His image of The Tempest holds the key to many of our mysteries."

"And what brought you to me?" He raised his head as he said this and those tiny pin-points fixed me in place.

Was I going to get away with the next part of my prepared story? It all depended on just how self-obsessed the man was.

"I had heard from adepts of the Rosicrucian mysteries," I said, "that there was a master who cultivated them in this city, and it did not take me long to identify the palace where these ceremonies took place." I drew from my satchel a small glass cross with an image of a triangle at each extremity, bought in a junk shop that afternoon. "Yesterday, as I passed to and fro before this palace in a gondola the glass of this cross clouded over. Local enquiries informed me, Excellency, of your position and your personal history and so this evening I took the liberty of endeavouring to attract your attention."

I thought I heard the faintest hint of a snort from the man with the lantern but I did not look towards him. The two brothers continued to stare out of the window. And I continued to gaze into the dark pits of nobleman Piero Garzoni's eyes.

He said nothing for a few seconds. Then he asked: "And what do you want from me?"

"Only to share in your ceremonies. And perhaps the grace of one or two days' hospitality before I pursue my journey."

"And where are you going next?"

"My final destination is Egypt, to see for my own eyes the great constructions raised by Thoth, or Hermes Trismegistus."

"You make the identification between the two, then?"

"Most surely, Excellency," I said.

"I have no idea whether you are who you say you are," he said. "Your drawing shows you have skills, and you are clearly steeped in these mysteries."

"Thank you, Excellency," I said.

"I think you should meet my current mentor."

"The count from Georgia," I said.

"You know him?" he said.

"I have heard of him," I said.

"Ah." That seemed to satisfy him. He turned to the man with the lantern. "Fetch the count, Luca."

Luca said nothing but his expression became even more peevish. He had no enthusiasm for the task, it seemed. He set off down the *salone* to the staircase. We were left in the semi-darkness, with just the occasional flicker from the storm outside. Amid the steady rushing sound of the rain I heard Luca's footsteps climbing the staircase to the next floor.

"Luca is my loyal servant," said Garzoni, "as are Gaetano and Giorgio," waving a hand at the motionless men by the window, who made no acknowledgement of their names. "Most other people have abandoned me." His tone was quite matter-of-fact; it was as if he were commenting on the weather.

I found myself shivering. My clothes were cold and clammy but I do not think it was only that.

He went back to studying the drawing. Now he read the English rhymes to himself. I could hear him muttering the words and it was clear that he knew enough of the language to follow them. "Where did you find these words?"

"They came to me in a moment of meditation," I said.

"Can you interpret them?"

"No," I said. This was a spur of the moment decision. "They were not destined for me, but for you. I am merely the conduit."

He made no answer to this but continued to mutter the words to himself. Then he said: "Did you know I had visited England?"

"I know little of your life," I said, "other than your service on behalf of the republic."

"The republic," he said. He merely repeated the words, with no special emphasis. But I guessed a certain animosity. I remembered the book on Marin Falier. The writer of that diatribe had been no lover of republican virtues.

We now heard footsteps descending the stairs. I turned and saw Luca entering the *salone* ahead of Count Gelashvili. The lantern-light brought out the silvery splendour of the count's attire; he was wearing the same shimmering coat and wig, but had toned down the powder on his face. His frothy poodle ambled by his side.

"Excellency," he said breathily as he approached us. "You wish to introduce me to someone?" He did not even glance at me. Perhaps my black garbs had made me invisible.

"This is Umbriel from the Scottish highlands," said Garzoni.

"Umbriel," repeated the count, and now he deigned to glance at me. He did not recognise me, which was not really surprising. I was attired very differently from our last encounter, which had in any case been brief. "What a charming name. Which clan do you belong to?" He addressed me in his breathy English.

"Umbriel is not the name I was given at birth," I said calmly in English. I used just the lightest Scottish accent.

"I imagine not," he said.

"This is a chart that Signor Umbriel has presented to me," said Garzoni.

The count moved to the other side of the table and bent over the table. "This is most curious," he said, returning to Italian. "Did you design it?"

"No," I said, remembering just in time to maintain a foreign accent. "No?"

"No. I drew what was dictated to me," I said. "There is no design to it. At least no design of my devising."

Suddenly he looked hard at me. "Have I not met you before?"

"I don't think so," I said. "Where?" I was glad we were now speaking in Italian. Hearing me speak in English might have jogged his memory of the encounter on the Liston.

"And you are a student of the mysteries of the Rosy Cross?"

"Hardly that," I said, with a light laugh. "I make no such claims. As I said to his Excellency, I consider myself a conduit. I know that at times I am chosen by the powers to communicate certain messages." I gestured to the document on the table.

"The message is not of the clearest," he said.

"I fear not," I said, with a light laugh.

"Can you give us any further proof of your powers?"

"I claim no powers," I said, modestly lowering my eyes. "I know only that I have moments of insight, which I cannot explain."

"You can't explain them," he said. "You make no claims to special studies. Your message is undeniably obscure." He gave a high-pitched laugh which was echoed by a sudden yap from his poodle. "Quiet, Zosimos."

Garzoni addressed the count. "What are you insinuating?" His voice was as quiet and unemphatic as ever.

"Oh, nothing. Just wondering." He gave a fluttering gesture with one hand and allowed his voice to fade away.

Garzoni turned back to me, those pin-point eyes transfixing me. "Do you have anything to say to the count?"

I thought of waving a hand dismissively myself but pulled myself up in time. I must not attempt to imitate the count in any way. I said simply: "I can only repeat: I'm little more than a conduit. But sometimes important messages pass through me."

"Can you give us an example?" said the count. "It would be helpful, you know."

"It often depends on the place," I said. "Certain places emanate suggestive auras." I glanced around the large empty room, lit by the flickering candle and by a final flicker from the storm outside. "This is indeed one such place. I can hear the voices of those who have lived here in former times. Time is in the end an illusion, after all."

Garzoni continued to fix me. "Please go on. Let us hear these voices."

I raised both arms suddenly so that raindrops spattered outwards from my shaken cape. Zosimos whimpered. I closed my eyes and raised my face to the ceiling.

"This is a palace where there has been much joy but also much pain."

"Like so many homes . . ." the count began to say, but Garzoni hissed for silence.

I swayed to left and right. "No, there is something that must not be said, that must not be uttered . . ."

I remained quiet for a few seconds. There was just the steady thrashing of the rain.

"A young bride," I said. "Brought to this house. Why is she wandering? At night? What is that in her hand?" I moaned. "No, it's gone."

"That's enough," said Garzoni. His voice was as unemotional as ever but the tone was peremptory. I gave another moan and came slowly out of the trance.

It had worked. I looked at Garzoni and saw him gazing thoughtfully at me. There was little likelihood that he would guess that one of the family servants had reported to the agents of the Missier Grande the strange circumstances of his wedding night, when his bride had been found wandering the palace in the middle of the night clutching a knife (file 362, page 96). As I well knew, this little family scandal had never become common knowledge.

Of course there was always the risk that he might be wary of taking into his home someone who could intuit family secrets from the very walls of the building, but I guessed that his fascination with such occult powers would outweigh his prudence.

The count looked at him in some consternation, but he did not dare say anything. Luca's characteristic air of irritation had also taken on a touch of obvious puzzlement.

"And can you do the same with objects?" said Garzoni after a long few seconds of silence.

"It depends on the object and its associations," I said.

"Obviously," he said.

"Obviously," echoed the count, attempting to add sceptical emphasis to Garzoni's observation but only succeeding in sounding flustered.

Garzoni stood up. He was surprisingly small; I wondered whether he always adopted a sitting position for a first encounter. "Follow me," he said.

He picked up the lantern and we all, with the exception of Gaetano and Giorgio, walked the length of the great hall until we reached the last door on the right. It led into a bedchamber which was only a little less sparsely furnished than the hall. A single bed was placed in the centre of the wall opposite the door; it looked forbiddingly hard. I guessed this was Garzoni's own room. There was a bookcase nearby; the dark tomes that caused the shelves to sag in the middle looked as forbidding as the bed. To soothe his eyes before falling asleep at night he had a tenebrous painting of the Flaying of Saint Bartholomew high on one wall, and a table to the right was cluttered with an odd assortment of objects: strangely shaped receptacles, miniature portraits, small bronze busts and statues of contorted mythical creatures. Odd as the collection was, one sensed that there was nothing random in it. Garzoni went towards it and picked up one of the bronze statuettes. He gave it to me.

It was a robed female figure with her raised hands joined in prayer and twisted to the right, while her body curved sinuously in the other direction. I knew that I knew it. It was very familiar to me . . . but where, when . . .

I turned it over in my hands and gazed at it. I could sense the others gazing with equal intensity at me.

Then I recognised it. It was the material that had confused me. It was a miniature bronze copy of a life-size marble original: the statue of Santa Giustina that stood over the monumental entrance to the Arsenale. The Battle of Lepanto had been fought on her feast day and ever since she had become another protector of the city – and more particularly of the Arsenale, where Garzoni had spent much of his life.

But there had to be more to it than that. I was not being asked as an expert on Venetian mannerist sculpture. There must be some personal link, something that made it important to Garzoni.

Despite the clamminess of my clothes I could feel sweat breaking out on my forehead. Well, I could at least disguise my panic by putting on a little show. Indeed, some histrionics were almost obligatory.

I closed my eyes and lifted the statue above me, holding it firmly in my left hand and gently stroking it with the other. At the same time I began to emit my all-purpose musical moan. Zosimos joined in with a high-pitched whimpering, until Garzoni snapped a savage "Quiet". I realised that, fortunately, it was addressed to the dog and not to myself.

I knew that I had seen the saint's name somewhere in those hundreds and hundreds of pages; just a minor reference – possibly in a parenthesis. But where, where, where . . .

I forced myself to apply reason. I did at least have the advantage of being able to take my time; no one, after all, knew how long such spirit messages took to reach this world. So taking things calmly, where was such a name likely to occur? Well, logic told me that it would not have been in one of the files devoted to Garzoni's home life. This must come from the file on his public role. That was the big grey folder, with the wax stain on the cover . . .

Just a passing reference . . . And suddenly the name leapt out at me: it *was* within a parenthesis, on a page talking about the innovations Garzoni had introduced at the Arsenale. None of these innovations was in any way connected with industrial procedures or techniques of craftsmanship: nothing so tediously practical. No, they were mostly to do with aspects of ceremony or hierarchical protocol. Everywhere there was an emphasis on absolute, blind obedience to authority, obedience that was formalised in repeated ceremonial gestures – including (and this was where the parenthesis came in) a daily act of homage to Santa Giustina. There it was: I could see the scrawled letters of the saint's name.

So what did this mean? Maybe Garzoni had introduced a practice whereby every day the arsenalotti had to bow to the statue of the saint . . . maybe as they entered the Arsenale in the morning . . .

No: I saw the handwriting again in my mind. It was not the bureaucratically neat calligraphy of Signor Massaro or any of his officials, which I had come to recognise; it was bold and casual, presumably that of the confidential agent himself. No humble arsenalotto would have written with such careless ease; it must have been someone higher up in the service who had reported the innovation. And now I remembered further details of the pages containing the reference: it had been a report on certain practices introduced specifically for the upper ranks of those employed in the Arsenale. And these practices were supposed to remain confidential, known only to those of that specific rank. This was a constantly recurring theme in the reports on Garzoni's life; there was nothing he loved so much as secrecy – specifically the secrecy of the closed circle of adepts. He had endeavoured to introduce such practices into the daily running of the Arsenale. And one of them must have been a daily act of homage to Santa Giustina. So it would not have taken place in the public square but in some private room: therefore the homage had not been paid to the large marble statue outside but to this small bronze copy. Which explained why it had been put into my hands.

There was a shuffling of feet beside me. I did not open my eyes but I could sense a growing feeling of scepticism around me. I had to say something.

It would involve a certain amount of guesswork. I let my moan modulate into articulate speech: "I see men. Many men . . . they approach . . . again and again, time after time . . ."

I swayed and let my speech blur into a moan again. Then I said: "They bow and they take a vow – but their hearts are not in it, no . . ."

"That will do," said Garzoni. There was a note of decision in his voice. I had convinced him.

I came out of my trance again and looked around. Once again the count was looking bewildered and Luca had an expression of suspicious curiosity on his face. He was probably one of the men who had sworn that daily oath – and presumably was one of the few who, at least in Garzoni's opinion, had actually meant it. So he knew I had divined rightly. What I did not know was whether Luca believed I had received the message about the oath from the spirits.

Garzoni now addressed Luca. "Signor Umbriel will sleep here tonight. Find him a room and give him a meal."

"Thank you," I said. "You are most hospitable."

"Your Excellency," said the count, "you are always most generous. But have you considered –"

"Count Gelashvili," Garzoni cut in – and though no louder than usual his voice was like honed steel, "you know that I do not seek advice."

"But I . . . I . . ." He sounded like his own poodle.

Garzoni walked out of the room. I glanced at Luca. It was dark in the room now but I thought that his expression became slightly less peevish as he observed the count's dissatisfaction. I was beginning to get a sense of the interactions in this vast gloomy building.

Luca said to me: "Gaetano and Giorgio will find you something to eat."

We returned to the great hall and, on Luca's instructions, the burly men were finally stirred from their seats. When they stood up it turned out that they were not in fact tall, just unnaturally broad; the breadth was all muscle. The red-haired man picked up a candle and we walked the full length of the hall to a door at the far end. The kitchen was surprisingly neat and clean at first glance: there was a general fishy smell, but that is standard in Venice.

The two men still said nothing. The one with greasy hair opened a cupboard and made a grunting sound, which I took as an invitation to examine the contents. One quick look and sniff were enough to illuminate the methods of whoever was responsible for orderliness in this building: the practice was to shove all superfluous elements out of immediate sight and close the door on them. The cupboard was crammed with greasy pots, pans and plates, many containing half-eaten fish, fragments of cheese or mouldering fruit. The smell was suddenly overpowering, and it was not appealing. As the red-haired man waved his candle around I thought I detected scuttling movements at the back of the cupboard and hoped it was just the effect of the flickering light.

I reached in and took the hardest-looking cheese and a slab of bread; I did not have the courage to use any of the plates so I took the food to the table in my bare hands; the table at least was spotless.

I sat down and tore off a hunk of bread. "Are you going to eat as well?" I asked.

The two men had returned to the doorway and taken up position there; they both gave slow shakes of their heads by way of answer. The expression on their faces was impossible to determine; it could have been anything from cunning wariness to bovine stupidity. I suspected the truth lay somewhere between: bovine wariness, perhaps.

Footsteps approached and Luca entered the room. He stood next to Giorgio and Gaetano and observed me for a few seconds.

"Is no one else going to eat?" I said eventually.

Luca did not answer this. "What do you want here?" he said. There was a fussily clerical note even to his voice, as if he had some especially pedantic form to fill out.

"I told your master," I said. I tried to maintain an unprovocative tone.

"We heard all that. We've heard the same stuff from the so-called count."

"You are not adepts of the mysteries?"

"Just answer the question," he snapped.

"Do you begrudge me the support of nobleman Garzoni?" I said.

"So you admit you're here to sponge off him?"

"I admit nothing of the sort. But if it were so, would I be the only one?" I said.

"We are his Excellency's loyal servants," he said, almost spitting the words out in what seemed to be barely suppressed fury. "We had the privilege of working under him at the Arsenale and now that he has retired from public life we are honoured to continue in his service. We will not permit anyone to take base advantage of his generosity."

Everything about Luca suggested that he had held an administrative position of some importance in the Arsenale. He was clearly not one of the caulkers or carpenters. Gaetano and Giorgio, on the other hand, were the sort of people one immediately associated with the Arsenale: burly and probably uneducated with large calloused hands. Not good people to antagonise.

I decided to try the soft approach. "I've no intention of staying here long. But you must understand that someone like me is naturally drawn to a man like your master. But now that I've seen him and spoken to him I have no need to stay long. You won't begrudge me a night's sleep, here surely?"

"What was that drawing all about?"

"I've told you, I'm merely the –"

"Yes, the conduit. I heard. What do you know about the Arsenale?"

"Only what a visitor to your city can learn from books. Why do you ask?"

He did not answer immediately. My knowledge of the secret ritual had clearly unsettled him. I could not be dismissed as merely a charlatan. He too seemed to decide at this point that a softer approach would serve him better. He came and sat down at the table opposite me and some of the petulance left his voice. "Never mind why. You need to understand that we are here to serve his Excellency and naturally we wish to protect him from anyone whose only aim is to sponge off him. The nobleman is of a generous nature and he has esoteric interests that –"

"You think the count is a *frappatore?*"

The direct question took him by surprise. But after a second or two he said: "What I think is neither here nor there."

"Why don't you throw him out?" I said. Maybe I could use his dislike of the count to my advantage.

He frowned, and glanced quickly at the two men by the door. Then he stared back at me. "The opportunity has not yet arisen. But if we could prove to his Excellency that he is a fraud . . ."

I was not yet sure I could take that "we" as including me. "He doesn't seem the type the nobleman would willingly take to his heart," I said. "Those silver clothes, the dog . . ."

"Nobleman Garzoni is a man of unpredictable tastes," Luca said. "As you seem to be aware, he is impressed by anyone of imposing presence. And he has his occult interests, which the count exploits skilfully." There was a sour note in his voice as he paid this tribute to the count's talents. "But when his Excellency realises he has been played upon he is ruthless."

"Ruthless?"

"Yes. Always." He stared hard at me; despite his sleek clerical appearance there was something very unsettling about him. I found myself strangely revolted by the way his pale cheeks glistened in the candlelight. "Remember that."

I swallowed a large piece of cheese and tried to appear nonchalant. "I will do so." Then I changed the subject. "Tell me, in this whole palace are there just the four of you? Or five, including the count?"

"We are the only servants who have remained faithful to his Excellency. He does not wish for other servants. He has no other family."

"A lot of cleaning," I said.

He did not bother to answer this. "If you are going to stay here you must remain in the room that is assigned to you until his Excellency summons you. You do not go wandering about the palace."

"I understand," I said. Wandering about, of course, was my duty as confidential agent. I glanced at the two hulking figures by the door and wondered whether I would have the courage to perform it.

"Gaetano and Giorgio will take you to your room now," he said. "Take your bread and cheese with you."

I followed Gaetano and Giorgio up the stairs to the next floor. The two men, for all their hulking shapes, moved lithely; they also seemed to move in natural harmony with one another – not exactly in step but with a sort of shared smoothness of stride. I was reminded of Walnut Face and the zany. Perhaps these men too had a background of athletic stage shows. During Carnival the arsenalotti would put on performances, like the famous Feats of Hercules, in which they created human pyramids; perhaps they had been part of the team: I imagined they would have been at the bottom of the pyramid.

The second floor had a large hall only slightly less impressive than the lower one. There were gaps on the walls where paintings had hung. Someone was selling off the palace's treasures, it seemed. But I guessed there were still enough valuables to keep this small group of residents in the style to which they had clearly grown accustomed for some time yet. To the left, at the end of the hall, a door was ajar and candlelight could be seen coming from the room. A single yelped bark told me that it was the count's chamber.

The red-haired man (I still did not know which was Gaetano and which Giorgio – but then perhaps they did not have a separate existence) pointed at the room on the opposite side of the hall and gave me a candle. I nodded and they turned round and went back down the stairs.

20

The room had a single bed, a couple of stiff chairs, a chest of drawers and a wardrobe, all with heavily frivolous decorations. There was a single window; I looked outside and saw far below the black surface of the side canal of Sant'Angelo. The rain was no longer falling torrentially but with a steady persistence which made me grateful to be inside.

But it was a limited gratitude. There were plenty of other buildings whose interiors I would have preferred: I could even look back on the prison cell in the Doge's palace with nostalgia. At least the company had been less menacing.

I took off my wig with some relief: not only was it tight-fitting but I was not too sure that I was the only living thing inhabiting it. I gave my head a vigorous scratching and realised that the prickling had at least taken my mind off the dampness of my clothes, which now returned to bother me.

I tried the bed. It had a rigid mattress and a single rough blanket. Luca did not need to worry that I was going to take up residence here.

I went to the doorway and looked across the hallway to the strip of flickering light from the doorway opposite. Well, what could I lose? I picked up my candle, strolled across and tapped at the door.

"Who is it?" came the count's nervous voice, together with a single yap from Zosimos.

"Umbriel," I said softly; I did not want to bring the two brothers up again.

"What do you want?"

"Just a word or two."

There was a rustling and bustling, a hissed "Shh", presumably to the dog, and then the door opened. The count stood there, his wig hastily placed on his head, and the dog in his arms. "We have nothing to say to one another, I think," he said, this time in his very good, breathy English.

"Now don't be so hasty," I said, injecting a slight Scottish tang into my voice. "There is no need for us to be enemies."

"I, sir, am a genuine adept of the mysteries. I do not –" And then he stopped and stared at me. "I *do* know you," he said.

I cursed myself for having taken off the wig.

"You're the guide. The h-onest guide." He had even remembered his laboured joke.

"Yes," I said.

"So perhaps not quite so h-onest after all."

"Well, perhaps I'm not only a guide."

"So what are you then, sir? Pray enlighten me." He had recovered some of his swaggering confidence.

"Well, I consider myself a friend of Mr Boscombe," I said. "And I'm eager to know what happened to him."

"What are you suggesting?" he said. He was suddenly wary again; even Zosimos sensed the change and whimpered in his arms. The count dropped him to the floor and the dog ran back into the room.

"Nothing. But I thought it worth talking to you."

"I have been questioned by the *sbirri*. Fortunately, his Excellency was able to testify that I was here in the palace that evening."

"Very good to have a nobleman on your side. Especially one you are currently gulling." I had decided to go for the straightforward attack.

"How dare you," he said angrily. The effect was slightly spoiled by the fact that he was evidently uncertain whether to pull himself up to his full height in outraged hauteur or lean towards me in aggressive confrontation; the result was an absurd bobbing movement, like a strutting pigeon.

"Listen, Count whoever you say you are, there's no point in either of us keeping up this pretence. You know I'm not a visionary, I know you're not a Georgian count."

"You know nothing of the sort," he said. "I won't listen to any more of this. In fact, I will denounce you immediately to his Excellency."

"He'll only put it down to envy," I said. "And remember, if you tell him about me I can tell him about your habit of fleecing tourists at the gambling tables."

This seemed to shake him for a moment. Then he said, "his Excellency knows better of me," and pushed past me on his way to the stairs. Seconds later Zosimos nosed the door ajar and went scuttling after him.

"It'll do you no good," I called out. But I was not feeling quite as confident as I tried to sound. Well, I could at least take the opportunity to have a look at his room. I pushed the door wide and shone my candle around.

The first impression was of great, almost excessive neatness. There were no loose items of clothing or bedding anywhere but in the proper places. A trunk was neatly aligned against the wall beside a round low basket, presumably Zosimos's place of repose. On the desk by the window were a few books of astrological lore and similar topics, all in a neat row and arranged in order of size, which irritated me to a perhaps unreasonable extent. He had been writing a letter; I walked over and looked down at the opening words: *Dearest Susan, you will know with what sorrow.* It ended there. He had been writing in English. I looked at his seal and the handwriting. I was trying to remember the letter Shackleford had picked up at the Queen of Hungary inn, but it was too long ago and I had only had a glimpse of it.

There was also a sheet of writing in an alphabet I could not begin to recognise, presumably Georgian. It was not enough to convince me of his nationality. In fact, a glance at the two sheets revealed that the Latin alphabet was written with the casual ease of a native, while the passage in the foreign alphabet testified to the laborious effort of a new learner, shaping each letter with painstaking care.

I decided I had seen enough. By now I felt that the count was the person I understood best in this household and whom I therefore least needed to investigate. I cast a perfunctory eye around the rest of the room and left, pulling the door to behind me. Soon I heard his footsteps clattering importantly back up the stairs, together with the clickety pattering of Zosimos's paws. I put my head out of my room. "Well?" I said.

"His Excellency was unprepared to receive me as he is about to go out but I will inform him as soon as he returns."

"Where is he going?"

"They frequently go out at night," he said. "It might be better if you are not here when he returns."

"You mean we're alone in the palace?"

"I don't know what you're thinking of but of course we're not alone. Gaetano remains here."

"Ah. Which one is he? The one with red hair?"

"Yes. So there is no point you thinking you can roam freely around the place." There was something rather pathetic in his self-satisfaction.

"You know sneaks never come to a good end," I said, perhaps rather childishly.

"Sneaks?"

"Don't pretend you don't understand. You're no more Georgian than I am. I'd guess you're from somewhere in the Midlands. Perhaps Birmingham."

"I see no point in continuing this conversation," he said, absurdly exaggerating his foreign accent and thus confirming that I had guessed correctly. He flounced into his room, followed by Zosimos, who raised his tail in clear imitation of his master's disdain.

I moved quietly towards the staircase and listened hard. I could hear voices from the floor below. There were also sounds of movement, with a downward tendency, I thought. I walked to the far end of the hall, where large windows gave on to the Grand Canal. The central one opened with only a minor scraping noise; a few windblown raindrops spattered me, but without too much conviction. I leaned out. I could see a gondola prow emerging from the water entrance below. A minute or so later the gondola set off down the Grand Canal in the direction of Saint Mark's Square. There was no way of telling who was inside the cabin. The gondolier was presumably Giorgio, but as he was swathed in a black cape and it was dark and wet it was impossible to be sure; if it had been Gaetano there might have been a gingery gleam amid the gloom to make identification easier

"U-u-u!" This was more less the utterance that came from the top of the stairs. I swivelled and saw red-haired Gaetano standing there, pointing at me accusingly.

"Just having a look at the view," I said soothingly. "Where are they going at this time of night?"

He did not answer, just came striding towards me. I closed the window and raised my hands appeasingly. "Don't worry, I'm going to bed."

He did not actually lay hands on me. He simply marched me to my room and waited till I had closed the door. Then I heard him move away. I did not hear his footsteps on the stairs again so presumably he was still in the hall. I wondered if he and his brother were actually mute. There was no indication that they were deaf; maybe they just did not have much to say.

I waited about half an hour, during which time I pondered on the question of what I was doing in this palace, and came up with no satisfactory answers. Then I picked up my chamber pot, which I had urinated in, and opened my door the slightest crack. I could see Gaetano sitting on a chair by the staircase. He was motionless. However, his eyes flickered towards my door. I put the chamber pot outside the door with an apologetic wave and closed the door again.

I decided it was worth exploring my own room, to see what opportunities it offered – for flight, if nothing else. I noticed that there was a trapdoor in the ceiling. The wardrobe was almost directly beneath it; the problem was to reach the top of the wardrobe, and that could be done, I thought, by sliding the chest of drawers towards it. I first checked the contents of the chest of drawers; it was fortunately almost empty, with the exception of some moth-eaten undergarments which I decided not to inspect too closely. Given its relative lightness, I was able to slide it along the floor without making too much noise by doing it as slowly as I could. Once it was in position I used a chair to climb on to it and scrambled from there to the top of the wardrobe. Not surprisingly the latter was covered with a thick mat of furry dust; my arrival on these unexplored heights created a good deal of resentment among the local spider population.

I reached up to the trapdoor, which was held closed by a simple bolt. When I pulled this the door swung down and I was able, with the assistance of my candle, to peer into the shadowy recesses of the loft. I could make out a dormer window about twenty feet away, which presumably gave access to the roof.

I climbed back down, leaving the trapdoor open. There was no knowing whether it might become necessary to make a sudden clandestine departure. I also left the chair in place alongside the chest of drawers.

About an hour later I had another look into the hall. I had no chamber pot this time but I could always pick up the old one with another gesture of apology for my incontinence. However, this time Gaetano gave no sign of life. I stood completely still and after a few seconds I caught the faintest rumbling sound. Was it a snore? I did not move. It might well be, but could I be sure it came from Gaetano? It might be the count in the room opposite. Or even Zosimos. A few seconds later I felt fairly sure that the dulcet sound was emerging from Gaetano's lips.

So. Did I really want to take this opportunity? Would it not be much easier just to wait in my room and go on pondering on the futility of it all? Yes, but it would not actually make me feel any more relaxed. On balance, exploring the palace would at least make the way I had spent my day (and much of my earnings) seem slightly less pointless.

I opened the door fully. Gaetano did not stir. I picked up my candle and moved towards the staircase, shielding its light with my hand, and started down the stairs. The palace seemed absurdly large now; my candle could not hope to illuminate more than the smallest circle around me. Beyond its flickering yellow light the shadows amassed. When I reached the first floor I felt sure that the whole building had expanded while I was waiting upstairs. Everything – the ceiling, the doorways, the paintings, the distances – was higher, broader, larger, vaster and more menacing than it had been an hour or so earlier. And the shadows were definitely thicker and blacker.

I headed for Garzoni's bedchamber. In the flickering light Saint Bartholomew's torturers seemed to be setting to their messy task with extra vigour; I shuddered and moved towards the cluttered table.

I passed my candle over the various objects, so that the bronze and marble caught the light and shadows swirled and swivelled, giving the impression of sudden scuttling movement, as in the kitchen cupboards. I identified statues of Egyptian deities, bejewelled representations of astrological signs, and busts of (I think) magi and occult thinkers. Some of them were certainly of value, even if not necessarily of great artistic worth. Part of the table was given over to writing materials and books; the latter were clearly what Garzoni was currently reading. My scroll had been placed on top of the pile, I saw, and felt a totally inappropriate glow of pride.

One of the books was open and I saw that Garzoni had written marginal annotations beside certain passages. The text appeared to be written in Latin, a language I could translate from given a desk, a good dictionary, a clear head and a free afternoon. For the moment I had none of these things, so I could only hope to get a vague notion of the subject matter. It was the names that caught my attention: I saw *Sereniss. Princ. Henrico*, and then, a few lines below, *imperator Rudolphus*. The only Emperor Rudolph I could think of was the eccentric Holy Roman Emperor of the previous century. I then saw some words whose meaning jumped out at me, coupled with a repeated name: *Horologium Drebbelianum. Telescopium Drebbelianum. Instrumenta Drebbeliana Sole lucente agitata.*

It had to be a scientific treatise of some sort – but one with royal connections, whatever that meant. I looked at the frontispiece, which told me the book had been published in Amsterdam in 1688. The title itself was in what I presumed to be Dutch and covered much of the page; I only recognised the words *ELEMENTUM* and below that *PRIMUM MOBILE*, Garzoni's annotations were incomprehensible, being written in some kind of shorthand.

I took my scroll off the other books and looked at their titles. More of the sort of stuff Fabrizio had lent me: *The Clavicle of Solomon*, *Picatrix*, the *Zecor-ben*. A quick glance inside the last one showed me it had been much read; there were the same incomprehensible marginal annotations on every other page.

This was getting me nowhere. I put the book back on the pile, then remembered the scroll. It had fallen off the table and, owing to the usual vagaries of Venetian floors, had rolled beneath it. I bent down and reached for it but it had gone too far. I had to get down on to my knees and grope in the dusty gloom and when I backed out I tried to get up too quickly and hit the back of my head on the edge of the table with a resounding thwack. I only just managed to repress the word that rose to my lips, and bitterly regretted the fact that I had not put my wig back on to carry out this little piece of reconnaissance work.

Before the sound of the thwack had ceased to resonate I became aware that it had caused a disturbance among the cluttered objects on the table, some of which were performing a juddering dance. My hand shot out to pacify a vibrating jar and my sleeve caught a heavy clock, delicately poised on the very edge. A second later the clock had tumbled to the ground, and the crash when it landed made the thunder seem like a mere amateur.

21

I stood absolutely still, waiting for the last echoes to die down, and then listened hard. There was complete silence for a few seconds, with just the faintest steady swishing of rain outside. And my heartbeats.

And then footsteps. They were coming down the stairs – fast. I snuffed out the candle and looked around. If I attempted to run towards the door I would be seen as soon as Gaetano reached the foot of the staircase. So a hiding place . . . under the bed seemed an obvious one.

I moved swiftly towards it and lifted the overhanging counterpane. The stench of stale urine made me hesitate – and another second of reflection made me decide against it; if I were to be caught my chances of talking my way out of the situation would diminish in counter-proportion to the embarrassing circumstances of my capture. Instead, I moved behind the door, to the blank spot invisible to anyone entering the room.

Gaetano had come down without a light, which was good. I heard him grunting his way across the hall and then pausing before entering the room. He was presumably screwing his eyes up in an attempt to pierce the gloom; I imagined he was already regretting his failure to bring a lantern.

He moved cautiously forward and soon I could see his lumbering form. He reached the table and his foot touched the clock, whereupon he leaned down to grope about before straightening up and looking around – at least I thought I saw his shaggy head turning slowly from side to side. It was possible he even stared straight at me, but clearly he saw nothing. He mumbled something and headed out again, presumably to make his way back upstairs in search of a lantern, which would give me time to make my escape.

And then there was a scrabbling clickety sound and something small and white came dashing into the room. It paused and sniffed and then swivelled and ran straight towards me, yapping shrilly. Seconds later the broad dark shape of Gaetano lunbered back into the room and his hands shot out and grabbed my shoulders.

"All right," I said. "No need for violence."

He jerked me forward and then twisted my arms behind my back and pushed me into the hallway. Flickering light now appeared from the staircase and I saw the count coming down with a lantern. He had clearly dressed in haste and his face looked pale and anxious as he peered towards us.

"Where is Zosimos?" he asked.

"Don't worry," I said, "the dear little thing has come to no harm." And Zosimos went running towards him yapping with smug triumph.

The count bent down and patted him and then looked back me. "What have you been doing?" he said, sounding every bit as pleased as his dog.

"I was just exploring," I said. I twisted round to look at Gaetano. "Could you let go of me now? I'm not going to run away."

"Don't trust him," said the count at once. "Keep hold of him."

Gaetano gave a grunt which made it clear that that was his intention.

"So how long are we going to stay here like this?" I said after a few seconds, during which Zosimos darted at my feet and yapped daringly.

"Until his Excellency returns," said the count. "And then he will decide."

"And how long will that be?" I said. "Why don't we wait somewhere more comfortable?"

Even Gaetano seemed to recognise the sense of this and shoved me towards the table where Garzoni had been sitting when I first entered the palace. He pushed me on to a chair and then took a seat by the window as before. The count took the chair furthest from me and picked up Zosimos, making soothing noises, as if the dog had been engaged in some life-and-death struggle. I drummed my fingers on the table. Conversation languished.

It struck me that I could try to establish a rapport with the count without Gaetano's following our conversation by speaking in English. "So what do you think is going to happen now?"

"I don't know what is going to happen now," he replied in deliberate and careful Italian, to make it clear to Gaetano that he was not going to engage in any subterfuge.

That put an end to that. We sat and waited for a long time, possibly as much as an hour and a half. I toyed with various possibilities, like suddenly springing towards the window and diving into the Grand Canal, or grabbing Zosimos and hurling him into Gaetano's shaggy red tangle of hair before sprinting to the staircase. But in the first case I would not have time to look before I leaped, and there were obstacles like poles down below which could prove painful if not fatal, and in the second case the outcome would hardly be fair on poor Zosimos no matter what he had done to deserve it.

So we continued to sit there and this time it was only Zosimos who fell asleep. Lucky brute.

At last we heard noises below: the water gate being opened from without; scraping, slithering and sloshing sounds as Garzoni and Luca stepped ashore; and then Luca's voice calling for Gaetano. Gaetano called something back in indistinct Venetian – probably "I can't come down" or words to that effect – and stood up to move to my side.

There was a buzz of disgruntled voices; they clearly could have done with help in bringing in the gondola. A minute or so later their lantern-light appeared at the top of the stairs and they entered the hallway. I stood up, as did the count.

Garzoni was wearing his nobleman's cloak while Luca was swathed in some shapeless dark garment that did not add to his dignity. Giorgio was behind them, holding a lantern.

"What is the matter?" said Garzoni sharply.

Gaetano put a hand on my shoulder. "In your room," he said to Garzoni, clearly enough.

"Explain," said Garzoni.

The count spoke up. "We caught him snooping in your room. It was Zosimos who sniffed him out. He broke something as well – Umbriel did, not Zosimos," he added hastily.

"Is this true?" said Garzoni, addressing me.

"It's true," I said.

"He's clearly not to be trusted," said the count. "I can also tell you that I first met him –"

"Silence," said Garzoni.

I had guessed that reticence on my part would provoke the count into ill-judged volubility. He fell silent, but it was clear that an accusatory torrent was waiting to burst forth. He resorted to making further soothing noises to Zosimos.

"You may return to your room," Garzoni told him.

"Very well, but –" Then he thought better of it and choked back whatever he had been going to say. He put Zosimos on the floor, picked up his lantern and set off towards the staircase, Zosimos by his side.

Garzoni called out after him: "Please leave your dog with us."

The count turned round, looking puzzled. He was clearly about to ask why, but again thought better of it. Bending down he nudged Zosimos in our direction. The dog gave a puzzled whimper but did not move. Giorgio strode forwards and grasped him by his collar and jerked him round. Zosimos gave another whimper but then resigned himself to the situation. The count walked towards the staircase and gave just one last puzzled look back at his pet before disappearing. Giorgio forced the dog to sit.

"Now let us hear what you have to say," said Garzoni. He walked towards the table and sat where I had first seen him, his back to the window. I remained standing before him, like a student at an oral examination. Luca, Gaetano and Giorgio were presumably the professor's research assistants.

"I'm sorry," I said.

"Is that all?"

"As I said before, I am a conduit. I can't always claim responsibility for my actions."

"That sounds very convenient."

I spread my hands out. "I know it must sound like an excuse. But there is little I can do when I am summoned. Your chamber is charged with great spiritual energy; as I lay in my room upstairs I could feel the call. I could not block it out, I could not ignore it. Even now the objects you keep there are speaking to me, as they did before, when your small statue communicated its secrets to me."

"Do they frighten you?"

"My gift frightens me at times," I said. "But I know it is also a privilege."

"But does this palace frighten you? Is the spiritual energy intimidating?"

"It would be absurd bravado on my part to say no. I'm sure you have used your own spiritual powers to good ends, but . . ."

"To achieve good ends we usually need to instil fear. In fact, I would say that we always need to do so. Do you think a parent can bring a child up properly without making him afraid?"

"No, of course not," I said. I was beginning to get quite frightened myself – or, to be more honest, *more* frightened.

"Do you know what is wrong with this city?"

I presumed he was not talking about the sanitary regulations or the price of coffee. "There are many things . . ."

"The people are not afraid."

"Ah."

"They are not afraid of their rulers. Oh, they may fall quiet when the Inquisitors walk through the Piazza, but that isn't real fear. Moments later they laugh about them. The Doge is the subject of popular jokes. Indeed, the Doge is himself a joke." There was an exceptionally bitter tone in his voice as he mentioned the Doge. I wondered if there were some personal reasons behind this contempt.

"I am rather ignorant of politics," I said.

"That is as it should be, for most people. Most people have no reason to know anything about politics. It is better that they should not. All that is needed is that they be afraid of their leaders. In Venice no one has been afraid of their leaders since the thirteenth century – since Doge Enrico Dandolo."

"Ah yes," I said. "The taker of Constantinople."

"That was true authority," he said. "The Venetians feared such a man. The Crusaders feared him. And the effete inhabitants of the Eastern Roman Empire were terrified. He understood the need for authority – and for the symbols of authority. The four bronze horses that he brought back to this city from Constantinople were such a symbol: the ruler holds the reins of the chariot of power and rides where he wills over the subject peoples. It was fitting that those horses were first placed outside the Arsenale, where our city's aquatic chariots were created – the ships which guaranteed our sway over the peoples of the Mediterranean. It was a mistake to move them to Saint Mark's Square, where they became just another item of picturesque décor."

"I see what you mean," I said. An occasional nod of agreement was clearly all that was required; he was certainly not looking for debate.

"Only one man after Dandolo showed anything like the same capacity for leadership, the same understanding of the need for authority."

I murmured: "Doge Marin Falier."

"Exactly. He saw how the true authority of the Doge – necessary authority if the Venetian state were to be respected – had been eroded. And when he himself became the subject of mockery he understood that drastic steps must be taken to re-establish that authority. Yes, it would have been a bloodbath if his plan had come to fruition. But in that bath the Venetian state would have been purified, the Doge would have become once again a formidable figure of authority, feared and respected by his subjects and by his enemies – not like the pathetic drooling figure he is today, dressed up for parades and processions. The beheading of Marin Falier was a tragedy. It showed how the city panicked when confronted with one who held the true gift of authority."

He liked that word. I remembered that it had appeared over and over again in the booklet on Marin Falier.

"Maybe it's time for a new Marin Falier," I said.

He looked hard at me. "Your drawing contained allusions to Marin Falier. Did you know I was an admirer of the man?"

"I was inspired to draw symbols of power, that is all. And the moving spirit undeniably came from this building, as I passed it on the Grand Canal."

"These emanations are strong then?"

"Overpowering," I said. I glanced at Luca, whose expression was growing peevish again.

"It is likely," Garzoni said. "It is a sign that our plans are gaining approval in the spirit world. Perhaps it is only meet that you should share in these plans."

"Your Excellency," said Luca, quietly but firmly.

I expected the usual explosion from Garzoni at the interference. But it seemed that Luca was the one person he would listen to. He glanced at him and said: "Luca is cautious, as ever. That is often a necessary quality. However, there are times when we have to take a decision which also involves a risk. This is one of them."

"I am honoured," I murmured.

"But I will not forgo one customary precaution. I require of you a test of loyalty. It is something I always insist on. As Luca, Gaetano and Giorgio well know, it was always my practice when I commanded at the Arsenale. I required proofs of unshakeable loyalty from all those beneath me. Disloyalty is to me the unforgivable sin."

I suddenly remembered the story of his sister's dress. Presumably, wearing it had been seen as an act of disloyalty to the family. Members of the Garzoni family simply did not do such things. I had a growing sense of dread.

He went on: "Luca, Gaetano and Giorgio have recently given undeniable signs of their loyalty to me. They have proved both their commitment to creating a new moral climate in this city and their willingness to go to any lengths to further this endeavour."

I could sense Luca growing uncomfortable, and Gaetano and Giorgio were now staring fixedly at me as well. I was clearly hearing something they would rather I did not hear. My mind flew instantly to the murdered *gnaga* in Saint Mark's Square. I tried not to look at any of them but mentally compared my memory of the menacing figure on the roof holding the severed head and the figures of these three men. I realised that it could have been either Gaetano or Giorgio. Luca had probably been the planner of the show.

"That is most commendable," I said.

"Such deeds are not mere random acts of terror," went on Garzoni, without explaining any further. It was not clear whether he assumed that I knew what he was talking about. "For what we are now planning it is essential that the city should be in a suitable state of fear. Fear is our element. It is an essential prerequisite for our great venture."

I glanced again at Luca. He was attempting to look as stony-faced as possible, giving nothing away, but I could sense his growing anxiety as Garzoni talked on.

"That is why I continue to explore the world of occult mysteries," the nobleman continued. "I am aware that Luca has his doubts about this area of my research . . ."

Luca gave a slight shrug, which could have meant anything.

" . . . but it is not mere eccentricity. Such mysteries can confer power on those who know how to harness them and certainly contribute to their ability to inspire fear. The Emperor Justinian commanded what were described as demons, but were probably familiar spirits. I will not be worried if my subjects think I consort with demons, so long as they *fear* my demons – and fear me at the same time."

"Your subjects . . ."

"Yes, that is what I said. You will understand what I mean – once I have put you to the test."

"You have seen my gifts."

"I have, and I believe in them. I have ceased to believe that the count possesses any powers that can be of any use to me. He impressed me at first with what I now realise were cheap conjuring tricks. I have no further use for him. You seem a worthy replacement. Your powers are undeniable. But I need to know if I can trust you to put them to my service – exclusively to my service. That would seem to be what you were called to do. I have no doubt you *were* called here. But I need proof of your . . ." He paused. "Of your reliability. What I am going to ask of you will not be easy."

As earlier, when Luca and the count had come with us to his chamber to witness my first test, I could sense the tension throughout the room. Gaetano and Giorgio had given up all pretence of being interested in the weather outside and were staring attentively at Garzoni. Luca's pale face was pushed forward as he stared at me. I could feel sweat running down from my armpits and I imagined that my forehead must be glistening in the lantern-light.

"Giorgio," said Garzoni, "give me the dog."

I was beginning to feel a little sick.

Giorgio picked up Zosimos, who had been watching us with wary curiosity. The dog made no protest as he was placed on the table in front of Garzoni, but lay down and turned over on his back, his four paws raised, in a pathetic attempt to curry sympathy. Garzoni put his hand inside his cloak and pulled out a dagger. It had an ornamental handle inlaid with gaudy jewels, but it was clearly not just ornamental. Seconds later its purpose was made quite evident.

With one vigorous plunge and swipe Garzoni cut the throat of poor Zosimos, who did not even have time to whimper. There was a spurt of blood and a sudden convulsion of the legs, and then it was over.

My mind was racing. There was one flickering moment of relief that I had not been asked to do the deed, and then came a great surge of dread as logic got to work, suggesting what the natural sequel must be.

"Your task is clear?" said Garzoni, wiping the dagger on Zosimos's belly, and leaving glistening streaks on the white fur.

"You wish me to do the same to the creature's master." I managed to say it without an audible tremor.

"If you cannot do it you are of no use to me. Is that clear?"

"It is."

"Gaetano, call the count," said Garzoni.

22

"I will fetch him," I said in a firm voice. I snatched up a candle, turned round and strode down the hall towards the staircase.

There was a moment of uncertain dithering behind me and then Garzoni said: "Follow him." I heard Gaetano's footsteps behind me.

As soon as I turned the corner and started ascending the stairs I increased my pace to a run, protecting the candle flame with my hand. I tried to make as little as noise as possible so that Gaetano would not be alerted and increase his pace as well. Everything was now going to depend on the count's swiftness of reaction. I did not have high hopes.

I reached the count's room and threw the door open. He was sitting at his desk, writing, with the lantern at his elbow. He spun round in alarm.

I grabbed his arm and tugged him to his feet. "We have to run," I said in English.

"What – where . . ." He spoke in English as well. His hand reached out to the lantern, as if its light might clarify things.

I yanked him to the door. "There's no time to explain."

"I don't understand . . ."

"They want to kill us."

"What are you talking about?" He jerked free of my grip.

Maybe I should have brought up his pet's corpse, I thought with savage anger. At that moment Gaetano appeared in the doorway.

"He doesn't want to come," I said to Gaetano.

Gaetano grunted and leaned forward and grabbed the count by his shoulder.

"What's the matter?" said the count, now clearly alarmed.

I said in clear English: "They have killed your dog. They are going to kill you."

He gave a whimper, rather like Zosimos himself, which suggested that perhaps he had taken in the message. Gaetano pulled him out of the room, holding his arm firmly. The count held his lantern up in his free hand, clearly desperate not to lose the benefit of illumination. I snatched up some sheets of paper from the desk and followed a couple of paces behind, holding my candle high.

I went on, still enunciating with special care, "When we reach the top of the staircase I'm going to attack Gaetano with fire. You will then run with me to my bedroom."

"Are you mad? What —"

"Just do as I say. It's our only hope."

We kept walking and I lowered my candle and set light to the sheets of paper. Gaetano turned round at the unexpected flare of light and I hurled the blazing sheets into his face. It did not set him ablaze; I had not expected it to. But it made him release the count so that he could bat the flaring paper away, and as he did so I gave him a shove so that he staggered backwards, losing his balance, and fell down the stairs. I did not stop to watch his crashing descent but grabbed the count and ran towards my bedroom.

"You could have killed him," gasped the count.

I did not bother replying. I was sure that Gaetano was robust enough to survive even such a fall. Seconds later his bellow of pain from behind and below us assured us he was still alive.

I slammed the bedroom door shut behind us and turned the key. Then I pointed to the open trapdoor above us.

"But —"

I jumped on to the chair, and from there to the chest of drawers, and said, "Follow me."

A few seconds later I was up in the loft and leaning down towards the count. "Give me the lantern." Whatever else, we did not want to be clambering around the roof space in the dark.

He did as he was told. He was evidently in a state of shock.

There was a rattling at the door. He turned round to face it, as if under some spell.

"Quickly," I hissed.

"Maybe I should . . ." He seemed to be wondering whether to open up to see what they wanted.

"They will kill you," I said, slowly and deliberately. "As they killed your dog."

There was a great crash against the door, and I could see it shake.

The count gave a little squeaking noise and then clambered on to the chest of drawers and stretched his hand up to me. A few seconds later I had managed to haul him up beside me. "Hold on to me," I told him, and lay flat on the boards. Leaning down as far as I dared, while the count held me in a less than Herculean grip, I managed to get a scrabbling grasp on the edge of the wardrobe-top where it flanked the wall and give it a sudden jerk. It was lucky that the wardrobe was not full and that the Venetian floor had the usual idiosyncratic contours; with just that one convulsive jerk I managed to tip it forward. The ensuing crash coincided with another one at the door, where there was a simultaneous splintering sound.

The overturned wardrobe would hold them up for a minute or two, at least, I hoped. I pulled myself back up and turned to see the count was kneeling like a child at his first communion, holding up the lantern and gazing around at the vast extent of the loft, the shadowy shapes of beams and rafters disappearing into the black depths. He was also noticeably shaking.

I pointed to the small dormer window I had seen earlier and we clambered across the boards, moving in a fast crouching walk and sweeping away cobwebs, imagined or not, from before our faces. The window had a bolt, which was rusty but opened with a screeching jerk. It gave on to the stone guttering that ran all the way around the edge of the roof. The cool fresh air that swept in was a relief; it had stopped raining.

"And then where do we go?" said the count; his body seemed to have stopped trembling, but the tremor had passed to his voice.

"We should be able to get on to the next building," I said, trying to sound more confident than I felt.

I stepped out on to the gutter, which seemed solid enough. To my left the tiles sloped upwards, glistening with rainwater. I leaned in towards the tiles, and propped myself against them, urging him to follow. There were agitated noises from the room we had just left.

With a slight moan he came out after me, holding the lantern up against the vast night sky, and we both stood there for a few seconds, breathing hard and taking in the spectacle. The moon had managed to rive a tattered passage through the storm-clouds and it cast a spectral light over the city. We were too far from the front of the palace to see the Grand Canal but we could make out the dark shapes of the city's towers and domes; to our left was the sharply leaning tower of Santo Stefano and straight ahead the great dome of the Salute, glistening with an argentine light. At any other time it would have been a privilege to be in this position.

I gazed to my right in the direction of the front of the palace. At a certain point along the straight stretch of the roof I thought I had seen a flicker of light. Then something dark and square thrust out from the tiles. What . . .

"Quickly!" I said. "Up the roof."

What I had seen was another dormer window being opened. A dark, hulking shape emerged, either Gaetano or Giorgio, and clambered out on to the coping. The light remained inside; presumably he was not bringing his lantern out with him.

We had an advantage of seconds and we scrambled up the wet tiles.

"If we slip . . ." said the count.

"Don't," I said curtly. I could not think of any better advice. Then I added: "Leave the lantern." He needed both hands free, and the light only made us easier to spot. He let go of it and it slid down the tiles to the gutter, where it went out.

We reached a large square block of bricks, capped by two chimneys, and scuttled behind it, lowering ourselves to a squatting position, and holding on to the bricks to steady ourselves.

I could hear the man below moving along the gutter, breathing hard and furiously. He must have seen the flaring path of the lantern and so knew more or less where we must be.

"He'll have a pistol," said the count in an agitated whisper.

"Then we need a weapon ourselves," I said, looking round.

"There," said the count. On top of the brick block, next to the curved cylinder of the chimney, was a loose curved tile, one that had been left over when the roof was last retiled, presumably. He picked it up.

We heard the man halt. He had reached our rejected lantern and he was presumably scanning the rooftop. It would not take him long to realise that the only possible hiding place was where we were. Seconds later we heard him start to scramble up the tiles himself, but he did not seem to be heading straight towards us. Probably he wanted to take us from the flank.

"They killed Zosimos?" said the count suddenly.

"Yes," I said, in some surprise. It was an odd question at that moment.

"Very well then," he said, and stood up straight.

"What are you doing?"

The count did not answer, but pulled his arm back and hurled the tile, just as a sudden loud bang came from the left, accompanied by a flash of light. I thrust my head round the side of the brick pedestal and saw the man reeling back, evidently struck by the tile; both his hands were still raised and clutching the just-fired pistol. He had been standing on the ridge at the top of the roof and now the pistol fell from his grip as, with both arms flailing wildly, he went tumbling down the tiles. He let out an absurd high-pitched wail, and disappeared over the edge of the guttering. Seconds later there came a great splash as he hit the water of the side canal.

I spun round to the count, who was leaning on the chimney-pedestal and panting. "Are you hurt?"

"I think it grazed me," he said, putting his left hand on his right shoulder.

"That was – that was very brave," I said. I could have said foolhardy, but brave seemed better. It had also been totally unexpected. Clearly, one should never judge from appearances. Certainly he did not now look like a hero; he had covered his face with one hand and the panting was modulating into the customary whimpering. Well, maybe it was a tribute to Zosimos – who could be proud of him.

There was a sound of splashing from the canal, mixed with a vague watery bellowing, suggesting that our follower had survived his fall. Maybe I should have felt relieved, but actually I did not give a damn.

"We'd better get away from here," I said, "in case anyone else comes after us."

We made our way back to the relative safety of the gutter and went all the way to the end of the palace. There was a drop of about ten feet to the roof of the next building, which fortunately had an *altana* resting more or less against the side of the Palazzo Garzoni: this was a wooden platform, where the inhabitants of the building could take the sun, dry their clothes or just enjoy the view. The *altana* had a protective railing all around it so it was reasonably safe for us to hang from our gutter and drop down onto it. I went first and was thus able to assist the count in his landing.

The *altana* was naturally near a dormer window that provided access to the roof. We had little choice but to break a pane and reach inside to open it, and once on the common staircase on to which it gave were able to descend to the street without arousing the curiosity of any of the neighbours. I thought it unlikely that Garzoni would have sent anyone after us, since their priority would be to rescue their fallen comrade. Nevertheless I insisted that we ran for at least two minutes, until I felt we had put a sufficiency of calli and campi between us and the Palazzo Garzoni. We halted in Campo Santa Maria del Giglio, the count complaining of a stitch.

We leaned against a shop front just in front of the church's façade; the pompous statues and curious bas-reliefs were dimly visible in the moonlight.

"Are you hurt?" I said.

He put his hand to his shoulder. There was a vicious tear in his jacket but no blood.

"No," he said. He seemed quite surprised.

"That was quite a throw."

"I've had experience," he said, not without a touch of satisfaction.

"I think you and I have a good deal to learn about one another."

"Well, you start," he said. He had dropped all pretence at a foreign accent; English was clearly his mother tongue and it had, as I had suspected, a hint of the Midlands about it.

"Maybe we should get to somewhere safer first. I suppose there's no reason why we shouldn't go to my house. They have no idea who I am."

"Ah," said the count.

"What do you mean by that?"

"Well, when you burst in on me just now I was in the process of writing a letter to his Excellency."

"I see. Telling him who I was."

"Well, yes. After all, I had no reason to be fond of you."

"The feeling was mutual," I assured him. "What had you written?"

"That I had recognised you as a *cicerone* – the same man who had been arrested with the English tourist."

"I see. And my name and address were probably in all the gazettes."

"Oh yes, no doubt about that. I saw them myself."

I thought of something. "When we left your room I grabbed some papers to set on fire. Could they have included your letter?"

"Where did you get them?"

"The corner of the desk."

"I'm afraid not. Those were – well, they were alchemical formulae I was trying to learn. The letter was in the middle of the desk, where I was writing."

So my house was clearly out of the question as a refuge. "You know," I said, changing the subject, "I was worried that it was going to take some time to convince you that Garzoni and his henchmen wanted you dead. But you accepted the idea very quickly."

"Well, I knew that Luca didn't like me. It was just a question of whether he would be able to persuade his Excellency."

"But you knew they might kill you?"

"Well, I didn't know for sure but I'd certainly picked up some hints that they were dangerous people. They were always practising with pistols. They have a whole armoury."

"And you still wanted to stay with them?"

"Where was I supposed to go? I don't have any money."

"And what do you mean by hints?"

Up to this point he had been talking in a low tone, his eyes unfocused. Now he looked hard at me. "Just who are you? And why should I tell you anything?"

"Well, if you want to know, I'm a confidential agent of the Missier Grande. And I was asked to investigate Garzoni."

"And I'm supposed to believe that? A *cicerone* and *frappatore*? Spying for the Venetian state?"

"It doesn't matter to me whether you believe it or not, but you might at least recognise the fact that I've saved your life. Just as I acknowledge that you've done the same for me. But let's find somewhere better to talk things over."

"Where?"

"We'll have to think," I said. I wondered whether we could go to the Missier Grande's office in Saint Mark's Square in the hope that Sior Massaro might be there, working through the night. But a second's reflection told me that it was an idea born out of wishful thinking. Then an alternative struck me. "How about an empty theatre?"

"Do you have a particular one in mind?"

"Yes. And you might as well admit it, such a place would be home from home for you," I said on a venture.

He looked sharply at me. "How did you —"

"It's come to seem inevitable in this whole business," I said. "Everything seems to lead back to theatre. I could tell you were an actor. You couldn't even stop yourself quoting Shakespeare when you were supposed to be a count from Georgia."

"Ah," he said, "did I? I don't recall . . ."

"*Julius Caesar*," I said. "Twice."

"Ah well, yes," he said, "that was one of my favourites." He gave a sigh. Perhaps he was recalling spellbound audiences and thundering applause . . . or perhaps he was just remembering getting a regular wage.

"But then," I said, "this city does bring out the histrionic in everyone." I gestured towards the niches in the church façade. "Just look at those statues there. Members of the Barbaro family, all ready to take a bow. Not one of them looking the least bit God-fearing, or even just suitably pious."

He looked at the posturing marble figures in some perplexity. He clearly did not see the point I was making.

"Come on," I said, sighing myself. "We've a long walk."

We headed east. A few minutes later we stepped out into the great glistening expanse of Saint Mark's Square. At the far end, towards the basilica, they had begun assembling the colonnade for Ascension, but at the western end the wooden planks and columns were still stacked along the sides of the square. There were plenty of people around, despite the late hour. Animated groups were clustered round the tables outside the coffee shops, although no one was sitting down, presumably because the chairs were still wet from the storm. I glanced up at the windows of the Missier Grande's offices. There was no light there. Sior Massaro did go to bed then, like other common mortals.

As we set out across the square I heard my name called by a female voice. "Mr Marangon!"

I looked towards the tables outside Florian's coffee shop. It was not difficult to spot Miss Boscombe; one only needed to follow the direction of most of the bystanders' eyes. There was no sign of her father. She appeared to be surrounded by young Venetian noblemen.

"Who's that?" said the count sharply.

"She is Mr Boscombe's cousin."

"I don't wish to meet her," he said firmly.

"Very well."

"I will wait beneath the clock tower." He strode across the square while I walked towards Miss Boscombe.

I bowed. "Miss Boscombe, a very good evening. I trust you will forgive me –"

"Anything, dear Mr Marangon. What have you been doing?" And she let out a little trill of laughter. I had the impression she must have been drinking. Two of the young men with her, who had been looking suspiciously at me, laughed as well, although I am sure they had not understood a word. They had certainly been drinking.

"I trust you will forgive me if I do not linger with you," I said. "I'm afraid I have been forbidden to speak to you."

"Oh, that nonsense," she said. "Never mind about that."

"Please give my regards to your father, as well," I said.

"Oh yes, of course. He's somewhere around," she said, vaguely gesturing at the whole square. "I just thought I'd tell you that I managed to speak to my cousin. We were allowed a brief meeting in the prison. Poor Frederick." She forced herself to look serious for a few seconds.

"So he has survived his ordeal," I said.

"He looked so pale," she said. "I don't know whether they've been feeding him or not. We protested to the Resident."

"I'm sure he's been given every –"

"Well, never mind all that. What have you found out?"

I felt startled for a moment. Did she know about my role as a confidential agent? I almost asked her who had told her but then she went on: "I hope you haven't given up your inquiries on my behalf."

"Miss Boscombe, I did explain to you –"

"I see. So you care more about what some petty Venetian official says than a lady in despair from your own country." Her tone was so clearly bitter that the young men around her looked hard at me. I think one of them even put a hand to his sword. Then she said meltingly: "And I had thought we could be such friends."

"Miss Boscombe, I'm afraid I must leave you. Give my regards to your father."

"Oh, go then. I suppose it's that wretched girl in the bookshop who's made you such a poltroon."

"Miss Boscombe, I will attribute your remarks to your distress over your cousin. Good evening." I realised that I had better get away before I exploded and possibly ended up on the end of some young hothead's sword. I bowed and walked away, while she let out a shrill peal of mocking laughter which seemed to be taken up by the whole square. I wondered where her father might be and guessed he was probably studying the sculptures on the basilica or the Doge's palace.

The count was waiting by the clock tower, as he had said, and he was eyeing the parade on the Liston, which was still quite animated. I wondered if he was thinking nostalgically of the splendid appearance he had made there just a few weeks earlier.

He pointed to the half-built wooden colonnade that had arisen just in front of the flagpoles. "What's going on?"

"Another piece of Venetian theatre," I said. "It's preparations for the Sensa."

"The what?"

"The Feast of the Ascension," I said. "One of the key dates in the Venetian calendar, when the Doge rows out to the Lido and renews the city's marriage vows with the sea."

He gave a frown. "I think I've heard Luca talking about this with his Excellency," he said. "I don't know what they were saying as they stopped talking when they realised I could hear."

"It's perhaps the biggest spectacle of all: the Bucintoro –"

"What's that?"

"The stage barge, every inch of it gilded and sculptured."

"Sounds rather gaudy," he said.

"That's an odd remark from someone who dresses in silver from head to toe."

He sniffed. "You know as well as I do the importance of putting on a little spectacle. I saw your performance on that gondola."

"Exactly," I said. "And no one knows its importance better than the Venetian state. So the Doge goes out in the Bucintoro to San Nicolò on the Lido, with all the city authorities on board, all in their finery, orchestras playing, the arsenalotti rowing, they celebrate Mass, the Doge throws a nuptial ring into the sea, and then the city has a few days' holiday."

"Very well," he said. "It all sounds splendid. But tell me, what did that woman want? What did you tell her?"

"She's come from Florence on account of her cousin. And that's something else we need to talk about."

"All right. But let's get away from here before someone else recognises us."

That was sensible. I was already regretting that we had passed through the square, even though avoiding it would have meant taking a circuitous route. We bought a lantern at an extortionate price from a young lad standing underneath the clock tower, simply because we did not have the energy to haggle, and because I happened to have the money in my pocket. The count did not offer to contribute. Then we set off down the Merceria, turning right by the church of San Zulian towards Campo della Guerra. From there we made our way to Campo Santa Maria Formosa and then the great square of Campo Santi Giovanni e Paolo. I mentioned to the count that it was near here that Mr Boscombe's unfortunate tutor had met his end. His face became particularly sombre and he simply murmured: "So I heard."

I did not press this point. We walked down the oddly named Barbaria de le Tole and finally found ourselves in the square where the old theatre stood. The square was completely quiet and as far as I could tell nobody saw us clamber through the window in the side alley.

We made our way into the auditorium. I could see no signs that Zanotto had managed to make any improvements in the décor; perhaps there were a few more ornamental pillars on the stage but they did little to combat the overwhelming sense of forlorn abandonment. A perfect place for the two of us to spend the night, I thought wryly.

"Why have you brought me here?" said the count.

"Have you any other suggestions?"

He did not attempt to answer that. He took a seat in the front row and leaned back wearily. I put the lantern on the stage and then heaved myself up on to the boards after it, remembering, with a tinge of envy, how the zany had sprung there in one simple leap. I sat down next to the lantern, my legs dangling over the edge of the stage; the position gave me a slight advantage, I felt, for the conversation that had to come.

"What's your real name?" I began.

"Does it matter to you?"

"Well, it seems like a good starting point. Why shouldn't I know it?"

"You can call me Alfred."

"And why a count from Georgia?"

"Have you ever met anyone from Georgia?"

"No," I said.

"Well, there you are."

"I see. And do you speak Georgian?"

"No. But I've learned the alphabet."

"And why did you do that?"

"A good way to communicate with someone secretly."

"Someone else who knows the alphabet."

He did not bother to answer this, which was fair enough. But I persisted: "And who would this other person be?"

"I suspect that you already know that."

"Shackleford."

"So why ask?"

"Well, I still haven't grasped the exact connection between you two."

He was quiet for a few moments. Then he said: "Well, you might as well know. He was my brother."

"Ah." I was quiet myself for several seconds. Then I said: "I'm sorry."

He started crying. He leaned forward in his seat, put his head between his hands and sobbed unashamedly.

There was not much I could do. I did not think that he would welcome a comforting arm round his shoulders, so I just waited.

Eventually his shoulders ceased to heave and the sobs became more intermittent. He looked up at me. "I suppose you never weep." The tone was somewhere between bitter and defensive.

"When I have reason to," I said. "And I can see you have."

"I'm all alone now," he said. It was said simply and was quite touching.

"Was he your only relative?"

"I have a sister, Susan, but she's married to a dolt of a clergyman and has never wanted anything to do with us."

I remembered the draft of the letter to Susan on his desk.

"And so you and . . ."

"Peter."

"You and Peter were close."

"We were," he said. "We did so many things together."

"And you always got on well?"

He took no offence at this, as I had thought he might. He seemed quite willing to talk about his relations with his much less flamboyant brother. "Well, we were obviously rather different characters. And there's no doubt that Peter was a little jealous of me."

"Was he older or younger?"

"Two years older. And he was always saying that I was spoilt because I was the youngest. Well, perhaps there was some truth to it. I was certainly the better-looking." And he put a hand to his face and wiped away the tears; he did it with delicate dabbing gestures, suggesting that he was worried about the effect of the tears on his make-up. However, as he had presumably removed the make-up before getting ready for bed, there was in fact no streaky effect. "But I used to tell him that looks weren't everything, and he shouldn't worry just because his face was so plump."

"I'm sure he loved you for that," I said.

The count (I could not stop thinking of him under that title) took this quite seriously. "Well, everyone likes to be comforted. And he was certainly cleverer than me – or, at least, more intellectual."

"So he was a real scholar?"

"He could always pass for one. That was his – his special line."

"But you were both actors."

"Oh yes," he said. "We belonged to a travelling company. It was quite successful – until the manager absconded with all the profits."

"I see. And that was when you changed your line of performance?"

He seemed to have accepted the inevitability of telling the whole story. I think it was even something of a relief. I was beginning to realise that without his brother he was quite a pathetic figure.

"Yes," he said. "We tried various things, even doing juggling tricks in village squares – that's where I learned to throw. But Peter wasn't very good at that sort of performance. Anyway, I wanted us to go to London and try to get a job with one of the big theatres there – Drury Lane, Haymarket – but Peter didn't think we would have a chance. He had always been a great reader and he thought he might be able to pass himself off as a scholar and get a job as a bear-leader."

"And that would leave you on your own."

"Yes," he said. He was clearly thinking back to that time and from the nervous note in his voice and the serious expression on his face I imagined it had been a moment of crisis. "And then I suggested that if he did find a rich pupil and take him abroad there would always be ways of making more than just the regular wage. After all, these young men often have far more money than is good for them."

"Oh, certainly," I said. "It does them good to be fleeced."

He looked sharply at me. "I imagine you've never been really poor. Not knowing where your next meal will come from."

I gave an apologetic shrug. "I've never starved." There was no point in antagonising him if I wanted to hear the full story.

"It was just a matter of indulging their caprices. They want to gamble. And often enough they're fascinated by someone who seems to have occult powers. It's surprising how many stories you hear of young men involved in such practices. We kept on the look-out for such people."

"So your brother would take them abroad and bump into you, in all your splendour."

"This was only the third time we had done it," he said. "It had worked well enough the first couple of times. And we never took all their money."

"They were able to get back to England," I said.

"Of course. And I'm sure they enjoyed it on the whole." He added this last with a little less conviction.

"But this time there was something else," I said. "There was the matter of the book your brother was bringing out."

He looked sharply at me. "How do you know that?"

"You'll remember that Mr Boscombe called on me after discovering the murder. He told me. But he didn't know what the book was – or rather he only knew what your brother had told him."

"Ah yes," he said thoughtfully. "Well, it caused far more trouble than it was worth." He clearly realised how inadequate this was as a comment on the events of the last few weeks and his face twitched in a sudden wince.

"So whose idea was it?"

"Peter found the book in the Boscombes' library after he had been accepted as tutor. He and I both know some Italian from opera libretti so he was able to read it and see what a – well, what a controversial book it was."

"Yes, I know."

"Have you seen the book, then?"

"Just an English edition that a friend of mine lent me. A bookseller in Calle dei Fabbri. Your brother knew him, in fact."

"Ah. Well, that's no surprise. But of course the English edition was published anonymously. The one the Boscombes had was different. For a start there were the signatures. It was an Italian edition, especially produced for James Boscombe, who had been friendly with a group of Venetians in London. And the three authors had all signed it, three Venetian noblemen. It so happened I was in London when Peter found the book and he sent me a letter asking if I could find out about the three names. I got in touch with a Venetian actor I knew and he was able to tell me who they all were. A certain Zanotto, a certain Garzoni and a certain . . ." He looked at me, to see if I knew.

"Go on."

"A certain Grimani."

I tried not to show my surprise. "The Grimani are a large family," I said. "You only need to see how many palaces there are with that name."

"Yes, well, this one was Pietro Grimani, the present doge."

"I see."

"When I told Peter this he got very excited. He said I must go to Venice and see what chance there would be of selling this book to one of the families. They would all certainly be embarrassed by it and possibly be willing to pay quite a sum to hush it up."

"So why didn't you bring the book yourself?"

"Peter couldn't run the risk of the family's noticing that it had disappeared before he and the boy left the house. So I came here ahead of them. I found out that Zanotto had no money and so wasn't worth bothering with. The Grimani family were – well, they were too important, too powerful. It had seemed like a good idea back in London but I didn't know how to approach them. So I went to Garzoni."

"And he wasn't embarrassed at all."

"No, he was delighted that the book had been found. He seemed quite gleeful."

"Rather disappointing."

"Well, so I thought at first. But it turned out he would be willing to pay to get hold of it since it would be a wonderful opportunity to expose the Doge as a hypocrite and a turncoat. Those were his words. He seemed to really hate the man. And he even contacted Zanotto, who he thought would be just as willing to expose the Doge as he was."

"But Zanotto then thought that if there was going to be any money in it, he should be making it."

"I suppose so. I never fully understood what was happening."

"And then the book disappeared."

"Yes." He frowned and went silent.

"Do you think it was stolen?" I asked.

"What else can I think?" he said. There was a touch of despair in his voice.

"Mr Boscombe told me he thought your brother had faked the burglary, presumably so that he could handle the sale by himself."

"But we always worked as a team!" he said. It was almost a cry of despair. To lose his brother so horribly was bad enough, I supposed, but to be forced to suspect that the beloved brother had also betrayed him was too much to bear. Perhaps it was no wonder that he had not found the strength to break away from Garzoni's house. The only alternative – that which now faced him – was a wide world in which he was utterly alone. He did not even have his dog.

I said none of all this. Instead I murmured: "Well, I suppose we'll never know. Not unless the book turns up again."

"I don't care about the wretched book," he said.

"No," I said. "I suppose not at this point. But clearly Garzoni does. It seems almost as if he had been waiting for just such an opportunity."

"He's mad, you know," he said. "Completely mad."

"I had an inkling," I said.

"And that man Luca just plays on his madness. I think he's hoping that Garzoni will adopt him eventually. He's already got his hands on most of his finances."

"And the two brothers?"

"Oh, they're not in it for the money. Garzoni clearly knew how to inspire total loyalty in the Arsenale. They're fanatical followers. They'll do anything for him. And Luca knows how to play on their loyalty as well."

I put the question as bluntly as possible. "Do you think their loyalty extends to killing?"

His face gave another twitchy wince. I had the suspicion that this was a question he had preferred not to pose to himself. "You mean those male prostitutes?"

"Yes."

"I don't know," he said after a long pause.

"Then what made you think immediately of the *gnaghe* the moment I asked if they were killers?"

He leaned forward, his forehead propped up on his hands and mumbled to the floor. "There just seemed to be some agitation in the palace on the days those . . . those things happened. Nothing I could point to definitely."

"And yet you stayed there."

His shoulders started to shake again. I went on regardless. "Even though they might have killed your brother."

"No," he said, looking up. "They didn't do that. I'm sure of that. They were in the palace that evening." He wiped his eyes again. "That's partly why I say I don't know about the other murders. Otherwise I would definitely have gone." A pause. "I don't know where."

"Oh, come on," I said, "the world's a big place. And there's always the theatre again."

"Yes," he said, looking around. "You know, I'm glad you brought me here. You think I could make it again? Be a success?"

"You're a fine performer," I said, quite sincerely. "I didn't doubt you were Georgian until today, you know." His range was probably limited, but I felt there was no need to say that. "Anyway, maybe we should try to get some sleep. Tomorrow morning you can come with me to the Missier Grande and tell him all you know."

"The Missier . . . You're not serious? Are you really an agent of his?"

"Yes," I said, and wished I could feel proud as I did so. "We'll have to tell them what we know."

"But we don't know anything," he said, his voice a little agitated.

"Well, what we suspect. That is almost as good, as far as they're concerned." Indeed, I could have added that the Missier Grande dealt almost exclusively with suspicions. But again this did not add to my self-esteem.

"I don't want any trouble," he said. "I just want to go away now. Back to England."

"You'll be able to do that, I assure you. But we must first do our duties with the authorities here."

He fell quiet. After a few moments he said in a resigned voice: "Very well. Now let's sleep."

I thanked him.

I should have remembered that he was a more than competent actor.

23

The next morning I awoke on the floor of the stage with the smell of sawdust in my nose and a crick in my neck. A quizzical rat was inspecting my foot. Otherwise I was completely alone.

A quick search of the auditorium, backstage and the dressing rooms told me that Alfred's desire to avoid trouble had clearly won out over his sense of civic duty.

I set out for Saint Mark's Square and the offices of the Missier Grande on my own. I suppose I could have taken the rat.

First, I visited my apartment, which was more or less on the way. There seemed to be nobody watching it, but when I opened the door I saw at once that there had been visitors – and that I was going to owe Sior Fabrizio a good deal of money. The books he had lent me were scattered over the floor, their spines cracked and pages loose. The damage had been wanton. I thought I recognised the hand, or at least the orders, of Luca. But then I suppose Gaetano and Giorgio had no reason to love me either. My other less esoteric books had been treated with less savagery; I suppose they had felt the need to avenge the fact that I had fooled their master with the aid of the occult works.

The means of ingress had been the window again. If I were going to continue in this line of work I would have to find an apartment on a higher floor, I thought resignedly.

Their revenge had not extended to my clothes, so I was able to change into something less funereal and to don a less itchy wig. The change did not exactly cheer me up but it left me at least feeling slightly less conspicuous as I set out for the square. There was also the fact that it was a gloriously sunny day; the storm had cleared the air and I walked down the Riva degli Schiavoni enjoying the morning sunshine on my back.

Preparations for the Ascension feast were now well under way. Numerous workmen were busily assembling the wooden colonnade; wooden vases, painted to look like marble, were leaning against the real marble pillars of the square's stone colonnade, waiting to be hoisted on top of the wooden columns. As I watched, a workman jocularly pretended to be staggering under the weight of a vase, which his colleague then picked up with one hand.

When I reached the offices of the Missier Grande I found that the Dante quotation still worked as the password. It seemed there had been a certain amount of exaggeration about the elaborate nature of the security procedures guarding the place. Sior Massaro greeted with me with some surprise. "We were not expecting to hear from you so soon," he said. "I'm not sure the Missier Grande will be ready to receive you just yet."

"I do bring important information," I said. "I think he must hear what I have to say."

"Well, I'll try to speak to him," he said. "Wait in the little room."

I went into the small room with the devotional paintings and gave a smile and nod to Saint Jerome, whose hand was still raised with the breast-beating stone.

Eventually I heard Sior Massaro's quick footsteps returning accompanied by the more measured pace of the Missier Grande.

I stood up as they came in. The Missier Grande sat down at the desk and looked hard at me. "You have been remarkably swift," he said. Sior Massaro sat down at his side and at once started writing.

"I was unable to stay any longer," I said. "Nobleman Garzoni wanted me to commit a murder and my failure to comply inevitably meant that I would be the next person to die."

"This is a very grave accusation you are making," he said, his voice as unruffled as ever.

"I realise that, Illustrissimo. I don't do it idly."

"So please explain."

I swallowed. I had rehearsed the story in my mind but now that it came to telling it I found my grand design crumbling away. It all seemed so absurd.

I began, trying to keep my voice as level as his own. "I decided that the best way to gain access to the palace was to pretend to possess occult powers. I drew on the knowledge I had acquired from the secret reports to persuade him that I knew things that only someone gifted with such powers could possibly know."

"Go on."

I told him of my spectacular entrance, of my trick with the statue of Santa Giustina and then of exploring Garzoni's bedchamber and being discovered there.

"You seem to have precipitated events with unnecessary haste," he observed. "Was there any special urgency that prompted you to explore the chamber on your first evening in the palace?"

"It seemed like a good opportunity at the time," I said.

"But it clearly proved not to be."

"I suppose so," I said, a little disheartened. Maybe the honest thing would be to tell him that I had had no desire to spend any more evenings than necessary in that house.

I went on to recount the test to which I had been put and my subsequent hairbreadth escape with the count. He listened with no sign of emotion as I told the story of our flight across the roof and the confrontation with the pistol-wielding *bravo*. Sior Massaro did look up momentarily, his quill pen hovering in the air as he looked at me, perhaps in awe but also perhaps in disbelief.

"And where is this so-called count?" asked the Missier Grande.

"I'm afraid he has run away. He told me he would come with me to talk to you, but then . . ." My voice tailed away feebly.

"You seem to have a remarkably trusting nature," he said. "Not the greatest asset in this line of work."

"Well, I certainly don't trust nobleman Garzoni," I said.

"No, that is clear. But I would like to know what evidence you have gathered of any actual nefarious activity. And I don't mean foolish but harmless games with occult symbols and the like."

"He asked me to kill the count," I pointed out.

"He said he wished to put you to the test," he said. "Do you have any concrete evidence that he would have let you carry out this deed?"

"But why would he ask me such a thing?"

"Nobleman Garzoni believes in unfailing loyalty. We know that. It might be just the kind of dramatic test he would put someone to, without letting them carry it through to the bloody denouement. You, of course, failed the test and so lost the opportunity to continue to observe him and his activities."

"So I should have agreed to cut the count's throat," I said.

"I can see the dilemma, but I suspect that you made a short-sighted and in the end unproductive decision."

"I'll remember to be more ruthless in future."

"I am not certain that you have a future in this line of work. It comes down to a question of assessing possibilities with the necessary detachment and intelligence."

Perhaps I should have felt relieved to learn that my career prospects were limited in this field, but actually all I felt was anger. I did my best to keep my voice calm. "Nobleman Garzoni is to my mind a dangerous man with an obsessive longing for power. He practically admitted to me that he had ordered the killing of the male prostitutes."

"This is new information," he said. "Why didn't you mention this earlier?"

"I was trying to recount events with the necessary detachment," I said, trying not to sound too sarcastic. "One thing at a time."

"So now tell me about the male prostitutes."

I reported Garzoni's words on the need to create an atmosphere of terror in the city. And I mentioned my suspicions that Luca and the two brothers had been responsible for the actual killings.

"You have no definite evidence for what you say?"

"He didn't show me the decapitated heads."

"I would ask you to restrain your impulse to give sarcastic replies," he said, his voice as flat as ever. "I am not saying your information is incorrect. I am simply pointing out, as before, that if you had not jeopardised your position in the household you could have gathered some concrete evidence to prove what you now only suspect. You may have a certain flair for the theatrical, as I said on the occasion of our previous meeting, but I fear that if it is not coupled with the necessary detachment and caution it is not of immediate use to us."

"I will be more careful next time."

"It remains to be seen whether there will be a next time," he said. "For the moment I would ask you to draw up a detailed report of what you have observed – keeping as closely as possible to the bare facts. This will then be filed –"

"Along with all the other gossip," I said. I did not care how bitter I sounded.

"Along with all the other unverified information," he said. "Then you may go."

"Illustrissimo, there is another reason why I thought it might be expedient to report to you as soon as possible."

"Yes?"

"I suspect that nobleman Garzoni is planning something to disrupt the Ascension Day festivities."

"And your evidence?"

"Nothing definite, just stray words about the need to make an impact."

"I see. Another of your intuitions. Well, write a detailed report. We will recommend vigilance to the arsenalotti on duty."

So he was not going to do anything.

"When can I return to my work as *cicerone*, Illustrissimo?" I asked.

"Ah, that too remains to be seen," he said. "Good day. Sior Massaro, please pay Sior Marangon whatever remains to be paid." He turned and left the room.

It took me an hour to write an account with the required detachment and caution. Sior Massaro handed me the rest of my wages, which I accepted with some relief, if not effusive gratitude. Then he thanked me and told me not to worry too much.

"Bark worse than his bite?" I said drily.

"Well, I wouldn't go that far," said Sior Massaro.

"No, I thought not," I said. "Well, thank you Sior Massaro. You've been very kind to me. Since it seems there's no future for me in this city you might as well throw away the file bearing my name."

"Oh no," he said. "Of course not."

"There is a future for me?"

"No, I mean we never throw anything away." He added rather awkwardly: "And of course, the best of luck."

24

I stepped out into the square and the sunshine hit me full in the face. I remembered how I had felt the previous morning, when it had struck me that I belonged in this city since I was, after all, being paid to protect it. Well, now I had been paid and the change of tense resulted in a distinct change of mood. I still had the money in my pocket to take a cup of coffee at Florian's if I wanted, but I had no idea whether I would in a week's time.

I decided to forgo the coffee and made my way towards Sior Fabrizio's bookshop. I was going to have to tell him what had happened to his books and work out some system of repayment.

I arrived just as Lucia was approaching the shop from the opposite direction carrying a basket of groceries. We paused outside the door.

"We didn't expect to see you again so soon, Sior Alvise," she said. "Surely you have not already read those tomes?"

"Well, you would be surprised to hear how much I did read of them," I said. "And how useful they've been."

"Useful?" she said. "So you have discovered the Philosopher's Stone then?"

"Not exactly," I said. "But before we go any further I have a confession to make."

"To me?"

"Well, to your father, since it was he who lent me the books."

She looked troubled at these words and glanced towards the shop window. Her father could not be seen inside. "What has happened?"

"The books have been damaged."

"Sior Alvise," she said, "what have you been doing?" Her dark eyes looked straight into mine, and their expression suggested that her mind was already at work, conjuring up sinister occult rituals.

"My apartment was broken into," I said, "and a good deal of damage was done. But I will repay your father in full."

"What sort of damage? And who did it?"

"It's a long story. I know who did it but the knowledge is not much use at the moment."

"Can you not denounce these people?"

"Siora Lucia, let me tell the story to both you and your father. It will be a relief to me and I will appreciate your advice, as ever." I had decided that if I was no longer a confidential agent there was no longer any reason to remain confidential; the Missier Grande would probably not have agreed but I was not going to ask his opinion.

"Let's go in." When we got inside her father was nowhere to be seen. "He must have gone upstairs," she said. "One moment." She ran up the stairs, and returned a few moments later with her father.

He looked perturbed. "Sior Alvise, my daughter tells me there has been trouble."

"I am extremely sorry for the damage to your books."

"It is not the material damage that concerns us."

"It is good of you to say so, sior. You both deserve a full explanation of what has happened to me."

It took almost twenty-five minutes (which included two intervals while Fabrizio dealt with customers) and they listened in silence, with just a few requests for clarification, an occasional *cospetto* from Fabrizio and an occasional intake of breath on Lucia's part (the killing of Zosimos, the escape across the roof). I tried not to overdo the drama but I cannot deny that Lucia's reactions were gratifying.

"So you are a confidential agent of the Missier Grande," said Fabrizio. He did not sound enthusiastic.

"I have been one," I said. "The Missier Grande himself made it perfectly clear that my days as such are over. Or rather my day as such is over."

"And I'm glad to hear it," said Lucia firmly.

"Well, so am I," I said. "Except . . ."

"Except what?"

"Well, everything is so unsatisfactory," I said. "I would rather have finished having at least concluded something."

"I'm sure your performance was splendid," said Lucia. She seemed almost radiant, now that she had learned the real explanation for my sudden interest in occult matters. This was more than gratifying.

"It was not bad," I said, "though I say it myself. But I wish there could have been a last act and final curtain."

She nodded. "Nobleman Garzoni clearly should be arrested, along with his *bravi*, from all you say. But I have no doubt that he'll be watched from now on. And I for one am glad that it is not you who has to do the watching." She smiled. "There may be a good deal of theatre in Venetian life, as you say, but things aren't usually as neatly arranged as in an opera libretto."

"Maybe not, but I can't get rid of the notion that some kind of grand finale is being prepared all the same."

"Yes, but you needn't be involved," said Sior Fabrizio. "Leave it to the *sbirri*. That's their job."

"But will they *do* their job?"

Lucia was looking at me seriously. "Sior Alvise, I can see you are troubled. What is it you really fear?"

"That Garzoni is planning something. And something imminent. Maybe . . ."

"Maybe what?"

"I don't know, but I suspect it's something to do with the Feast of the Ascension."

"Tomorrow?" she said.

"Exactly."

"Then you must do something about it," she said.

I looked at her with some surprise. "But didn't you want me to keep out of trouble?"

"Out of unnecessary trouble," she said, and she smiled. "And anyway, I've come to realize that that sort of advice doesn't work with you."

"I don't go looking for trouble," I protested.

"No, but when it comes, perhaps you don't do all you could to avoid it. Though maybe . . ." She stopped.

It was my turn to pick up the unconcluded sentence. "Maybe?"

"Well, maybe it depends on the person who asks you to get involved."

I felt myself grow red. "Siora, I assure you –"

"Oh, don't bluster," she said. "I don't blame you. It was natural enough."

"Lucia, my dear," said Fabrizio, "if you're referring to Siora Boscombe, I think you're being a little unfair."

"It was merely an observation," she said, "not an accusation. And in the present case the young lady's charms clearly have nothing to do with anything."

"No," I said, "they don't."

"And in this case I think you do well to get involved. I don't see what else you can do. Not if the safety of the city depends on it."

I looked at her a little warily, wondering if she was making fun of me, but she was entirely serious. "It may sound absurd," I said, "but I think that it quite possibly does." I turned to Fabrizio. "Can you tell me anything about a certain Drebbel? Apparently he invented a kind of clock or a telescope, and was connected with the Emperor Rudolph. And with Prince Henry, although I don't know who that would be. They're names I saw among Garzoni's papers."

He tried the name over and over. "Drebbel, Drebbel . . ." It sounded quite charming in his Venetian accent. "I think I've come across it but I couldn't say where. Give me time for a little browsing and I'll see if I can come up with anything."

"All right. I'm going to try to find out about Garzoni's time at the Arsenale."

"And how will you do that?" said Lucia. "You no longer have any official status."

"I hardly had any before," I said. "I wasn't allowed to tell anyone I was a confidential agent. I'll just have to rely on my natural charm of manner."

"Well, I'm sure you'll find out all you need to know," she said. It was not clear how ironic she was being. "Who are you going to ask?"

"I'll start with my old gondolier's brother, who works there."

"Ah, Bepi," she said, with a smile. She had always liked Bepi. "Give him my best wishes. And if I can be of any help . . ."

"Lucia, my dear," said her father, in a vaguely admonitory tone.

"Don't worry, father, I'm not intending to storm Palazzo Garzoni."

"They wouldn't stand a chance if you did," I said. And I was not sure how ironic I was being.

"How sweet of you," she said, with a bow. "Let us know what you learn from Bepi's brother."

"I will do so," I said, and took my leave.

I made my way to Bepi's usual waiting place near San Moise. He was there, apparently playing the same game of dice with the same two gondoliers.

"Are we back in business?" he said.

"Not yet, I'm afraid."

"Ah."

"No. I was wondering if I could talk to your brother."

"Which one?"

"Is it Giacomo? The one who works at the Arsenale?"

"That's right. What do you want from him?"

"Oh, just a chat. I'll explain it all later."

"Well, they come out early today. La Sensa, you know." He glanced upwards to see where the sun was. "Should be coming out in about an hour and a half. Do you want me to take you to the Arsenale?"

"That would be very good. I don't want to drag you away from your game, though."

"Don't worry. I sometimes think I play too much."

The larger of his two companions said: "What that means is he's losing."

Bepi gave a shrug and a smile and pushed a small pile of coins in the direction of the man who had spoken, which suggested there may have been some truth in his remark. "Come back in half an hour," he said. "Give me time to win some back."

I did as he said. He was looking calm enough when I returned, so I imagine he must have had some better luck. He bade goodbye to his companions and then strolled with me in the direction of his mooring place.

"Have you found any other work?" I asked him.

"Nothing regular," he said. "I'll be ferrying people for the Sensa later this afternoon and evening."

"Yes, of course," I said, stepping into the gondola. "Sure I'm not taking you from business now?"

"Wasn't planning to start work till later in the day," he said. "Tell me what you want with Giacomo." He untied the mooring rope and leaped lightly to his post.

"It's complicated," I said. "I was asked by the Missier Grande to investigate nobleman Garzoni."

"You?" he said.

"Yes," I said. "There's no need to sound quite so surprised." Actually he had merely uttered the second-person pronoun in a mildly interrogative tone: "*Ti?*" "I wasn't supposed to tell anyone but now that I've been dismissed from the job I see no reason to keep quiet."

"But you're still investigating," he said as he pushed us away from the mooring poles towards the Grand Canal.

"Well, yes."

"Is that a good idea?"

"I think so," I said. "Something's happening that is a long way from the Lepanto spirit."

He gave a kind of all-purpose grunt, which might have been an acknowledgement of the justice of my remark but might equally have been an expression of disgust at my shameless exploitation of that one time he had revealed something of himself to me.

I chose to believe in the former possibility and went on: "I need to know something about some of the people around Garzoni. Your brother might remember them."

"He might. He doesn't notice much, mind you."

I hoped that this was just an elder brother's typical lack of appreciation of a younger sibling. And I remembered that Bepi tended to regard most people born more than three years after him as hopelessly ignorant, even if they were not wholly to be blamed for their condition; as I myself was nearly ten years younger I sometimes marvelled that he had ever agreed to work with me. But possibly he put me, as a semi-foreigner, in a different category.

We travelled past the church of the Salute, and the wide basin of the lagoon opened up before us. There were more craft than usual on the water, as people were making their preparations for the great celebrations the following day. Some of the more elaborate ceremonial boats were already being tried out, so that the lagoon seemed suddenly to have spawned hosts of golden-bearded deities and mythological creatures, all tossing and tumbling on the glittering water.

"Some of these people," muttered Bepi.

"What's the matter?"

"You'd think they'd never been on the water before," he said, gesturing towards a flamboyantly decorated boat to our right, with ten oarsmen who, despite having Neptune as figurehead, did not seem very familiar with the aquatic element.

"Well, you know how it is," I said. "Every guild likes to have their representatives out on show for the big day. I expect they're bakers, or barrel-makers . . ."

"They could hire proper gondoliers," he said sourly.

"Anyway, it looks as if it should be a good day for the ceremony," I said. The Bucintoro, the ceremonial boat that bears the Doge to the Lido for the wedding ceremony, is so overloaded with gilded carvings and allegorical ornaments that it is unable to venture outside the lagoon, and even within the lagoon it cannot sail if the water is at all choppy. Gaudily splendid but impractical, confined to its own native waters, it is perhaps all too suitable a symbol for the city as it is today. And even as they enjoy the spectacle, I suspect many Venetians secretly realise this.

"We won't be able to go up the Arsenale canal," said Bepi.

"No, I suppose not," I said. It was usually off-limits to private boats and this was even more likely to be the case today, since all sorts of preparations would be under way. The Bucintoro is moored throughout the year in the docks within the Arsenale itself, but tomorrow it would make its stately way down the canal into the lagoon, ready for the Doge and assembled dignitaries to board it near the Piazzetta.

Bepi steered us in towards the poles alongside the Riva. He tied up the gondola and we disembarked and set off down the narrow Calle del Buso. A minute later we emerged from the gloom of the alleyway into the sunlit animation of the square, directly opposite the magnificent entrance into the Arsenale, guarded by its impressive array of marble lions. I could not help glancing up at the statue of Santa Giustina, perched on top of the tympanum above the gateway; every curve and fold in the saint's form had become very familiar to me.

The workers were already emerging from the gateway, with that extra spring in their legs bestowed by the knowledge that several days of holiday awaited them. Bepi greeted a number of them in his usual laconic fashion (a nod and a *bondi*, sometimes accompanied by a name). At last he said, "*Bondi, fradeo,*" and introduced me to Giacomo. Apart from a slight facial similarity, it was difficult to believe they were brothers.

Where Bepi was unemphatic in movement and voice, Giacomo was expansive and noisy. He greeted his brother with a loud salutation, throwing out his arms in a gesture that combined welcome and surprise; his arms seemed to be too large for his body and were in constant motion. Although he must have been in his late twenties, his whole demeanour was that of an enthusiastic child let out of school early.

He greeted me with a vigorous handshake and said, "Ah yes, you're the *foresto*," beaming happily as if my presence were the crowning touch to the day's joy.

I guessed that *foresto* was how I was known in the Zennaro family. "Well, yes, but my parents are Venetian. Anyway, do you mind if I ask you some questions about some people who used to work here?"

He did not stop beaming but said: "What's it about?"

"It's unofficial inquiries for the Missier Grande," I said, in as vague and unofficial a fashion as possible.

"You can trust him," said Bepi. "He's not a *sbirro*."

"Well, all right," he said; but his broad smile had become a trifle wary.

"Let's walk towards Bepi's gondola," I said. "You do all live . . ."

"We all live together," said Bepi. "One big happy family," he added, in his flattest tone.

"That's right, *fradeo*," said Giacomo, and gave him a jolly fraternal punch on the shoulder, which merely caused Bepi to raise a weary eyebrow.

We crossed the square to the corner where Calle del Buso began, walking behind a number of other workers. It was too narrow for us all to walk side by side so we waited till we reached the sunlit Riva to begin the conversation. When paused by Bepi's gondola I said: "The Missier Grande is interested in nobleman Garzoni."

"Oh, God," said Giacomo.

I looked at him. The expression of amiable cheeriness had sagged somewhat. "Did you have any dealings with him?"

He laughed. "I'm not that grand. Just a caulker, me. But we all knew him.

"Was he respected?"

"He was feared," he said.

He would have been pleased to hear that, I thought. But then he undoubtedly already knew it.

"Most of us hated him," Giacomo went on. But then he added: "There were some who respected him. Even worshipped him."

"And how many would they be?"

"A handful," he said, indicating a tight-knit group by cupping his hands together. "And they stuck together. Like a – well, like a secret society. Even had their own codes." He paused. "Or so people said. I was never close enough."

"Doesn't sound good for the overall spirit of the place," I said.

"It wasn't. That's why people were so glad when at last they managed to get rid of him."

"And do you think he kept up contacts with any of these people? The ones in the secret society?"

"Look, I'm not saying it was a real secret society. Just acted like one."

"I understand," I said. "But did these people stay in touch with him after he had been dismissed?"

"Well, I've heard stories . . ." He paused. "And there were those who joined him when he left."

"Right," I said. "Luca, Gaetano and Giorgio."

"That's right," he said. "Nice trio." He gave a guffaw: "I don't think!" He was one of those who like their irony to be well signalled. His brother rolled his eyes to heaven and then bent down to the rope and began to unmoor the gondola.

"What can you tell me about them?"

"Well, Gaetano and Giorgio were both haulers."

"Haulers?" I said.

"They do all the heavy lifting around the place. Barrels of pitch. Uncut poles. Iron hoops. You want something carried, you point it out to them and they carry it wherever you want it. You have to tell them exactly where. Can't let them work it out for themselves. Story goes that Gaetano once carried a barrel right out of the Arsenale all the way to the Piazza because no one told him to put it down." He threw out his arm, pointing all the way down the Riva, and guffawed again. "Probably would have gone on walking all the way to Santa Marta and then into the lagoon if a guard hadn't stopped him outside the Doge's palace."

"And they respected Garzoni?"

"Loved him. Knew where they were with him. They wanted orders. He gave orders."

I said hesitantly: "Were there ever any rumours about . . . about their relations?"

He guffawed again, as if it was the funniest thing I'd said so far. "Garzoni couldn't stand inverts. You heard about the man who was flogged."

"Was that for sexual practices?" I said.

"Well, not officially. The poor man had been late three days running. But people say that there was also a rumour that he liked bending over and that was what made Garzoni come down so hard on him." He suddenly realised the possible double meaning of what he had said and roared with laughter again. "If you know what I mean!"

Bepi looked up from the rope and said, "Sometimes the people who speak out the most against it . . ." His voice tailed away but his point was clear enough.

It was obviously a new thought to his brother. "Do you think so? You mean . . . Cospetto!" He seemed quite flummoxed by the idea. Then he said, "Anyway, I can't imagine Gaetano and Giorgio getting up to that sort of stuff."

Bepi shrugged. "I'm not saying they do. But maybe Garzoni likes having them around, all the same."

"What about Luca?" I said.

"Oh, Luca Sartori," Giacomo said. He sounded contemptuous. "He was master of ceremonies, responsible for all the spectacles that get put on."

"Is that an important job?"

"Well, it never used to be, but under him it became all-important. I mean, we arsenalotti have always taken part in the city's ceremonies – rowing the Bucintoro, escorting foreign diplomats into the city, acrobatic displays in the Piazza . . . you know the sort of stuff."

"Yes, I know," I said.

"Well, Garzoni seemed to decide that that was what the Arsenale was all about, and Sartori spent all his time preparing the shows. Even if you weren't directly involved you had to take part in the drills every morning. Can't deny that it impressed foreign visitors when they came. They would see us all marching to our work places in step." He did a strutting parody of a military march for a few paces to make the point. "But it got too much and people started asking when we were going to try to design something useful – a ship that could really take on the Turks, for example. Somebody told me once that Sartori had actually worked in the theatre and it sounded likely. He certainly didn't know much about ships."

"Does anyone in there?" asked Bepi.

"Yes, I know, I know," said Giacomo, "only you gondoliers understand anything about boats. If it weren't for the gondoliers the city would come to a halt." He gave his brother a playful slap on the back, which Bepi accepted with a resigned wince. I gathered this was a running joke in the family. "But the Arsenale used to be the power-house of the city." He paused, evidently feeling this was a little feeble. "Of the Mediterranean."

"Go on, say the world," said Bepi.

"Yes, well, why not? But the point is that under Garzoni and Sartori all that counted was the spectacle. And loyalty to them. Or rather to him. No worker was ever supposed to question any order. Now that wasn't the real spirit of the Arsenale, was it?"

"No," I agreed. "Nor of Venice."

"Exactly. You're a *foresto*, yet you can see that."

"Well, as I said, I'm also a Venetian."

"Yes, of course you are," said Giacomo, as if indulging me in a personal whim.

"So people were glad when he was forced out?"

"Most people. There was always that group."

"The secret society."

"Well, if you want to call it that."

"That was your description."

"Oh, you're a sharp one!" he said, with another loud laugh. This time he slapped me on the back, almost knocking me over. Bepi gave me a wry smile, as if to say, "Didn't I warn you?" I gave him an answering nod. We boarded the gondola, Bepi quietly but firmly refusing his brother's exuberant offer to help with the rowing.

Giacomo and I passed through the cabin to the far end, so that Bepi could continue to hear our conversation. We remained on our feet, steadying ourselves by resting our hands on the roof of the felze.

"So how many would there be in this . . . this group?" I asked.

"Oh, probably about twenty or so. And as I said, there have been stories about them recently."

"What sort of stories?" I said.

"They've been meeting up with Sartori after hours."

"Where?" I said.

"Oh, it's probably nothing important. Just keeping in touch with him. Why shouldn't they?"

"Yes, of course. Perfectly normal. But do you know where they've been meeting?"

"Well, there's the floating stage."

"The what?"

"There, look," he said, pointing eastwards.

"Oh, that thing," I said. It was a floating platform about the size of half a tennis court, moored to two huge poles about twenty metres from the boat yards and fishermen's houses that straggled down to the lagoon in the area around the churches of Sant'Isepo, Sant'Antonio and San Nicola di Bari. It held a wooden theatrical stage, and a number of covered booths. "It belongs to the Arsenale, doesn't it?" I remembered having seen arsenalotti perform acrobatic feats on it during the celebrations for the arrival of a foreign dignitary some months earlier.

"Yes. Sartori had it built a couple of years ago. But since he left it hasn't been used officially. The new master of ceremonies seems to have forgotten about it."

"So what's the story about these people meeting him there?"

"Oh, I heard it the other day. Apparently people saw torches there some nights ago. And somebody said Sartori wants to put on a last show for the Sensa, even though he no longer works for the Arsenale."

"And there were definitely arsenalotti involved in this?"

"Oh, nothing's definite. You know what it's like. Tizio says it to Caio, and Caio says it to Sempronio . . ." he said, using the Italian equivalents of Tom, Dick and Harry.

"And Sempronio said it to you," I said.

"That's right," he said, and laughed uproariously at the sheer comedy of this sequence.

"Bepi," I said, "can we go and have a look at the platform?"

"Why not?" he said.

When we approached, the platform appeared to be empty. The stage contained no ornaments or properties; the area beneath it was completely closed off.

"There's a sandolo," said Bepi, nodding towards a slim boat moored to the back of the platform, on the landward side.

"So maybe there's someone there," I said.

At that moment a door underneath the stage opened a few inches and in the dark crack a figure could be seen looking towards us. I ducked and entered the felze. I had only caught a glimpse but I was sure I had recognised Gaetano's red hair.

"What's the matter?" said Giacomo, bending down to peer in after me.

"Take a good look," I said. "Is it Gaetano?"

He straightened up and I heard him say, "The door's closed again."

"Bepi," I said, "we'd better move away. Don't let him think we're spying."

Bepi rowed us out to the open lagoon.

"I have to find out what's going on there," I said. "If we can manage to distract Gaetano's attention . . ."

"Just tell him to carry something somewhere," said Giacomo, and laughed.

"Maybe," I said. I addressed Bepi: "This evening, do you think you could drop me there? After we've got rid of Gaetano?"

"Got rid of him?" he said.

"Oh, I'm not planning to kill him," I said. "As Giacomo suggests, we'll just give him a task to perform."

"Well," he said, "the evening before the Sensa is usually fairly busy . . ."

"Yes, of course," I said. "Forget about it."

"Perhaps at the end of the day," he said. "When I'm going home."

25

We arranged a time and a meeting place and then Bepi took us to his usual mooring-post near the church of Sant'Isepo and I set off back to the centre of the city. From the Arsenale onwards the crowds grew thicker. In addition to the usual Venetian, I could hear the accents of the islands of the lagoon, Murano and Burano and Pellestrina, as well as those of the mainland, the harsher consonants of Padua, the rolling vowels of Treviso, the sing-song accents of Feltre . . . The Feast of the Sensa brings in people from all around, to sell their goods in the great fair in and around Saint Mark's Square, to find bargains, enjoy the spectacle or take advantage of the crowds for less commendable purposes. I checked that my wallet was safely lodged in my inner pocket.

There were many people already wearing masks, even though mask-wearing did not officially begin till the day of the Sensa itself; for many Venetians being unmasked is an unnatural state of being and they cannot wait for the opportunity to return to the freedom bestowed by stiff pieces of pasteboard tied to their faces.

Wherever space permitted it, jugglers and singers and pipers and strummers and assorted mountebanks had set up their miniature stages and were doing their best to attract the fickle attention of the ever-jostling crowd. I wondered briefly whether I should simply forget all about Garzoni and his machinations and set up my own booth as Umbriel the Rosicrucian fortune-teller. But a moment's reflection told me that without the assistance of the Missier Grande's archives my skills in that direction were fairly limited, and Venetian crowds are not kind to those whose performances do not match their promises, as a Trevigiano juggler who had dropped two coloured balls was discovering at that very moment.

It took me quite a while to make my way back to Fabrizio's shop, even though I had taken what I thought were the less frequented back streets. His shop had a few customers, people from the mainland who probably did not get many opportunities to see new books in their villages. Lucia was persuading a young couple with Preganziol accents of the virtues of Richardson's *Pamela*. Maybe she might even convince them they should read it in English.

Fabrizio greeted me. "How is it out there now?"

"Crowded," I said.

"I think I'll miss the celebrations this year," he said. "After fifty odd years the novelty begins to wear off."

I remembered that he had said the same thing the previous year. Possibly he had been saying it, with slight variations, for the last thirty years.

"I've found out something about this Drebbel," he said. "I knew I had heard the name."

"Ah," I said, "I was sure I could rely on you."

"Cornelis Drebbel," he said. "He was born in the Netherlands and was an inventor and scientist. He was invited to the court of King James of England and lived there for some years, becoming friendly with Prince Henry, the King's eldest son. But he was also summoned to the court of Emperor Rudolph II in Prague. And, as you suggested, he designed telescopes and a clock. But probably what will most interest you is that he designed a boat that could travel underwater."

"Underwater?" I said in surprise. "The whole boat?"

"The whole boat."

"And what would the purpose of that be?" I said. "How would the passengers breathe?"

"Well, now you're asking me things that my sources do not tell me. But I imagine the purpose could well be military. Think of the advantage of being able to approach an enemy ship unseen."

"Yes," I said, thinking of this possibility. "And did Drebbel actually create such a craft, or just design it?"

"It's said he actually built one and that King James himself travelled along the River Thames in it."

Well, this was a piece of English history I had missed out on.

"Where did you find this information?" I asked.

"Travel books," said Fabrizio. "A Dutch traveller who knew Drebbel in England wrote an account of his meeting with him." He made a vague gesture heavenwards, which I had come to recognise as an indication that he had been reading in his own private library, conserved in the apartment upstairs, rather than in any of the books on sale in the shop. I had come to suspect that the books above our heads greatly outnumbered those that surrounded us.

"I must inform the Missier Grande," I said.

"You think he will listen?" said Lucia, who had succeeded in selling the lachrymose volume to the visitors from the mainland (as far as I had been able to gather, she had succeeded in convincing the young lady, who had then instructed her husband to make the purchase; I imagined that Richardson would have little to teach her about marital relations).

"I can only do my best," I said, my voice already faltering as I imagined the cold eyes of the Missier Grande on me.

"Is such a thing possible?" said Lucia. "A boat that goes underwater?"

Fabrizio spread his arms. "I'm only telling you what I learned from an account by a Dutch traveller who heard of such a thing in England over a century ago. I know no more than that."

"Well," I said, "I'll pass on the information and if they don't listen I'll see if I can get more solid evidence."

"How will you do that?" asked Lucia.

I told them about the floating platform and said that I had agreed with Bepi to investigate it that night. "But maybe I'll have to anticipate things," I said thoughtfully.

"Little point in my telling you to be careful," she said.

"I count on your telling me so," I said, keeping my voice light.

Fabrizio spoke up at this point. "Sior Alvise," he said, "let me join my voice to my daughter's. Do nothing foolish."

"Thank you, both of you," I said, quite seriously now. "I do appreciate your concern. I really am going to do nothing dangerous; I'm just going to see what is happening on that platform – in the full light of day, what's more."

I left the shop feeling absurdly heartened by their words of concern. It was good to know they cared. And I had to acknowledge it: it was especially good to know that Lucia cared. There was so often that touch of irony in her voice; I could never tell how seriously she took me. All I knew for sure was that she did not greatly approve of my line of business. It was not likely that she would consider my having become an unofficial *sbirro* as much of an improvement. But at least it seemed that she cared enough about me not to wish to read of my body having been fished up from a canal the following morning.

I should propose marriage to her at once, I said to myself. Ironically, of course. And then, less ironically, I found myself wondering whether it was likely that Sior Fabrizio would consider a semi-*sbirro* a suitable match for his daughter.

Once I had started this line of speculation I realised that I was not going to be able to stop it. Lucia was on my mind. And if I heard a sentimental enough song I would probably have to admit she was in my heart too.

Very helpful thoughts, I told myself. Just what I needed to be doing at this point in Venice's history.

I walked to Saint Mark's Square, scarcely noticing the jostling crowds this time. They had simply become the element through which I had to make my way, just as a fish has to move through water.

I found the door to the Missier Grande's offices locked, however, and there was, of course, no indication of any alternative address to which informants and confidential agents could apply. I thought of trying my luck at the Doge's palace, but realised that on a day like this it would be very difficult to gain an audience with anyone of any importance. When Venice gives itself up to pleasure it does so thoroughly and wholeheartedly.

So I made my way pensively towards the Riva, possibly the only person in the whole crowd not enjoying the music and the spectacle. Perhaps I should have equipped myself with a plague mask and a bell to mark myself off all the more clearly.

I called in at home, half thinking that I might tidy up the mess there. It might be one way of calming myself. However, the sight of the damaged books and scattered clothes was so dispiriting that I decided it would be easier to go out and save the city from destruction. I put a few possibly useful objects in a satchel and set off again. Down in the *magazen* I took a glass of wine from Giovanna, who was too busy with the mainland visitors to be her usual motherly self (which was a relief), and a slice of sausage from the *luganegher*, and then set off eastwards.

It was with some relief that I reached the eastern portions of the Riva, where the crowds began to thin out and the extra breathing space seemed to allow my brain room to develop more consequential lines of reasoning. I could not wait until the evening, when Bepi would be free. I would have to find another way of approaching the platform. I jingled the coins in my pockets. They did not play such a rich and varied medley as they had some days ago but there were still enough of them to have an effect in this less prosperous area of the city, I thought.

I made my way down to the boatyards that looked out on to the lagoon. As I expected, activity had ceased for the Sensa, but amid the overturned boats and the stacked piles of wood there were three boys aged around ten or eleven in ragged clothes playing some elaborate game, which seemed to involve pebbles and mud – mainly the latter. They looked up at me with wary suspicion, clearly expecting me, as a member of the adult world, to tell them to stop whatever they were doing.

"*Bondì, fioi*," I said casually.

They muttered a few surly words of greeting, and then returned to their slimy activities. Apparently the aim of the game was to see how deeply one could thrust a pebble into the mud. This explained the fact that the right arms of all three of them were caked in the stuff up to their elbows.

"Listen," I said, "have any of you visited that platform?" I gestured towards the object moored some twenty metres away.

"They won't let you," said the sharpest-looking of the three, a boy with a red Castello cap and a liberal application of mud around his mouth and eyes, as well as his arms.

"Who won't?"

"Arsenalotti," he said. The other two nodded agreement.

"We tried it once," said the smallest boy, in a very high-pitched eager voice. "And they really thrashed us. We were only going there to dive off it. Half killed us, they did."

"Anyone want to earn a half lira?" I said.

They did not immediately clamour for it, as I had expected them to do. They narrowed their eyes and the sharp-looking boy said: "What do you want?" Castello boys were cautious, it seemed. I should probably learn from them.

"I'd just like one of you to take a message to the man on the platform."

"A message?"

"Yes. Have you got a boat?"

"We can get one, Sior."

"Good. So just row out and tell him that they've found Umbriel and the count on the Giudecca."

"They've found what?"

"Umbriel and the count." I said it very carefully and then got him to repeat it. Then I said: "He must go to the Redentore at once. And show him this." I showed him a scrap of paper on which I had drawn Santa Giustina. I was sure that Gaetano could not read, but he would certainly recognise the saint that Garzoni had elected as a symbol of personal loyalty. The boy stretched out his mud-caked hand and I told him to clean it first. He accepted this as reasonable and dipped his hand into the lagoon water and then shook it dry.

"The lira?" he said.

"First deliver the message," I said.

And that too was clearly considered reasonable. They had good business sense in this part of Castello.

The other two boys clamoured to be part of the expedition. The sharp boy accepted their proposal but said firmly: "I choose what we spend the money on." They nodded. Garzoni himself couldn't have hoped for more loyal henchmen. On the other hand, presumably the sharp one had earned the trust through merit, not fear.

"And what if he asks who gave us the message?" said the leader.

"You tell him another boy brought it to you and he had been given it by someone in town."

He considered this for a few seconds and eventually nodded. "All right, that'll do."

They scampered over to an ancient-looking boat propped up against the wall of the boatyard and proceeded to drag it down to the water. Half a minute later they were heading towards the platform, with the tallest boy standing up and handling the oar in truly professional fashion. I watched until they bumped up against the side and Gaetano emerged to engage in conversation with them. I saw how skilfully the children handled his foreseeable initial reaction of angry and gesticulatory dismissal, remaining just out of reach, while one of them stood up and waved the piece of paper; I could not hear any words but saw Gaetano gradually calm down, listen to what they had to say, accept the piece of paper, scratch his red hair over it and then dismiss them. Even as the boys headed back towards me, Gaetano was unmooring his sandolo.

A couple of minutes later he was rowing doggedly in the direction of the Giudecca. As far as I could tell from this distance, he had no sign of injury from his fall and immersion the previous night. But I had no doubt that he had a keen memory of those who had been responsible for the ignominious episode and an equally keen desire to meet them again in less disadvantaged circumstances. And that perhaps helped to explain the ease with which he had been gulled. Of course, there was also the fact that he was, as Giacomo had suggested, immensely stupid.

"Now, boys," I said, "for another lira you can row me out to the platform. You can leave me there, and when I wave you can come and pick me up again. I'll pay you when we get back, all right?"

They agreed, and two minutes later I was clambering up on to the platform. I told the boys to go back to their game in the boatyard. I did not want to be responsible for anything that might happen should anyone – Garzoni, the brothers, Sartori or any stray arsenalotti – turn up unexpectedly. I told them to keep an eye out and I would wave to them when I wanted to return. They seemed happy enough with this arrangement and rowed back to the boatyard.

I suddenly felt very lonely and exposed.

I made my way to the stage; it occupied the northern half of the platform, with its back to the shore, and looked out over the lagoon. Two staircases rose up to it, one on either end. It was a few feet higher than me and presented an apparently unbroken wooden wall. However, I had seen earlier that there was a doorway a few feet from the western end of the stage; it was from this that Gaetano had emerged. I walked towards it. It had a simple handle, which I turned. The door, of course, did not open.

I would have to use the tool I had brought. I extracted from my satchel the iron bar I had taken from the window shutter in my apartment. It had proved useless at its job there so it might as well earn its keep here.

Knowing what theatrical constructions are like I did not expect the task of forcing the door to be especially difficult, and so it proved. I had to decide whether to attack the lock or the hinges. In the end the lock proved easier, yielding to the superior strength of the bar after a couple of minutes of wrenching and splintering. I put the bar back in the satchel.

I pushed the door open, and stepped into the gloom. I had a tinderbox and candle in my satchel, but enough sunlight came through the open door and filtered through gaps in the planks that formed the ceiling to provide a grey half-light. I just needed to wait for my eyes to grow accustomed to the dimness.

My first impression was of clutter. There were large dark shapes on every side, and they all looked menacing. Gradually the half-light bestowed more definite contours and removed much of the menace; many of the objects were nautical tools, such as oars, furled sails and *forcole*. There were also workbenches and a collection of carpentry tools and some stacks of uncut wood. There were coils of iron chain and hanks of rope. To all of these I attributed non-threatening intentions. It was the large object in the centre of the room that remained menacing even after it had acquired clearly visible outlines.

In shape and posture it was something like an enormous seal. As for size, it was about twice the length of a gondola and the height of a man at its point of maximum elevation, in its very centre. It appeared to be cased entirely in leather and at first I could see no apertures. Eventually I made out a round hole on the side of the craft that I was inspecting, which I presumed was for an oar. The leather around the hole seemed to be loose but I imagined there was some method of pulling it tight from inside the vessel once the oar was in place and thus sealing the hole in waterproof fashion. At the front of the boat protruded two small prong-like instruments like crab claws. I puzzled over these for a while: were they purely ornamental, or were they intended to intimidate, like the dragon prows of Viking ships? But how would that work, if the boat was underwater? Was the intention to scare the fish? I put this problem to one side and studied the upper part of the vessel. On the top of the curved roof was a hatch. I managed to clamber up the side and lift it; it opened without any problems and I peered into the darkness. There was little point in entering, since without a candle I would learn very little, so I closed it again and dropped back down to the floor.

I examined the floor beneath the craft; I could make out the edges of a very broad trapdoor, presumably ready to open and allow the boat to sink into the water.

One thing I could do was sketch what I was seeing. That would provide some sort of starting point when I eventually managed to communicate my discovery to someone in authority. I pulled out my sketchbook and a crayon and positioned myself near the door, so that I would be able to hear any approaching boats.

However, I had failed to take into account my tendency to become totally absorbed when at work with a crayon, pen or brush. I may be a mere dilettante, but when I do take up my instruments I have the total dedication, if not the skill, of the professional artist. And so it was that when my rough sketch was only half complete I suddenly heard voices very close to me, and realised I had failed to pick up the noises that must have preceded them: the swish and scrape of the approaching boat and the scuffling, sloshing sounds of disembarkation.

As soon as I had forced my heart back into its regular position and picked up the sketch from the floor where my startled fingers had dropped it, I looked round for a hiding place. There was really only one, I realised with the dismay of inevitability.

The voices were calling out for Gaetano; they had begun with puzzled tones and were now becoming urgent.

I crammed my sketching material into my satchel and scrambled up the side of the craft. I heaved the hatch open, said a brief prayer and lowered myself in. The floor was not as far down as I had expected, and when I had come to a steady standing position I could still reach up to the hatch, which had a handle on the inside, and lower it shut behind me.

Now I was really in the dark. In so many ways.

I reached out with both hands to steady myself and to explore my new environment. The walls were of rough wood, curving inwards. As I shuffled forward I encountered a bench set crossways, presumably for the rowers. I sat down. It also had the advantage of being close to the oar-hole, through which came a little air and the voices of the new arrivals.

I first recognised the fussy clerical tones of Luca Sartori. "So someone has broken in. I don't think we need fear too much from that. They won't have understood what they saw."

"Gaetano will have to explain his abandonment of his position." This was the quiet voice of nobleman Garzoni. As usual the low tone of his voice only made what he said sound all the more menacing.

"Excellency," came an indistinct growl. That was presumably Gaetano's brother, Giorgio.

"Silence, Giorgio," said Garzoni. "Your brother will speak for himself when he returns."

There came a grunt from Giorgio, whether of assent or of protest it was impossible to tell. However, he said no more.

"Have they stolen anything?" said Garzoni. "Or broken anything?"

"Everything looks all right," said Luca. His voice was alarmingly close. Presumably he was inspecting the submergible boat. I hoped my footprints were not visible. And I hoped even more fervently that he would not decide to inspect the interior as well.

Then I heard his footsteps move away and I released my breath, gratefully and noiselessly.

"What time are they delivering the gunpowder?" asked Garzoni.

"Not till nightfall," said Luca. "We have to be careful."

"I suppose so," said Garzoni. "Soon things will be very different."

"Of course, Excellency."

There was a pause, and then Garzoni spoke musingly. "It seems a pity that such a well-crafted instrument will have such a short life."

"We can make it again," said Luca. "In fact, when we no longer have to make them clandestinely we can make hundreds of them."

"No," said Garzoni. "The greatest advantage of this craft is that it *is* unknown. It must remain so even after tomorrow. Those who made this one swore an oath of secrecy. That will remain binding. If we do make more of them, it will continue to be in secret, unknown to the ordinary workers of the Arsenale."

"Of course, Excellency," said Luca, as if no other possibility had ever crossed his mind.

"Secrecy. Authority. Fear. The three keys to effective government." Garzoni was clearly saying something he had said many times, and Luca's response was yet another automatic "Of course".

"Together with firmly controlled instruments of fear," said Garzoni.

"You mean more submergibles?" said Luca, a little uncertainly.

"I mean the human equivalent, our Varangian guard."

"Ah yes," said Luca.

"They will be under your direct control, of course," said Garzoni, "but I would like to address them before our enterprise begins."

"Of course. They'll be assembling here at dawn."

I was thinking hard. The Varangian Guard: if I remembered rightly, this had been the Byzantine Emperor's personal bodyguard, formed by Vikings. It seemed unlikely that Garzoni had managed to find a troop of Scandinavian warriors in Venice today; presumably this was his way of referring to those arsenalotti who had remained faithful to him. I remembered his admiration for Doge Dandolo, who had taken Constantinople in 1204 and thus more or less assumed the control of the Byzantine Empire, even if he had not taken the title of emperor. The man's ambitions were becoming clearer – and more frightening.

I had certainly heard enough by now to have an alarming, if not immediately believable, story to tell. The problem was how to escape in order to tell it. A sudden dash for it would be foolish, with both Luca and Giorgio around, and possibly armed. I put my eye to the oar-hole. I could only see a small section of the room; fortunately it included the open doorway, where I could see Giorgio standing with his customary idle vigilance. Neither Luca nor Garzoni was in sight.

"I am going to rest for a while," said Garzoni, somewhere to my left. "Please stay vigilant. We can't afford to make any mistakes at this point."

"Of course not, Excellency," said Luca.

Garzoni moved off somewhere, presumably to a seat of some sort. I heard Luca continue to pace nervously. Then I saw him move towards the doorway and talk to Giorgio in a low voice. I could not hear any words.

It was noticeable that none of them chose to pass the time outside in the sunshine. They presumably did not wish to call attention to their presence on the platform. As they were apparently using it as the base for a conspiracy to overthrow the Venetian state this coyness was understandable enough.

Luca moved back into the room, walking to the left and out of my sight. Perhaps he too was going to have a rest. I sat still and prayed for a reassuring sound, like a steady snoring.

Of course, no such noise came. I heard occasional footsteps and some other unidentifiable quiet movements. I imagined him moving around the dark space with his usual fussy precision, as if measuring the room as he walked. Perhaps he was nervous.

I was certainly not feeling calm myself. Among other things my shirt was being transformed into a wet rag pasted to my skin and sweat was trickling down both sides of my cheeks. I would have to get out of this place or faint from heat exhaustion. I preferred to think of it as that, rather than terror.

I tried to distract myself from this physical discomfort by getting a better sense of my surroundings. I began to grope around, making as little noise as possible. Underneath the seat I felt something soft and flabby; it reminded me of the innards of animals. Groping further, I discovered that this flabby material ran around the bottom part of both sides of the boat.

Several minutes passed. Then I heard a grunting noise from Giorgio's direction. I peered out and saw that he was waving to someone out on the water. He looked back inside and made an utterance that probably corresponded to an announcement of his brother's arrival, although no consonants were distinguishable. I heard Luca walking with his quick steady pace across the room towards the door. Then he and Giorgio both walked out into the sunshine.

I guessed I was not going to get a better opportunity. I stood up and pushed the hatch. As I did so the thought came into my mind, together with a sudden sickening surge of terror, that perhaps I would not be able to open it from the inside. Fortunately this proved not to be the case and with just the slightest scraping sound it jerked up and I felt the cooler air brushing my face.

I heaved myself out, still trying to make as little noise as possible. I slid to the side of the hatch and reclosed it as softly as possible.

I peered to my left and saw the small dark shape of nobleman

Garzoni sitting on a rigid chair with his hands on his lap and his head tilted back. In any other circumstance it could have been a touching picture of the frailty of old age.

I could go across and simply brain him with one of the large hammers lying on the nearby workbench; that would solve a lot of problems. Of course, it would create one or two as well.

I did pick up a hammer, but moved swiftly away from Garzoni. Just as I reached the doorway a croaking cry came from behind me. "Stop him!"

Why hadn't I brained him?

I burst out into the sunlight, screwing my eyes against the dazzle, my hammer-wielding arm already raised. To my left I saw the shapes of Luca and Giorgio swivelling round to stare at me; they were close to the southern edge of the platform, presumably greeting Gaetano. Even as I turned to run to the western edge I had a glimpse of Giorgio already lumbering towards me. I dropped the hammer at this point – since my sole aim was flight, it was only a hindrance – and also tore my satchel off, hurling it into the water.

Seconds later I had followed it, in an embarrassing flat flop of a dive. Elegance, however, was hardly my priority. I was a fairly experienced swimmer, but this was the first time I had done it fully clothed. After the first moment's sheer relief at the coolness of the water my next sensation was panic, as I realised just what an impediment water-sogged breeches, shoes and jacket were. There was clearly no time to try to remove any of them. I had already heard another resounding splash as Giorgio followed me. Still, the brevity of the time gap between my immersion and his told me that he had not removed any clothing either, so we were equally impeded.

He, however, had probably twice the muscle-power. By the time I reached the boatyard, where the three boys were staring open-mouthed at me, I could hear his snorting breath just behind me. I scrambled up the muddy slipway and gasped, "I'll pay you later, boys," and ran up the nearest alleyway.

Those few words probably saved me. A few seconds later I heard a fierce protesting grunting noise and I spun round to see Giorgio attempting to get a foothold on the slipway while the three boys pelted him with mud and pebbles. Loyalty to one's employer is obviously another quality of eastern Castello. Those boys would get a lira each, I told myself, if I lived.

Their defensive barrage was not likely to hold him up for long but it was just enough for me to turn a few corners in the warren of alleyways and courtyards and get out of the sight and hearing of my pursuer.

Women in courtyards, busy stringing beads on necklaces, gazed at me in frank amazement. Children in ragged clothes laughed and pointed. I bestowed apologetic and benevolent smiles on all and kept running.

After I had passed the church of Sant'Isepo I put my hand to my hip, as I felt a stitch coming on, and slowed down to an urgent walk. Continuing at the same pace I reached the broad canal of the Arsenale and walked along its fondamenta towards the lion-guarded entrance. There were a number of gondolas and sandolos moving along with me. The great wooden gates into the dockyards themselves were closed but one could sense the activity going on behind them, as the Bucintoro was prepared for its annual excursion.

After the Arsenale the crowds grew thicker and now I felt grateful to them, blessing the inhabitants of Mestre and Dolo and Mira and Mirano who had decided to cross the lagoon and fill the streets of the city with their quaint rustic capes and caps, their coloured ribbons and their baskets of garden produce; it all helped to distract attention from my mud-bespattered, soaking clothes, and their chattering voices and occasional raucous songs drowned out the rhythmic squelch of my shoes.

I reached my own street just as the clamminess of my garb was beginning to make me shiver. I could not wait to tear it off.

Unfortunately Giovanna caught sight of me just as I made for my front door. Although she was holding three tankards in her hand, for a group of Trevigiani who seemed already to have had quite enough to drink, she paused to chat.

"Fallen in the canal?" she said.

"Just a joke with some friends," I said, with a fixed grin to show how very humorous it had been.

"You young people," she said, with an indulgent shake of her head.

"I really have to get changed," I said apologetically.

"I'm sure you do," she said. "Dress up nice for the Sensa, won't you?"

I ran upstairs. No kindly fairy had visited in the last few hours and miraculously restored order. The room was the same disaster area, with the torn books still strewn around the floor, and the black garments that I had worn the previous day adding their extra touch of stygian gloom to the chaos. I stripped off my soaked garments and attempted to dry myself with the only small towel I possessed, which was woefully inadequate to the task. At least I did not have the problem then of choosing what to wear next. My only option was to put back on that funereal garb; I stopped short of the dark wig, however. Instead, I pulled from a drawer a bright red Castello cap which I had bought before I had been able to afford the wig. I had no other shoes, unfortunately, so would just have to continue squelching until the last drop of moisture had been squeezed from the old ones.

I would win no prizes for sartorial elegance but there was no reason why the authorities should refuse to speak to me, I thought, as I headed back down the stairs.

As I stepped out into the street two squat revellers moved towards me. They were wearing masks, and waved their hooded cloaks in vaguely antic movements.

"Looks as though your friends have come to meet you," said Giovanna, with a benevolent smile.

I turned instantly to run back upstairs but the nearer of the revellers grabbed my arm and jerked me back.

"Siora," I shouted, "they're not my friends – they're not –"

"Go on with you," she said, and laughed. "I know you young people."

A gloved hand was put across my mouth as I continued to yell and struggle. The two men – and their lithely coordinated movements, together with their broad bulky shapes, told me they were Giorgio and Gaetano – flanked me and my arms were pinioned behind my back. I felt something prick into my side and total panic seized me. Behind me I could hear Giovanna laughing. However, as I was carried away, with my legs barely touching the ground, I heard her laugh become uneasy and she called out, "What are you doing to him?"

But then they had taken me round the corner. I made one last squirming attempt to free myself and out of the corner of my eye I saw the figure to my right raising his arm. Then there was a crashing blow on my head and blackness swallowed me.

26

I was vomited from the belly of blackness some time later. I had no idea how long it had been. Time and space had become indistinguishable entities in which I spun dizzily, my body and mind pulsing and throbbing, with shafts of pain stabbing repeatedly into my skull. I was aware that a boat had taken me across water, that numerous rough hands had grabbed and jostled and heaved me about, like an inert but pain-receptive sack of coals.

Then I found myself in a familiar place: dark, musty-smelling, gently rocking on water – even though the last sensation could just as easily have been the effect of the pain. A lantern approached me and the light was like another explosion inside my skull; I squeezed my eyes tight and moaned. The light was withdrawn.

A voice spoke: "Can you hear me?"

I said, "Yes." Or at least I attempted to say it. My tongue had apparently been replaced by a slab of uncooked meat, which had no wish to be disturbed. I managed a spray of saliva, I think, but they seemed to take that as assent.

"Have you spoken to anyone about what you saw here?" The voice was Garzoni's. I felt proud of myself for having recognised it.

"Excellency," I attempted to say. And I must have been trying to say it in English, because it became another spattering surge of sibilants.

The question was repeated and I tried again to indicate my awareness of his social status, with no coherent result.

"Lay him on the floor. We will have to wait until he recovers sufficiently to question him properly."

I found myself stretched out on the wooden floor, next to the wall, with a folded cloak underneath my head. I presume this solicitude was connected with the need to extrapolate information from me, which they would be unable to do if I died on them. I was lying on my left side, since it was the right side of my head that had received the blow.

Time passed. I closed my eyes, paying grateful homage to Pluto for the gift of darkness. However, even with my eyelids lowered a display of pyrotechnical effects seemed to be constantly manifesting itself before me, and I began to wish for simple oblivion. This did not come but I did fade in and out of consciousness; occasionally I was aware of footsteps and lamplight approaching and of people looming over me. I also grew aware that the darkness out of which these light-bearing figures emerged had grown thicker. Night had come on.

The throbbing had grown less intense and I found I could open my eyes and even contemplate the distant lantern-light without feeling as though it were ablaze inside my head. I did not yet care to do anything too rash, like moving my head. That would have to come with time. Perhaps by Christmas, if things proceeded well . . .

The thought of Christmas reminded me that there was some other festivity approaching. Easter? Shrove Tuesday? The Feast of Saint Mark? The Salute? The Redentore? No shortage of holidays in Venice.

The Sensa . . . that was it. Charming festival. All those boats. The splendid Bucintoro. The Doge and the wedding ceremony . . . The submergible boat . . .

The what? That was not right.

No, that was not part of it. But it was connected somehow . . . I must think.

A few more fireworks scattered spangled light in my skull as my brain did its best to focus on this intrusive presence.

Yes. I had seen this boat. I had even climbed inside it. Maybe I was in it right now and that was why things were so strange and fluctuating.

No. That had been earlier. Before the explosion.

Explosion. Gunpowder.

Someone was waiting for gunpowder. To blow up my brain again. No. To put inside the submergible boat.

Yes. It was a boat for the Sensa. And it was going to be filled with explosive. And then the Varangian Guards were going to take over.

The Varangian Guards? Where did they come in? Intriguing name . . .

"Oh my God," I said. I think my tongue even formed the words, even if they did not emerge audibly from my lips.

It was all coming together. The submergible boat was going to be used to blow up the Bucintoro. That was the plan.

As simple and as spectacular and as murderous as that.

I got no satisfaction from having put these scattered fragments of knowledge together, just a sudden sickening sense of urgency and panic. I was the only person who knew about this conspiracy and I had just had my head blown to pieces and replaced with a jar of maggots.

Or maybe not. I gently tried moving my head to left and right and found that it functioned as a head. I could even use my eyes to see where I was and who was there with me.

I was underneath the stage on the floating platform where the submergible boat was concealed and with me were Nobleman Garzoni (sitting in a chair near the aforementioned boat and gazing into the darkness, presumably dreaming of unlimited power), Luca Sartori (pacing up and down) and the two brothers, sitting on a bench by the door. There was a lantern on the table near Garzoni's chair. It provided the only light.

Given that my head was apparently still attached to my body, maybe I could make a sudden dash for freedom. Well, if not a dash, a steady crawl.

I attempted to move my legs – and was unable to do so.

The panicky thought that I was paralysed was swiftly dismissed, to my great relief, as I realised that there was a constricting force of some sort around my lower ankle. Just the left one, I realised after another experimental wriggle. I lifted my head a few inches (by no means as easy as it sounds) and peered down my body; despite the darkness I thought I could make out a chain, snaking away from my ankle to a hook in the wall.

I was going to have to think very, very hard about all this. Such a pity my brain had been blown up. I winced. Why these constant images of explosions?

Unfortunately, the answer to that was all too easy. Less so, the answer to the question of how to prevent the explosions – both from coming to my mind and from taking place. But I had to persist. My mind was the only thing that I could rely on. My shattered mind. I would have to piece it together again, just as I would have to piece together all I had learned so far.

Normally I liked to walk around when thinking hard about

problems. This time I was denied that option and so I had to find a substitute. I must walk up and down mentally: pace up and down past all the facts I had learned, and scrutinise them thoroughly, from all angles . . . including all I had learned about the various participants in this whole affair, and their likely role.

I do not know how long I spent in this mental activity. I know that I saw that Garzoni had fallen asleep in his chair and that Luca stood gazing down at him. The lamplight was behind him so I could not see the expression on his face, but there was something supercilious and almost proprietorial in his stance as he stood over the older man. It suggested quite a different relationship from the one I had presumed to exist between the two of them. One can learn a good deal from the way one person looks at another when the person observed is oblivious of the fact.

Some time later there was a stir of movement at the door.

Gaetano and Giorgio had seen something outside and they summoned Luca, who picked up the lantern and walked briskly towards them. I could hear the sound of a boat bumping up against the platform. All three men walked out into the open air. Now was the chance for me to –

I did not know what. To inspect my bonds perhaps. I managed to crook my body and stretch one hand down to my foot.

There was a shackle around my left ankle, not so tight as to chafe me but not loose enough for me to remove it without a key. The chain that snaked from it to the wall was about ten feet in length.

I heard noises of strained physical activity – heaving, scraping and grunting – together with a murmur of voices. Then lantern-light approached the doorway, together with heavy footsteps. Gaetano and Giorgio came in carrying stout barrels, their arms wrapped around them and their bodies leaning back with the weight. Luca followed close behind with the lantern.

They set the barrels down on the ground near a table some fifteen feet from me. Garzoni gave a twitch in his chair but did not awaken.

I saw Lucas's head turning in my direction and closed my eyes just in time. I saw no advantage in establishing communication – at least not until I had worked out what my strategy might be. That could be a very long way off.

It seemed the three men had enough to occupy themselves with in any case. Even without opening my eyes I could follow most of their movements for the next couple of hours. They continued to busy themselves in and around the submergible. I could hear buckets of water being carried to and fro, and when I half opened my eyes I saw Giorgio standing by the side of the craft and handing a bucket up to Gaetano, who was leaning out of the hatch at the top of the craft to receive it. The boat seemed to be very thirsty.

The heavy barrels they had brought in from outside remained where they were on the floor; presumably they would be the last thing they loaded, so as to avoid any dangerous mishandling.

It had grown light outside, I realised, although the oil lamp remained alight on the table a few paces from where I lay.

Luca glanced towards me and clearly realised that I was conscious again. He approached.

"Can you hear me?" he said in a low voice.

"I need water," I said. That was what I intended to say; it's possible that the only distinct word was the last one. I propped myself up on my elbow; I felt slightly less vulnerable in that position.

"We brought you here just to ask if you have spoken to anyone. I think it's clear by now that you haven't or they would have found us by now. There really is no need to keep you." As usual his tone was precise and businesslike.

"Thanks. I'll go then," I croaked.

"No need to keep you alive," he said, spelling it out very carefully for me. "Gaetano will be very happy to kill you."

"His Excellency will wish to speak to me," I said, as loudly and distinctly as I could. It was still a spluttering croak but it seemed to work. I saw Garzoni twitch in his chair again. "Excellency!"

Garzoni sat up and turned in my direction. He was instantly alert. There was no senile grogginess or confusion. He knew where he was and why he was there. And he knew why I was there. A look of irritation flickered over Luca's face, but only for an instant; then he became his usual deferential self.

Garzoni rose and moved towards me. "Have you recovered sufficiently?"

"For what?" I said. I needed to get myself into a more suitable position. I heaved myself up and sat with my back against the wall. My head started throbbing again at the movement but the pain faded as soon as I had settled back.

"For our questions."

"I think so. I need water."

Garzoni bade Gaetano, who was standing by the submergible with an empty bucket, bring me a mug of wine. They had not brought any drinking water with them, it seemed. Gaetano obeyed, but from the expression on his face it was clear that there were many other things he would rather do to me.

The wine proved restorative. Against my instincts and my desires, however, I restrained myself to a few sips. I needed all my wits about me. I put the mug down beside me, still half full.

"So, Signor Umbriel," Garzoni said, pronouncing the name sarcastically, "it seems you were not what you claimed to be."

"My name is not Umbriel," I admitted.

"Why the lie?"

"It was expedient," I said. I felt quite pleased with myself; if I could produce a word like that without drowning myself in spittle then perhaps I was going to be able to manoeuvre my way through this very tricky conversation.

"Clearly," he said. "But for what purpose?"

"To gain an audience with you," I said, as if this were obvious.

"And why was your real name not good enough?"

"I feared that you might not be so welcoming to a mere *cicerone* from Castello."

He did not attempt to deny the well-founded nature of my fear. "And that is all you are?"

"Excellency," I said, "you saw what I can do. My powers are undeniable."

"I saw that you have access to certain knowledge. But what good is that if you do not have the courage to put it to good use?"

"Excellency, I will admit that I was afraid."

"And I trust you are even more afraid now," he said.

"Have no doubt of it," I said truthfully.

"You failed the test."

"I failed that one. It was unexpected."

"I do not usually allow second chances," he said. "Do I, Luca?"

"No, Excellency," Luca said, with intense satisfaction. "Never."

"Excellency," I said, "you see that I am still drawn to your circle of power. Why else am I here?"

"That is what I wish to know. How did you know to come here?"

"As I said to you in your palace, the places associated with you are charged with great spiritual energy. I could feel the pull."

"Did you speak to anyone about what happened in the palace?" he said.

They were all waiting to hear my answer. Until that moment I had not decided on an answer. The only reason to answer affirmatively would be if I thought that the fear of being arrested would make them give up their plans. While that might be true for Luca, perhaps, it certainly did not apply to Garzoni himself, who by now had too fully committed himself. Whatever happened he was not going to apologise meekly to the Doge and go back to his cabalistic games in the privacy of his palace.

And so, on the strength of that argument, I decided to answer in the negative and see where that would take me.

"No, Excellency."

I sensed rather than heard a general expulsion of breath. There could be no possible reason for me to lie about this, I imagine they were all thinking.

"Excellency, there is no reason to keep this man alive," said Luca. He sounded too eager, which was unusual for him.

Garzoni at once frowned. "That is for me to decide."

"Of course," Luca said. It sounded as though he was on the point of adding a but . . . and then thought better of it.

"Excellency," I said, and was surprised that I managed to say it not only without spluttering but also without a tremor, "I can make a forecast, one that you cannot afford to ignore."

"Go on," he said.

"This is not a small matter, Excellency," I said. "You will need to listen most attentively. I believe I know your plans – but I also see a potential flaw."

"'There are always potential flaws," he said, "for any man who dares something truly extraordinary. But there comes a point when one has to believe that destiny is on one's side and take the necessary risk. That moment has come for me – and for Venice."

I must be careful not to sound too damping or I would get no hearing. This was going to be the performance of my life – quite literally. The two little shows I had put on in the palace were mere conjuring tricks by comparison. I felt the throbbing in my head returning but I forced myself to ignore it.

"Excellency, this is a flaw that can be eradicated, once it has been identified. It would be absurd to fail out of an excess of pride."

His face grew dark and I wondered if I had gone too far. I could tell that Luca thought so and was almost rubbing his hands in glee. But Garzoni said quietly: "Go on."

"You will need to listen to me to the end," I said.

"Go on," he said again.

At that moment Gaetano gave a grunt from the doorway. "*Eccoli,*" he said. Here they are.

Luca and Garzoni at once turned towards him. These must be the arsenalotti: the Varangian guard.

Garzoni said: "Your story will have to wait. I must greet these men."

He gathered his cloak around him and went towards the sunlight. Luca gave me a grim look as he followed him out but said nothing; he presumably thought that a little mime of my imminent strangulation would be too vulgar.

I sat back, feeling absurdly relieved. Or perhaps it was not so absurd: I needed the pause to gather my forces. My heart was beating hard, my head was throbbing and I could feel my shirt growing damp with sweat again. How could anyone ever envy the life of an actor?

I listened hard to what was happening outside. I heard Luca's voice, suddenly brisk and firm, issuing orders. This must be the part of the work he most enjoyed. There was clearly a whole troop of men out there, who had presumably disembarked from a barge of some sort. I could hear them clumping on the planks, and the platform was swaying slightly to their footsteps. As Luca continued to issue orders their footsteps became regimented. They mounted the two staircases at either side of the stage and suddenly their marching feet were above my head.

A minute or so later I heard Garzoni's voice addressing them. I could only catch occasional words: "historical moment ... transform the city ... glory ... authority ... authority [again] ... no pity ... instruments of fear ..."

So those were not just abstract concepts. He meant them quite literally – and was making it clear to these men that he meant them.

There were no other voices – or, at least, there were no other voices from above me. I could now hear a general human clamour from the direction of the city. The lagoon was clearly filling up with crafts of all sorts. Musicians were trying out their instruments – instruments of pleasure, I thought wistfully. I could hear distant trumpets and pipes. Ragged choruses from the various guilds and schools. People just shouting. Everywhere a great desire to enjoy the day.

Everywhere except on this platform.

Garzoni was clearly getting carried away now. It was probably a long time since he had been able to make a full-length speech to a whole troop of men. He was making the most of it. I could hear the occasional shuffle of feet. These were men whose military discipline was perhaps a little rusty.

After a crescendo of steadily rising sentences, his voice came to a sudden climactic pitch. I heard the words "death or glory" and guessed that this must be the final choice he was offering them. There followed a loud but ragged cheer. They seemed to like their chances. After this his short, light footsteps came down the eastern staircase first, followed by Luca's quick precise pacing. Then there was the general tramping of the men as they re-descended both staircases.

At this point the confused rumbling of voices, footsteps, splashing and scraping suggested that the men were re-embarking. I imagined there was a prominent place left on the boat for Nobleman Garzoni and his eager follower Luca Sartori.

A minute later the two men came back into the room, together with Gaetano and Giorgio.

"Prepare the boat," said Garzoni to Gaetano and Giorgio.

"Are you going to listen to me?" I said.

"Yes. But the preparations will go ahead."

"Would you please untie me?"

"That is not necessary. Your mouth is not fettered, is it?"

I had not really hoped I would be released but I had thought it worth trying. "I would like to stand up, at least," I said. "And a little freedom to move my legs."

"I'm sure your chain will not impede you."

I slowly got to my feet. The room swayed as I did so and everything became blurry, with the exception of the oil lamp on the table, which flared with a fierce intensity. I closed my eyes and leaned against the wall.

"Well?" said Garzoni.

"One moment," I said hoarsely. Then I gathered my thoughts, my willpower and whatever residue of courage I still had. "Excellency, I can see your intention. You wish to do what Doge Falier failed to do."

"That is so," he said calmly.

"You are going to destroy the city's entire ruling class in one mighty conflagration, just as Doge Falier intended to do with the sword."

As I was speaking Gaetano and Giorgio were clambering up on to the submergible.

"And to do this you have ordered the creation of an entirely new kind of craft – new to Venice, that is. You first heard of it in England, during your stay there many years ago."

"You are well informed."

"People have said you brought in few innovations at the Arsenale in terms of ship-building design."

He gave a contemptuous laugh. "All they wanted were better boats for commerce. Or imitations of English and Spanish galleons. What use to us are ships designed for the Atlantic Ocean?"

"You proposed something that was truly revolutionary, that could truly create fear, and it was dismissed as a fantasy." I was working by intuition now, but I felt fairly confident I was on the right lines. The fact that the room was still swaying around me was actually helpful; in these unreal circumstances bold speculation seemed the reasonable course of action. "And so you decided that this craft should remain your secret."

"Young man, I'm beginning to suspect you have inside information."

"Call it what you will," I said. "Inside information. Insight. Intuition. I know what I know but I do not always know how I know it."

"Continue," he said.

I glanced at Luca. He was gazing quite impassively at me, but I thought I spotted a tremor at the corner of his lips. Gaetano and Giorgio continued their preparation of the vessel quite unperturbed. Gaetano had climbed into it and Giorgio was leaning over and handing him a lantern.

I went on: "And for this purpose you needed an inner circle of people you could trust entirely – people who would never reveal the secret. People who would take the oath to Santa Giustina."

"That is correct. No venture can ever succeed without the undying loyalty of an inner core of believers."

"Given your high rank, your social position, you required at least one entirely trustworthy subordinate, who could act as your delegate in all administrative matters, who knew the employees of the Arsenale and who could choose the most trustworthy of them as your followers. A man who had been with you through your career at the Arsenale, of great organisational skills, whom you trusted implicitly." I did not look at Luca as I said all this but Garzoni did and I followed his eyes. Luca was just gazing at me, his eyes slightly narrowed in his round bland face.

I went on: "He it was who chose the carpenters who could make the submergible boat. As the man in charge of all ceremonial matters at the Arsenale, he could set up this floating platform and use this under-stage area as a secret workshop."

"So far all you say has been correct," said Garzoni. "When are you going to reveal this flaw?"

"I have already done so," I said.

"Explain yourself."

I swallowed. I was now coming to the dangerous part. "Luca Sartori is the flaw in your scheme."

Luca took a step towards me. Garzoni barked: "Stay there." Then he turned to me. "Explain what you mean."

"I will do so, but I require that you listen to me to the end. Do not allow Luca to cut me off."

"Luca will do nothing without my permission," he said grimly.

"Excellency," said Luca, clearly struggling to keep his voice calm, "this man is a dangerous liar, who will say anything to –"

"Excellency," said I, "so far I have spoken nothing but the truth. I only require that you listen to me for another minute. Then you can take your own decision."

"Go on." His voice was quiet but firm.

I noticed that Gaetano and Giorgio had stopped work too. Giorgio was standing by the craft and Gaetano had hoisted himself up and was sitting on the hatch, with his legs dangling down into it.

"First of all," I said, "let me just make sure that I've understood how today's enterprise will work. The submergible boat will be launched through a hatch in the platform here. It will sink because the bladders underneath the seat and along the sides of the craft are now filled with water."

There was a stir among those listening. For the first time they took in the fact that I had inspected the interior of the craft.

"At the opportune moment Gaetano and Giorgio are going to row the boat in the direction of the Bucintoro. They will have to do this blindly, simply relying on a mathematical calculation of the number of strokes required to reach it."

The silence that greeted this suggested that I had guessed correctly.

"When they reach the Bucintoro they are presumably going to attach the submergible to it in some fashion." I was imagining the purpose of those claw-like protuberances at the front of the boat.

"There are two extendable clamps that will seize hold of the keel, operated from inside the craft," said Garzoni. He had clearly studied the technical details of all this carefully. "It's possible that those on board the Bucintoro will notice something, but they won't have time to do anything about it."

"Gaetano and Giorgio will then ignite the fuse to the barrels of gunpowder," I said. "Now I am presuming that, loyal servants though they may be, they are not intending to immolate themselves for the cause."

"There is a hatch in the floor of the craft by which they can leave it."

"Won't that simply flood the boat? And so put out the fuse?"

"There is a sealed chamber beneath the floor of the boat. They enter that, close the hatch above them and then open the exterior one.

We have tried it and it works. If the correct procedure is followed the water does not enter the inner chamber."

"I see," I said. "So at that point the Bucintoro will explode, killing the Doge and all the most important luminaries of the Venetian state."

"It will be a glorious moment," said Garzoni, his eyes gleaming with anticipatory joy.

"And you, Excellency, will be near by in a boat rowed by your loyal arsenalotti, and amid the ensuing panic you will proclaim yourself the new ruler of the city."

Garzoni picked up a large pistol from the table. "This will be my immediate symbol of rule," he said. "And I will use it fearlessly should there be any opposition. As will my followers, all of whom are also armed. But the people will already be in a suitable state of fear and so I anticipate little resistance. They will, in fact, no doubt welcome a strong ruler."

"Everything seems perfectly planned," I said.

"It is. And so the flaw you indicated . . ."

"Ah yes. Luca Sartori has been a most loyal servant in every way," I said.

"He has."

"His virtues have always been those of the diligent clerk – but a clerk with a gift for spectacle and an understanding of how to make a good impression."

"What are you insinuating?" said Garzoni. Luca himself merely breathed hard and heavily.

"Excellency," I said, "I have been inside your palace. I have even been in your kitchen. The kitchen presents a gleaming outward appearance. But if you open the cupboards you will find rotting food, filthy implements and maggots."

"What does that matter?" Luca said, unable to restrain himself.

"Silence," said Garzoni. And then to me: "What do you mean?"

"Luca Sartori is a man of spectacle," I said. "He also knew how to impress foreign visitors to the Arsenale: employees marching in step, polished boots and belts . . . but no new ships, no innovations. With the exception of the secret weapon for the inner circle."

"Spectacle has its role too," said Garzoni. "The people need outward signs of power."

"But here there are *only* the outward signs. There is no power. I have been inside that machine," I said, waving towards the sinister seal-shaped vessel. "Again, it looks very impressive from the outside. Menacing even. But . . ." I paused.

"But what?" said Garzoni. "What you are saying makes no sense. That machine is not supposed to be seen. That is the paradox of its power." He clearly liked this alliterative phrase and I got the impression he was even contemplating repeating it. I cut him short.

"Oh, but it is, Excellency. It is supposed to be seen." I paused again. "By you."

"The man is raving," said Luca furiously. "Don't listen to him."

"Silence!" Garzoni's tone was peremptory.

"Excellency, you have put almost unlimited power into the hands of this man. At the Arsenale he was just another functionary from the citizen class. Diligent, respectful, respectable. You turned him into a man who could decide the fate of others. He it was who decided who belonged to your inner circle and who must remain outside. And when you left the Arsenale he came with you and took full charge of your palace. Palazzo Garzoni. A splendid building on the Grand Canal of Venice. Which belonged to the Garzoni family, who fought in the battle of Lepanto. Who captured Constantinople."

"I know what my palace is and what my family is," said Garzoni quietly and deliberately.

"Well, to all intents and purposes it now belongs to a man of the citizen class who comes from eastern Castello."

"Belongs to him?" said Garzoni, in an offended and incredulous tone.

"How dare you –" began Luca.

"Silence," said Garzoni. "I will handle this. What do you mean?" he said to me.

"I'm sure that if you study the deeds and legal documents you will find that it will pass to him on your demise. But even if that were not the case, he has been treating your property as if it were his for a long time now. Selling the family paintings."

"That was on my authority," said Garzoni. "Our enterprise needs funding and frivolous paintings of pagan deities are of no concern to me."

"Maybe not," I said, "but it would be interesting to see just where all the money has gone. Undoubtedly some of it has gone to pay those actors outside, but certainly not all."

"Actors? What do you mean?"

"Oh, they're arsenalotti, of course. And probably they feel a certain loyalty to you. But they're Venetians. And Venetians are not by nature subversive. Luca Sartori is not a subversive man. His instinct is always to obey. He has, indeed, always obeyed you. Just think of the history of this city. Apart from Marin Falier, the last time the Venetians tried to overthrow their government was in 1310, under Bajamonte Tiepolo. And on that occasion the handful of insurgents were put to flight by an old woman with a stone mortar. The Venetians have no rebellious urge. They may grumble about taxes and tell cosily frightening stories about the Inquisitors and the Ten, but they don't want to overthrow them."

"I am going to change all that," said Garzoni in a grim menacing tone.

"And these men you have chosen are all happy to tell you that they agree. They go along with you. Who are they to disagree with a Venetian nobleman? And one who used to be their commander? But they don't mean it. And you only need to look carefully at that craft they have built for you to realise it." Again I gestured at the submergible.

"What about it?"

"It won't work," I said. "It is built to impress you but not to sail underwater. For months, years perhaps, you have talked about this heroic enterprise, and Luca Sartori realised there was no way to discourage you from it."

"Of course not."

"And so he had to convince you that he was with you, heart and soul. He got the best of the loyal followers at the Arsenale to make this vessel for you to admire. They convinced you that it would work underwater, in some carefully controlled experiment, presumably at night." I looked at him as I said this and his lack of reaction persuaded me I had guessed correctly. "And then the plans were made for today. All those men in the large boat outside are here to cheer you, to testify to their loyalty . . . But when the Bucintoro fails to explode they will commiserate with you and then happily go off home, back to their wives and families. After all, they're arsenalotti, employed by the Venetian state, with regular wages. And the men rowing the Bucintoro are their own colleagues, fellow arsenalotti –"

"Those men are the servile followers of the new commanders at the Arsenale: wretches who showed no loyalty to me."

"Despicable people, no doubt. But your loyal followers none the less work alongside these wretches every day. Even if they have their disagreements, they are likely to have qualms about seeing them all murdered in an instant. Think of it, your Excellency."

When I stopped for a moment he was uncharacteristically silent. It was quite probable that the thought of such qualms on the part of his followers had never crossed his mind. Luca said, "Excellency . . ." Garzoni merely put up his hand and Luca fell silent too.

I went on: "As I say, I've seen the interior of that contraption. The wood is rough, the oar-holes are jagged and I'm sure will not remain waterproof for long, and it will be impossible to control the direction they row in. I am sure too, that those metal claws are impossible to operate from inside the boat. But in any case I doubt they will get as far as the Bucintoro. I think your two loyal servants will simply suffocate." I paused. "For Gaetano and Giorgio are entirely loyal, I'm sure of that."

There came a grunt from the two men. I was not sure how much they had followed of all I had said but it was clear they were gratified, or at least relieved, to hear they were not included among the traitors.

I wondered whether I should add that I knew that they had loyally carried out the murders required by his campaign of preparatory terror, but decided there was no reason to raise that matter. That would seriously compromise my chances of survival.

I went on: "I suspect that the craft will not even move successfully away from the platform. Gaetano and Giorgio will simply suffocate conveniently close to home. That will make it all the easier for all traces of this episode to be concealed afterwards."

Garzoni spoke at last. His voice was somehow both distant and bitter. "What proof can you offer for all of this?"

Now came the biggest gamble of all. I had to pray that I was right in this last guess of mine. If I was not, it would put an end to the whole thing – for all of us.

"I can offer you some immediate evidence," I said. I stretched my hand out and grabbed the oil lamp that stood on the table. I had calculated correctly and I could just reach it. At once, I hurled it straight at the nearer of the two barrels, which were both still standing where Gaetano and Giorgio had set them down.

Garzoni gave a shrill cry of alarm and a strange whimpering noise came from Gaetano and Giorgio.

The lamp shattered, spraying its oil, and instantly the flame enveloped the top of the barrel. I looked at Luca and saw he had not moved. I had guessed correctly.

There was a cracking sound as the wood caught fire and then the flames settled down to a steady but undramatic crackling.

"What is it?" I said to Luca. "Pepper? Sawdust?"

He let out an enraged snarl in which no words were distinctly audible and suddenly snatched one of the pistols from the table and aimed it directly at me. I must have made some sound myself but the next noise I heard was a loud bang, which resounded as I fell backwards. By the time I lay sprawling on the ground I realised I had not in fact been hit. But the sudden movement had set my head throbbing and aching again, and it took me some seconds to scrabble to a sitting position.

Then I saw that Luca was lying on the ground, with a dark pool widening around his head. Garzoni was holding a smoking pistol.

I spoke in an uncertain voice: "Thank you."

"I did not do it for you," he said. His voice was still strangely remote.

"Perhaps we had better put the fire out," I said.

"No," he said. "It's better as it is."

There were footsteps on the platform outside and two men peered in. "Everything all right, Excellency?"

"No. Your treacherous master is dead. You can go back to your –" I think he was on the point of saying "wives and children", but I'm sure he did not want to repeat my exact words, and so after a pause he said, "your comfortable lives."

"Excellency?" said the nearer man, who had now seen the dead body, and was clearly alarmed.

"It's over! The whole farce is finished. Be off with you!" He waved the gun at them.

That persuaded them and they ran off. Seconds later we heard a hubbub of alarmed voices and then the sounds of the boat pushing off and away.

"Cowards. Traitors." He did not yell the words, just uttered them as simple statements of fact. With one last remaining impulse of curiosity, he turned to me and asked: "How did you know about the barrels?"

"Excellency, I saw Luca come in after Gaetano and Giorgio, holding the lantern right next to the barrel. I knew how unlikely it was that a man like Luca would be so careless with gunpowder."

"Very well." He was reloading his gun as he spoke, which did not reassure me. Meanwhile the barrel had settled down into a steady blaze. A little tongue of flame set out across the wooden floor, following a trail of oil drops, and reached the table.

"Gaetano, Giorgio," he said.

The two men lumbered forward. Their faces looked grim. Perhaps they had never liked Luca, but they had respected his orders. They probably respected any orders that were clear and simple.

And now Garzoni gave such orders. "Prepare the gondola."

"Where are you going?" I said.

"We may not be able to blow the Bucintoro up but we can do some damage with these things." He indicated his pistol and then bent down and picked up the one lying by Luca's body. "Since it seems the end has come for me, I will make it a glorious one. I will kill the Doge." He said this as mere matter of fact. He added: "I always had a contingency plan in reserve."

"Will you release me before you go?" I said. I was looking at the table, which was now ablaze.

"I'm afraid not," he said. He called to the brothers, just before they passed out into the open air: "Gaetano, Giorgio, set fire to the submergible." They paused, looking at each other uncertainly; clearly the arrival of a new order before the previous one had been carried out added unwelcome complications to their lives. However, after a moment of agonising mental struggle they turned round and headed towards the submergible.

Garzoni looked straight at me. "You opened my eyes to the treachery of my lieutenant. That does not make me love you. I'm keeping my bullets for those on board the Bucintoro, otherwise you would share Luca's fate. However, you will certainly now share the fate of his dead body – and that of his false invention. No doubt Luca often laughed to himself at my expense. I won't allow anyone else to do so."

He looked around, as if to see whether there were any other weapons he could use. Then he continued: "Fire will accomplish that for me. I just wish I could apply it to the whole city."

I did not attempt to plead again. The only likely result, I thought, would be his instructing Gaetano or Giorgio to finish me off; they would have no trouble in doing so without the waste of a precious bullet.

Gaetano, meanwhile, had carried a blazing stave from the barrel over to the submergible. Giorgio had torn Luca's cape from his body and he dipped it into his brother's flame. Then he reached up the side of the boat and launched the flaring object into the hatch. With this team effort the whole craft began to crackle. I could already feel the heat on my own body.

The two large men hurried away from the fire and joined their master at the door to the room. Before they passed through it Garzoni paused. "We might as well make sure of things. Gaetano and Giorgio, put him into the submergible."

27

I think I screamed. The next few seconds were a confused and painful blur of sights and sensations. Gaetano came over and simply wrenched from the wall the hook to which the chain was attached while Giorgio picked me up. I did my best to resist but my best was definitely inadequate. Within ten seconds I had been hoisted up, carried like a sack of coal and dropped feet first into the hatch of the blazing boat. If I had not been in a weakened condition perhaps it would have taken them as many as fifteen seconds.

I landed on top of the fiery remnants of Luca's cape. My shoes, still water-logged, proved effective in stamping out the final sparks, which fortunately had not succeeded yet in setting fire to any of the interior fittings of the craft. But I could already see flames in the forward section of the boat and the noise and heat were tremendous.

I remembered the bladders filled with water along the sides of the boat and attempted to burst the nearest one, using the end of my chain. I managed to penetrate its skin and the water spurted out but at once dribbled away ineffectually into the floor. It was clearly going to be inadequate against the flames that had gripped the upper portions of the boat.

I reached up and gripped the edges of the hatch and tried to hoist myself out. But my arms refused to do my bidding; it was as if my muscles had simply been replaced with jelly. The very effort caused my mind to swim. I did the only thing I could and screamed for help.

The flames were now surging towards me and as I opened my mouth again for another last scream smoke filled my lungs. I was about to drop to the floor, in the hope that the smoke would smother me before the flames reached me, when I thought I heard a voice.

"Alvise?" it seemed to say.

Somehow I found the lung power and the energy for another scream. "Here!"

A familiar and very welcome face appeared in the hatch above me, shining in the flamelight.

"Bepi!" I reached up to him.

Somehow, with the combined forces of a final desperate effort on my part and a vigorous tug on Bepi's, I found myself hoisted from the blazing pit. Bepi then leaped down to the ground while I simply rolled down the side of the boat, through the flames.

I lay on the floor for a second or two until Bepi jerked me to my feet.

"Quickly," he said. "The whole place is going to collapse."

There were more flames than walls now, and the cracking sounds of beams giving way behind and ahead of us indicated that he was not exaggerating. I staggered after him, curiously aware of the clanking sound of the chain dragging behind me at my ankle.

We plunged through the doorway and I gasped with a mixture of relief and awe and disbelief as I saw the blue sky above me and felt the cool morning air around me.

"This way," said Bepi, pulling me to the right, where I saw his gondola bobbing innocently alongside the platform.

I grew gradually aware of other sights and sounds. The lagoon was thronged with colourful vessels, of all shapes and sizes. To the west of us, in the direction of the Piazza, the Bucintoro took pride of place, its golden decorations glittering in the sunlight, its countless red oars moving in perfect synchrony like stiff but graceful wings. The great red and gold banner of the republic streamed in the wind above it. The sound of triumphal trumpets became audible over the crackling of the flames behind us.

"My God," said Bepi, "you look terrible." We were standing beside the gondola and he at last had the time to take a good look at me.

"But better than I would have done if you . . ." I could not finish the sentence; it was the wrong moment to have embarked upon such a complex grammatical structure. I concluded with a simple "Thank you".

"My pleasure," he said. "What have you been doing? What have *they* been doing?"

"Bepi," I said with sudden urgency, "there's no time. We have to get after them."

"Who? The old man and the two *bravi?*"

"Yes, them. Did you see where they went?"

He pointed to the other side of the platform. "They had a boat over there."

There was no sign of them. They had disappeared amid the bobbing masses of other gondolas, barges, sandolos and sailboats; everywhere we looked were fluttering pennants, gilded statues, and liveried oarsmen. To the right I saw a large boat with about thirty men in uniform heading back towards the Arsenale. Everyone else, as far as I could see, was moving in the direction of the Lido.

"They're heading for the Bucintoro," I said. "He has a gun – no, several guns – and he intends to shoot the Doge."

Bepi did not seem over-surprised. However, he demurred. "I don't think so. They set off the opposite way, towards the Lido."

I turned and stared in that direction. There were fewer boats in that stretch of water but still enough for a single gondola to be difficult to spot.

"Maybe," I said, and then paused.

"Maybe what?"

"Well, clearly, attacking the Bucintoro in a single gondola would be a rather hopeless venture. He's mad but he's not stupid – and he certainly doesn't want to *look* stupid. Presumably he's going to make his attempt when the Doge disembarks on the Lido. Let's go in that direction."

Bepi asked no further questions. He bade me get in, loosened the mooring rope, swung himself into position at the stern, snatched up his oar and pushed off. Seconds later we had joined the thick of the nautical throng making eastwards. Few people paid any attention to us; their eyes were all on the roaring fire behind us.

Once we were far enough from the flames to talk more coolly I said: "How did you come to be there?"

"I was worried when you didn't turn up at our meeting point last night. I tried to tell myself it was nothing but I couldn't put it out of my mind, so early this morning I went to your house. And the woman in the tavern said she was a little worried too, since she'd seen you go off with two men and she wasn't sure you had really wanted to."

"Oh, she spotted that, did she?"

"So I wondered if it had anything to do with the platform and

I thought I'd investigate. But when I got here it was swarming with arsenalotti and they weren't too friendly. I wasn't sure what to do but I hung around, and soon enough they all left and then the place went up in flames. I was thinking, well, that's that, but then I thought I'd better check . . ."

"Thank God for second thoughts, Bepi. And thank you."

"Yes, well." He did not exactly shrug; that is not easy to do while you are rowing, but he intimated clearly enough that he had no wish for further effusive displays of gratitude.

I was still peering into the mass of boats ahead of us but could not make out the distinctive squat shapes of Giorgio and Gaetano, nor of Garzoni; he, of course, would probably be concealed within the felze, busily loading and cocking his pistols.

"Can we get there before the Bucintoro?" I asked.

"Me against sixty-eight arsenalotti?" said Bepi. "Shouldn't be a problem."

"Well, I suppose the Bucintoro isn't built for speed," I said with some anxiety. "But it's still coming on at quite a rate."

We were now passing the marshy area between the end of Castello and the island of Sant'Elena, with its Gothic church and Benedictine monastery. Alongside the landing stage was another large boat with gilded decorations and a splendid golden banner. Just beyond it lay a slightly lower boat, no less splendidly decorated.

"Of course!" I said. "The Bucintoro stops at Sant'Elena first."

"That's right," said Bepi. "The Patriarch meets him there and blesses the ring."

I peered towards the two large boats. Presumably the larger belonged to the Patriarch. It was already full of people, probably all clerical; I could see dark vestments mingled with dazzling white cassocks and the purple of the Patriarch himself. The other boat had fewer people, and there seemed to a mixture of lay and religious people aboard.

"What's that banner?" I asked, pointing to the one flying from the smaller boat.

"It's the Worshipful Company of Santa Giustina, protector of the guild of customs officials." He said it with a rather dismissive note, as if he felt the saint was wasting her protective powers. I could now see the symbol of the martyr's palm on the banner.

"Why are they there?"

"It's their special privilege on the day of the Sensa, to be alongside the Patriarch when he blesses the Bucintoro. I guess they have a boring enough job, so it makes a nice day out for them."

"Wait, wait, wait," I said, putting my hand up. I was thinking hard. "Bepi, let's head for Sant'Elena. Aim for the customs boat – I mean the Santa Giustina boat."

"You sure?"

"No, not sure, but I have an idea."

There was a cluster of smaller boats bobbing around the two larger ones, most of them gondolas. I could not identify Garzoni's gondola but neither could I say, at this distance, that none of them was his.

"Does the Doge disembark?" I asked.

"No, the Patriarch's boat comes out and meets him and the Patriarch blesses him from his own boat."

"And what about the Santa Giustina boat?"

"That will go to the other side of the Bucintoro, and then all three will head towards the Lido side by side."

In fact, even as we approached Sant'Elena I saw the boat with the great banner of Santa Giustina move out into the lagoon, so as to be on the right of the Bucintoro when the latter arrived. It had a high castle-like structure towards the stern, where were clustered the dignitaries of the Worshipful Company: a group of men in splendid light-blue coats and large wigs, together with a number of priests in dark vestments. There were ten oarsmen per side, all clad in dark clothes with light-blue sashes, all standing in the usual Venetian rowing position. It was impossible to recognise anyone at this distance. The one thing I could see was that the people on the high bridge of the boat would be more or less on a level with the Doge's throne on the Bucintoro.

"Bepi, we've got to get aboard that boat," I said.

"Oh yes?" he said. "Sure you're dressed for it?"

"Never mind," I said, "somehow we've got to manage it."

"I'll get us alongside," he said, "and then you see what you can do."

He veered to the right, away from Sant'Elena, squeezing between a boat rowed by men in strange orange and yellow liveries (the guild of citrus-fruit sellers?) and a gondola bearing a squabbling family. The large Santa Giustina boat had come more or less to a halt, with all its oars resting in the water.

I turned to look behind us. The Bucintoro was approaching in stately fashion, the dazzling red oars steadily and gracefully rising and falling. We could hear the trumpets and drums now, which mingled with the harmonious voices of the choir on the shore of the island of Sant'Elena. It was a pity we could not just sit back and enjoy the visual and aural feast.

I turned back again and stared at the Santa Giustina. The most obvious point of approach would be the stern, but here both the lower and the upper deck (the upper deck being the castle-like structure) were crowded with people gazing either at the fire or at the approaching Bucintoro. It was not likely they would fail to see a gondola sneaking up from the same direction.

"Let's go on to the front of the boat," I said to Bepi.

He had already come to the same conclusion and we now skirted the row of oars, which were barely stirring in the water along the starboard side. None of the oarsmen paid us any attention and we reached the prow, with its gilded carvings; in pride of place was a protruding recumbent lion, looking rather inappropriately soporific. I hoped the members of the crew would be equally slow to react. I moved to the front of the gondola and prepared myself; I picked up the chain dangling from my ankle and wound it round my waist; there was enough to go round twice and I tucked the loose end in between the two circles. It might even become fashionable.

Bepi swung us until the lion was just above me. Still no one seemed to be watching. I reached up and gripped the front paws. From somewhere strength was returning to me and I managed to hoist myself up until I was astride the lion, which took things philosophically. I slid forward and dropped onto the deck.

"What the devil . . . ?" came a voice from halfway down the deck. A sailor strode forward and gazed at me in perplexity.

"Inspection for the Missier Grande," I said haughtily. "Out of my way."

One thing I had learned in the past few days was that people used to taking orders will go on taking them if they are issued in an authoritative enough tone, no matter what the circumstances. It did not matter that

I was dressed in filthy charred rags and had no wig, blood-caked hair and a chain round my ankle, so long as my voice remained that of a man used to command; it did not need to be loud, just firm. Once again I thanked my days watching actors play Coriolanus and Henry V.

He stepped back nervously and I strode past him.

Once he had given way the oarsmen and other sailors did the same and I made my way to the staircase that led to the upper deck; there were two flights, one on each side of the boat. The people up there still had their backs to me but I now recognised the red hair of Gaetano. He was wearing the long clerical gown of a priest. The clerical garb must have been waiting in the gondola. Presumably this was all part of Garzoni's contingency plan. I could not see him yet but I knew he must be up there.

I started up the right-hand staircase. There was now a stir among the oarsmen and people at the top were beginning to realise something strange was happening. A man who looked as if he must be the captain of the ship appeared at the top of the staircase and stared down at me.

"Who the devil are you?"

"I come from the Missier Grande," I said, continuing to mount the stairs. "No time for explanations. You have an assassin on board."

"Just stop there," said the captain, barring the way, as I reached the top. He put a hand to my chest and a burly sailor loomed up at his side.

I needed to play this carefully. All they needed to do was push me and not only would I fall but I would lose all possible claim to authority. Sprawling on the ground in tattered clothes and an ankle chain never looks impressive.

I did not attempt to barge past them. I just stood still and said calmly: "You will answer to the Missier Grande." Strangely enough, I felt calm. Too many infinitely worse things had happened by this point for this setback to disturb me unduly.

"You don't look like a representative of the Missier Grande," said the captain, but I was pleased to note there was a hint of uncertainty in his voice.

Other people were turning round and staring at me. These included Gaetano, who stared at me open-mouthed. I resisted the temptation to wave at him. I still could not see Garzoni, but a large group of people remained clustered around the rails at the stern, watching the approach of the Bucintoro – and, of course, the fire, which was still blazing merrily.

"If I don't," I said, "it is because I have come from that fire over there, which was set by the assassins."

Gaetano turned round and walked away, presumably to find his master. "And that man there," I said, pointing after him, "the one with the red hair, is one of the assassins."

"Come, sior," said the captain (the "sior" was promising), "he is a priest."

"He is wearing a priest's garb," I said. "Arrest him now!" And I gave these last words as an order.

"I will leave you to do that," said the captain, evidently feeling this was the easiest way out, and stepping aside. "His Excellency nobleman Zanotto welcomed him and his companion aboard himself."

I had guessed right. On hearing his name Zanotto detached himself from the people at the stern and came towards me. He was now wearing what were obviously his robes of office as a member of the Worshipful Company of Customs Officers. They were distinctly less shabby than his nobleman's cloak, as I remembered it, so that his elaborately curled wig no longer seemed quite so ridiculous. His face was extremely worried as he came towards me. He clearly had not recognised me yet.

"Excellency," I said, and bowed.

"It's you," he said, with clear dismay. "But what are you doing here?" Looking like an escaped madman, his tone added.

"Excellency," I said, "I presume you extended an invitation to nobleman Garzoni to join you on this boat for the ceremony."

"And if I did? If I did?" His voice was now clearly agitated and he glanced back towards the people at the stern. Garzoni had still not manifested himself; I could see Gaetano's red hair amid a cluster of powdered wigs, and I could only presume that one of them belonged to Garzoni. But the faces all remained resolutely turned away from us.

"Are you aware that he is armed? With several pistols?"

Zanotto's agitation increased. "What are you suggesting? What are you suggesting?" Perhaps he thought that by saying things twice he could remove the danger.

"I'm not suggesting. I am telling you. Nobleman Garzoni intends to murder the Doge."

There was a general gasp from those around us. Zanotto's expression said clearly that he had suspected as much. I almost began to feel sorry for him.

At that moment Garzoni emerged from the crowd of people at the stern, flanked by Gaetano. He was wearing his nobleman's cloak, which was well wrapped round him, despite the warmth of the morning. He walked unhesitatingly towards me, his dark pits of eyes fixed on me.

"What is this ruffian suggesting?" As usual, his voice, although quiet and marred by his sparseness of teeth, somehow managed to cut through the tumultuous noise all around us and cast a chilly spell. At least that was how I felt it.

"I am telling everyone that you are armed and dangerous," I said, staring straight into his eyes.

"I ask you all to look at this poor wretch, who has clearly escaped from San Servolo." And he made a contemptuous gesture with his right hand in the direction of the madhouse. "Throw him off the boat," he said, and turned away.

There was a moment's pause and I sensed that everything would turn on my next decision. If I did nothing there was no doubt that Garzoni's order would be obeyed, dubious though his authority was.

If I attempted violence against him I would look like a madman, attacking a venerable nobleman. If I merely blustered I would lose all advantage. What was needed was some demonstrative action, one that would carry its own authority.

I raised my left hand in as authoritative a manner as possible (I was remembering a fine performance of Mark Antony's funeral speech) and with the other I unwound the chain from round my waist. For the two or three seconds it took me to do this people wavered. And then suddenly I began swinging the chain in a vicious whooshing circle. All those closest to me stepped back in alarm.

"Take this as my chain of office," I announced, scarcely knowing what I was saying. "I say again that I speak with the authority of the Missier Grande." This time I said the name as loudly as was possible without sounding hysterical.

Suddenly Garzoni spun round and this time he had drawn a pistol from underneath his cloak. I had been expecting this and before he had time to level the weapon I lashed the chain forward with a vicious jerk of my arm. The far end caught the pistol and sent it flying into the air, while Garzoni gave a cry of pain and tumbled backwards. There was a general gasp all around at what had probably appeared to be a sudden and brutal attack on my part. This lasted a split second until the pistol fell to the ground in everybody's sight. And then all eyes swivelled to where Garzoni lay sprawling, with his cloak spread out. Three other pistols were visible, tucked into his belt. Even as he lay there his uninjured hand moved towards one of them.

Zanotto gave a sharp cry and dashed towards him.

"Careful!" I screamed.

There was a loud explosion and Zanotto staggered back, gazing in horror at his left arm. His fine robes of office had been sliced open and a bloody stain was spreading there. Amid more gasps of horror a couple of the more courageous bystanders sprang forwards and pinioned Garzoni before his hand could proceed to another of the pistols. Somebody else pulled the guns from his belt.

At this moment the Bucintoro came alongside us. The pistol shot had clearly been heard even above the trumpets and drums, and the rails were lined with curious faces. The castle was higher than ours, of course, and the dignitaries massed upon it stared down at us, clearly with some perturbation. The Doge himself could be seen, his usually benevolent face looking a little perplexed as he gazed in our direction.

I moved towards Garzoni. The people around him stepped back, as if acknowledging my official role in this affair – or perhaps just worried that I might lash out with the chain again. Only Gaetano was now left crouching by his side and Garzoni was speaking urgently to him, his face contorted with rage and hatred. He had seen the Doge, I think.

"Stop that man!" I cried, pointing towards Gaetano.

Gaetano had pulled a pistol from his own belt and pointed it unwaveringly towards me. I stood dead still. So did everyone else.

Garzoni said: "You know what to do."

Gaetano gave a grunt.

My eyes darted to the right, towards the Bucintoro. The Doge was now in plain sight, on a little platform above everyone else, peering vaguely in the direction of his would-be assassins. Gaetano's eyes flickered from me to the Bucintoro and back again.

Perhaps he was going to shoot me and then the Doge; I had no doubt that he had another pistol in his belt. Or perhaps he would go for the Doge first . . .

I knew that if my hand holding the chain so much as stirred I would be a dead man. I stayed rigidly still and ran a thousand calculations through my mind. None of them worked out well.

Then Gaetano suddenly swung the pistol, placed the muzzle next to Garzoni's head and pulled the trigger.

Gaetano dropped the gun by the side of the bloody mess that had been his master's head and stood up, his own head drooping in silent surrender. When the screams had died down I moved forward and put a hand on his shoulder, turned to the captain and said: "Take this man into custody."

And they did it. Three sailors gripped him and hustled him away. His face remained inscrutable. I wondered if he had carried out Garzoni's final instructions or acted on his own initiative. Then I realised that the latter notion was absurd.

Of course, it was always possible he had misunderstood his instructions. There was a cry from another boat to starboard. "What is going on?"

I recognised the voice and moved towards the railings. Below us lay a *dodesona*, its twelve oarsmen all in splendid white with red trimmings; the Missier Grande was standing bolt upright in the middle of the boat, with two men in white liveries in front and another two behind. Each of the liveried men had a musket by his side.

I leaned out and said: "It's a long story, Illustrissimo."

Amid all the hubbub – trumpets still playing, drums pounding, excited voices gabbling on all sides – the Missier Grande stood absolutely still, a slight frown on his upturned face. Then he said: "I have no doubt it is. Four of my men will board your boat and restore order. You will join me and give me a condensed version. The celebrations will continue."

And once again orders were obeyed – particularly the last one. Such is the Venetian desire for pomp and spectacle that nothing – not even an unexpected conflagration, an assassination attempt, the wounding of one nobleman and the murder of another – could divert the course of events by so much as a minute.

However, it was the end of my involvement in the festivities.

28

I spent much of the rest of the day being interrogated by the three Inquisitors. It was quite surprising that they were prepared to devote their time to the case that same day, since everyone else of any importance was taking part in the grand banquet in the Sala del Maggior Consiglio. The sounds of merry feasting were perfectly audible to us, and I saw at least one of the Inquisitors cast an occasional wistful glance in the direction of the noise. However, the case was clearly considered serious enough to warrant not only their full but also their immediate attention. I imagined that a few spare lobsters and chicken legs would be put aside for them.

Being interrogated by the Inquisitors is probably most Venetians' worst nightmare, but I had been through too much by this point to feel any special terror. And it was undeniable that the strange circumstances of the interrogation robbed it of some of its power to awe.

In any case, as the Missier Grande was there as well, I was able to see the curious relationship that bound them to him: formally they were, of course, his superiors, in rank and prestige, but they clearly depended on him for most of their information and also, it seemed, for a good many of their policies and decisions. He maintained a tone of deferential respect towards them but never at any point did he seem intimidated – not even when they criticised him for the decision he had taken to investigate nobleman Garzoni without first referring to them. He bowed his head respectfully and acknowledged the licence he had taken but it was evident – to me, at least – that he would do exactly the same thing next time round.

Curiously, they asked fewer questions about nobleman Garzoni than they did about the murders of the *gnaghe*. I think there was a natural embarrassment on their part about having to question a member of the *popolo* regarding one of their own rank. With the question of the *gnaghe* they felt more comfortable, since those murders had clearly been committed by Luca, Gaetano and Giorgio. However, I pointed out that the arcane symbolism of the murders – the references to the legend of Saint Isidore, for example – pointed to the fact that, despite all that Garzoni had said about the aim of creating a general sense of terror in the population, the real aim of the actual perpetrators (or, at least, of the planner) of the murders had been to impress *him*. It was exactly the same logic that had led to the creation of the wholly impractical submergible. The purpose was simply to keep Garzoni happy – and thus to keep his coffers for ever at the disposal of Luca. Obviously Gaetano and Giorgio had been mere tools (although willingly murderous ones).

The Inquisitors did not exactly thank me for my intervention but they acknowledged that it had been timely. An excess of gratitude or praise would probably have seemed too much like endorsement of the Missier Grande's tendency to independent enterprise. I was finally allowed to leave their august presence, but the Missier Grande made it clear that he wished to speak further with me, and so I remained in his private office, in the company of Sior Massaro.

Nobleman Zanotto was then questioned by the Inquisitors; his arm had been bandaged and it seemed the wound was a superficial one. Naturally I was not present during his interrogation – they would hardly allow a *popolano* to witness the interrogation of one of their own rank. However, Sior Marasso discreetly let me know the broad outcome of the interrogation. It seemed that Garzoni had asked Zanotto to allow him to join the boat on the day of the Sensa, although he had not specified a purpose; Zanotto had had no idea of Garzoni's intentions. This last seemed likely enough, even if Zanotto had reason to know that Garzoni harboured no friendly feelings towards the Doge. He had probably thought that the public nature of the occasion would have been enough to deter Garzoni from any open manifestation of hostility, not realising just how seriously deranged the latter had become by this point. In any case, Zanotto was dismissed from the Inquisitors' presence without charge. He actually walked past me on his way out of the Doge's palace, and merely gave me a stiff nod of acknowledgement. I returned the compliment wearily.

Sior Massaro was also kind enough to arrange for the chain to be removed from my leg, for my own wounds to be cleaned and for a simple change of clothes to be provided. The substitute garments clearly belonged to an artisan employed in some menial capacity in the palace; I was left to wonder what circumstances lay behind their ready availability. They were clean enough and more or less of the right size.

The Missier Grande arrived at last from the Inquisitors' chamber, looking totally unruffled.

I stood up as he entered the room. "May I go now, Illustrissimo?"

"Before you do I wish to remind you that you are a confidential agent. Nothing must go beyond these walls. This vow of silence includes your gondolier friend and your bookseller friend."

"Without their help I would have got nowhere," I said.

"That may be so. But they need know no more of this business than they know already."

"Am I to be allowed to return to my former line of work?"

He seemed to consider this for a moment. Then he said: "I think the state would have no objections."

"That is very gracious of the state," I said.

"I have told you before to restrain your impulse to sarcasm. If you have been expecting fulsome expressions of gratitude and rewards, please remember you were acting without due authority and the state can hardly be expected to encourage such behaviour."

"I thought the state paid more attention to results," I said. "After all, no one authorised the lady to drop her stone mortar on Bajamonte Tiepolo's standard-bearer."

"No," he said. "But neither had she taken a vow of silence before being involved in the matter."

"I see," I said.

"You can take comfort from the fact that you are not to be in any way castigated or reprimanded for having continued to concern yourself in this affair after an explicit instruction not to do so."

I remained silent, since I could not think of anything to say that was not sarcastic.

"I will add," he said, making it sound like a casual afterthought, "that you showed remarkable initiative. We may need your skills again."

"Thank you," I said. "I'm not sure that —"

"I did suspect that my warning to stay clear might not prove totally effective. It probably proved a good spur to action, in fact."

"Illustrissimo, are you saying . . . ?" I was truly startled this time.

"Never mind that. You may return to your former employment as a *cicerone*. That is to say, until such time as we shall require your services again. And Sior Massaro can perhaps find suitable precedent to award you compensation for the losses you have sustained, including, it seems, your wardrobe."

Once again I found myself unexpectedly saying thank you. He gave a stiff bow and was about to leave when I said: "And the English gentleman in custody?"

"We will see to that."

"We know that nobleman Garzoni's staff were responsible for those murders," I said.

"They have confessed as much," he acknowledged.

Both Gaetano and Giorgio had been arrested. I could not imagine that theirs had been a gushing or a lengthy confession.

He went on: "Arrangements will be made for the release of the English gentleman. He will be allowed to re-join his relatives and they will all be invited to continue on their way to Florence."

"I'm sure you will not have to invite them very hard," I said.

He did not reply. I think he felt he had already exchanged enough banter with me. He gave another stiff bow and I was left alone with Sior Massaro.

"Well, that's remarkable," said Massaro.

"I beg your pardon?"

"The Missier Grande is rarely as complimentary as that. He likes you."

"Likes me?" I said with astonishment.

"Well, perhaps that's a slight overstatement. Let's say that he approves of what you've done."

"I'm pleased to hear it," I said, rather warily. Still, since it would probably have its effect on the amount of my compensation I allowed myself to be gratified by the news.

"I expect we'll be seeing more of you," he said.

"Oh, wonderful," I said. I did not try too hard to make it sound sincere.

29

I was rather more sincere in my gratitude when Massaro arranged my compensation. The amount he stipulated, after consultation of a ledger and some mental arithmetic, would certainly make up for all the incidental expenses, such as my broken windows and depleted wardrobe; it would even help me to pay for Fabrizio's books. And I would certainly be able to compensate Bepi for any loss of earnings he had incurred (it would be difficult to persuade him to accept payment for saving my life).

I left the Doge's palace thoroughly exhausted and not a little hungry. The post-Sensa celebrations were under way and the Piazza was full of masked revellers, dancing and prancing under the swinging lanterns strung between the various booths. I gazed blearily at the scene and decided I had to get away somewhere quiet. The easiest thing would have been to go home, I suppose, but I knew that the merry-making in the *magazen* beneath my apartment would be equally hearty; the fact that there would only be about fifty people perpetrating it rather than ten thousand would make little difference to the amount of noise that penetrated through the floorboards and broken windows.

I treated myself to some biscuits and a glass of malvasia from a stall near the clock tower. A masked lady with both breasts emerging from her tight bodice asked if she could have a nibble of the biscuit. I was too tired to do more than acquiesce to the literal meaning of this request, which seemed to disappoint her. She took one bite from one of the biscuits and then left me to enjoy the sensuous delights of the remaining ones by myself. After finishing the wine I found myself sufficiently revived to take a decision on my next move. I needed quiet and I needed thoughtful conversation.

So I made my way towards Fabrizio's shop. It struck me that I could also deliver a first instalment of my reimbursement for his destroyed property. And both he and Lucia might still be concerned over my safety. Despite the Missier Grande I could always let fall a few modestly unassuming words that would give some hint of the perils I had faced and overcome.

When I reached the shop I saw that it was entirely dark. I was mildly surprised, since I thought that Fabrizio might have wanted to continue to profit from the influx of visitors from the mainland. But I suppose he was entitled to a holiday like everyone else.

I saw that there was a light in the apartment above the shop and so I knocked at the door. A few moments later Lucia's head appeared at the window above me.

"Siora," I said, "excuse the hour. I thought you might welcome some news."

"Sior Alvise," she said, "I will come down at once."

Moments later she was opening the door; the lantern in her hand revealed her face to be pale and anxious.

"Siora," I said, "is there trouble?"

"My father has been attacked."

"No! How? Where?"

"Here in the shop. A couple of hours ago."

"Is he all right?"

"He's resting. It's not a serious injury – a blow to the head – but it was an unpleasant shock . . . but Sior Alvise, you too?" She raised the lantern to study my face. "And what are you wearing? Is this for Carnival?"

"No," I said, "it's a long story. But let me hear about your father first."

"Come into the shop. I cannot invite you upstairs. Father needs rest." She stood inside and I entered the shop.

"No, of course not. What happened?"

"He was alone in the shop. I had gone to the Piazza. A customer came in. A foreigner. English, I think." She was talking in clipped sentences. It seemed to be the only way she could keep the panic out of her voice. She was able to maintain control over short groups of words. "Father asked if he wanted anything. He said he wanted to look around. So Father left him. The man went over to that bookcase there. A minute later Father was sure he saw him putting something into his pocket." This slightly longer sentence came out in a single rush and she paused for a while before continuing. "And so Father asked him to put it back. The man denied it. Father insisted. And then he suddenly hit Father and ran out."

"Hit him? How?"

"Just a punch. Perhaps more of a push. But Father fell over and banged his head. When I came back he was still groggy."

My mind was racing. The malvasia had set little wheels in motion. "Did your father describe the man?"

"He was masked. But he was about thirty. English, as I said."

"With a breathy voice – like this?"

"Yes."

"This was Shackleford's brother," I said. "Retrieving his brother's property."

"His . . . ?" She looked puzzled and then, with an expression that indicated sudden realisation, she said: "Oh, you mean . . ."

"The book was there all the time. Shackleford needed somewhere safe to hide it from his own pupil. Where better than among other books? Presumably on a high shelf at the back, among . . . among . . ."

"Among our stock in less frequent demand," she said drily. The revelation seemed to have momentarily relieved her anxiety.

"When I was talking to him the other evening and I mentioned your brother's visits here he must have suddenly realized. I can't think why I never thought of it. Well, I suppose the book had come to seem of secondary importance and so I more or less forgot about it."

"And what does he want it for?" she said.

"I think I know," I said slowly. "He's going to try to complete his brother's plan."

"But his brother got killed."

"Well, I think he thinks . . . No, I'm not sure that I do know. But I think I can guess where he's gone."

"Well, I'm going to go too," she said.

"But Siora Lucia," I said, "your father . . ."

"Father is being looked after. My aunt has come over. She's a – well, it doesn't matter; she's a very good nurse." I suspected her first description had been going to be of a less flattering nature. "I want to see this man and I want to speak to him."

"I'm not sure this is a good idea," I said. "Not if I'm right about why he's gone there."

"Sior Alvise, I am going to speak to this man. And I will go there alone, if you won't take me."

"You don't know where," I said.

"No, but you are going to tell me. Or you are going to take me."

So of course I took her.

After she had let her father and aunt know that she was just slipping out for some medicine she joined me at the door and we set off, each holding a lantern.

I told her where we were going and gave her my reasons for thinking it was the most likely place to find the younger Mr Shackleford. She gave a sigh and said, "Everyone's a performer in this city. Even the visitors. Either the city infects them or it invites visitors of a certain kind."

"Probably both," I said.

"Of course, you too," she said. "You're no minor performer yourself. And you haven't even told me of your adventures today. Were you right? About nobleman Garzoni? Planning something for the Sensa? I only heard wild rumours and then my father's accident put everything out of my head."

"I was right," I said.

"Tell me all," she said, after I had allowed an intriguing pause to create suspense.

I had been intending to drop no more than a few laconically enigmatic remarks, but pressed in this insistent fashion what could I do? My account of the events of the night and day took us all the way to Campo Santi Giovanni e Paolo.

"So that was what the fire was," she said. "I saw it and wondered if it was just a new part of the celebrations."

"Well, that's what it became in the end," I said. "I think that's the destiny of everything in this city."

There were a few booths set up in the square, and the smell of fried fish and cheap wine hung over them. Masked revellers were dancing the *furlana* around the statue of Colleoni to the music of a few violins. We paused to watch for a few moments and she said: "We may be frivolous pleasure-seekers but no one can deny we do it with great style."

"Siora Lucia," I said, turning to look at her.

"Sior Alvise," she said, "if you are going to ask me to dance, let me remind you that we have urgent business."

"Let me just ask if you will dance with me afterwards," I said, in some confusion. Dancing had not actually been the first thing on my mind.

"Afterwards I wish to return to my father," she said. Her face was serious.

There was silence between us for a few seconds. The violins continued their insistent tune. Then I said: "I think I've bungled it." I made no attempt to hide my disappointment. The carnivalesque atmosphere, together with weariness and slight inebriation, all combined to make me say quite openly what I was thinking, something I had never done in her presence. "I suppose a *cicerone* should not aspire so high –"

"Sior Alvise, I have the utmost respect –"

"I don't want respect," I said. "I want –" And then I halted. I realised I was about to go too far.

She obviously realized it too and simply said: "Let's go."

We walked the length of the Barbaria delle Tole in silence. The music died away behind us so I could meditate on my clumsiness in relative tranquillity.

We reached the Teatro Santa Giustina. It was as quiet as it had been the other evening when the count and I had broken in. I was about to direct her to the alley alongside the building when I noticed that the main entrance door was slightly ajar.

"I hope we're not too late," I said, in sudden alarm.

"You mean ..."

"I don't know who else could open the door," I said. My intention had been simply to warn Shackleford of his danger.

I ran up the stairs and pulled the door open. We entered the foyer, our lamps casting flickering light on the dusty stucco and dim frescoes. We stood still and heard surreptitious movements from the direction of the auditorium.

"Shackleford!" I called. "Is that you?"

There was a moment's silence and then a breathy voice from within the auditorium said uncertainly: "Who's that?"

Lucia and I moved towards the grand colonnaded doorway that led into the auditorium. The vast space was lit by a single lantern balanced on the edge of the stage. A cloaked figure was standing above it, next to the wings of the stage, as if wondering whether to take a last bow or not. He wore a tricorn hat and the face beneath it was masked.

"Come down from there," I said.

"Why should I? And what are you doing here?"

Lucia spoke up: "I want the book that you stole from our shop." She strode down the central aisle and I followed her until we were beneath the stage.

"It wasn't your book," he said, clearly rather disconcerted by her demand.

"That did not give you the right to attack an elderly man."

"I didn't mean to hurt him," he said. "I – I panicked."

"Did you come in here by the front entrance?" I said.

"No, of course not. How could I?"

"It's open now. That means your . . . your potential client has arrived." I spoke quietly.

"Zanotto? So where is he?" He looked around, making it clear that he had not been lying about his tendency to panic.

"That's what we need to know," I said, still speaking quietly. "He clearly came in as quietly and discreetly as possible."

"Well, that's understandable," he said. "I made it clear this was to be a discreet transaction. That's why I chose this place."

"How did you communicate with him?"

"I sent a boy to his house with a message. I didn't expect him to get here so quickly."

"He is as keen to get his hands on that book as you are to sell it to him. Only I don't think he intends to buy it."

"What do you mean?"

"He intends to kill you just as he killed your brother."

"What?" This was said in a high-pitched screech. "I thought that was – I thought . . ."

"You suspected the Grimani family," I said.

"Well, yes."

"Because they're big, they're powerful, they can probably hire any number of *bravi*."

"Yes."

"The point is," I said, "they are so big that the accusation that one of their members, however prestigious his present position, wrote an absurd poem in an absurd history book thirty years ago is of no significance whatsoever. The mistakes of youth; look at all the positions of responsibility the foolish young man has held since that time. He would probably be more embarrassed by the bad rhymes than by the contents of the book that contains them." Among other things, Doge Pietro Grimani was known to write poetry.

"But Zanotto . . . it wasn't even he who wrote it, it was his brother."

"So he has told us all. Have you checked that fact? There was a brother that went to England, it seems. But it is quite possible that our Zanotto visited him while he was there. Remember, it was *this* Zanotto that Garzoni contacted about the book, when you told him about it. Of course, it was ingenious of Zanotto to accuse himself of blackmail. That apparently shameful confession prevented us from thinking of anything worse. But think about it: would he really dare to blackmail the Grimani family? And we know he couldn't blackmail Garzoni, since Garzoni was actually proud of the book. So there had to be another reason he wanted to get hold of it. The point is that Zanotto is a man of almost no accomplishments, a man who has lost most of his family fortune and who, towards the end of his life, has finally managed to obtain a minor post in the customs office . . . a post that guarantees a modest but certain income, just enough to buy a new cloak and a veneer of respectability. But his hold on that office is precarious enough to mean that should a whiff of scandal about unorthodox political positions emerge he could lose everything. *This* is the kind of man who would kill to suppress that book. Who *has* killed to suppress it. And who means to do so again."

Shackleford let out a kind of whimpering sound and started looking around again; more than ever I was reminded of Zosimos.

I went on: "Your brother made the mistake of agreeing to meet him alone. He probably thought that if he went there without the book, which he had hidden in the bookshop, he would hold the whip hand. Perhaps he took a dummy copy and Zanotto killed him for it – and only then discovered his mistake. But Zanotto had gone there quite clearly with the intention of killing; that's why he set up the whole secret meeting, using his undeniable acting skills with the woman who rented out the *casino*, and then taking along the *gnaga* costume, so that he could disguise the nature of the murder. After all, he certainly couldn't afford to *pay* for the book."

Lucia moved a little closer to me. She whispered: "Do you think he's listening to us?"

"I'm sure he is," I said.

"And do you think he's armed?" Her voice did not quaver but it had a note of fiercely controlled urgency.

"I don't think he'll have a pistol," I said.

"Where is he?" said Shackleford. "Where is he?" He was staring about in a hunted fashion.

"Come down from there," I said. "We had better stay together."

"You come up here," he said.

"You only make a better target –" I began to say.

Shackleford gave a sudden yelp and disappeared. One moment he was standing above us and the next there was just the vanishing flick of his black cloak. His yelp ended in a sickening crunch as his body hit the ground beneath the stage.

"Trapdoor," I said, staring stupidly.

"My God!" screamed Lucia. "Save him!"

I remembered the zany's sudden effortless leap on to the stage but realised I could never manage anything similar. Instead I ran up the stairs at the side of the stage, and scrambled towards the square black hole that was the open trapdoor, holding my lantern over it.

I could just see a large shifting dark form below; there was a last whimper from Shackleford and then a gurgling sound. The dark shape separated into two, one lying inert and the other moving swiftly away. I thought I could see a dark sheen of blood around the neck of the motionless body.

I was about to drop down in pursuit when Lucia called out: "What can you see?"

"He's dead," I said.

"Alvise, don't go down there."

It was absurd, but somewhere in my mind I registered the fact that she had called me, for the first time, just Alvise.

She went on: "That would be to take part in his performance. Come back here. Quickly." Her voice was urgent but firm.

I realised she was right. Zanotto would undoubtedly be waiting with the same bloody knife. And that would then leave Lucia out in the auditorium on her own.

I darted back across the stage and jumped down, which was not as light a feat as I had imagined. The jar to my body set all my aches and pains jangling again.

She said: "Remember he knows this theatre. He's desperate but he's also determined to put on a last performance. We have to refuse to take part in it." She sounded remarkably calm. "First we had better put out the lanterns. They are just making targets of us."

She extinguished her own. With some trepidation I did the same to mine. As we stood there, waiting for our eyes to grow accustomed to the darkness, her hand brushed against mine and then held it.

I decided it was not a good moment to renew the invitation to dance. I whispered: "Let's try to make our way out."

"All right. Don't let go of me."

"Never," I said, gripping her hand more firmly.

I made for the central aisle, allowing my shins to tell me the way as they scraped against the seats. My other hand was still holding the extinguished lantern, which prevented me from groping my way forward manually.

We were halfway down the aisle when Lucia suddenly screamed and her hand was jerked away from mine. I swivelled and I could just see her thrashing around. As I lunged towards her she suddenly went rigid and Zanotto's voice spoke: "I have a knife to the young lady's throat. Do not move another step."

"It's true," she said, her voice wavering just slightly.

"What do you want, Excellency?" I said.

There was a pause. The problem, I think, was that Zanotto really did not know what he wanted. His only chance had been to split us up and then kill each of us separately. We had thwarted that plan, and now he could kill Lucia but it was unlikely that he would then be able to kill me. Battered and bruised I might be, but I was at least thirty years younger than he was. On the other hand, he might be tempted to try, simply on the grounds that he had nothing to lose. Somehow I had to persuade him that it would not be in his interests.

"Excellency, there is no point in any further bloodshed," I said.

"Why did you have to interfere?" he said. His voice had its usual petulant tone, as if he were complaining about nosy neighbours.

"Excellency, if you give yourself up now you can ask for clemency, given that your victims were both dishonest foreigners."

"Despicable people. Blackmailers. *Frappatori*. The ruin of the state."

"Exactly," I said. "No one will blame you."

"I had earned a respectable position. People looked up to me."

"I'm sure you'll be able to make a case for yourself," I said. "The Inquisitors are reasonable people." Then I added in English, praying that Lucia's reading of *Pamela* would have familiarised her with these words: "Lucia, his left arm is injured."

"What did you say?" said Zanotto, immediately suspicious.

"The left arm, just below the shoulder – *ferito*," I said, pronouncing the English words as clearly as possible, and adding the Italian word for "injured".

There was a sudden high-pitched shriek from Zanotto, telling me that Lucia's linguistic skills were up to the challenge, and at once I hurled myself forward. The next few seconds were a hectic confusion of tangled bodies, cloaks, thrashing limbs, a slashing knife, and some grunting and screaming. Zanotto and I both tumbled to the ground and at a certain point, with a sharp piercing pain to my palm, I managed to jerk the knife from his hand. I heard Zanotto's head hit the floor with a crack and disentangled myself from him; he remained still.

Lucia was sobbing. I put my arms round her and felt the throb of her convulsions against my chest. A few seconds later the spasms diminished in intensity and she detached herself from me. "Is he . . . is he . . . ?"

"I don't know," I said. "I certainly didn't stab him. But he's an old man. Being thrown to the ground like that might have been fatal."

"He could be performing again," she said; there was an uncharacteristically bitter note in her voice.

I bent towards the recumbent figure. "I can't detect any breathing."

"Stay away," she said, tugging at my arm. "I have no doubt he has another knife concealed. We are not playing his game any longer. Let's get out of here."

It was good advice.

When we returned a few minutes later, with lighted lanterns and accompanied by three of the least drink-befuddled arsenalotti we had rousted out of a nearby tavern, we found Zanotto still lying on his back, his face contorted with pain and rage, and his right hand clutching a knife: Lucia had been right. He was now breathing stertorously and was unable to move anything but his eyes, which flickered malevolently from one to another of us. His arm and his upper body were liberally splashed with blood, though this turned out to be Shackleford's rather than his own.

It proved impossible to remove the knife from Zanotto's clutch, and he was still holding it when the priest from Santa Giustina came to read the last rites over his body. Only when I was sure he was dead did I extract it delicately from his fingers, even then half expecting one last, rancorous lunge.

30

I awoke and found myself surrounded by books. I was lying between sheets of a crisper candour than anything my body had ever experienced, wearing a nightshirt of similar purity. My head had ceased to throb for the first time in centuries. Clean linen and all the reading matter one could ever want. Perhaps this was heaven.

Lucia rose from a chair in the corner of the room. It *was* heaven.

"How do you feel?" she said.

"Perfect," I said. Then I added: "And puzzled."

"You collapsed in the Doge's palace. We got permission to bring you home with us. You've slept through a whole day."

Vague memories of the confused hours that had followed the death of Zanotto flickered before me. I remembered the lantern-lit faces of *sbirri*, the lean features of the Missier Grande, and endless nagging questions. At one point, if I remembered correctly, Signor Massaro had spoken up to suggest I should be allowed a respite. I hoped he still had a job.

"How was I . . . how did you . . ."

"The *sbirri* carried you here," she said. "On a stretcher."

"I'm so sorry," I said.

"What for?"

"Well, the inconvenience . . . the . . . the . . ."

"It seemed less inconvenient to have you recuperate here for a day or two than to have to arrange your funeral," she said, with a quick flash of a smile. "And the Missier Grande seemed to appreciate that too."

"Does your father mind?"

"He's in the next bedroom." She lowered her voice. "I think he's hoping that having another invalid in the house will reduce the intensity of his sister's solicitude."

I gazed at the walls of books on both sides of the room. "There *are* more books than in the shop," I said.

"And this is just one room." Then she said: "There are some people here who want to thank you."

"Who are they?"

"The English family."

"Ah. All of them?"

"Well, the three we've met. The young man is out of prison. He's the most vociferous in his gratitude."

"Yes, I can imagine. Should I get dressed? Do I have any clothes?"

"I see no immediate need for that."

If only she were Miss Boscombe, I thought; I would be able to read all sorts of suggestive possibilities into that remark.

"I'll call them," she said after a pause, during which she gazed at me with a slightly wary expression. Perhaps my face had given away my thoughts. "They're taking lunch nearby."

Some minutes later, during which I drifted in and out of sleep, I heard brash English voices on the staircase. I raised myself to a sitting position and wondered whether a pose of weary languor or Bourbonic hauteur would be more impressive. In the end I think I just looked harassed.

I had probably done better not to dress; I certainly could not compete with the frilly frothiness of Mr Boscombe's silk shirt. He did not appear to have suffered any great deprivations in prison; he was certainly no thinner or paler and his laugh was as explosive as ever. He released it immediately on seeing me, as if nothing could be more comic than finding me once more in bed.

Miss Boscombe was dressed in a magnificent confection of blues and pinks, which provided a neat contrast with the drab greys of her father's outfit. He stood by the door with the peevish expression of one who would far rather be studying an Etruscan tomb.

"Just wanted to say how grateful we all are, you know," said young Mr Boscombe, and gave another bark of a laugh. I wondered whether the other prisoners were missing his cheeriness.

"So grateful, so very grateful," said Miss Boscombe. Even the elder Mr Boscombe let out a grunt of vague acknowledgement.

"Good of you all to say so," I began.

Young Mr Boscombe cut me off. "And I've been thinking. I know my troubles have, um, caused you some troubles of your own."

"Well, one or two little problems," I said.

"So brave, so very brave," murmured Miss Boscombe.

There was the faintest sound of a sigh and I darted a glance at Lucia, whose face was expressionless but who none the less managed to communicate the suggestion that were she not bound by the rules of courtesy she would be rolling her eyes.

Mr Boscombe continued: "So I have a proposal to make to you."

"Yes?"

"Well, after the tragic death, you know, of, well, of Mr Shackleford . . ."

"And his brother," I said.

"Yes, of course, his poor brother as well."

"Scoundrels the pair of them," put in the elder Mr Boscombe.

"Oh, Father," said Miss Boscombe. "De mortuis, you know."

"Neither of them was so very bad," I said. "Certainly not so bad as to merit such appalling ends." I had even come to feel some kind of sympathy for the younger brother. I have no doubt that Lucia would say it was because we were fellow performers.

"Yes, well, be that as it may," said young Mr Boscombe, "I was wondering whether . . . Well, the thing is, I'd like to continue my tour. At least as far as Rome."

"Yes?" I said.

"Well, would you care to take Mr Shackleford's place? Miss Busetto tells me you're also a fine artist. You could make some kind of record of our travels . . ."

I looked back at Lucia, who was looking encouragingly in my direction.

"Mr Boscombe," I said, "it is a very generous offer, but I'm afraid I can't answer immediately."

"No, I see that," he said. "Wouldn't dream of pressing you."

"It would be marvellous," said Miss Boscombe. "I was so impressed by your artistic knowledge, you know, in the little house we explored. Such an eye for detail." And her own innocent blue eyes gazed straight into mine.

I realised I could not meet them without a blush that would give to all present the impression that Miss Boscombe and I had done far more than just appreciate artistic treasures in the little house. I gave her a vague smile and nod and then pleaded general fatigue to cut short the meeting.

The Boscombes left the room with further fulsome expressions of gratitude and another laconic grunt from the elder Mr Boscombe. Lucia remained in the doorway and gazed at me.

"You're not going to turn down this opportunity?" she said.

"I seem to remember you referring to such young men as being in search of nothing but gambling houses and the stews," I said, pretending to be a little puzzled.

She made an impatient puffing sound and said: "It would be a chance to travel, to see the great cities of Italy, to develop your talents . . ."

"I know," I said, "I know."

"Well?"

"You heard what the Missier Grande said last night."

She stared at me without saying a word.

"He wants me to become a permanent *confidente.*"

"A *sbirro,*" she said. She took care not to say it in too loaded a fashion, but the word already bore its own burden of derogatoriness.

I could have prevaricated, pointing out that my role would be above that of the regular *sbirri,* who would have to defer to me. Instead I said: "If you like."

"Sior Alvise," she said, "you have artistic gifts, you have intellectual curiosity . . ."

"Siora Lucia," I said, acknowledging with a pang of regret that we had returned to the formal relationship, "I will retain these things. The Missier Grande says I can continue as a *cicerone...*"

This time the impatient noise was an out-and-out snort.

" . . . but I must be prepared to be on hand for occasional operations, if they should be required to preserve the security of the state. It seems I also have a talent for that."

"Yes," she said sadly. "So it seems."

"You do see," I said, earnestly now, "that if I turn down the proposal of the Missier Grande, I might not be able to work in Venice again, as *cicerone* or artist or anything."

"That is how they blackmail you," she said. There was a bitterness to her tone. She went on: "Sior Alvise, I won't deny that I admired your bravery the other night. And your selflessness. But I was just slightly perturbed . . ." She paused.

"Go on," I said.

"Well, I was perturbed by the suspicion that you actually enjoyed what you were doing." She fell silent, but her eyes remained fixed on mine.

"Enjoyed it?"

"Oh, I'm not saying you were getting some grotesque pleasure from the violence or from the terror. But you were . . . you were somehow in your element."

"And that element is . . . ?"

"I think I said it that night. Performance. You enjoy pretending to be what you are not. And, of course, that is a very useful skill in that line of work. But if I made one contribution that evening it was to warn you of the risk of entering too fully into a world solely of performance."

"You saved our lives," I said.

"Thank you. Possibly I did. And now I wish I could save you from returning to that world."

"Lucia," I said, not even noticing that I had omitted the siora, "I appreciate what you say. But I think I belong to that world."

"Yes, I think perhaps you do." She turned to the door. "Shall I inform them of your decision?"

"You may as well," I said. Was it worth telling her that it was partly the thought of being exiled from the city where she lived that had driven me to this choice? Ironic, since my choice now seemed to be driving us further apart. "Oh, and you could also tell them, if they ask, that their precious book has not been found."

"Is that true?" she asked.

"It is what the Missier Grande has told me to tell them," I said.

"I see." Here she could easily have given another snort – or, at least, a slow sad shake of the head. However, she did not. She probably considered it a waste of time. She left me to my thoughts.

They were not comforting ones. I told myself that time might be on my side. After all, there was always the chance she might need my help if she ever started to read *Clarissa*.

But tomorrow I would go back to my own apartment, with its torn books, filthy rags and grey sheets; these things, too, were my world. No point in my getting used to cleanliness.

My last thought before I drifted off to sleep again was that I must not forget to reward those three boys at the water's edge. Resourceful lads: playing with mud and getting well paid for it.

End note

I have done my best to convey the atmosphere of eighteenth-century Venice as accurately as possible. I have allowed myself one or two chronological liberties. John Murray's term of office as British Resident in Venice actually began shortly after the Dogeship of Pietro Grimani. Reports of *gnaghe* are most common in the 1780s, although occasional references to them can be found earlier in the century.

Most of the locations mentioned in the novel are real. The only major exception to this rule is the Teatro Santa Giustina. The square and the church of that name exist, just where I have placed them, but the theatre is purely imaginary.

Glossary

Words that are Venetian rather than standard Italian are indicated by V in brackets.

altana (V)	a wooden structure on the roof of buildings, used for various purposes (drying of clothes, taking of sun)
arsenalotto (V)	a worker at the Arsenale
barnabotto (V)	a Venetian nobleman fallen on hard times and granted cheap rented accommodation in the parish of San Barnaba
bauta (V)	white face-mask
Bondì (V)	Venetian for Buongiorno (good morning)
bravo	a hired thug
calle (V)	a narrow street
campo (V)	a city square (in Italian the word indicates a field)
canalazzo (V)	alternative name for the Grand Canal
capocomico	director of a theatrical company
casino (V)	small room or set of rooms, used by Venetian aristocrats for various purposes, including gambling
cicerone	tourist-guide
codega (V)	"link-boy" (hired escorts holding lanterns)
cospetto	mild imprecation
felze (V)	the cabin of a gondola
fioi (V)	Venetian, corresponding roughly to "lads"
fondamenta (V)	road running alongside a canal
forcola (V)	the carved wooden structure on gondolas acting as a rowlock
foresto (V)	Venetian for foreigner
fradeo (V)	Venetian for *fratello* (brother)
frappatore	Tuscan word for a swindler; used as the title of a play by Goldoni
furatola (V)	a cheap tavern

ganzer (V)	literally "hookman"; the man who pulls gondolas to the shore; often retired gondoliers
gnaga (V)	male prostitutes, who dressed in female clothes with cat-masks
illustrissimo	most illustrious or eminent; a term of respect, generally used in Venice to address those not of noble rank.
Liston (V)	in Saint Mark's Square, the area between the clock-tower and the pillars by the water-front, used as a fashionable parade-ground
luganagher (V)	sausage-maker
magazen (V)	cheap taverns, not allowed to serve cooked food
malvasia (V)	malmsey wine; also used as the name of taverns that served such wine
Nicolotti (V)	inhabitants of western Venice (around the parish of San Nicolò dei Mendicoli); traditional rivals of the *Castellani*, inhabitants of eastern Venice.
piano nobile	the first floor of a Venetian palace; containing the principal rooms.
popolano	member of the lowest order of Venetian society
provveditore	superintendent
rio (V)	Venetian word for a canal
salizada (V)	a broad street in Venice (one of the first to have been paved)
sandolo (V)	flat-bottomed Venetian rowing boat, of simpler build than a gondola
sbirro	officer of the law; often used derogatorily
scalco	high-ranking official servant
scudo	coin worth seven lire
sguazzeto (V)	boiled pig trotters and veal
Sior/Siora (V)	Venetian for *Signor/Signora*. (They did not generally distinguish between signorina and signora)
sottoportego (V)	archway or passage under a building
tabarro	cloak
zaffi (V)	see *sbirro*; also often used derogatorily
zecchino	the principal Venetian coin, worth twenty-two lire (origin of the word "sequin")